LAST STAND
AT MAJUBA HILL

LAST STAND AT MAJUBA HILL

JOHN WILCOX

headline

First published in 2007
by HEADLINE PUBLISHING GROUP

1

Cataloguing in Publication Data is available from the British Library

Typeset in Sabon by Avon DataSet Ltd,
Bidford on Avon, Warwickshire

978 0 7553 2718 8 (ISBN-13)

Printed and bound in Great Britain by
Clays Ltd, St Ives plc

Headline's policy is to use papers that are natural, renewable and recyclable
products and made from wood grown in sustainable forests. The logging
and manufacturing processes are expected to conform to the
environmental regulations of the country of origin.

HEADLINE PUBLISHING GROUP
A division of Hachette Livre UK Ltd
338 Euston Road
London NW1 3BH

www.headline.co.uk
www.hodderheadline.com

In memory of my son,
Paul Leonard Wilcox, 1959–1979.

Acknowledgements

My thanks, as always, go to the helpful staff of the London Library, whose shelves have given me a contemporary, as well as retrospective, view of the events I have described in 1880–81. They are due also to Sherise Hobbs, my editor at Headline, for her creative suggestions and her impeccable eye for the non sequitur.

In South Africa, I found the most exemplary and informative guide in Dave Sutcliffe at Newcastle, who knew more about the Majuba campaign than I shall ever learn and who, somehow, hauled, pushed and goaded my wife and me up the steep slopes of Majuba Hill to the summit in afternoon temperatures of more than thirty degrees. Back home in peaceful Salisbury, I was grateful to Edward Beauchamp of the famous Greenfields company of gunsmiths, who explained how Jenkins could cause the Baron to misfire in the duel on the Nek.

And, as ever, my love and thanks go to my wife Betty, who fought the Majuba battles with me on site and who read and often corrected every word that I wrote.

I tried to read as widely as possible during the research for the novel and I found the following books particularly helpful:

Egypt	*Cairo*, by Andre Raymond, Harvard University Press, 2000
	Cairo, by Stanley Lane-Poole, Virtue and Co., London, 1892
	Egypt's Belle Epoque, by Trevor Mostyn, Quartet Books, 1989
Duelling	*By the Sword*, by Richard Cohen, Macmillan, London, 2002
The Transvaal War	*Life of Sir G. Pomeroy-Colley*, by Lieut. General Sir William Butler, John Murray, London, 1899
	The Battle of Majuba Hill, by Oliver Ransford, John Murray, London, 1967

Commando, by Deneys Reitz, Faber and Faber, London, 1929
The South African Military History Society (several pamphlets)
The Colonial Wars Source Book, by Philip J. Haythornthwaite, Arms and Armour, London

Some of these, alas, are out of print now, but they can be found in the London Library.

J.W.
Chilmark
April 2006

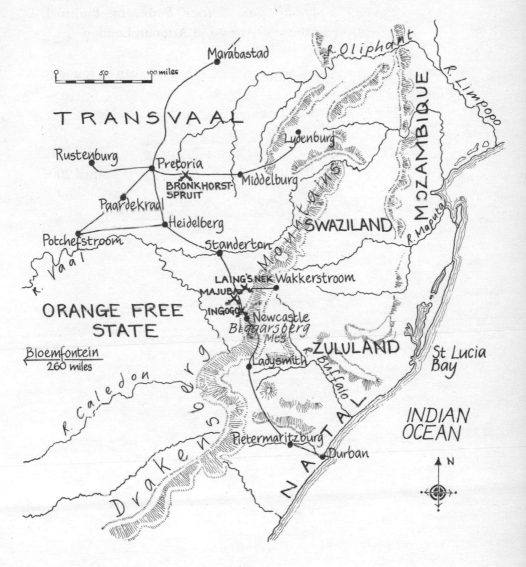

Location of First Anglo-Boer War, South-East Africa, 1880–81

TRANSVAAL

Marabastad

R. Oliphant

R. Limpopo

MOZAMBIQUE

R. Maputa

Rustenburg

Pretoria

BRONKHORST-
SPRUIT

Lydenburg

Middelburg

SWAZILAND

Paardekraal

Heidelberg

Potchefstroom

r. Vaal

Standerton

Wakkerstroom

LAING'S NEK

MAJUBA

INGOGO

Newcastle

Biggarsberg
Mts

ORANGE FREE
STATE

Bloemfontein
260 miles

R. Caledon

Ladysmith

Buffalo

ZULULAND

St Lucia
Bay

INDIAN
OCEAN

Drakensberg

Pietermaritzburg

Durban

NATAL

N

0   50   100 miles

Chapter 1

Cairo, 1880

The Honourable Edward Ashley-Pemberton, First Secretary to Sir Evelyn Baring, British Representative on the Egyptian Commission of Public Debts, screwed his monocle more securely into his eye socket and dabbed his brow with a handkerchief, woven, of course, from the finest long-staple Egyptian cotton. Although the new mechanical fan creaked in the ceiling over his head, its effect was to stir only marginally the heavy, humid air that clung like swamp fever around him and his two visitors. Even in early October, Cairo was hot. Damned hot.

'Dashed if I know why the Consul General sent you to us,' he drawled. 'Dashed if I do.'

'He told me that nothing concerning the English here happened unless Sir Evelyn approved.' The response came from the slimmer and taller of the two men sitting opposite the First Secretary, in tones similar to his own: those of an upper-class Englishman who would consider it very bad form to betray any hint of emotion or, indeed, any great interest in what was being said.

Ashley-Pemberton's top lip moved fractionally. Given a touch more energy it could have been a sneer. 'That's all very well, but Sir Evelyn has just been posted to be Finance Secretary in India. Went off yesterday, as a matter of fact. No replacement yet. Anyway,' he looked down at the single sheet of paper on his desk, 'says here you want employment in the Khedive's army. Eh? What?'

'Yes.'

'Yes. Well then.' He paused for a moment and took a good look at

1

the two men opposite. The word 'adventurers' flashed through his mind and left a sour impression. In truth it was not surprising, for his visitors seemed an ill-assorted pair.

The slimmer and taller was obviously a gentleman, not only because of his accent and tone of voice but also because behind the veneer of indifference – or was it genuine diffidence? – could be detected an air of command. He carried himself well, sitting upright in the chair, and although the cream cotton suit was anonymous enough, it was well made and sat easily on his wiry but broad-shouldered frame. It was the face, though, that was most arresting. Burnt black by the sun, it was high-cheekboned, clean-shaven – unusual for this hirsute age – and the nose had been broken at some time, leaving it slightly hooked and bestowing a lean and predatory look on his appearance. He could have been a young hunter – perhaps in his mid-twenties – from the middle of the great continent, or even a haughty, well-bred Arab from the Saharan wastes, dressed well for the civilised city. Yet the eyes were brown not black, the thin-lipped mouth was more sensitive than cruel, and underneath the burnishing which the sun had given it, the hair was clearly brown.

The other man was decidedly different. Certainly no gentleman, he sat leaning forward on the chair, his great hands resting on his knees, a cheerful, enquiring grin bending upwards a huge black moustache that seemed to touch his ears. These were eyes black enough to match the short-cut, bristling hair, and they sparkled like an urchin's marbles in the somnolent atmosphere of the room. The suit was of similar cut to that of his companion but it clothed a muscular body clearly not used to being confined by such sartorial discipline. He was short – at five foot four perhaps some five inches shorter than his companion – but he exuded great strength. He seemed, in fact, like an errant bruiser confronting a magistrate. But in no way fazed for all that. A strange pair indeed.

Ashley-Pemberton cleared his throat and repeated, 'Yes. Well then. Can't be done, y' see. Consul General should know very well. This city is teeming with ex-officers of the Egyptian army – Gyppies, I mean, not Europeans – who have been thrown out of work because the Egyptian Government can't afford to keep 'em on. You must know that the whole damned country is still virtually bankrupt and we and the French are tryin' to haul 'em out of it.' He looked again at the paper on his desk. 'Y' see, Mr . . . sorry, Captain Fonthill, and . . . er . . .'

'Three five two Jenkins,' said the broad man. 'Late of the 24th Regiment of Foot and Royal Corps of Guides, Indian Army. Same as the captain 'ere.' His voice carried the lilt of the Welsh valleys and his tone was cheerful, anxious to please.

Fonthill felt it necessary to intervene. 'Sergeant Jenkins is always called 352 because there were so many Jenkinses in the 24th – a Welsh regiment – that the last three figures of his number had to be used.'

'Really.' The word expressed disdain. 'Well, although there is plenty of work for soldiers to do, particularly down south to the Sudanese border and here in the desert where the damned Bedawis are raiding villages and caravans, there's just no money to pay 'em.'

'I see.' Fonthill leaned forward. 'But we walked here through the new city, with all the fine buildings and that fantastic Azbakiyya Square, with its fountains and plants. The whole place seems crowded with well-dressed people and fairly buzzing with prosperity.'

The First Secretary allowed his monocle to fall and polished it with his handkerchief. 'Bit of a façade, I fear,' he said. 'The American Civil War brought great prosperity to Egypt as a result of the North's blockade of the Southern ports. Manchester couldn't get cotton for love nor money, so we had to buy it from India and Egypt, and this lot's long-staple stuff fetched a pretty penny, I can tell you. It rose from sevenpence ha'penny a pound to nearly two shillings and five pence within a few months.' He sniffed. 'But Ismail Pasha, the Khedive, blew it all on trying to make Cairo like Paris.'

Fonthill smiled. 'Sounds good to me.'

'Well it wasn't. The Egyptian National Debt soared from four million pounds to a hundred million, and it got to the point where Egypt couldn't even pay the interest on the bonds let alone begin repaying the debts.' Ashley-Pemberton's voice registered indignation. He was clearly shocked. 'We and the French were the main bankers, so we had to foreclose, of course.'

'Of course.'

3

'What?' The First Secretary looked up sharply. But Fonthill's face betrayed no sarcasm. 'Quite so. We appealed to the Turks – they still formally own this damned country, y' know – and got Ismail out and put his son in his place. As you can see, we're now running the finances here and trying to sort things out. Trouble is, we're getting the blame for the fact that the *fellaheen* – the peasants – in the fields are hungry. Which reminds me. You're staying at Shepheards, of course?'

Fonthill shook his head. 'No.'

'The Continental? Savoy?'

'No.'

'What . . .?'

'We are in the Metropolitan in Bourse al-Gadid Street.'

'Yes,' Jenkins chimed in. 'Nice little place, see. Two pound ten shillings a week for two rooms, a bath, light and breakfast each. Worth rememberin' it is, look you, in case you're ever 'ard up, like us at the moment, see.'

Ashley-Pemberton slowly replaced his monocle, his face set. 'How kind of you to let me know,' he murmured.

Jenkins beamed back. Irony was always wasted on him.

'What I was going to say,' continued the First Secretary coldly, 'was that there is considerable anti-British feeling in Cairo at the moment and I recommend that you don't stray into the Old Town after dark. But you seem to be living there at the moment anyway.'

'Thank you,' said Simon. 'It's good of you to advise us.'

'Hmmm.' It was clear that Ashley-Pemberton's worst apprehensions about his visitors had been confirmed by Jenkins's happy explanation of their financial condition. 'I'm afraid,' he continued, his voice now quite remote, as though he was making an aside in his club, 'I cannot help you in your search for employment. Under the circumstances, I could not possibly recommend you . . .' As he spoke, his eyes strayed down to Simon's letter and then his voice tailed away. He looked up again with a frown. 'Captain Fonthill, did you say? Ah, Captain Simon Fonthill?'

'Yes, that's right.'

'Would you, by any chance, have made the acquaintance of

General Sir Garnet Wolseley, the Quartermaster-General at the army's headquarters at the Horse Guards, London?' He asked the question as though there was only the faintest chance of the answer being in the affirmative. Wolseley was the best-known soldier in Queen Victoria's army, and after a series of brilliant successes against her enemies in various parts of the Empire, he had recently returned in triumph to London to be fêted, and, indeed, to be genially satirised by Gilbert and Sullivan in their latest musical *The Pirates of Penzance*, as 'the very model of a modern major general'. It seemed quite impossible that these two penniless adventurers could know this hero.

'Yes. Knew him very well. We served with him in the Sekukuni campaign in South Africa, on the Mozambique border, a few months ago.'

'Ah.' The First Secretary's jaw didn't exactly drop but his mouth opened perhaps an inch and stayed that way for a moment. Then he spoke again, this time with an air almost of urgency. 'I say. I do wish you'd said . . . or at least made clear . . . Do forgive me, Fonthill.' He picked up a small silver bell on his desk and tinkled it, 'I . . . er . . . think we may have something for you, don't you know.'

Within seconds an Egyptian in loose garments topped with a red fez materialised and Ashley-Pemberton addressed him sharply in a language unknown to Simon. The man returned equally quickly with a single sheet of paper and gave it to the First Secretary, who perused it briefly and passed it over the desk.

'Cable, from Sir Garnet,' he said. 'Came about a week ago. Addressed to you but we didn't, of course, know you from Adam so we just hung on to it, so to speak. Slipped my mind. I do apologise.'

'Good lord.' Simon took the cable. 'He must have contacted my parents. They're the only people who knew we would call here. Excuse me for a moment.' Companionably, Jenkins leaned over his shoulder and they read the cable together:

GENERAL POMEROY-COLLEY NOW C-IN-C DURBAN
STOP GOOD MAN STOP TRANSVAAL BOERS
THREATEN WAR STOP HE NEEDS GOOD SCOUTS

STOP HAVE RECOMMENDED YOU STOP IF INTERESTED CONTACT HIM MARITZBURG SOONEST STOP REGARDS WOLSELEY END

'It seems,' murmured Ashley-Pemberton, 'that you are in demand.'

'Yes. More than here, anyway.'

Jenkins took the cable and his lips moved slowly as he followed the words again. Then: 'We'd better get goin', bach sir. Back the way we came, I suppose?'

Ashley-Pemberton's brows rose – threatening the security of the monocle – at the familiarity between the two. 'You'll need to take the train back to Alex,' he said, 'and then on to Port Said to board a steamer going to Durban down the Canal.'

Simon was frowning and spoke almost to himself. 'Yes, dammit. It'll take at least a month and it's damned expensive.'

'Can't help there, old boy, I'm afraid.'

Simon stuffed the cable into his pocket and rose. 'Wasn't asking for it. Thank you. Good afternoon.' Then he spun on his heel and walked through the door.

Ashley-Pemberton belatedly got to his feet and raised a finger. 'I say . . .' he began.

Jenkins gave him a beatific smile. 'Cheerio, old top.' Then he too was gone.

Outside, under the high white sun, the pair walked together in silence back to the green shade of the Azbakiyya Square, Ismail Pasha's twenty-acre folly, where one could buy anything from a live tiger in a cage to the services of an Italian whore. They found a stone bench and sat beneath an Australian gum tree, imported at great expense. Doves above them moaned to each other in gentle courtship and tame crested hoopoe birds speared insects in the lush, well-watered grass at their feet. The traffic around them belied the reality of national bankruptcy. Dandy fezzed *beys* rode by on prancing, well-groomed English stallions, fastidiously avoiding the street hackneys carrying Mr Cook's tourists eager to spend their inflated sovereigns. Arabs of the Nejd mingled with *fellaheens* astride donkeys and locals

6

in caftans, sheikhs in green turbans and Bashibazouks idling in their tall hats and swathed cummerbunds, daggers peeping from the folds. Cairo seemed a fecund crossroads, where there was money to be made and spent.

'Are you thinkin' what I'm thinkin'?' asked Jenkins.

Simon nodded. 'We have exactly nine pounds, twelve and sixpence between us. How the hell are we going to get to Durban and then 'Maritzburg?'

Jenkins broke the silence again. 'I don't like suggestin' it, see, but you could mail your folks again . . .'

'No.'

'Well, I understand, bach sir. They'd only say "Come 'ome, then", wouldn't they? An' I suppose you still don't want that, eh?'

Simon didn't reply, but stared ahead unseeingly at the passing throng, his elbow on his knee and his chin resting on his fist. Jenkins knew very well that he couldn't go home. Alice Griffith, his long-time love, would be getting married at about this time, in the little parish church near her parents' home on the Welsh–English border, only some ten miles away from his own parents' house. Alice, with her fair hair and steady grey eyes, would be walking down the aisle at the side of her husband, Colonel Ralph Covington. This wounded hero of the Sekukuni campaign, his former commanding officer, who had long persecuted him, was marrying the woman whom Simon loved more than life itself and who loved him in return. He wouldn't want to be even in the same country when the nuptials were celebrated.

'No,' murmured Simon, contemplating but not absorbing the saffron-clad hips of a dark-skinned woman walking by. 'We can't go home. This offer is just what we want – working for the army, doing what we do best, but on our own, not serving within that bloody institution. We've got to get down to see Colley as soon as we can.'

'What? On nine pounds, twelve shillings and sixpence?'

Both had received good back pay as army scouts, working for Wolseley in the Sekukuni campaign, and Simon also had a fair allowance from his father. He had insisted some time ago, however, that he could earn his keep and that the latter should be banked at home for his return – minus the hundred pounds that he had asked

7

his mother to use to fund a good wedding present for Alice (he had not specified what it should be, nor did he care). His pride forbade him now from requesting that his allowance should be restored. It savoured, somehow of failure. Unfortunately, since the end of the Sekukuni war nearly four months before, he and Jenkins had lived comparatively high on the hog, going on safari to the north-west of Zululand, and then, not finding congenial employment in South Africa, making the long and expensive journey to Egypt, where Simon had felt sure they could serve the Khedive in some adventurous capacity or other. Now their funds were virtually exhausted. But not quite.

Simon turned to Jenkins. 'You know what we could do?'

Jenkins grimaced. 'Oh yes. But I thought we were going to keep them for a rainy day?'

'As far as I am concerned,' Simon looked up at the brazen sky, 'it's pissing down. Come on.'

With a new certainty, the pair joined the milling crowd and made their way back to their modest hotel in Old Cairo. Bourse al-Gadid Street was as unlike the wide boulevards beyond the Azbakiyya in Ismail's new town as a Bombay bazaar was Haussmann's Paris. It sat on the edge of the labyrinth of narrow lanes but the upper storeys of its houses leaned towards each other so that a leap, it seemed, could easily take one across the gap, and indeed, so thick was the traffic of the pedestrians below that it appeared to be the quickest way of crossing the street.

The two men climbed the stairs to the second floor of the building where the corridor opened out to a surprisingly cool and spacious reception area. Jenkins was right. The Metropolitan was indeed 'a nice little place', modest but clean and ideal for two ex-soldiers down on their luck. The white-gowned manager beamed at his two guests from behind his reception desk. 'Tea, *effendi*?' he enquired of Simon. He had been delighted that the slim English gentleman and his servant had chosen his hotel for their stay in Cairo, rather than any of the gilded palaces usually favoured by the Europeans. This young man was a person of taste and culture, obviously.

'Thank you no, Ahmed,' said Simon. 'But you can help us.' He

8

looked around to ensure that they were alone. 'We have a mind to buy a little jewellery to take home to our wives. Something – what shall I say? – ah, ethnic, perhaps, that we would not normally find in the shops near the Azbakiyya. Is there a jewellery quarter in the old part of town?'

Ahmed's teeth flashed. 'Oh indeed, indeed, *effendi*. Here. Let me show you.'

He reached below his counter and pulled out a flat board, scuffed at the edges, on which had been pasted a street map of Cairo. It had been hand-drawn with no obvious reference to scale and it was much thumbed, but Ahmed exhibited it with pride.

He jabbed a finger down. 'We are here,' he said. 'Now, just here,' he pointed to a long thoroughfare which cut arrow straight through the hatchwork of narrow alleys that constituted Old Cairo, 'is the Musky, a very fine street indeed. It goes right the way through the city to the East Wall here at the Bab El-Ghurayib, so. But here, observe closely, you must turn right into the Ghuriya, and around here,' his black fingernail circled a maze of little lanes leading off the Musky, 'is jewellery quarter. Many fine shops there, *effendi*. You will surely find what you want, but,' he squinted up to where light filtered through the *mushraybia* screen from the lane, 'go soon because the sun will be setting in an hour.' He wrinkled his nose. 'And it is not perhaps wise for you to be there after dark. You understand . . .?'

Simon nodded and smiled. 'That is most helpful. We will go immediately.'

But first they had to visit Simon's room. Once inside, Jenkins quietly turned the key in the lock and Simon reached inside the single wooden wardrobe and withdrew a dirty rolled shirt. Three of its six buttons were missing, the collar was torn and it had clearly not seen water or soap for weeks. It was no prize for even the most indigent thief, but Simon handled it with care, opening it out so that at each armpit, where the fabric of the sleeve met the body of the shirt, small patches could be seen, as though they had been sewn there to soak up perspiration.

''Ow many, do you think?' enquired Jenkins.

'Not sure. Maybe two. Certainly no more.' Simon picked away at the stitching delicately with the end of his pocket knife, so that, eventually, one of the patches fell on to the bed, revealed as a tiny fabric bag. A moment's more work with the knife opened one end, and as Simon shook it, two small stones rolled out on to the cotton blanket. They lay there, irregular in shape and dull-looking, though they winked now as a stray shard of sunlight filtered through the wooden screen into the room.

Simon held them to the light. 'Let's see what these two are worth,' he said. 'I would rather keep the other two in reserve.' He looked across at Jenkins and grinned. 'Till it really rains.'

The Welshman frowned. 'But why do we 'ave to go into these back streets to sell 'em? Why can't we go to a proper merchant or whatever? Get a better price, wouldn't we?'

'Maybe.' Simon rubbed at the larger of the two diamonds with his thumb. 'But I'd rather not risk it. A pukka merchant would have to ask questions about how we had acquired two uncut diamonds, and when it emerged that we had been in Kimberley, we would bound to come under suspicion as diamond thieves. You heard what old tight-arse said about the English being unpopular here. I don't want to end up in an Egyptian jail just when we've got the chance of a decent job in South Africa. No. Let's take our chance in the bazaar.'

Jenkins sniffed. 'All right, bach sir, but I don't much fancy roamin' about in these streets after dark without a bit of protection, look you.' He walked back to the cupboard and, standing on a chair, reached to the flat top and drew down two long, thin objects, loosely wrapped in blankets and tied with cord. 'Let's take the rifles, eh?'

'Good God, no. We can't walk through the streets of Old Cairo carrying two Martini-Henrys.'

'Suppose you're right.' He replaced the rifles. 'Better be knives, then. I've got a spare.'

Simon shuddered. 'Ugh. I'm no bloody back-street knife-fighter, 352. You know that. You can fight with the damned things, but I wouldn't know where to start. We weren't taught how to use knives at Sandhurst, only nicely polished sabres. No. I'll do without. Anyway, I don't want a fight. I want to keep out of trouble.' He shot

10

a keen glance at his servant. 'These diamonds have enough blood on them as it is.'

Jenkins's nose buried itself in his moustache as he made a face and nodded. 'You're right about that, bach sir. That you are.'

Before keeping their promise to scout for General Wolseley in his war against the Sekukuni nation, some ten months before, the pair had risked their lives in the brutal diamond-mining town of Kimberley and then on the veldt of the Transvaal to rescue their old friend Nandi, a young half-Zulu girl, from the clutches of Mozambique diamond smugglers. The girl had insisted on giving them four diamonds, as 'keepsakes'.

Now Simon jingled the two stones together in his hand for a moment. 'God knows what they're worth,' he mused. 'But the bastards who stole them defended them stoutly enough. They should get us back to Durban.' He replaced the gems in their little sack, put it in the breast pocket of his shirt and carefully buttoned it. 'Come on. Let's try our luck at diamond trading.'

They found the Musky easily enough and followed it to the junction described by Ahmed. There they took a right turn, plunging into the narrow alleyways where only a thin streak of light above marked the narrow space between the lattice windows of the overhanging storeys. Almost immediately they were in amongst the traders. There were no street stalls, as they had come to expect from places like Bombay and Durban – indeed, if there had been, there would have been no space for customers to pass by. Instead, the ground floors of what seemed to be private houses, constructed of large stone slabs climbing up to the balconies above, had been opened out to create small shops, often only some six feet high and eight feet deep and seemingly unconnected to the living quarters within the house. The shopkeepers lounged on their steps, smoking pipes or more elegant cigarettes and seemingly quite uninterested in selling the wares that choked the interiors of their little cubicles.

Fascinated by the bustle, sights and smells of the crowded thoroughfares, Simon – his hand nonchalantly protecting his buttoned-down shirt pocket underneath his jacket – and Jenkins made their way through first the cotton market, and then the tinned goods *suk*, where the products of the West were piled high, leading on to the armourers' section, with its old chain-mail shirts, curved scimitars that the hand of Saladin might have gripped and elderly muskets, their butts worked in silver. Simon had no idea in which direction they had wandered or how far when, on impulse, he stopped and bought a sturdy ebony walking stick, with a bulbous hand grip. He staggered the vendor by paying the asking price without demur and then enquired of him the location of the jewellery quarter. The man raised a languid hand and motioned that they should take the next turn to the right. They did so and immediately found themselves in another marketplace. This one glittered and sparkled with the skills of the jeweller and silversmith, with each alcove a treasure trove of bangles, baubles, beaten copper, elegant silver and shining gold; trinkets and more precious objects mixed in a seemingly haphazard fashion.

'Blimey,' said Jenkins. 'It's Aladdin's cave!'

They shuffled along, heads turning, until they came to a shop which seemed a cut above the rest, in that, tucked away in the dim recesses of a deeper than usual cavity, they could see what seemed like precious stones arrayed in various settings and displayed on cushions along a series of shelves which themselves had been draped in fine silks and cottons. Sitting on the edge of his shop, his back to a huge hinged shutter, sat the owner, puffing a long, curved pipe. His blue turban was elegantly wound and his long white robe was gathered in at the waist by a knotted black cord that glittered with gold tassels. His beard was white and he looked up at the two Europeans with black eyes that seemed quite expressionless.

'Good evening, sir,' said Simon. 'Do you speak English?'

Perhaps a little surprised at the politeness of this Englishman, the old man struggled to his feet, put his hands together in an almost Hindu gesture and bowed his head slightly. 'Yes, *effendi*. You are welcome. What can I do to help your honour?'

Simon gestured to the shallow interior. 'May we step inside for a moment?'

'Of course.'

'They moved three paces into the dim interior, where two oil lamps shed a little light, sufficient, however, to elicit a myriad sparkles from stones set in exotic bracelets, necklaces, pendants and rings, all ranged along the shelves without thought of security. Used to window-shopping in London's Bond Street, where widely spaced jewels were exhibited in locked glass cabinets, Simon was struck by how easy it would be to scoop up these Eastern treasures and be off down the street. A glance at the sauntering crowd outside, however, made him realise that one cry in Arabic of 'Stop, thief!' would result in a dagger in his back within seconds.

'Do you purchase precious stones, as well as sell them?' he enquired.

Immediately the old man's posture changed slightly. It was almost imperceptible but sufficient for him to establish that he was dropping the role of supplicant and assuming that of reluctant purchaser. The black eyes seemed to harden as he took in these two Englishmen. 'Sometimes, *effendi*,' he said, 'but not often, and as you can see,' he indicated his emporium, empty although in truth there was room for perhaps only one more person to have entered it, 'trade is not good.'

'Very well.' Simon took out his small sack. 'I have two uncut diamonds here, which you may care to look at.' He rolled the stones out on to his cupped hand. Dirty as they were, with traces of yellow Kimberley clay still adhering to them, they glinted promisingly in the half-light.

The old man produced a jeweller's glass, screwed it into his eye and examined each stone in turn. His nose wrinkled and he looked up at Simon. 'You wish to sell these, *effendi*?'

'Yes, but only if the price is right. I appreciate that I could probably receive more for them in Amsterdam or London, but I do not wish to return to Europe yet and the money in hand would be useful.'

The Egyptian resumed his study of the stones for a moment and murmured, 'You realise that these are not top-quality diamonds? They are uncut and must be cleaned and polished as well as fashioned, and the price must recognise this.' He put down the glass and his black eyes shot a glance first at Jenkins and then at Simon. 'May I ask how you came by them?'

13

'They were given to me by a diamond merchant in Kimberley in return for a service I was able to render him. He assured me that they were worth one hundred English pounds each.'

Jenkins nodded gravely, both in support of his master and in admiration at the impudence of the lie.

'Ah.' The old man hesitated, then returned to his examination for a moment. Then: 'I fear that you were misled.' He held up his hand as Simon made to interrupt. 'Oh, they are genuine diamonds, but they are of a very poor quality and are worth much less than your friend's estimation. I fear I could offer you nothing that might interest you.'

Simon nodded. 'I understand. Thank you for your time. I shall try elsewhere . . .' and he made to take the diamonds back but the shopkeeper held up his hand and gave a wan smile.

'Perhaps, however,' he said, 'you would allow me to examine them properly in good light at my workbench in my house.' He waved a hand to the interior. 'And while I am doing so, perhaps you would do me the honour of taking a little tea there. It should not take long. It might be that we can do business, although I doubt it.'

Simon inclined his head. 'Very well, but I do hope that we can be quick. We have other business to conduct this evening.'

The old man half bowed. 'Of course. Here, take your stones and let me close these premises.' He ushered them outside and then, with some difficulty, swung across the thick wooden shutters – more like two heavy doors – which covered the opening. He clicked and locked an ancient padlock to secure them, then beckoned for Simon and Jenkins to follow him a couple of paces towards where, recessed into the blank stone wall, an equally old and formidable door led into the house behind the shop. He had no key but pulled on a cord that jangled a bell above his head. This led eventually to the door being pulled back by an elderly and incredibly fat shaven-headed retainer.

They entered a charming inner courtyard, in which a fountain tinkled. The shopkeeper took off his slippers and left them on a marble slab outside a door, and Simon and Jenkins did the same with their boots. ' 'Ope we don't 'ave to run for it,' murmured Jenkins, but he followed Simon into a narrow carpeted corridor which led into a

14

square room whose floor was covered with rugs and furnished with a low divan around three sides. Dim illumination – for the light was now rapidly fading outside – was provided by small pieces of coloured glass let into a framework of stucco high on the wall. The elderly servant, however, lit candles and revealed a room with whitewashed walls and a ceiling formed of planks laid on massive beams and painted a dark red. Shallow recesses framed fine-looking examples of the goldsmith's work.

The old man gestured for them to sit on the divan and whispered something to his servant. He turned to his visitors. 'Tea will be brought to you very soon. It will be from India and served with milk and sugar in the European style.' The last sentence was added with a touch of pride. 'If you will trust me with your diamonds for a moment longer I will examine them and rejoin you within ten minutes.' He smiled and gestured to the artefacts in the recesses. 'As you see, if I fail to return you have adequate securities.'

Simon smiled in response and gave him the diamonds. Then the two men sat in silence for a moment until a half-stifled giggle made Simon look up. A *mushraybia* screen – the interlocking lattices made of finely carved knotted wood, the traditional Ottoman and Mamluk method of allowing warm air to cool as it passed, while preventing outsiders from seeing through – had been set into the top half of the wall facing them at mezzanine level. It was clear that they were being observed.

'Well I'm dashed,' said Jenkins in a loud stage whisper. 'Is it the harem, then, bach sir? I always wanted to 'ave a peep into one o' them, see.'

'Probably, but I shouldn't try to climb up.' Simon's response was barely audible. 'I understand that the ladies are usually fat and a bit unwashed. But keep your voice down. I don't want to give offence – or be overheard for that matter.'

Tea came very quickly, but they hardly had time to sip it before the old man returned. He sat down beside Simon companionably, and produced the diamonds.

'It is as I thought, *effendi*,' he said. 'They have not the value given to them by your friend. Here, take the glass and examine them closely.

15

I have taken away a little of the clay and you will see that they have a slightly yellow appearance. This is typical of South African diamonds – we call them "Cape Yellows" – and it lowers their price. Now, also observe,' he put a finely manicured finger to the edge of the slightly larger of the two stones, 'the bearded girdle there. There are what we call tiny hairline fractures at the edge of the stone. You may also see one or two carbon spots in the gem itself.'

Simon carefully examined the stone but could see none of this, although there was, perhaps, a slight yellowish tint to the gem. Damn! The prospect of them buying tickets for Durban seemed to be receding. And yet the *suks* were renowned for sharp dealing. And the English were universally disliked in Cairo . . . He decided to bluff it out.

He returned the glass. 'I see,' he said. 'It is kind of you to point out these imperfections. Perhaps, after all, it would be best for us to take our chances with the market in Amsterdam, because I cannot believe that the gems are worthless. So,' he rose to his feet, 'we shall bother you no more.'

The old man laid a hand on his arm. 'I did not say, *effendi*, that your diamonds were worthless. I merely pointed out that they were not worth two hundred of your English pounds.' He smiled, gesturing for Simon to regain his seat. 'I can have these stones mounted in a way that will, to some extent, conceal their imperfections, but the processing – the cleaning, the cutting, the polishing and then the mounting – will be an expensive matter. I could offer you no more than fifty pounds for the two.'

Simon made a quick calculation. Their railway fare to Suez, then the cost of third-class tickets down the Suez Canal, through the Red Sea and on to the east coast of South Africa would cost at least sixty pounds for the two of them. The bargaining must continue.

'I quite appreciate, of course, that your processing costs on the gems must be included in the price,' he responded, 'but I cannot believe that my merchant friend in Kimberley, who deals in world prices, would have been so wrong in his estimation of the worth of the diamonds. Perhaps I could accept one hundred and twenty pounds, but no less.'

Jenkins blew his nose. He was clearly enjoying this.

The Egyptian shook his head sorrowfully. 'It would give me great pleasure to be able to meet your request, but I cannot do so. If I did business in that fashion, *effendi*, my wives would grow thin and my children would have no shoes for their feet. I will offer sixty pounds but no more.'

Simon screwed up his eyes. 'I understand your problems, but unfortunately I have difficulties of my own. One hundred pounds is the least I could accept.'

'Alas, we are too far away on this puzzling question of price. Let me, then, make one last – and very generous – offer, which must be regarded, *effendi*, as positively my last. I will give you seventy-five pounds.'

Simon noticed that there was no light now filtering through the stained-glass diamonds on the walls. It must be dark outside. Time to go. He waited a moment longer, then, with a great show of reluctance, nodded his head. 'I fear I cannot accept,' he said. 'But I am prepared to take ninety, if you pay me in sovereigns, for where we must travel paper money will be a hindrance. I presume that this will be no problem?'

The old man inclined his head. 'You drive a hard bargain, but very well. It will take me a moment longer, *effendi*, to get the coins, that is all. Allow me to take the diamonds.' A final thought struck him. 'Where are you staying? Shepheards, of course?'

'Of course.'

'Then I shall send two of my men to guide you. It will not be easy to find your way in these lanes after dark, particularly,' he smiled, although it did not reach his dark eyes, 'carrying your precious burden.'

'Oh, that will not be necessary, thank you. I believe we shall find our way safely.'

'No. I insist. It will be safer and quicker.' With a half-bow, the old man left the room, leaving the two friends sitting side by side, staring straight ahead and trying to retain straight faces.

'Well,' whispered Jenkins after a moment's silence, 'I know you can't sit a horse properly nor shoot straight to save your life, but you lie and argue beautifully, bach sir. I'll say that for you.'

'Thank you, 352,' Simon murmured to the wall opposite. 'I've probably been diddled out of a fortune but the money will get us safely out of here.' Another subdued giggle from beyond the lattice above them could have either confirmed or refuted that.

Eventually the shopkeeper returned clutching a goatskin containing the coins. With him were two black-bearded men, tall for Egyptians, with visages that seemed permanently set in scowls beneath their black turbans. One would have been forgiven for thinking that they resented the tiresome business of escorting two infidels back to their marble-pillared hotel.

'Please count the coins, and I insist that Sulimein and Abdul accompany you,' said the old man. 'I would not sleep if I thought that you had left here without escorts to guide you and keep you safe.'

For the first time Simon thought that he detected a faint hint of irony in the old man's tone. But, as ever, the black eyes remained expressionless and the half-smile that played around the thin-lipped mouth seemed genuine. He counted the coins quickly, replaced them in the bag and wrapped the cord which secured the puckered top around his wrist. Then he offered the shopkeeper his hand. 'Thank you for the tea and for trading with us. May God be with you.'

The old man took his hand and then that of Jenkins. He did not speak but gestured down the passageway, and the bald-headed servant led the way into the courtyard. There they regained their boots and the man slid open the bolts on the old door, and the four of them stepped out into the alleyway. They found that the narrow street had been transformed. In the gloom – for there was no lighting – they saw that all the shops had been boarded up and that the alley was now completely deserted. Where once the trinkets of the silversmiths had glittered, now each shop presented a dead façade, with crude wooden shutters bolted and barred. The stone walls of the houses, looming so close together, seemed to form narrow canyons. The *suk* now seemed an alien, unfriendly – even dangerous – place.

'Blimey,' said Jenkins. 'What's 'appened to all the fairy caves?'

Simon strengthened his grip on the ebony stick and tucked the cord of the goatskin through his trouser belt, securing it with a knot.

He spoke softly to Jenkins. 'I may be completely wrong, 352, but I don't like the look of these two. We need only one man to guide us to the hotel, so why give us these two great bruisers? It doesn't seem right. It would be the simplest thing in the world for them to lead us into a dark cul-de-sac, cut our throats and take the money back to our white-bearded friend. Let's see where they lead us, but if they are making for Shepheards Hotel, then we should be on that main street, the Musky, or the other wide one, the Muhammad Ali, within about three minutes. If we're not, we had better prepare for trouble.'

Jenkins nodded. 'Right you are, bach sir. If it comes to it, look you, I'll take that big bugger on the right. You take the littler one, though 'e's big enough.' He shot a quick, concerned glance at Simon. 'Remember, if there is a fight, look at their eyes. That'll tell you which way they're goin' to jump, see.' He snorted. 'Bugger it, I told you I should 'ave brought me extra knife.' And he unbuttoned his jacket to free the handle of the knife protruding from his trouser top.

It soon became clear that if they were being led to Shepheards Hotel, then they were certainly not being taken by the most direct route. It was no use relying on Jenkins. This impeccable horseman, crack shot, alley fighter, dedicated washer of shirts and polisher of boots had no sense of direction and had, in fact, taken the Queen's shilling in Birmingham when he thought he was in Manchester. All Simon's instincts told him they should be turning right. Instead, however, the two men ahead of them now turned left again into what seemed to be the heart of the tangle of alleyways in the Old Town.

The walls above them seemed to lean in closer and only a sliver of moonlight, catching the top of the stonework high above them, cast any light at all on the street down which they were now being led. The echo from the clump of Simon and Jenkins's boots on the cobblestones was the only sound and, screwing his eyes to peer ahead into the gloom, it seemed to Simon that the alley ended in a blank wall.

'It'll be now,' whispered Jenkins.

Suddenly both men whirled round, knives appearing in their hands as if by magic. The bigger of the two sprang at Simon in an obviously prepared plan, but in doing so, he had to pass Jenkins, who had moved a pace ahead of his partner. The Welshman's boot caught the shin of the big Egyptian, who cursed and lashed backhandedly at his assailant, but Jenkins had slipped aside so that the knife swung harmlessly down and in front of the other attacker, thus hampering that man's own attempt to close in on the elusive Welshman. Simon took advantage and slashed the weighted head of his stick across the second Egyptian's face. The force of the blow was partly softened by the end of the man's turban, but it was strong enough to send him staggering back.

The advantage of surprise had been lost to the attackers and now the fight had been reduced to two separate encounters, so that, despite the narrowness of the alley and the closeness of all four men, each pair of antagonists had only eyes and ears for his opponent. It was as though two separate duels were taking place, at venues far from each other.

Certainly Simon had no sense of how Jenkins was faring, for with throat dry and perspiration trickling down his forehead, he was fiercely concentrating on the man confronting him – a man who was now softly approaching him again, his left hand extended as though to maintain balance, his right hand held slightly back, with the long, curved blade of the knife glinting in the half-light. Simon licked his lips and found them as dry as sandpaper. He felt fear all right, for he remembered what it was like for sharp, hot steel to cut into soft flesh. That had been a Zulu assegai two years ago, but at least he had had a weapon of sorts to defend himself then. Now he had only a walking stick and no training in this disgusting alley-cat, knife-in-the-ribs warfare to fall back on. Or was that quite true . . .? He remembered the fencing master at Sandhurst encouraging him after hours with foil and sabre: 'You've got talent for this, Fonthill. You could make a swordsman.'

Simon immediately reversed his grip on the ebony stick, which he had previously used two-handedly as a cudgel. Holding it only with his right hand, his left held high behind him, he bent his knees and presented the sharp end to the Egyptian and stood waiting, *en garde*. The latter halted in his advance for a moment, clearly puzzled. What was it Jenkins had said? Ah yes, watch the eyes. Simon looked hard at the dark visage opposite him, the face exuding hate and determination, the whites of the eyes standing out.

Now those eyes glanced quickly at the end of the stick. Simon realised intuitively that his opponent was going to grab the end of that piece of wood, pull Simon towards him and then swing his blade from the side deep into the ribs. And so it proved. Quickly the Egyptian feinted to Simon's right with his left hand and then swung it back to clutch the end of the stick. But Simon was even quicker. Now perfectly balanced, he lifted the end of the stick marginally, took a quick fencer's step forward and lunged in the classic style, left leg braced behind him, right leg bent to its fullest extent, his sword arm stretched to the limit. The thrust was made with the speed of a cobra striking and the end of the stick took the assassin directly in the left eye as he swung forward. The man let out a howl of anguish and staggered back, clutching his eye with his free hand. Quickly reversing his grip, Simon now brought the club end of the stick across the wrist of the Egyptian's knife hand, splintering the bone and sending the blade spinning across the cobbles.

A cry behind him made Simon spin round, his heart in his mouth at what he might see. Jenkins and the big Egyptian were locked together in a strange embrace against one wall of the alley – strange because the big man was half draped across the Welshman's broad shoulders, so that Jenkins's head protruded from under the other's armpit. As Simon watched, the Egyptian uttered another cry, more a half-sigh this time, and gradually crumpled to the floor, Jenkins seemingly helping him down with his shoulder but in fact sinking his knife even deeper into the other's stomach until, with a twist, he sent him crashing on to the cobblestones.

Jenkins withdrew the blade and looked up, his black hair matted across his forehead. His face distorted, he cried, 'Look out, bach!'

Simon instinctively ducked his head and twisted low, but there was no threat. The second assassin, still clutching his eye, was running as fast as he could down the alley, away from these foreigners who looked so easy to take but who fought like tigers. The encounter had lasted less than a minute and now the street was silent again, apart from the heavy breathing of the victors.

'Bloody 'ell, man,' gasped Jenkins. 'You only 'ad a bit of wood. What did you do?'

'Just watched his eyes,' said Simon, both hands on his knees, trying to regain his breath. 'Good advice. Thanks.' Then he looked across at the inert form of the big man, blood oozing out of two wounds, one in the chest and the other in the stomach. 'Oh hell, 352,' he wheezed, 'did you have to kill him, for God's sake?'

Jenkins drew himself up to all of his five feet four inches. 'Well, as a matter of fact, bach sir, I bloody well did, saving your presence, like. The bugger was trying to kill me an' 'e 'ad a knife and 'e was bigger 'n me as well, see.' His tone grew grudging. 'I'm surprised you 'ad to ask that, look you.'

'Sorry, old chap. You're right, of course. Lordy, I wouldn't want to go through that again.' Simon hitched up the goatskin of coins which was now hanging down his thigh and looked again at the dead man. 'I'm afraid we'll just have to leave him and get out of here before my one-eyed friend gets back to the shopkeeper and starts a hue and cry.'

Jenkins sniffed, only half mollified, but he bent over the corpse, wiped the blade of his knife clean on the dead man's *burnous* and slipped the weapon back beneath the band of his trousers. Together the two friends walked quickly down the silent street and began the difficult task of finding their way back, out of the maze of *suks* and alleys, to one of the main thoroughfares.

They were lucky, and after some ten minutes of squinting up at what stars could be seen in the narrow slits of sky they emerged on to the Musky. There, in a doorway, they jettisoned Jenkins's blood-stained jacket and did what they could to smarten their appearance before hailing a late hackney cab to take them back to their hotel. Jenkins, typically, seemed quite unperturbed by their desperate encounter and hummed tunelessly – he was one of the few Welshmen who could not carry a tune to save his life – as he sat back on the buttoned cracked leather. Simon's mind, however, was racing.

'That nasty business means that we must change our plans,' he said eventually.

'Why? We've got our money and that killin' wasn't our fault.'

Simon sighed. 'Look. Despite the English influence, Egypt is a

Turkish possession and not part of the British Empire. We are unknown here and must appear as just a pair of penniless adventurers. You have killed a man and I've injured one and, more to the point, let him get away to tell the story. The body will be found in the morning. That villainous shopkeeper will want his money back, and in this city with its strong anti-British atmosphere he could spin any story and raise feelings against us. I am not sure that old Ashley-Pemberton would raise a finger to help us – in fact he'd probably throw us to the dogs to placate the authorities – and Wolseley is too far away to help, even if he could.'

Jenkins sucked in his moustache. 'Ah. Right. So what do we do, then?'

'Well . . .' Simon mused. 'We will have a few hours in hand anyway, because I told old greybeard that we were staying at Shepheards. First thing in the morning I shall cable General Colley in South Africa that we are on our way to serve him as scouts, following Wolseley's message to us – that will put him under some sort of obligation and make sure that we get work. But Ashley-Pemberton knows that we intended to go back to Alexandria and pick up a steamer going down the Canal from Port Said, and I don't trust him not to pass this on if he is questioned.'

'So?'

'So we won't take the train across the desert to the mouth of the Canal.'

'What? Are we goin' to march through the jungle to South Africa, then? It'll be a bit 'ot.'

Simon smiled. 'You're not far off, 352. But no. Not through the jungle. We're going to go due east across the desert to Suez at the southern end of the Canal and pick up a steamer from there. No one will think of looking for us there. The train will be too dangerous, but I would think that there will still be traders crossing the desert. We will buy passage on a camel train.'

Jenkins's jaw dropped. 'What? Ride on camels?'

'Certainly. It's the only way.'

'But with respect, bach sir, you can barely sit on a horse when it's movin' a bit. You'll just fall off a camel.'

23

'Don't be impertinent. Anyway, I'm much better on a horse now. A camel goes slower. They must be easier. You'll see.'

They found Ahmed still at the reception desk on their return – in fact, he never seemed to leave it. If he was surprised at Jenkins's appearance in shirtsleeves and their general air of dishevelment, he gave no sign. 'Whisky, *effendi*?' he enquired.

'Yes please. Two large ones, in my room, please. But Ahmed, there is one further service you can render us.' Simon placed two gold sovereigns on the desk.

'Ah sir, you are very kind, but no.' He gently pushed the coins back. 'We are honoured to have you stay at the Metropolitan. No extra payment is required. I shall be glad to help you further.'

'Good man. I knew we could rely on you, but I do insist you take this as a small token of thanks for what I am now asking you to do.' Simon pushed the coins back and leaned forward conspiratorially, beckoning Ahmed towards him. The Egyptian, eyes wide, inclined his head across the counter.

'Now, Ahmed,' continued Simon in a low voice. 'With your intelligence and sharp eye, I know you will have realised that we have been here in Cairo these last three days on special work.' Ahmed, his mouth open, began to shake his head in denial, then switched to nodding in happy agreement. 'Of course,' said Simon, 'I knew you would. Nothing escapes you. In fact, we have been liaising between the British Government and the Khedive on matters of the utmost secrecy. Now, can I rely completely on your discretion?'

Ahmed looked quickly to his right and left. 'Of course, *effendi*. Oh yes, indeed.'

'Good. It has now become necessary for us to leave Cairo early in the morning to take a steamer from Alexandria to Italy. But for reasons which you will understand I cannot reveal . . .' the Egyptian nodded his head solemnly, 'we cannot take the train to Alexandria. This means we must somehow cross the desert to Suez at the southern end of the Canal and pick up a northbound boat from there. Is it possible to do this?'

The Egyptian frowned. 'Let me see . . . what day is it? Ah yes, Monday. You are in luck, *effendi*. There is a camel train which leaves at about ten o'clock tomorrow, from the Bab El-Ghurayib gateway in the East Wall, right at the end of the Musky. The caravan takes goods to the little villages at oases on the way to Suez. The leader of the train is Mahmud Muharram and he is my brother. I am sure that for a fair price he will take you across the desert. I can go now and arrange it for the morning, if you wish.'

'That would be very kind of you, Ahmed. I knew we could rely on you. But there is one last task I ask of you.' Simon added another sovereign to the little pile. 'We must travel incognito until we reach Suez, you understand?' Ahmed nodded his head vigorously. 'Do you think that you could procure for us some Arab garments? Nothing elegant, just something so that we do not stand out from your friends conspicuously as Europeans. Mahmud can know that we are English, but until we leave Cairo, no one else must. Yes?'

'Of course, *effendi*. That will be no problem. No problem at all.'

Simon leaned across and shook his hand, and equally solemnly, so did Jenkins. 'Thank you, Ahmed,' said Simon. 'You have done our two countries a great service.'

'It is nothing, sir. Nothing at all.'

Jenkins gave him a great grin. 'And don't forget the whiskies, bach. Right away if you can. Bit parched, see.'

Chapter 2

Ahmed was as good as his word, and shortly after dawn they found small bundles of clothing outside each of their doors. He knocked on Simon's door shortly afterwards – did the man never sleep? – and assured him that his brother would take them on the journey with his *funduq* for six English sovereigns. Then he showed him how to dress, displaying the delight of a mother arraying her child for the school fancy dress.

Simon was allowed to keep his plain white trousers, tucked into his riding boots. It was not possible, explained Ahmed, to find Egyptian slippers to fit, but the boots would merely show that he was probably from the northern coast, more accustomed to riding horses, and he would pass. His tailored shirt was replaced by a simple cotton garment, buttoned to the neck, worn under a voluminous and unstructured white robe, gathered at the waist by a red sash. A head cloth of undyed cotton, allowed to flow over the forehead to the eyes and also over the shoulders to offer protection against the sun, but loose enough to be tucked across the mouth to keep out sand, was kept in place by two plaited cords tied around the crown of the head. To Simon's untutored eye, this seemed more the dress of an Arab than an Egyptian, but he was relieved to be spared the great Egyptian turban, wound precariously round the head like a bundle of washing, which he knew, from previous experience with something similar in Afghanistan, Jenkins would be unable to keep in place. Ahmed assured him that the dress was typical of a desert traveller and would fit them for the eighty-mile journey across the plains and sand dunes to Suez.

Once Jenkins had been similarly equipped, they shouldered their duffel bags, took down their still-wrapped Martini-Henrys, paid their bill, shook hands warmly once again with Ahmed and left the little hotel before the other guests were up and about to marvel at their transformation. Within the hour they had passed through the great gate of Bab El-Ghurayib in the East Wall to where a bewildering number of camels and men were milling about on the scrub and arid shingle that lapped the walls of the city. The activity seemed haphazard, with camels snarling their yellow tombstone teeth and refusing to rise from their kneeling positions, tents being struck and household utensils being rolled into untidy bundles. The smell of camel dung forced the two men to wrinkle their noses.

They soon found Mahmud Muharram – not difficult in that he stood tall in the chaos, shouting words of command and swishing in emphasis with a long frayed whip. He was a big man and wore a black beard behind which his teeth flashed in welcome as he nodded in approval of their garb.

'Good, you are dressed for the desert,' he said in excellent English. Then he frowned and pointed at their awkwardly wrapped rifles. 'What are they?'

'English army rifles,' said Simon. 'We have no wish to use them on this journey but they will be necessary when we reach our final destination.'

The frown remained. 'You are soldiers, then?'

'No, although we used to be. We have been asked to work for the British army as scouts.'

'I do not know what that means. But I want no shooting on my *funduq*. Show me the rifles, but not here. Come.' He beckoned to them to follow him to where one tent was still standing. It was long and shallow, secured by a seemingly random web of ropes tied to pegs in the ground or pinned down by rocks, and it had no defined shape except for a low peak in the middle. It looked as though the first breath of wind could blow it away, but Simon and Jenkins were to come to respect its strength and resilience to desert storms. One end had been left open and they ducked their heads and followed Mahmud into the interior. There they sat on cushions and Simon carefully unwrapped his rifle.

The Egyptian took it and his eyes lit up as he weighed it in his hands, worked the ejector lever behind the trigger and then lifted the stock into his shoulder and sighted along its barrel. He raised an eyebrow towards Simon: 'It is the latest, I think?'

'Yes. We have used it in the Zulu War and last year against the Afghans.'

'Ah.' The big man nodded his head slowly. 'Then you are truly warriors.'

'Well,' said Jenkins, 'used to be, that is. We've sort of retired now, see.'

The smile returned to Mahmud's eyes. 'Good. I am glad to hear it. I do not want any soldiering on the journey to Suez.'

'Of course not,' Simon hastily agreed. 'We will keep the rifles out of sight, of course. But there will be no danger in the desert, surely?'

The Egyptian shrugged his shoulders. 'If we are lucky, no. But there are always the Bedawis.'

'Who are they?'

'They are not Egyptians.' His lip curled. 'They are from the south and they are nomads, desert dwellers. They have drifted up from the big desert lands above the Sudan and they look after small herds of sheep and cattle. But that is not all they do. Some – the bad ones – raid small villages and steal and they sometimes stop caravans like ours and demand payment to allow us to progress.'

'Good lord. They are just pirates, then?'

Jenkins's moustache bristled. 'Why don't you just send them off with a bloody nose or whatever, eh?'

Mahmud looked from one to the other uneasily, as though acknowledging a weakness. 'Ah, unlike you, my friends, we are not warriors. We are just traders. My people are not brave. It seems easiest just to give them what they want and then get on with our business. You see, these Bedawis are cruel people. They will kill if they are opposed.'

'I understand,' said Simon. 'It is not easy for you. But you deserve protection. Why does the army of the Khedive not give you that protection?'

The big man shrugged again. 'There was a time when the army

sent out patrols to keep the camel routes open. But now we see very few soldiers. The Bedawis know this and they are growing more . . . what do you call it? . . . yes, arrogant. They stopped me a month ago and also last week, on the way here. But,' he opened out his hands in a fatalistic gesture, 'that was unusual. Perhaps Allah will be good this time.'

Simon involuntarily put a hand on his pack, where a slight bulge revealed the presence of the gold sovereigns. He exchanged glances with Jenkins. 'When they stop you, what do they demand?'

'Ah, nothing particular. They just go through our wares, taking what they want. But they are not stupid. They do not take everything, for that would mean the end of our journeys and the end of their income. It is best to let them have their way. It is like a tax that we pay. But,' he frowned again as he ran his hand along the steel-blue barrel of the Martini, 'keep these out of sight. They will want them.'

'Hmm. How are they armed?'

'They have muskets – our traditional *jerzail* – but I am not sure how good they are at shooting. The weapon, you know, is not accurate like these rifles of yours. What I *have* seen them use is the scimitar, their curved swords. Three years ago they took off the head of one of my men with one sweep.' He shuddered. 'After that I do not oppose them.'

Simon nodded slowly. 'I see. Right, Mahmud, if they show up we will adopt a very low profile, I promise you. And we will keep our rifles under wraps. Now, here is the payment for our journey. Tell me, how many miles must we travel and how long will it take?'

The Egyptian gave a half-smile. 'I do not know your miles,' he said. 'I count journeys in time, and this one usually takes about ten days, depending upon whether we have a windstorm. If we do, it is longer.'

Simon made a quick calculation. 'Good lord. That's less than nine miles a day!'

'There's slow for you,' agreed Jenkins, curving up his eyebrows.

'Ah, but you forget that we must stop at five or six villages by the wells to trade and to water the camels. And our beasts are not racing camels. They . . . er . . . what is the English word?'

'Plod?'

'Plod, yes. A lovely word. You have both ridden camels before?'

Jenkins coughed and Simon interjected before the Welshman could speak, 'I am afraid not. But Jenkins here can ride anything.'

Mahmud smiled. 'That is well. Camels are not difficult to ride when they . . . er . . . plod. But it is different if we have to make them go fast, although that should not be necessary. Time in the desert should not be bullied or hurried. You will see. Now, I will find you camels and show you how to mount and sit. Bring your bags – and wrap your rifles and put them away.'

The two Britons did as they were bid and exchanged glances as they followed the big man outside into the burning sun. Simon was glad that Mahmud had shown not the slightest interest in why two Europeans should wish to adopt Arab disguise and take the slowest way across the desert to Suez. Perhaps Ahmed had put his finger to the side of his nose and implied great affairs of state. If so, Simon's admission that they were on their way to work as scouts with the British army would have sat ill with that theory. Simon sighed. What the hell! He was tired of spinning lies and just wanted to get out of Egypt. Yet he liked what he had seen of Mahmud. When he was speaking he had given no hint of dissembling and he had looked Simon directly in the eye. He had an air of command, and certainly the men, women and even children who were loading the camels and packing the tents seemed to possess a sense of purpose and urgency about them that was not typical of Egyptians, in Simon's brief experience. They seemed to respect and unhesitatingly obey the big man. He was surely to be trusted.

The Bedawis were a different matter. By the sound of it, it would be difficult to conceal the rifles *and* the sovereigns from them if they came calling. Simon bit his lip. There was no way that he and Jenkins could allow either to be taken. Low profile or not, they would fight if they had to, even if it meant compromising Mahmud and his people. The prospect of that worried Simon. If there was a fight – and they must do all they could to avoid it – and if he and Jenkins survived it, then they would move on, leave the caravan at Suez, board ship there and depart from Egypt and the desert, probably for ever. But the

31

families of the little caravan had to make the return journey. The aggrieved Bedawis would surely attack them again, and without the two well-armed Englishmen, what would happen to these gentle traders? He sighed, for he could think of no obvious solution. Then he shrugged his shoulders. He would have to find an answer to that question when and if it arose. Perhaps, as Mahmud had hoped, Allah would intervene.

The camels, however, were a more immediate problem.

Despite years of riding as a boy in the Brecon Hills and his time spent on horseback at Sandhurst and in the Regiment, Simon was a poor horseman and he knew it. In fact, if the matter ever slipped his mind, Jenkins – a superb natural rider – was there to remind him. Falling off a horse seemed as instinctive a course of action to Simon as staying on was to the Welshman. It was true that gradually, over the last two years in South Africa and Afghanistan, his seat in the saddle had become a little more secure. But these sky-high, lolloping, unempathetic creatures were a different proposition altogether, and he approached the smelly camels with a sinking heart. There was that distinctive hump to start with – how was he to sit on that? And how the hell was he to get on in the first place?

Most of the trading goods, the tents and the other paraphernalia of the little column now seemed to be loaded on to the pack camels, and the packs of the newcomers, the wrapped barrels of the rifles poking through, were added to the wide, many-layered burdens that projected above the animals by some four feet and by a similar distance on either side of their flanks. Everything – including the camels – looked most unstable. Mahmud pointed with his whip to two beasts, slimmer and taller than the pack animals, who were waiting in the couched position, their legs folded under them. A small boy stood on the doubled foreleg of each camel.

'These are for you,' he said. 'Egyptian camels are not the best but they can carry loads well enough. For riding, animals from Arabia are preferable and she camels better than males. These are from Syria. They will do.'

Jenkins approached the nearest camel with an appraising eye. At that moment, the beast turned towards him and emitted a huge belch and began chewing as a green sliver oozed over her loose lips and dripped down to the ground. The Welshman staggered back. 'Bloody 'ell,' he said, holding his nose. 'What's she been eatin', then?'

Mahmud grinned. 'Too much grass,' he said. 'They half digest it and then bring it back to chew again. She must walk it down. Now I show you how to mount and control. Watch.'

He seized the saddle pommel, dug his left knee into the side of the animal and nodded to the camel boy to stand aside. Immediately the camel unfolded her bent legs, and as she rose clumsily, Mahmud swung his other leg across the animal's back, tucking his robe under his bottom as he did so, and settled into the saddle in one smooth movement.

'Easy, eh?' he grinned.

Jenkins shot a worried glance at Simon. 'Bloody sight better if we didn't 'ave to wear these nightshirts,' he muttered.

Mahmud coiled his left leg around the front cantle of the saddle. 'Better to ride like this,' he said. He picked up the rein linked to the head stalls and shouted to the boys. Immediately, each gave Simon and Jenkins a short stick. The Egyptian gestured with his whip. 'Use those to give directions. Tap on the camel's neck to go left or right and so . . .' he tapped on the top of the neck, 'to go down.' Immediately the beast lurched forwards and then backwards and was kneeling again. Mahmud skipped off. 'You will get used to it. One important thing.' He knocked on Simon's chest with his whip in emphasis. 'Always keep up with the caravan. It is easy to drop behind, and suddenly the camel train is lost in the heat haze. You are alone and soon you are lost. If you are lost in the desert you will die.'

Simon nodded and looked across at Jenkins. The little Welshman blew out his cheeks and nodded even more vigorously.

'Good.' Mahmud looked around him. The first camels were making their way in stately line away from the city walls. 'Now mount and ride in the middle of the *funduq*.' He flashed his teeth. 'And God be with you.'

The camel boys gave reciprocal grins and gestured to the two Europeans to mount. Somehow they did so, although Jenkins's camel rose a little too quickly, leaving the Welshman's short legs waving in the air until he was able to get purchase and pull himself across the saddle. Once astride, however, it was as though he had been born there. He slapped the camel's haunch instinctively with his stick to set her moving and then tapped more gently on the left side of her neck so that the animal immediately fell into line.

To Simon, the impression was one of sitting on the cross trees high in the rigging of a heeling, pitching sailing ship, with one leg coiled around the mast as the only way of avoiding falling off. He shot a quick look around. No one seemed to be clutching the saddle pommel, not even Jenkins, who was now sitting grinning and swaying in complete unison with the gentle, undulating movement of his mount. Simon grabbed the pommel and clung on, hoping it would get better.

In fact it did, and it was not long before he began almost to enjoy the swaying, soporific gait of the strange beast he was riding. It was not unpleasant to allow his eyes to close as he reflected that it looked as though they had slipped away from Cairo before they could be connected with the dead body in the alley. And they had sufficient funds for the passage to South Africa! He opened one eye and patted the little goatskin bag of sovereigns that he had taken from his baggage roll and secured firmly to the saddle cantle. He squinted ahead at the squat figure of Jenkins, the cords securing the little man's headdress already slipping down his back, and the future definitely looked brighter.

The caravan had quickly left behind the Nile-watered lushness of the country around Cairo, and now, with the high white sun beating down, the camels were picking their way across a stony plain, broken here and there by dry wadis, irritatingly difficult to negotiate. It was a relief, then, when the sand underneath the animals' pads began to increase until it formed a soft white carpet over a harder stratum. It was perfect terrain for the beasts, and without urging, they picked up their pace. The particles of sand were clean and polished and Simon found that they reflected the sun strongly, forcing him to pull his head sheet low over his eyes to reduce the glare.

A midday break was taken in the shade of a few stunted scrub and palm trees, solitary in a moist depression. Handfuls of dates and raisins were shared, a little water sipped – although the camels were still replete from their stay at Cairo – and then the people of the *funduq* hung blankets across the scrub and curled up like scorpions in the scraps of shade so formed. Simon, his left leg now aching from its position coiled around the saddle pommel, followed suit, as did Jenkins, who was asleep within seconds.

The break lasted little more than an hour and then the caravan resumed its gentle progress across the desert, which had now truly become a sea of sand, with long, slowly rising waves of dunes reducing visibility to some two hundred yards all around. Simon, head swaying on his precarious perch, became almost hypnotised as he watched his camel place each splayed, padded foot on the sand, allow it to sink through the surface and then retrieve it with a flick that sent sand crystals spraying to all sides. Monotony seemed to be the main feature of desert travel.

It was another blessed relief, then, when, at about four p.m., palm fronds standing clear above the next sand dune announced that they had reached their first village – also their first trading point and overnight stay. They topped the dune and looked down upon a verdant patch of life set amidst the arid whiteness of the surrounding sand. The village consisted of about thirty huts made of crudely cut blocks of dried mud, set around a number of wood- and stone-lined wells and fringed with the tall date palms. Narrow irrigation channels spoked out from the wells and meandered between the palm roots, allowing enough moisture to sustain the trees and what Simon presumed to be tiny rice patches and clumps of fig trees.

The arrival of the caravan was obviously a cause of great joy to the little community, for children of all sizes ran out to meet the leading camel, women appeared smiling at the doors of the huts and swathed men, working the buckets at the wells, straightened their backs and grinned. With practised ease the leading camels were unloaded and blankets spread upon the ground beneath what little shade could be gained from the palms above. Minutes later the blankets were covered with a glittering cornucopia of products from beyond the shores of Egypt: knives, axes, nails and hammers from Birmingham; tinned food from France, set beside a delicately arranged pyramid of can openers; gaily coloured shawls, gowns and headdresses from India and Manchester; musket balls from Morocco; and drinking mugs from Stoke-on-Trent. These were supplemented by artefacts of more ethnic and regional origin: refurbished *jerzails*, daggers set with fake jewels, curled slippers, rings and bangles that radiated shafts of sunlight and bags of flour that wheezed white dust as they were set down.

' 'Ow the 'ell do they pay for this stuff?' wondered Jenkins.

The answer was provided within seconds as the village brought out its own produce: mainly dates, figs, and bags and baskets woven from palm fronds. Some coins exchanged hands, but at least half of the business was a matter of bartering, and it all proceeded so smoothly that it was over within the hour. What was left was immediately repacked for loading again on to the camels the next day and the payment in fruit was carefully covered in muslin, sprinkled with water and put away in one of the huts until the morning.

While the men were trading, the women of the *funduq* were smoothly unloading the tents and erecting them under the palms, while the children relieved the camels of the remainder of their burdens and then knee-haltered them.

Simon and Jenkins stood a little to one side, observing the disciplined muddle with interest and admiration. The scene was one of civilised but traditional behaviour and must have been repeated, except for changes in the products bartered, for hundreds of years previously. It was clear that the arrival of the caravan was an event – Simon presumed that Mahmud varied his route, so that each oasis was visited probably only once a year – and part of the long-nurtured culture of the desert. Looking at the bright eyes of the women and children of the village as they eyed the treasures on the blankets, Simon's thoughts returned to the conversation of the morning.

He turned to Jenkins. 'Are you thinking what I am thinking?'

The Welshman nodded slowly. 'This is good, this is, bach sir. Bit like the market on Saturday mornings in Rhyl, with the kids 'n that. What right 'ave them Bedwhatsit people got to spoil it, eh?'

'Quite. I still hope that we don't meet them because I don't want to cause trouble for Mahmud and his people. But if we do, perhaps we should give them something to remember us by.'

'Well, look you. I'll go along with that.'

The money that Mahmud had received from Simon paid for food for the two passengers and also overnight accommodation for them in the caravan leader's big tent. When all the work was done and the sun had gone down, bringing an immediate drop in the temperature, the pair gathered around a big fire lit outside Mahmud's tent with the leader and his brother Abdul – a younger replica of the big man, matching his cheerful smile but lacking the leader's gravitas – together with the elders among the men of the *funduq*. They all sat cross-legged in a circle, sipping syrup-like green tea from elegant little cups.

'Do 'emselves well on this caravan thing, don't they?' whispered Jenkins. 'Though I wouldn't mind a drop of something stronger, look you.'

'No chance of that. They're Muslims and never touch the stuff.'

'Blimey. There's strange for you.'

When the food came, it smelt delicious. One of the older women – she could have been Mahmud's wife, or one of his wives – brought a steaming bowl of saffron rice, over which pieces of boiled lamb had been spread. Then boys carried in small cauldrons and copper vats from which they ladled out over the main dish shreds of offal from the lamb, swimming in cooking fat in which pieces of butter were fast dissolving. Immediately Mahmud intoned some kind of grace in his native tongue, quickly translating it as 'In the name of God, the merciful' for his two guests, and then the men squatted around the central dish in a ring, peeled back their right sleeves to the elbow and began dipping their thumbs and first two fingers into the rice and meat, cautiously, for the fat was scalding hot.

They made room for Simon and Jenkins and the two copied the eating procedure of the others. Carefully using only thumb and two fingers – it was clear that it was impolite to soil the palm of the hand – they kneaded rice and small pieces of meat into a package, dipped the result into the fat, squashed the ball into the curved forefinger and then flicked it into the mouth with the thumb. Although Jenkins became impatient with the ritual and eventually began using all of his fingers, no one seemed to mind. After a considerable dent had been made in the rice mound, Mahmud produced his knife and began cutting away pieces of meat from the larger bones left and spearing treasured portions of liver and kidneys and placing them all on the plates of Simon and Jenkins. When it seemed that there could be no more room in their bellies for further food, watermelons and pistachio nuts were produced. It was hospitality of the most gracious kind and Simon warmed anew to the ways of this desert Egyptian and his happy band of travelling families.

After they had rubbed their hands with soap cake and rinsed them in wooden bowls of water, they sprawled contentedly on rugs alongside Mahmud, drinking more green tea. Simon thanked him for the hospitality they had received.

'I envy you your way of life,' he said.

Mahmud sipped his tea and grinned. 'Ahmed makes more money from his hotel in a month than I will in two years of leading my camels across the desert, but I would not change my life for his.'

'Were you born in the city?'

'No, the three of us grew up in a little village on the green edge watered by the Nile. Our father was a poor farmer whose bit of land was on the higher section, away from the main canals fed from the dams. He could not afford to pay the bribes to the water engineers, so we had to take water to irrigate our land up from one level to another by buckets. It's called *shaduf*. You know,' he shook his head, 'the *fellaheen* of this country have a terrible time of it.'

'Because of the water problem.'

'Of course. With that *shaduf* system, it takes six *fellaheen*, working from dawn to dust, to water two acres of barley or one of cotton or sugar cane. As there is only about one able-bodied man to three acres of cultivated land in Egypt, it is clear that *shaduf* cannot irrigate the whole country.' He spat away from the rug. 'That is why most of the country is desert.'

Simon wrinkled his brow. 'But modern methods of water pumping – I've seen them in operation in South Africa – could change things in less than ten years.'

'Ah, but who is going to pay for this big – what do you call it? – capital investment? I will tell you who. The financiers of Europe, the very same people who built what is supposed to be *our* great Suez Canal, the Canal which poor old Ismail Pasha had to sell back to the bankers in London and Paris before they kicked him out.' Mahmud threw away his tea dregs in an angry gesture. 'Give them any more chance of moving into this country and they will take it over completely. No.' He shook his head. 'It is better that we carry on bucketing our water and the desert stays the desert so that I can trade across it.'

A silence fell on the little group. The other men had listened in silence to the strange language spoken by their leader, not understanding a word, but they realised that he had been expressing views of great profundity, and as he finished, they nodded their heads in solemn agreement. It was Jenkins who broke the silence.

'That's all very well, Mah . . . er . . . Mah . . . mate,' he said. 'But what about these bandits that rob you all the time? You can't put up with them for much longer, can you?'

The Egyptian's face clouded. 'That is true. If it gets worse, something will have to be done. Maybe we fight. Maybe the Government sends soldiers again. I don't know. Allah will provide. He always does.'

Hearing the name of the deity, the others nodded their heads again.

Simon stood. 'Thank you again. Now I must sleep. What time tomorrow do we load up and move on?'

'I do not have a watch, but we keep God's time. We move at dawn.'

The pattern of the first day was repeated on the next and the next, with the caravan winding its way sinuously across the dunes, sometimes making faster time over harder, pebble-strewn terrain, sometimes stopping to trade at a village overnight, sometimes at midday. Once a fierce sand storm whipped up from nowhere and the camel drivers were forced to turn the rumps of their beasts towards the direction of the wind, bow their heads, cover their faces with their head shawls and wait until it had passed. On the fourth night, a similar blast hit them from out of the darkness when everyone was asleep. But the tents stood firm, their low profiles allowing the sand to sweep over them and away, so that little discomfiture resulted for those inside.

By the sixth day, Simon had even stopped scanning the desert behind them for a band of police pursuing them with questions about an affray in the jewellery *suk* of Cairo. They had successfully slipped away, it seemed, from that trouble in the city. Suez and a steamer south beckoned from just over the horizon.

Yet they had not left danger behind.

It was the sharp-eyed Jenkins who first saw the Bedawis. Leading as usual, he turned back to Simon and pointed to his right, to where the dunes had flattened and a plain of sorts had been formed by a freak of the wind. Simon shielded his eyes and squinted into the glare. Far away – perhaps a mile to the south – he could make out six tiny black figures, approaching them at some speed. A shout from Mahmud showed that he had seen them too.

Immediately the caravan lost its air of somnolence. Riders slipped from their camels and began tucking away under the loads items of particular value which could be easily hidden and so avoid the casual acquisitive eye. Simon had long since divided their gold coins into two small bags and he now gestured to Jenkins to untie his bag from the saddle pommel and tuck it away beneath the folds of his robe. He did the same himself and then looked at their rifles, on the camel ahead, still wrapped in their hessian coverings in the middle of the packs but protruding provocatively. He sighed, for there was nothing to be done about them.

Turning to his right, he tried to focus again on the intruders. They were now much nearer, of course, for they were clearly urging on their camels, but they were shimmering in the heat haze so that heads were horizontally parted from bodies and the bodies severed from the animals that bore them. It was an eerie, menacing illusion and Simon licked his lips – abortively, for he had no saliva to moisten them. Jenkins gently eased his camel back so that he was shoulder to shoulder with Simon.

'What do you think, bach sir?' he said. 'Challenge 'em right away?'

Simon shook his head. 'No. We promised Mahmud that we

wouldn't cause any trouble. Let them have anything they want except the coins and the rifles. If they take our gold we'll never get to South Africa, and if they have our rifles they will certainly use them against these people, probably for years. Is yours loaded?'

'Yes. One up the spout.'

'Hide a few cartridges in your left hand in case it becomes a shooting match. I'll do the same.' He gulped and tried to keep his voice steady. 'Don't act until I do.'

'Very good, sir.'

After the initial consternation, the caravan had resumed its even progress, as though the Bedawis had not even been noticed. But there was a definable air of tension among the Egyptians and some of the men, Simon noticed, had even produced old *jerzails* and slung them across their saddles. Would they fight if they had to? Certainly young Abdul, Mahmud's brother, looked in the mood. He was visibly excited, his eyes wide, and he kept twisting in his saddle to observe the approach of the Bedawis.

They were now close enough to be individually defined. They were completely shrouded in black, with headscarves wound low over their foreheads and around their lower faces, so that only their eyes could be seen. Each man carried a *jerzail* in his right hand, but these muskets looked far more lethal than the old weapons carried by the Egyptians, and the handles of long, curved scimitars poked from the sashes round their midriffs. Despite the pace at which their tall camels approached, these men rode indolently, at ease on their high wooden saddles. They looked like what they were: predators.

Mahmud pulled his camel out of the line and urged it towards the visitors. But they completely ignored him and spread out, seemingly to inspect the line of pack animals. Mahmud called after them, but the Bedawis paid no attention. It was as though the leader of the caravan was a person of no relevance to them. Instead, the six men slowed their camels to a walk and, without dismounting, began moving slowly along the caravan line, poking and prodding the packs, slashing at the binding cords with their sharp swords and inspecting the goods strewn on the sand.

It was too much for Abdul. He urged his camel forward with hand upraised to intervene. Immediately, the Bedawi behind him swung his sword and sent the flat of his blade crashing into the young man's head so that he tumbled from his mount and lay still on the sand. A young boy, no more than five years old – Simon recalled that he was one of Abdul's many progeny – ran forward with a cry and knelt by his father's side. The raider calmly leaned down from his high saddle and swung his sword again, this time with the blade aimed directly at the boy's neck. A cry from Mahmud made the lad jump to one side and the blade whistled by his face. It was a deliberate attempt to kill.

Immediately a hiss – of horror, outrage, fear? – rose from the traders along the line. The Bedawis paid no attention, but continued to work their way along the loaded camels, pulling away coverings and indicating with peremptory gestures the objects they would take. The swordsman took his place among them, as though the attempted decapitation of the boy had been merely an idle indulgence, not worth repeating.

'Bastard,' murmured Jenkins. 'I'll 'ave 'im, see if I don't.'

'Keep your temper, 352,' breathed Simon. 'I don't see how we can take them all on.'

So they waited in line. The man who had knocked down Abdul now shouted in impatience at finding nothing that interested him and he pulled out and looked down the line. His eye lit on the bound end of the rifle sticking out of Simon's pack. He urged his camel forward, and as he did so, Simon prodded his own beast into action so that he plodded forward to meet the Bedawi.

Without moving his head Simon whispered to Jenkins: 'While I divert this bastard's attention, see if you can quietly withdraw your rifle. Don't make a fuss now.'

'An' don't you do anythin' stupid. I told you 'e is mine.'

Simon greeted the swordsman with a half-bow.

'Good morning, arsehole,' he said, his face breaking into a beaming smile worthy of Jenkins. 'Pray tell me why you are such an ugly bugger.'

The Arab checked, frowned at the sound of the strange language and then waved Simon aside with his sword and reached for the rifle.

'Ah, the rifle. Does this interest you, sir? Then allow me to

42

demonstrate.' Still smiling, Simon slowly reached forward and tugged out the Martini. Engaging the eyes of the Bedawi, he began unwrapping it. The brigand shook away the lower folds of the headdress which obscured his jaw, mouth and nose, and Simon saw that his face was as black as his eyes. He was, indeed, from the south. Those eyes now gleamed avariciously as the long barrel of the rifle was revealed, then the loading and cocking lever around the trigger and the oiled stock.

'Look, arsehole, let me show you.' Still smiling, Simon produced a cartridge from the palm of his left hand. 'See, this is what you do, you piece of camel dung.' He cocked the lever and inserted the round into the slot behind the backsight of the rifle. Then he pointed to his right, across the plain, and as the Arab turned to look, Simon noted from the corner of his eye Jenkins slipping his own rifle free from his pack. Simon put the rifle to his shoulder and pulled the trigger.

Far across the plain – perhaps four hundred yards away and certainly well in excess of the range of the Bedawis' own *jerzails* – a spurt of dust and rock fragments showed where the bullet had struck home. A deep murmur rose from the intruders and Mahmud's men alike.

Simon turned his gaze back on to the black eyes facing him. The man's jaw had dropped and he seemed almost mesmerised by Simon's air of confidence, the strange, unintelligible words he spoke and the ever-present smile. Taking a deep breath, Simon produced another cartridge, slipped it into the breech, cocked the mechanism and made as though to offer the rifle to the swordsman. Then, as the man narrowed his eyes and reached forward for the rifle, Simon's smile disappeared and he suddenly reversed the gun and rammed the muzzle into the Arab's chest.

'Now,' he said, 'drop that damned sword.' Without removing his eyes – now as cold as those of his opponent – he nodded towards the sword and indicated the sand. 'Drop it now.'

Simon saw the expression in the man's eyes change suddenly from puzzlement to fury. Whatever he was, he was not a coward. He quickly moved his left hand to push away the rifle barrel and flung up his sword arm to bring the blade crashing down on to Simon's shoulder. But the move was all too predictable and in the time that it took for the sword to be lifted, Simon swung the Martini muzzle back and upwards and pressed the trigger. At point-blank range he could not miss and the bullet tore through the Bedawi's lower arm, shattering it and sending the sword twisting high into the air, its blade twinkling in the sunlight as it arced towards the sand. In almost the same movement, Simon brought the butt of the gun round to crash into the man's head, sending him too to the ground.

A great shout came from Simon's right, followed by the deep crack of a *jerzail*, and Simon felt the ball whistle past his head. Then Jenkins's rifle barked almost simultaneously and one of the Bedawis, his musket still smoking, slowly crumpled over his saddle and slid to the ground, a neat black hole in his forehead.

Simon quickly reloaded and pulled his camel away so that he could cover the remaining four intruders. 'Mahmud,' he shouted as he squinted down the barrel, moving the muzzle slowly to threaten all four. He was aware that Jenkins was now at his side in a similar posture.

'Yes, *effendi*.' There was a new note of respect, if not fear, in the Egyptian's voice.

'Tell these men to throw their muskets and their swords to the ground, then to dismount slowly. If they do as I say then they will not be harmed, but if they try to harm anyone else or to ride away, tell them that either I or Sergeant Jenkins here will kill them. Is that clear?'

'Yes, *effendi*.'

Mahmud's voice was hoarse but the orders were conveyed and the four brigands, all traces of arrogance now long since gone, threw down their weapons and dismounted. They stood together, surly but apprehensive.

'Now, Mahmud, tell them that they must go along the line and pick up all the possessions that they have thrown to the ground and then, with the owners telling them exactly what to do, they must repack all those things on to the camels. When they have finished, they must bury the man that the sergeant was forced to kill. Tell them now.'

'Blimey, bach sir.' Jenkins's voice too was now a little hoarse. 'You're certainly rubbing their noses in it.'

Simon lowered his rifle and realised that perspiration was rolling down his cheeks. 'Do you realise, 352,' he said, his voice unsteady, 'that that man tried to kill that little child?'

'I do indeed, bach sir. That's why I wished you'd left 'im to me. But I must say, you 'andled 'im beautifully. And your language . . . my word! I thought you was supposed to be a gentleman. I don't know where you picked up them expressions, indeed I don't. Dear, dear me.'

The look of lugubrious offence on Jenkins's face broke the tension and Simon was forced to grin. 'Must be the company I keep,' he said.

Mahmud relayed Simon's orders and slowly the Bedawis moved along the line of camels, picking up the goods they had thrown to the ground and, with the timid help of the families, packing it all up again in great loosely bound bundles. It was clear that Mahmud's people were still in awe of the brigands. They averted their eyes from them and no one was taking great care about the repacking. Abdul, however, had recovered from the blow to his head and was determinedly collecting the discarded *jerzails* and scimitars and stacking them well away from the camels.

A worried-looking Mahmud walked across to Simon. When he spoke, his voice was angry. 'I do not think that what you did was wise,' he said. 'Killing a Bedawi is a terrible thing to do. It will bring retribution on us. Now we will all probably be killed by the brothers of these people. And,' he gestured to where the man shot by Simon lay on the sand, his face contorted with pain as he held his shattered arm, 'what do we do with him?'

'Ah yes. We will talk in a moment about the Bedawi, Mahmud.' Simon spoke with a certainty he did not feel. 'But first, the injured man. Do you have someone – perhaps one of the women – who knows a little about healing?'

'Yes. My chief woman knows a little but she is not a doctor.'

'Good. Tell her to bring water, cloth and something we can use as a splint to support the broken arm. I will help her. Sergeant Jenkins will stay here and make sure that the Bedawis do not make trouble.

45

Perhaps Abdul can bring one of the captured muskets and stay with him. I don't want them to get away, for I have something to say to them.'

Frowning – he who had always been in complete control of his caravan was now being told what to do by this Englishman who could not even sit on a camel properly – Mahmud nodded and walked away.

Jenkins leaned forward and gestured to the injured Arab. 'Better, surely, to finish off that devil now, before he can cause further trouble, eh? I could do it quietly with me knife, look you. 'E deserves it well enough.'

Simon sighed. 'He probably does, but I want to set these bastards some sort of example. We've got our Egyptian friends into enough trouble as it is. Keep an eye on the repacking – and on Abdul. He's in the mood to knock somebody on the head.'

Unwinding the sling of his water bottle from the saddle pommel, Simon tapped his camel on the head, awkwardly slid to the ground as it knelt and approached the wounded Bedawi. The man watched him approach with eyes that expressed hatred and apprehension – a fear confirmed when Simon knelt by his side and produced a knife. But the blade did not go to his throat but began gently sawing away at the sleeve of the injured arm. When the wound had been completely exposed, Simon put his arm under the Bedawi's head, cradled it and put his water bottle to the man's mouth. He gulped eagerly, never for a moment taking his eyes off Simon's face.

At this point Mahmud's wife arrived and Simon recognised the large woman who had served the main dish on the first night of the journey. She was carrying a white cloth slung over her shoulder, a bowl of water and a small goatskin bag. Nodding to Simon, she knelt and spoke softly and vehemently, presumably in Arabic, to the Bedawi who had attempted to decapitate her nephew, then, none too gently, she seized the injured arm and began to bathe it in the warm water. The Arab rolled back his head and gritted his teeth in agony, but made no sound.

Simon noticed that his bullet had not hit the bone in the centre, luckily, for at that range it would have completely severed the arm. Instead, it had caught it on the edge of the forearm, splintering it and

46

setting the wrist askew. As he watched, he realised that Mahmud's wife was not bereft of skill, for she was now deftly removing small bone splinters with a pair of tweezers. Eventually satisfied, she again bathed the break with water, then dipped into her bag and, gently this time, smeared some kind of ointment over the wound. Next she applied what appeared to be green moss to it. A rough dressing of white cotton completed the treatment. Then she motioned Simon to hold in place the small piece of wood she had brought and tied it to the arm with shreds of cloth to act as a splint. Gathering up her bits and pieces, she squatted for a moment and addressed the wounded man in guttural tones before clearing her throat and deliberately spitting into his face. Then she rose to her feet and walked away, her great buttocks swinging as though in derision.

Simon could not help grinning, but he took out his handkerchief and removed the spittle from the Bedawi's face. 'That'll teach you to swing your bloody great sword at a little boy,' he murmured. The Arab continued to stare at him, his black eyes now showing puzzlement.

Although the reloading of the camels had been completed, Simon noticed that no attempt was being made to bury the dead man. Mahmud explained that the Bedawis had requested that they be allowed to carry the body away back to their camp. 'I think it would be wise to allow this to happen, *effendi*,' he said.

'Very well. Perhaps it will serve as a warning. Now, Mahmud, I want to talk to them – and I want your people to hear and understand as well, so ask them to gather around. Perhaps you would be kind enough to interpret what I have to say?'

Mahmud bowed, his face still showing surprise at the crisp air of command Simon had adopted since the arrival of the brigands.

Simon insisted that everyone gather around the wounded man on the ground. The Bedawis did so with some signs of returned truculence at the humiliation they had been forced to endure. They glowered at Simon through the slits in their headdresses. The Egyptians had eyes wide with puzzlement and anticipation. Jenkins, his rifle at the ready, took up position at Simon's side.

'Now,' began Simon, 'I am Captain Simon Fonthill of the British

Army, and this is Sergeant Jenkins, who also serves the great British Queen.' He waited while Mahmud interpreted. The Bedawis still glowered but Mahmud's men uttered a communal 'Ah!' and nodded their heads, as though they had known the strangers' identity all the time.

'We serve our Queen as soldiers but we also serve the Khedive and we were specially selected to travel with the *funduq* to give protection to these good, honest traders against criminals such as you. From now on, all caravans that cross the desert will have at least two – and often more – British soldiers with them, dressed like Egyptians but armed with the latest weapons, to kill anyone who tries to rob the camel trains.'

Simon swallowed. There was still no reaction from the Bedawis, but the men of the caravan were clearly impressed. They nodded their heads solemnly and uttered words of obvious approval.

'That is not all,' continued Simon. 'Any Bedawis who rob the people of the villages at the oases will be hunted down by the British soldiers serving the Khedive and killed. Now,' he nodded down at the wounded man, who was sitting up and listening attentively, 'this man attempted to kill a small child. If he had succeeded I would assuredly have hanged him like a dog. He was lucky in that his sword missed. I have therefore only shattered his arm. He will not use that sword for many months now.'

He paused again and heard Jenkins chortle quietly.

'But it is the way of my people to bind the wounds of our enemies and send them on their way.' At this translation, the Bedawis exchanged glances. 'You too will be allowed to return to your camp and tell your families of my words. But you attempted to rob this *funduq* so you will be fined. You will forfeit your *jerzails* and swords and you will pay an additional fine of three camels. Now you may go, and take my warning back to your people. Go in the name of Allah. See to it, Mahmud.'

With a backward glance at Simon – half in wonder, half in consternation – Mahmud broke out three of the intruders' camels and gestured to the Bedawis to mount. The wounded man, none too gently, was thrust aboard one camel with the dead body slung behind, and the four unwounded Arabs mounted, two to each animal. Then, with what sounded like a cry of derision, they loped away.

'Bloody 'ell, bach sir,' gasped Jenkins, 'that was well done, that it was. Ah, you're a lovely liar when you get goin' like. But do you think they'll be back?'

'God knows,' said Simon, wiping the back of his hand across his brow. 'But I couldn't think of anything else. I think I'd better apologise to Mahmud.'

The two approached the big Egyptian, who was talking animatedly to his men. Mahmud turned to meet them. He spoke quietly but sternly. 'I wish what you had said was true but it was all lies. What do we do when they come back and you are not here with your big guns, eh? What do we do then?'

Simon sighed. 'I am sorry, Mahmud, really I am. But I could not let them have our rifles. If we had meekly turned the other cheek, as our Christian religion urges us to, then they would have become better armed and much more arrogant. Their attacks on you would grow. At least now perhaps we have warned them off.'

The big man remained silent for a moment. 'You were brave there to stand up to that man.' A wide smile suddenly split his beard. 'And I have never heard an English gentleman use those rude words. I am glad that my women could not understand.'

Simon blushed under his tan. 'Ah yes, sorry about that. But I lost my temper. It never does to do that. But look, Mahmud, I – we – never intended to endanger your people. It was rather forced on us. And I did not wish to speak as though I was leader here. You are in charge. Yet I had to pretend that I was still a British officer. Now, do you think they will return?'

The Egyptian tugged at his beard. 'I do not know. When they rode away, they cried that we were all sons of dogs and that they would come back. So yes, I think they will. Then what will we do?'

'Ah, yes. Well let me think about that. Perhaps we had better get moving again?'

They were interrupted by the arrival of Abdul, a cheery grin back on his face underneath a gull's-egg lump which had appeared on his right temple. Unlike his two older brothers, Abdul's English was poor, but he approached now with his arm extended and shook hands warmly with the two ex-soldiers. 'Good thing,' he said. 'Good thing. Brave thing. Good. No more Bedawis, eh?'

Mahmud spoke sharply to him and, only slightly crestfallen at the rebuke, the young man waved and remounted his camel. Slowly the *funduq* resumed its slow progress across the desert, leaving two large bloodstains behind on the sand.

Simon pondered as his camel plodded along in the middle of the line. If the Bedawis attacked in more force, this long single column was completely vulnerable. He and Jenkins could not gallop – gallop? Oh lord! – up and down the line firing their Martini-Henrys. Somehow he must define a system for defending the caravan. But how?

Then he remembered an old Afrikaner in Kimberley telling him of how, some forty years before, a Boer commando of only about two hundred men had defeated a Zulu impi of some two thousand warriors at Blood River. They had circled their waggons and fired their muskets from behind this makeshift fortress, with the women reloading the guns. And hadn't the pioneers crossing the North American plains done something similar when they were attacked by Indians? Simon looked along the line and frowned. It would take ages for this single-file column to wind itself into a circle and the fast-moving Bedawis would be upon them before the manoeuvre could be completed. Then his mind went back just under two years to the battle of Ulundi, when the Zulus had been finally defeated. The British General Chelmsford, remembering the disaster at Isandlwana, had actually advanced his army in a cumbersome square. The Zulus had flung themselves unavailingly against the British square and been shot to pieces. Now, the Egyptians lacked the firepower of the British army, but if they could be persuaded to resist – for he and Jenkins could not do all the shooting – they would have the advantage of firing their muskets from behind the cover of the camels, which, if the caravan was moving in a loose square, could be made to kneel before the attackers were upon them. It was worth a try!

Simon slapped the haunches of his camel, indicated Jenkins to follow and then drew level with Mahmud. 'If the Bedawis come, will they attack at night?' he asked.

Mahmud shook his head. 'No one moves at night in the desert if they can help it,' he said. 'It is too cold and difficult to find the way.'

'Good.' Simon explained his plan. At first the Egyptian was doubtful that his people would have the discipline to move in a square, for it was traditional to cross the desert in single file. Simon pointed out the advantage of the formation, given that the best marksmen would be placed at the right angles of the square, so that they could direct their fire through ninety degrees whichever way the attack materialised and so enfilade the enemy. Mahmud grudgingly conceded the point.

'But they have fast camels, and amongst the dunes they could be upon us before we have time to kneel the camels.'

'I've thought of that. You must put up outriders. Four men. One in advance of the caravan, one in the rear and one on either flank. Far enough out so that they can give adequate warning but close enough to ride back to safety. I know that your chaps are not soldiers, but they could do this, couldn't they?'

Mahmud frowned in silence for a moment.

'You should listen to the captain,' said Jenkins. ' 'E's a fine soldier. This is brainwork, see. It's what 'e does best.'

The big man nodded. 'Very well. We will try. I have about half a dozen men who can shoot quite well – and we have the Bedawis' *jerzails*. They are better than ours. And . . .' his eyes brightened, 'perhaps if we do well then they will not attack us again, eh?'

Simon grinned. 'That's the spirit. See if you can form the square now.'

On broken ground it would have been impossible to have advanced the caravan in this new geometric form. But on the wide swelling desert dunes, and given that no specific road was being followed, it proved to be quite feasible, once the excited Egyptians had grasped the idea. In fact, they enjoyed the new, more sociable formation, which allowed families to converse more conveniently.

The square was maintained that night, for they camped in the open, and guards were mounted. But it seemed that Mahmud was right. If the Bedawis were going to attack the caravan again it would not be at night.

It was, in fact, at mid-morning.

The caravan had been on the move for about two hours, the formation of the square slipping a little here and there as confidence set in and chatting took over. The outriders had been dispatched and four good men, armed with the Bedawis' *jerzails*, had been put at the corner points of the square, with Mahmud, Simon and Jenkins riding in the centre. All seemed peaceful under the brazen, harsh sky when a signal shot came from over the dunes to the right, closely followed by one from the left.

'Damn,' said Simon. 'They've split their force and are going to attack us from two sides. Clever bastards.' He held up his hand as Jenkins went to move. 'No, stay here until we see how many there are on each side, then we can take our positions accordingly. Mahmud, get those blasted camels kneeling and the men and families behind them. We can't waste a second.'

The Egyptians, however, whether from fear or recalling their instructions, had couched the camels quickly, the men levelling their muskets across the saddles, the women gathering the smallest of the children to safety and the biggest of the boys kneeling with spare *jerzails* and ramrods and powder horns, ready to reload the guns. The square, in fact, was perfectly formed and Simon felt a sudden surge of pride at the way this bunch of listless camel traders had been transformed, for the moment at least, into sturdy defenders. As he strode around the inside of the square, indicating by gesture where gaps should be filled, the four outriders came galloping sequentially down the dunes, waving their *jerzails* and kicking their mounts so that those old plodders moved at a pace that would have graced racing camels. Once inside the square, the rider from the right, who had fired first, vaulted from his saddle and shouted excitedly to Mahmud.

'About twelve of them coming this way,' Mahmud relayed.

A moment later, the front and back outriders came in, and then the picket from the left, his eyes wide, either in fear or exhilaration – probably both, Simon decided – arrived and screamed at Mahmud.

The big man gestured for him to dismount, patted him on the shoulder encouragingly and directed him to one of the sides of the square.

'He says about ten that way,' Mahmud said. 'What do you want us to do? Just wait?'

'Wait a moment,' said Simon. 'I want to see what they are going to do and whether there are any more of them.' He looked round the square. There were perhaps thirteen or fourteen camels on each side, couched comfortably, chewing and quite unaware, of course, that they had suddenly become ramparts and the first line of defence against musket balls.

Simon turned again to Mahmud. 'How much time have we got?'

'Perhaps three or four minutes. They were some distance away.'

'Right. Tell everyone to push bundles and whatever they can in front of the camels to shield them from the gunfire. Those old *jerzail* balls won't have too much penetration. They must be quick.'

Mahmud raised his voice and suddenly the square was a mass of activity. Most, although not all, of the loads had been pushed to the outside of the square when, to the right, a line of black figures materialised over the top of the sand dune. Immediately all activity within the square ceased and a hush fell upon the little community. Slowly the Bedawis urged their camels forward until they were fully revealed and then they paused on the crest of the dune, the stocks of their *jerzails* resting on their thighs so that the barrels pointed to the sky as they looked down on the caravan, like ravens waiting before pouncing on worms. There were, indeed, about a dozen of them.

Simon turned as he heard a murmur behind him. The second band had mounted the dune crest on the other side of the square, and they too sat waiting. Simon hurriedly counted. Nine. Were there any more?

Mahmud turned an anxious and questioning face to the two Europeans.

'How many men have we got with muskets?' asked Simon.

'About thirty. Another ten or so without.'

'More than enough.' Simon spoke with a confidence he did not feel. How many could shoot, and would they break and run when the Bedawis charged? And what would happen if the square was broken? He dared not think about that. The attackers were about two hundred and fifty yards away, out of the range of muskets but not of the Martini-Henrys.

'Mahmud, we three will stay in the middle here as reserve and rush to help whichever side of the square is under the fiercest attack. But don't move unless I tell you to. Understood?'

'Yes, *effendi*.'

'Where is Abdul?'

'He is one of the corner men. He is a good shot.'

'Splendid. Now, explain to your chaps that Jenkins and I are going to try and teach those devils a lesson for trying to frighten everyone by standing like bloody statues up there. So they will hear us shoot. But no one is to waste ammunition until I shout "Fire!" very loudly. Please interpret.'

Mahmud nodded and began relaying the instructions.

'Now, 352.' Simon turned to Jenkins. 'You look after this side where the greatest numbers are. It doesn't look as though they are going to split up and attack on more than two fronts – there aren't enough of them anyway. So when I give the signal, pot as many of the bastards as you can before they either charge or slip away. I will do the same from the other side. Understood?'

'Very good, bach sir.'

As always when danger appeared, Jenkins was imperturbable. His eyes had narrowed and he was already singling out the target for his first shot. Simon wished his own heart would stop beating so loudly that he felt sure everyone within the square could hear it. The odds were stacked against the defenders, he knew that. There were more Egyptians than Bedawis, of course, but he doubted whether many of them could shoot straight, and the attackers had the advantage of looking down from the crests of the dunes, over the camels, to the traders crouched behind. If they chose to dismount, they could direct strong fire on the defenders. But they would have to move nearer first to get within range, and the alternative – charging straight in – meant that they could mount no sort of fire while they did so. Even the

Bedawis would not be able to fire accurately from a moving camel. Yet could the Egyptians stand up against such a charge?

As he watched, he heard a single command from up on the crest and each of the Bedawis drew their scimitars. Ah, the direct attack! Simon shouted to Jenkins: 'Whenever you like now, 352,' trying to keep his voice level.

Immediately, Jenkins's rifle fired. Simon directed his own Martini at a black-veiled figure in the centre of the row above him and saw dust spurt up near the camel's front legs. Damn! Hurriedly he inserted another round, pushed the trigger guard forward to cock the mechanism, aimed a little higher and saw his target start back and then slump to the ground. Eight left. The startled camel veered to its right and pushed into its neighbour, so upsetting the geometric precision of the line that had now begun to advance slowly down the slope.

'Now, *effendi*?' cried Mahmud, anxiety cracking his voice.

'No. Too far away. Tell them to wait until I shout.'

Two more reports behind him showed that Jenkins was firing coolly. A shout from the advancing line gave the signal now for the Bedawis to charge. Eight scimitars were raised on high and the camels were galvanised into a lumbering trot and then a sliding, surging gallop as their pads plunged deep into the sand. It was not exactly a disciplined cavalry charge such as British lancers might have produced, but Simon could not help but suck in his breath in exhilaration at the sight of the eight tribesmen thundering down the slope, shouting some kind of battle cry, their swords held on high and their camels snarling.

'Fire!' he shouted.

Perhaps a dozen *jerzails* coughed from Simon's side of the square and he saw one of the attackers fall. Only one. Poor shooting, as he had feared. His own third shot brought down another camel, sending its rider cartwheeling down the slope – damn, still shooting low! – and he heard the wall behind him also open up. But he had no time to turn and assess the situation there. There were six of the riders still crashing down the dune towards him and all of the muskets along his wall were being reloaded. At least the attackers presented an easier target now, and he brought down another with a bullet squarely in the chest this time. A *jerzail* fired from the corner of the square – Abdul, for sure – and a fifth man toppled from his saddle.

The remaining four were brave men, however, and they did not falter in their charge. Leaning low to present a smaller target, their scimitars whirling, they reached the line of the defenders' camels, couched behind their baggage. And there they were forced to stop, for camels do not jump. Impotently, the Bedawis ranged along the line, their swords flashing in the sunlight, vainly trying to reach the defenders, who had all instinctively retreated a few paces as the riders met the barrier.

The momentary impasse allowed Simon to steal a glance behind him and to either side, for it was possible that the dozen attackers from that side could have spread out to attack the north and south walls of the little square. But they had not, and the sight that met his eyes gladdened his heart. The dune on Jenkins's side of the wall seemed to be strewn with inert black-swathed figures, their swords lying yards away from them, and riderless camels plodding away back up to the crest. Three riders were urging their beasts away from the square, their heads down and the flats of their swords slapping into their camels' flanks in a desperate attempt to escape the fire of the *jerzails*. Jenkins was standing outside the square on what appeared to be a pile of carpets, aiming his rifle at the three departing Bedawis.

A crash of musket fire behind him made Simon spin around again to see, as the smoke cleared, two Bedawis fleeing as fast as their camels could take them. It was a third, however, who caught his eye. Somehow, flailing his scimitar in his left hand, he had broken through the barrier and reined to a halt in the middle of the square, turning his head. The man's eyes seemed to light up as they settled on Simon and immediately he urged his camel towards him, veering to Simon's left to give himself room to swing his sword. Simon saw the bandage and splint on the rider's right forearm and he immediately knew the identity of his adversary. He fumbled beneath his robe for a cartridge but realised that there was no time to load or even to run, so he crouched, both hands spaced out along the rifle to block the swing of the scimitar. Within seconds the man was upon him. Simon smelt the foul breath of the camel and looked up at the bared teeth of the rider as he began his backhanded swing. But the sword slash never materialised, for Jenkins's bullet smashed into the Bedawi's chest and sent him crashing to the ground.

Suddenly all seemed silent within the little square. And then a great *huzzah!* arose from the defenders, as they realised that their attackers had now fled and that they had won the first battle of their lives. Small boys ran towards Simon, skipping and bouncing and waving their musket ramrods, women wept with relief, and thirty *jerzails*, their muzzles still smoking, were raised in the air in triumph.

Simon looked for Jenkins, and the little man, his Arab head cloth now hanging by one cord down the side of his head, came walking to meet him, his face split by that huge grin. Silently the two shook hands. 'Once again . . .' Simon's voice tailed away.

'Ah, think nothin' of it, bach sir. You'd 'ave bashed 'im with your rifle barrel anyway. Couldn't 'ave that, 'cos I told you the perisher was mine, so I 'ad to shoot an' deny you the pleasure, see.'

They were interrupted by Mahmud, his face smudged with black powder. Silently he offered his hand to each of them.

'Have any of your people been hurt?' asked Simon.

'Just one man has a sword cut on his shoulder, but it is nothing much.' He shook his head in disbelief. 'Who would have thought it? We beat more than twenty Bedawis. Well . . .' he smiled, '*you* did.' He gestured towards Jenkins. 'Do you know, this man must have killed six of them on his own.'

'The best soldier in the British army,' grinned Simon. 'Well, he used to be, before he took to the soft life.' He looked around. 'I would have thought that there was no chance of them coming back, Mahmud, is there?'

'Allah be praised, no. We must have killed eighteen of them and that means virtually all of the men – certainly the young men – in their camp. No one that I know of my people has ever stood up to them before. It is not good to kill, but these were evil men and they have been taught a lesson that will be sung about throughout this desert. And they have lost many of their camels, which will hurt those who are left.' He reached out and shook Simon's hand again. 'We owe you a great debt.'

Simon coughed. 'No. You did it yourselves. You must remember that. *You did it yourselves*. Congratulations.'

The evening meal that night was a noisy affair, as were their arrivals at the villages at which they stopped on their continued journey to Suez. Somehow, as Mahmud had prophesied, the news of the Bedawis' defeat had spread throughout these scattered communities, and Simon and Jenkins's wooden plates were piled high with the choicest morsels at each feast. It was as if, Simon confided to Jenkins, they had slain some great dragon in mythological times.

'Aren't we supposed to get a virgin maiden as a reward each then?' sniffed the Welshman. 'I don't see many of them about 'ere, look you.'

The remainder of the journey proved to be uneventful, although Simon insisted that the caravan should keep its moving square formation and Mahmud and his men happily humoured him. It seemed clear, however, that the danger of attack had been removed and Simon sensed that after their departure the caravan would fall back into its traditional single-line pattern for its long journeys. After all, that was the way it had always been done.

The farewell from the traders in Suez was quite emotional. Mahmud presented each of his passengers with identical jewelled daggers and insisted on refunding the six sovereigns paid for their passage. Each man, woman and child lined up and moved by the two friends to shake their hands. 'Good thing, good thing,' said Abdul with tears in his eyes.

To Simon's relief, there was a ship at the quay with steam up waiting for permission to leave Suez for its onward passage to Durban in Natal, and its captain was happy to take on board two last-minute passengers for the journey, however dishevelled they appeared in their creased cotton suits. Better, felt Simon, to be away before news of their triumph over the Bedawis reached Cairo.

As the SS *Belvedere* pulled away, Mahmud and Abdul stood waving on the dockside until they disappeared in the heat haze.

Chapter 3

The voyage down the stiflingly hot Red Sea and then along the seemingly endless east coast of Africa was uneventful and boring. During it, Jenkins reverted to his role of officer's servant, washing and ironing Simon's two shirts and pressing his one pair of duck trousers every evening (they were travelling third class, so there was no need to dress for dinner).

With little to do, Simon had plenty of time to reflect on matters he had been trying to forget: the depth of his love for Alice Griffith and the agony of contemplating her marriage to Covington – was it happening this very day, or perhaps the day after? This, together with the awful, dreadful prospect of the consummation of that marriage, made him morose and monosyllabic. It had been just before the end of the Sekukuni campaign, which Alice had been reporting on for the *Morning Post*, that she had confessed her love for Simon and promised to break off her engagement to Covington as soon as the battle was over. But in that fierce attack on the bePedi tribe the Colonel had lost his hand and his eye, so ending his glittering army career – and prompting Alice to make the agonising decision that she could not now abandon the man she no longer loved. Simon, heartbroken, had accepted her choice, but could not face returning home while the nuptials were being celebrated. The novelty and then the danger of the journey across the desert had lifted his spirits for a time. But the heat and boredom of the voyage brought back his misery and made him a withdrawn, sad companion. When the familiar sight of the rollers crashing on to the beach at Durban eventually hove into sight, then, Jenkins was hugely relieved.

Indeed, the excitement of the landing, with the rollercoaster longboat ride over the surf on to the open beach, and the sweet smell of the sugar cane fields that met their nostrils as they walked through the little town, helped to bring a spring back into Simon's step. Enquiries at Natal's administrative centre met with the expected news that General Pomeroy-Colley was at his army headquarters inland at Pietermaritzburg. Simon sent off a brief telegram to indicate their arrival and then set about equipping the pair for the journey to the north and the renewal of their lives as army scouts.

Sufficient of their haul of sovereigns remained for them to buy two good horses, a mule to carry their baggage, saddles and harness, ammunition for their Martini-Henrys, and appropriate dress for a life in the saddle – wide-brimmed slouch hats, Boer-type corduroy breeches and flannel shirts. Jenkins ventured into the Indian bazaar and received two pounds ten shillings for their Arab dress. He returned from this venture two days later, eyes rheumy, hair dishevelled, reeking of cheap whisky and beer. Simon decided to issue no rebuke. Better to let the little man get it out of his system before their excursion back into army territory.

'Look well if this general doesn't want us,' said Jenkins, surveying their new gear. 'What are we goin' to do then, after comin' all this way? Take up farmin'? I don't want to go back to ploughin', see. I was no good at it anyway.'

'Oh, I think he'll want us all right. From what I've heard, Colley has done what General Wolseley has suggested to him for much of his time as a senior officer.'

Simon had first heard about Major General Sir George Pomeroy-Colley when serving his apprenticeship as a young subaltern in the 24th Regiment, and the picture had been rounded out during his time in Afghanistan, when Colley was acting as Military Secretary to the Viceroy in Delhi. A distant cousin of the Duke of Wellington, Colley had won a reputation as being a brilliant organiser with an intellect far higher than that of most senior officers. He had had a distinguished early career in fighting the Bantus in the Transkei and later serving in the China War of 1860. But he had gained the greatest fame on Wolseley's staff during the Ashanti War, when he had kept

60

the army supplied through months of difficult campaigning in dense jungle. As a result, he had become a member of Wolseley's 'Ashanti Ring', a small group of officers who had fought with the great man and who had accordingly been marked down by him for preference.

It was no surprise, then, when Colley had been appointed to succeed Wolseley when the latter had returned to London from South Africa, after the successful completion of his Zulu and Sekukuni campaigns, to become Quartermaster General at the Horse Guards. Now Colley – 'the Pillar of Empire', as he was known back home – was High Commissioner and Army Commander-in-Chief for South-East Africa. His territory covered Natal and Zululand but he was alleged to have a 'dormant authority' over the Transvaal in the north, only to be exercised in case of emergency. How close was that emergency?

Simon had gained some knowledge of the political situation in the Transvaal some months ago at first hand when serving as a scout for Wolseley in the Sekukuni campaign on the Transvaal/Mozambique border. The Boers of the Transvaal, he knew, were regarded as the main ingredients in a simmering pot that was likely to boil over at any moment. He also knew their history.

It dated back to the Great Trek that had begun in 1836, when more than twelve thousand descendants of the original Dutch population in the Cape had abandoned their farms to escape from British rule and consequent taxation. In their canvas-covered waggons and taking their oxen and other cattle with them, they had migrated north into the unexplored hinterland. There some had branched off to form the Orange Free State; others had crossed the Drakensbergs into Natal and Zululand. The biggest group of the trekkers had negotiated the River Vaal and pressed on north to settle in the Transvaal, a vast tableland of veldt rising over four thousand feet above sea level, broken only by the occasional valley or odd shaped kopje – a small, usually cone-shaped hill. To the conventional traveller it appeared to be the very incarnation of desolation. To these Boers, however, it represented heaven – as promised and promising a land as that Zion being settled at roughly the same time by the Mormons in Utah, across the Atlantic.

The British had followed them but granted them a treaty of independence, similar to that which had been accepted by the Orange Free Staters. The Transvaalers, however, made poor administrators and the state eventually lapsed into virtual bankruptcy, from which the British rescued it by annexing it in 1877. Yet fiscal security had brought no happy acceptance of the colonial yoke and the Boers of the Transvaal had been restless ever since. Simon knew that Wolseley's campaign against Sekukuni had really been launched as a show of power to impress and daunt the Boers of Pretoria, who had themselves failed to quell this marauding chieftain. It had worked for a while, but now, it seemed, the pot was boiling again. Would it boil over into war?

That was the question that occupied Simon's mind as he and Jenkins rode into Pietermaritzburg on that bright late spring day in November 1880. Certainly, the little town did not seem activated by the threat of conflict. Although this was Colley's military head-quarters, there was no great military presence evident as the pair walked their horses gently down the wide main street with its little white-painted wooden houses gleaming in the sunshine. Here and there horsemen in military scarlet or blue clipped by, their backs erect as ramrods, their tightly trousered buttocks bobbing up and down to the canter. Black levies in nondescript uniforms sauntered in the sunshine. But there was no rattle of mounted artillery, no marching columns, no limbers or army waggons to be seen. This didn't seem to be a town preparing for war.

'Blimey,' said Jenkins. 'Bit quiet like, innit? Doesn't exactly look like they've been waitin' for us, does it?'

Simon nodded slowly. He had to agree. The last time they had been here, after Wolseley had successfully mopped up after the Zulus' defeat at Ulundi, 'Maritzburg had been all abustle with army activity. He frowned. But of course there had been a great exodus of troops after that war. Following the tragedy of Isandlwana, the Empire had heaved itself upright in all its wrath and sent a large army to Zululand to seek revenge. Pride regained, the cost had been counted and London had quickly recalled its forces and sent them back to their duties in India and at home. There would be few enough battalions left in South Africa now. Which posed the further question: would there be enough to take on the hard-riding, sharp-shooting Boers if it came to it?

Once in the main square of the town – big enough, as with most South African townships, to turn round a veldt wagon pulled by twelve oxen – Simon asked Jenkins to find a small hotel where they could stay cheaply and set off in search of the Commander-in-Chief's headquarters. He found it situated in a modest clapboard house that, if it were not for the sentry and flagpost by the front gate, could have been a bed and breakfast *pension*. Here, Simon waited in a small anteroom while his name was taken through to Pomeroy-Colley.

He was ushered into the C-in-C's presence almost immediately. The general stood to receive him, his hand outstretched. Simon had time to take in the fact that the office resembled a study in a country home in that the walls were lined with books, although an unusual feature was the collection of contemporary prints, whose bright colours lit up the room. One of them, behind Colley's head, seemed to depict a skirmish with the Ashanti.

'W-w-welcome, Fonthill,' said the general, revealing his slight stutter. 'Kind of you to come all this way to give me a hand d-d-down here.'

In appearance the general seemed a gentle warrior. He had the upright bearing of a soldier and his body was short but well proportioned. His features were strong and evenly balanced, with kindly eyes set beneath a rapidly receding hairline which gave him a massive brow. This and the full dark brown beard bestowed upon him the air of an intellectual. He seemed more like a university professor than a professional soldier – or perhaps a successful musician, for the fingers extended were long and delicate. Simon remembered that Colley played the flautina.

He grasped the general's hand and immediately felt an empathy with this strange soldier of empire. 'That's very kind of you, sir. I hope you don't feel that we have rather pushed ourselves on you – my man and I, that is.'

Colley gestured to the button-backed armchair that sat before his desk. 'Ah, the famous 352 Jenkins. Quite a character, I hear.'

'Good lord, General. I didn't know he was famous.'

'Oh yes. I have heard a lot about the two of you. Mainly from General Wolseley, but also from General Roberts in India. It seems that you both gave great s-s-service to these outstanding soldiers.' The general smiled. 'Though I understand that some of your methods were – what shall I say? – perhaps, ah, a little unconventional, eh?'

Simon shifted on his chair. He felt daunted for a moment, particularly remembering his brushes with 'General Bobs' on the North-West Frontier. Then a prickle of indignation stirred within him. 'I am afraid, sir, that the roles we had to play in Zululand, Afghanistan and, indeed, the Transvaal, could not be fitted within the strict bounds of conventional soldiering. We were on our own, you see, often behind enemy lines. We had to establish our own rules of engagement. But,' he paused for a moment and looked the general directly in the eye, 'we stuck to them. We did nothing of which we were ashamed.'

The two men regarded each other in silence for a moment. Then the general gave his warm smile. 'My d-d-dear Fonthill. I did not wish for one moment to impugn your conduct. As I understand it, you behaved with great courage and resourcefulness in all of these campaigns. In fact,' he lifted his eyebrows in an infectious display of mock astonishment, 'Wolseley tells me that you instructed him in how to attack the Sekukuni stronghold, and 'pon my soul, he followed your advice.'

They both laughed. 'It wasn't quite like that, sir.'

'Well, no more of that. Right.' Colley leaned forward. 'I can certainly use you down here in just the sort of role that you . . . er . . . seem to specialise in. Do you know much about the situation in the Transvaal?'

'I know the territory well enough and I was roughly au fait with the political situation with the Boers up there until a few months ago, but I am a little out of date now. Do you think it will come to war, sir?'

'I v-v-very much hope not. I don't want it and neither does the Government back home. And as a matter of fact, I still don't believe that these Afrikaners would dream of taking us on, despite what the papers say. So the odds are against it. But the s-s-situation is a touch tricky all the same. Let me bring you up to date.'

The general walked over to a large wall map and gestured to Simon to follow him. 'I know you know the Transvaal, but it doesn't do any harm to take a look at the map. First thing is – the size of the dashed p-p-place.' His pointed finger described an arc. 'Huge. Bordered in the north here by the Limpopo, with the warlike Matabele tribe on the other side; by the Vaal in the south, beyond which is, of course, the Orange Free State; a small border here with Natal and a longer one with Zululand in the south-east. Due east we've got Portuguese territory and to the west the land of the Bechuanas, with the British protectorate of Graualand West to the south-west. As you can see, damned place has got b-b-borders with everybody and is roughly twice the size of the Free State and respectively Natal and Zululand.'

He sighed. 'Second thing is here.' He ranged his finger over the suspiciously white and unmarked hinterland of the state. 'Nothing. I know and you know that that doesn't mean there really is nothing there. Place will be full of rivers, kopjes, farms, native villages and whatever. But we just don't have maps of the Transvaal. If I have to campaign there I shall be lost, metaphorically and ph-ph-physically.'

Theatrically the general raised his hands and let them fall to his sides. 'Neither the Colonial Office nor the Horse Guards in London can help, so I have had to send to Berlin, of all places, to beg maps. What a state of affairs! Do you know, I have just heard that one of our chaplains was ordered to conduct a service at one post in the Transvaal in the morning and evens-s-song at another five hundred miles away in the evening. That just shows how well we know the country. But enough of all that. Come and sit down.'

'Now,' he continued, 'back to the d-d-dashed politics. The Transvaal state acquired huge debts, as you probably know, from attempting to fight your old friend Sekukuni, the bePedi chief. The Boer president in Pretoria, Burgers, levied a tax of five pounds on every burgher. Most refused to pay, and the national debt reached two hundred and fifteen thousand pounds.' Colley gave a sad smile. 'At this point, I understand that the state coffers contained only twelve shillings and s-s-sixpence, so the Transvaal was, in effect, bankrupt. Trouble was, it was surrounded by potentially hostile neighbours and just couldn't be left undefended. The result was that, in 1877, we bailed 'em out by annexing them. There was absolutely no resistance.'

Simon nodded. 'But now, just three years later, there is. Why?'

Colley pulled on his beard. 'A combination of circumstances. By beating the Zulus, we have, of course, done the Boers a favour. This big threat to their south-easterly b-b-border has been removed. Sir Garnet's defeat of Sekukuni to the east has removed another threat. So two of the main reasons why these strange people were happy to have our protection have been removed. The other thing is the old problem of taxation. Whoever forms their government, these dashed farmers just do not comprehend that they need to pay for the s-s-services that a civilised country must provide for its citizens, such as schools, drainage, a police force of sorts and even a small military presence. In other words, they won't pay their taxes.'

'Ah.' Simon nodded his head. 'The trouble is, I should imagine, that most of the Boer population are farmers who won't see the benefit of the services you name. They make their drainage and protect themselves at their own cost.'

Colley shook his head. 'They live by their guns for their meat. But they have to come into town to buy ammunition. The s-s-same applies to flour and other basic essentials such as clothing. They can't maintain a completely insular lifestyle.'

'Yes. I understand that. So what is happening now?'

The general closed his eyes and leaned back in his chair for a moment. Then: 'Sir Garnet tells me, Fonthill, that you were not just an ordinary army scout. He wrote and explained that you had a fine head on your shoulders and that, despite your insistence on maintaining your independence from the conventional lines of army command, you were capable of understanding strategic matters of some complexity.'

Simon felt himself blushing. 'That's very kind of him, sir.' The feisty little man who was now back home in London and well on his way to becoming the Chief of the Imperial General Staff had certainly never shared this confidence with him.

Colley sat forward again. 'Look here, Fonthill, can I count on your discretion?'

'Of course, sir.'

'Right. Well. The man nominally in charge of affairs based in Pretoria is Colonel Owen Lanyon. He's now been given a knighthood and the formal title of Governor. Frankly, I am afraid that he is a bit of a hard hat and is riding rather roughshod over the Boers on this taxation business. I have some sympathy with him, because they must be the most confoundedly awkward people, but I would have applied a s-s-softer rein.'

'But with respect, sir, don't you outrank him?'

'In the army, of course, yes. But he is the civil g-g-governor, and in any case, my military responsibility for the Transvaal is only to be exercised in the case of an emergency. In other words, F-F-Fonthill, I get the worst of both worlds. I can't stop the potato falling into the fire, but when it falls I must pull it out before it gets burned to bits.'

Simon grinned. 'From what I've heard about you, sir, you've had worse jobs.'

The grin – though rather more a rueful smile – was returned. 'The difference now, though, is that Mr Gladstone is riding on my back and he doesn't like colonial wars. And the overseas p-p-press is on *his* back.'

'Quite. I think I understand your difficulty.'

'Mind you . . .' the soldier in Colley returned and he sat upright, a wide smile upon his face, 'if these chaps do want a f-f-fight I shall certainly give them one and see them off. Everyone tells me that the Boers are really just an undisciplined rabble who will run at the first sight of professional soldiers – just as they did, more or less, at Boomplats in '48. Our revered C-in-C back home calls them "an army of deerstalkers".'

Simon frowned. This man was shrewd and far less jingoistic than most senior officers he had encountered, but at the phrase 'undisciplined rabble' Simon heard again the doomed colonel at

Isandlwana: 'I hope Johnny Zulu does attack. I've got seventeen hundred men here to give 'em a bloody nose.' He cleared his throat.

'I am not sure that that is true, sir,' he said. 'They may be undisciplined in terms of conventional soldiering and so on, but they are wonderful horsemen – probably the best irregular light cavalry in the world – and magnificent shots. I have stayed on Boer farms. The children are brought up in the saddle with a rifle. A boy will be sent out on to the veldt with only one bullet. If he misses, he won't eat when he gets home. These boys are trained to hit the small knucklebone of an ox at eighty paces.'

'Really?' Colley seemed genuinely interested. 'What about their weapons?'

'Well, sir, I've seen the modern American carbines, the Winchester repeaters, and some Enfield Sniders, but mainly they have Westley Richards. They are deadly at up to six hundred years, but our Martinis should be superior in terms of loading rate and range.'

'So I have understood. And, of course, they have no bayonets and should be inferior at close-quarter fighting.'

'Quite so, sir. Their argument, however, is that they can have three of our men down before they get anywhere near them. And when our chaps do arrive to threaten with the cold steel, the Boers just hop on their ponies and get away. They will fight in open country, you see. I suppose you would call it guerrilla warfare.'

Colley grimaced.

'But you were talking of potatoes, sir. Will they be roasted?'

'All in all, I think not, because as I say, I don't think the Boers, for all their talk, will take on the British army. But there is a f-f-flurry in Pretoria at the moment which is proving a little difficult. There is an Afrikaner up there called something unpronounceable – ah yes, it's B-B-Bezuidenthout; goodness, sounds like a sneeze, eh? Anyway, this Boer has been arraigned for not paying arrears of tax of some twenty-seven pounds. He has been able to prove in court that he only owes fourteen. That's been accepted but he has been charged costs, which brings the total back to twenty-seven. The d-d-dashed man refuses to pay, of course, so his waggon was seized. Now about a hundred of his countrymen have taken the thing back.'

The general sighed. 'Stupid, isn't it? But wars have been started for less.'

'What's the present situation, then?'

'Lanyon is supposed to be sending men to repossess the b-b-blasted waggon. He is assuring London and me that nothing will come of it and that it's just a storm in a teacup. In f-f-fairness, I believe it probably is. Now, young man.' Colley straightened his shoulders. 'This may all have seemed very discursive but I wanted you to have as much background as possible.'

'Thank you, sir. I appreciate that. But what exactly do you want of Jenkins and me?'

'Damn good scouting, that's what I want. I have about eighteen hundred men in the Transvaal, but no regular cavalry at all. Pretoria has a garrison of f-f-five hundred men, with four guns and f-f-fifty horsemen. The rest are scattered about the place, garrisoning six outlying posts at Potchefstroom, Standerton, Lydenburg, Rustenburg, Marabastad and Wakkerstroom. They're not good men and desertions are constant. They're all at least two hundred miles from each other and they have no cavalry to operate outside the township walls. If there is an uprising they will probably all be cut off and besieged.'

Simon raised his eyebrows. 'Sir?'

'If that happens – and, to repeat, I don't think it will – I shall have to invade the Transvaal from Natal. You've heard me say we don't have a decent m-m-map in the place. There seems to be only one way to take a military force – can't exactly describe it as an army – into the Transvaal, and that's up through Newcastle. I want you to get up there as soon as possible and survey the route, over the border and right through into the Transvaal. Sketch as you go. Particularly note the places where the Boers might try and stop me. I don't want uniformed soldiers doing this work – even if I had reliable people to do it, which I don't. And that brings me to one further point.'

Simon noticed that the general's stutter seemed to have disappeared now as he began issuing his orders.

'You know the country and you seem to know the Boers – as well, that is, as any European can – and your brain doesn't seem to have been atrophied by the demands of regimental duty.' Colley gave a half-apologetic smile. 'I don't want chaps in red coats blundering around the Transvaal, because, don't forget, I have no formal remit for the territory. This is Sir Owen Lanyon's country and he would be rightly furious to hear that I had sent spies in mufti into his backyard to sniff out the situation. On the other hand,' the general's smile disappeared and his eyes grew hard, 'I don't want to be caught napping when those potatoes fall into the fire. So, Fonthill, in addition to reconnoitring the ground on the border, penetrate into the Transvaal. Keep your eyes and ears open. Stray off the beaten track and talk to the farmers you meet. Short of riding as far as Pretoria and confronting the Boer leaders there, try and gauge the degree of support for war that exists in the country. I can't see things coming to a head within, say, the next six weeks, so you can take that long, but then I want you back to report. Understood?'

'Understood, sir.' Simon reflected that, when it came to it, the scholar had a decisive air about him. After all, he would not have been known as the army's coming man without reason.

Colley stood and offered his hand again. 'You will receive a captain's pay and your man that of a warrant officer, but . . .' he smiled, 'as I think you would wish, you will not hold rank in the army. You will, my dear Fonthill, be independent. Which means that I can disown you if I have to.'

Simon shook hands. 'I have no problem with that, sir. Thank you.'

Chapter 4

Simon reined in his horse, cupped his hand over his brow the better to focus and looked at the dust cloud behind them. 'How many, d' you think?'

'Oooh, I'd say twenty, twenty-five.' Jenkins puckered his brow. 'Bit too far away to be sure, see.'

'Well, one thing is certain. If we can see them, they can see us.'

'Not necessarily, bach sir. We're not kickin' up dust like a municipal rubbish cart, now are we?'

'Hmm.' Simon concentrated hard. 'Too many to be farmers and they don't look like British troops – no sun reflecting off polished brass and that sort of thing.'

Not for the first time, Simon wished he had brought his army field glasses with him. He had not done so because their presence would almost certainly have linked him with the military, but on these vast spaces of the veldt, they were needed. Particularly now, because there seemed something menacing about that dust cloud. The people of the Transvaal moved in ones or twos, or maybe in families. Not in the size of cavalry troops. He made a quick decision.

'I think we'd better get off this track,' he said. 'Quickly, but carefully, so that we don't raise dust. Let's drop into that donga over there.'

He pulled the head of his horse round and Jenkins followed, tugging the lead rein of their packhorse. They allowed the animals to pick their way down through the stones until they were below the level of the dried-up watercourse and wound along it until they were away from the track.

Simon looked across at Jenkins and held a finger to his lips. The Welshman pulled a lugubrious face and nodded.

Despite their wide-brimmed hats, the faces of both men were deeply tanned by the African late spring sun and they were covered in dust. They had been on the road now for five weeks and Simon had made the decision to turn back and report to Pomeroy-Colley. They had predictably found that the only route from Natal into Transvaal for a sizeable body of troops lay on the existing south–north road that crossed the border where it narrowed just north of the small town of Newcastle. To the north-east lay Swaziland and to the west the Orange Free State, owing allegiance to Britain but independent enough not to allow British troops to march through it to attack their brother Boers in the north. Simon and Jenkins had trekked along the face of the Drakensberg mountain range but had found no pass to provide a suitable alternative passage to the north.

What they had found, however, was that the conventional route across the border into the Transvaal provided plenty of opportunities for a determined enemy to hamper Colley's advance. They had also discovered, on ranging across the veldt of southern Transvaal, a unity of opinion among the Boer farmers that the time had come for their state to be independent again and free from the burden of British taxes. In all, in fact, it had been a dispiriting foray for the two men, and Simon had turned back an hour ago with relief, although he was not looking forward to reporting so negatively to the general.

Now they sat wearily in their saddles, waiting for this strange party to pass. Where was it heading and what was its composition? It was not like the Boers, who had no standing army, to send out military patrols, even to police their border, which, in this case, was some fifty miles to the south. Simon decided to let the party go and then trail it until he could discover its destination.

After fifteen minutes or so, he saw the dust cloud pass across the lip of the donga and move away. He was about to pull out to fall in behind it at a discreet distance when a voice came from above, speaking in clipped Afrikaner tones. 'Good day, gentlemen.'

Simon and Jenkins looked up to see three rifle muzzles pointing down at them. The rifles were held by three Boer horsemen, all dressed typically: battered wide-brimmed hats above seamed long-bearded faces; shapeless black jackets; corduroy trousers; and filthy laced-up boots. Unusually – and menacingly – their jackets were criss-crossed by bandoliers all studded with cartridges.

Surprised as he was, for there had been no sound to betray the approach of the horsemen, Simon retained presence of mind enough to notice that they were not being addressed in Taal, or Afrikaans, the Dutch-based language of the Boers. It must seem clear that they were English so there was no point in lying. 'Good afternoon,' he replied.

'Now,' said the man in the centre of the trio, 'would you like to tell me what you're doing skulking here, hiding from us in this donga?'

Simon allowed indignation to creep into his tone. 'We're not hiding from you and we are certainly not skulking. We are English and this territory is under English jurisdiction, so it's a free country.'

The Boer showed dirty teeth as he exchanged grins with his companions. 'Well,' he said, 'we can talk about whose country it is in a minute. But you still haven't answered my question. What are you doing here?'

'We are running low on water and we came down to see if there was a trickle still remaining from which we could fill our bottles.'

'Well,' the man regarded him silently for a moment, 'if that's true, you certainly don't know the territory. Everybody who knows the veldt in summer would know that unless there's been a storm, these dongas run completely dry. Now who are you and where are you going?'

Simon shot a quick glance along the three faces. They were all set hard and the rifle barrels had not dropped. 'My name is Fonthill and this is Jenkins. We are both English – well, not quite true, because Mr Jenkins is Welsh.'

'I'm glad you've remembered that, bach,' interjected Jenkins.

'It's true that we don't know the territory, because we are on our way from Durban to Kimberley, to try our hand at a bit of diamond mining.'

The blackened teeth were revealed again behind the beard. 'Kimberley! Well, man, you are way off trek.'

Simon thought quickly. 'We were advised not to head directly through Basutoland because the Sutos were not friendly but instead to cross the Free State. But I guess we have come too far north.'

'Ya. And you with those nice army Martini-Henry rifles, too. Where did you get those, then? From your boss – a fat old British army general, eh?'

'Certainly not. You can get these in Durban if you know where to go. And we did.' Simon adopted an indignant frown. 'Anyway, why the hell are you questioning us like this? What right have you?'

The Boer nodded to his own rifle. 'These give us the right. Now, very gently, toss up those nice guns of yours and then very slowly walk along the drift until you climb out the way you came in. We shall follow you from up here.'

Jenkins caught Simon's eye and raised a questioning eyebrow. Almost imperceptibly, Simon shook his head. These men had the air of brigands – Bedawis who spoke English and had better rifles. From their demeanour, they would have no hesitation in shooting if the pair showed any signs of resistance. He slowly withdrew his rifle from its saddle holster and threw it up. Jenkins did the same. Then they turned their horses and climbed out of the donga. About a quarter of a mile down the track, the main Boer party had stopped. Simon realised that they must have been seen from the beginning – what sharp eyes these men of the veldt possessed! The three must have been ordered back to pick them up.

As they cantered their horses towards the waiting group, Simon saw that a covered waggon, unusually pulled by horses instead of oxen, brought up the rear of the little party. All of the men waiting for them were dressed similarly, with crossed bandoliers at their chests and Westley Richards rifles at the ready. But it was the rear of the waggon that made Simon raise his eyebrows. Attached to it was a light field gun. It was of foreign manufacture – German? – so Simon could not define its calibre, but it looked menacing enough as it rested on its large unshod wheels. Standing behind the gun and attached to it by a long rein stood probably the most magnificent horse Simon had ever seen. It was a beautifully proportioned chestnut, with a fine head, arched neck and bulging muscles and tendons in its fore- and hindquarters. It carried a saddle that was a work of art in its own right, with an unusually high pommel, intricate carvings in its leather and silver discs worked into the fringes of the horse blanket underneath. The stirrups were hidden behind what looked like buckskin covers and the bit and bridle were also decorated with glittering silver roundels. At the rear of the saddle hung a long rifle holster, also made of soft buckskin, with fringes hanging from its length. Simon recognised the stock of what was undoubtedly an American Winchester repeating rifle peeping from its top.

'Bloody 'ell,' said Jenkins. 'That could be a circus 'orse, look you. But is that a circus cannon, eh?'

The two men were taken round to the head of the group, where the leader of the trio reported in Afrikaans to a small man, dressed like the others except that he wore riding boots and his moustache and beard were neatly trimmed in Vandyke fashion. He nodded slowly and then urged his horse forward, hand outstretched.

'Good afternoon,' he said. 'Sorry that you have been brought in like this. My name is Schmidt.'

Simon took the proffered hand. 'Fonthill,' he said curtly, 'and Jenkins. May we please have our rifles back?'

'I am afraid not.' Schmidt had clear blue eyes and there was an air of command about him. 'But we will keep them safely for you. Now I must ask you to dismount and get into the back of our waggon. It may be a little uncomfortable – we already have one guest and you will have to sit on top of our supplies – but we cannot afford to run the risk of you galloping away.'

Simon frowned. 'Why ever not? Who are you? Why are you keeping us in this fashion?' He did his best to feign total naivety.

'Ach, arguments now will only delay us, and I want to find a good place to camp before nightfall. You will join us then and all will be explained – including, I hope, what you are *really* doing here. Now. Please dismount and get into the waggon. Quickly, please. We haven't got all day.'

With ill grace, the two men slipped out of their saddles and climbed between the canvas sheets that hung down at the rear of the waggon which, after they had entered, were tied together behind

75

them. The pair found places to sit on top of assorted sacks and dimly made out a figure sprawled in the gloom at the far end.

'Howdy, folks,' boomed a deep voice.

The man crawled towards them and they realised that he was tall and slim as a beanpole – but an exquisitely dressed beanpole. The hand held out to them was encased in soft leather gauntlets, fringed at the wrist, and the man himself wore the same heavily fringed golden buckskin fashioned into jacket and riding breeches, the latter tucked into finely worked riding boots that had high insteps and heels that boasted spurs with spiked roundels as big across as apples. He had laid aside a white Stetson hat that carried a band at its base in bright geometric patterns. As he moved towards them, Simon saw that slung low below his hips were two empty handgun holsters, the bottoms tied closely to his thighs. A shaft of light caught his face. His hair was long and grey and pulled back into a tail behind his head and the pointed beard and long moustaches appeared to be white.

'Blimey,' said Jenkins. 'It's Buffalo Bill! I saw you in a picture book in Shrewsbury, fightin' the Indians an' all.'

'Close, mah friend, but not close enough. Ah ain't Bill Cody, though ah've met him sure enough. No. Mah name's Al Hardy, from Texas, and ah ain't never been to Shrewsbury. Pleased to make your acquaintance.'

Simon suddenly realised that his mouth was hanging open. 'Oh, sorry,' he said, grasping the gloved hand. 'Simon Fonthill, and this is Jenkins . . . er . . . 352 Jenkins.'

'Wow.' White teeth flashed in the semi-darkness. 'Ain't never met a feller before with a number 'stead of a name.'

'Well you would, see, if you 'ad my name. I'm 'appy with my old army number, look you.'

'Oh, sure. Glad to meet you folks anyway. Guess you're Limeys, uh?'

'Limeys?' Jenkins had never heard the term.

'Britishers. You don't sound like them South African fellers.'

'Yes,' Simon interceded, 'we are British. But what on earth is a Texan doing here? And how did these Boers capture you, and why are they keeping you for that matter?'

'Okay, son. Lotta questions there.' Hardy eased himself against a sack of flour and made himself more comfortable as the waggon jerked into motion. Simon's eyes were becoming used to the dim light and he noted that the Texan's face was open and pleasant, but it was lined and he was probably older than he looked, though his movements in the crowded waggon were lithe enough. 'Now you guys listen 'cos I got somethin' important to tell yah. Forget what ah'm doin' in this heah Africa. That can come later. How I got lassoed by this posse is as follows.'

He spoke now without languor, in a voice low enough so that anyone listening outside the canvas walls would not hear. Two days ago, he recounted, he had been heading east from Pretoria – 'nasty, stuffy little town, full of guys with long beards' – towards the mountains which fringed the Mozambique border, where he hoped to hunt. As he camped, a large column of armed Boers had overtaken him, accused him of being a British spy, and kept him in the waggon. The next day, at a place called Bronkhorstspruit, they had ambushed a British column of soldiers, marching 'band an' all' towards Pretoria. Watching from the waggon hidden in trees, he had heard the Boer commander warn the English colonel that the Transvaal had declared its independence and established a republic and that if the British column of about two hundred and fifty men continued its march then that would be interpreted as an act of war.

At this, Simon frowned and shook his head in exasperation. 'Ah, so the silly bastards have done it. What happened then?'

'Colonel said he'd gotten his orders an' sure as hell he was goin' to go to Pretoria. Then the firin' started. Man . . .' It was the turn of the American to shake his head, but he did so with what seemed like genuine sadness, 'I ain't never seen shootin' like it. Them Boers fired from the trees an' the Limeys never stood a chance. The shootin' was so damned accurate that them redcoats never had a chance of formin' up, takin' cover or even shootin' back properly. The killin' was bad worst ah've seen since the Little Bighorn.'

'Good lord,' said Simon.

'Sounds like a massacre, like,' whispered Jenkins, his eyes wide.

'Yup. That's the size of it. After it was over – only took about three minutes, or so it seemed – ah hollered from the waggon and said ah should help the wounded. So they let me. Not that there was much ah could do, 'cos there weren't many wounded, y' see. They was mostly dead, often with four or five slugs in the head – in the head, ah'm telling yah. Them boys can shoot right 'nuff. Mind you, the Boers were good after it was over. Rushin' to help the few that were wounded an' allowin' a coupla fellers to go to Pretoria to get medical help. Mebbe they was a bit ashamed, y' know?'

The waggon bumped along in silence for a while as Simon and Jenkins digested the news. So it was war, after all. And what a brutal way to begin it! Simon eventually lifted his head and asked why the American had been detained.

'Waal, they soon realised I weren't no Limey spy, but they said they couldn't allow me to wander round the country in time of war, so they stuck me with these fellers headin' south to the border. There, they said, they'll give me back mah horse 'n' guns and release me into Natal as a neutral.'

Simon's interest quickened. 'Do you know what they're going to do at the border? And why they've got this cannon?'

'No, sir. Don't suppose they're goin' to invade just on their own, huh?'

'No, of course not.' Simon put his chin in his hands. 'Their obvious role is to stay on the border to give warning of a British advance and even to act as skirmishers when that happens. But . . .' he mused in silence for a moment, 'they wouldn't need one cannon for that and there aren't enough of them to delay Colley seriously. No,' he looked up, 'I believe that they are going to reconnoitre a forward position, probably just on this side of the border, from which the Boers will launch an invasion into Natal.'

'Blimey,' said Jenkins. 'Now don't you start thinkin', bach sir, that we can stop them doin' that all on our own, like.'

The big Texan looked from one to the other. 'Say,' he said, 'who are you fellers anyway? What's this sir stuff? You army or what?'

Simon did not reply directly but regarded Hardy intently. The man seemed honest enough, even ingenuous, but he seemed too incongruous a figure to be taken seriously. What was he doing wandering around southern Africa, looking and sounding like a character from one of those penny Western frontier booklets that were beginning to circulate in London? Wasn't he too good – or bad – to be true? Yet Simon had never been to America, although he had studied the Civil War campaigns at Sandhurst and had read with fascination about the recent Indian wars. Perhaps this was what the men of that frontier were really like? He decided to probe.

'Mr Hardy,' he began.

'Al.'

'Very well. Al. I will happily tell you about us in a moment. But fair trade. You promised a moment ago to tell us about you. Did you say that you were actually at the battle of Little Bighorn?'

The Texan nodded. 'Sure was,' he said. 'Rode in with the general and rode out without him.'

'But every man with Custer was killed.'

'Yep.' Hardy seemed not at all fazed. 'Ah was scoutin' fer the general, and with one of our Injun scouts ah was one of the first men to find all them Sioux an' Cheyenne, campin' by the river there. Ah reckon it was the biggest gatherin' of the plains Injuns there's ever bin. Yessir. I led Custer and his men into that valley, but then the general split his command. Ah didn't go with him when he went up over the hills to wheel down on the varmints. Ah was ordered to lead Reno and three troops in, along the creek, yah know. Sure was tough fightin' down there, but in the end we just about got away with our hair.'

'Ah yes.' Simon remembered that Major Reno, Custer's second in command, had been pinned down by the Indians and had narrowly escaped, with severe losses. He had been pilloried for not going to his general's aid, but Simon had always felt that Reno was blameless and that Custer's death and those of his men lay at the door of his own vanity and ambition. Hardy certainly seemed to know more than the basics of the battle and it looked as though he really had been at one of the most famous engagements in recent history.

'Fascinating,' Simon continued. 'But what brought you to Africa?'

'Waal . . .' Hardy looked around the waggon as though he wanted to spit but then thought better of it. 'After the battle ah reckoned ah'd had enough of workin' fer the army, so I quit and wandered around fer a while and got me a stake silver minin' in Nevada.' He smiled softly – he had a gentle face, in repose not at all unlike that of General Colley. 'Did quite well, s'matter of fact. Ah sold up an' decided to take a look around the world with mah money afore ah turned mah toes up. Heard about all them diamonds in Kimberley, so came down to try mah hand, but found that there was no place there any more for the little man. Mainly it's the big corporations now, like them de Beers fellers.'

Simon nodded his head in acquiescence and shot a glance at Jenkins, who nodded back in agreement. From their own experience there, under a year ago, Simon knew that Hardy was painting a fair picture. Despite his colourful talk and appearance, the man seemed to be genuine.

'But your magnificent horse – you certainly didn't find him in Kimberley, surely?'

The Texan nodded equably. 'Surely didn't, son. Ain't he wonderful? Name's Custer, o' course, and ah bought him in Arabia on the way down here. Pure-bred stallion. Got a nice little Arab feller to make me the saddle 'n' stuff to match mah Western pants 'n' all. O' course, ah brought mah pearl-handled Colts 'n' Winchester with me from the States. Man,' he shook his head slowly, 'there'll be a hell of a row if ah don't get them all back. Oh lordy, yessir. Though I got a fair idea where they're keepin' mah pistols.'

Simon took a decision. 'Al,' he said, 'we too are army scouts; as with you, we are not exactly soldiers ourselves, although we used to be.'

'Yes,' Jenkins added, his proud grin seeming almost to light the interior of the waggon, 'we both fought the Zulus at Isandwannee, an' the captain 'ere was at Rorke's Drift as well.'

Hardy's eyes widened. 'Gee,' he said, 'I heard all about that. Both of them places musta been worse than the Little Bighorn.'

'Well, I don't know about that,' said Simon. 'But we were sent here from Natal by our army command there to scout possible routes for an advance, should it become necessary. We didn't know that war had been declared but it's clear from what you have told us that such an advance will certainly now have to be made.'

He studied the Texan's face carefully. 'Now, Al, I believe that the Boers in this party will let you go at the border. Despite what sounds like disgusting behaviour at that ambush, I believe them to be honourable people, fighting for what they believe in. So I think you'll get back your weapons and your horse. But I am sure that they will ship us back to Pretoria as prisoners of war, if they don't shoot us as spies. After all, we are not in uniform. I don't intend to let them do that. Will you help us get away?'

The tall man's face broke into his gentle smile. 'Waal,' he drawled, 'I didn't take too kindly to bein' bundled into this waggon and I'm kinda tired of sittin' on potato sacks. Also I didn't like the way these fellers shot at your redcoats without much of a warnin', so,' he stretched out his hand again, 'okay, pardners. I'll join your war.'

The three exchanged grins and handshakes.

'Now,' said Simon, 'all I have to do is work out how to get out of here.'

'Oh, 'e'll do that all right,' said Jenkins. 'The captain's good at that sort of thing.'

The waggon creaked along, going at a fair pace, Simon realised, though he could hear the cannon behind bouncing and pulling at its connection, so that the rear end of the wagon kept yawing under the strain. He removed from his hip pocket the little notebook in which he had made his sketches and extensive captions and carefully tucked it into his boot. He had decided that they must maintain their identity as would-be diamond prospectors. The alternative could be a firing squad or a noose slung from a tree. These Boers sounded ruthless.

In fact, Schmidt, their leader, proved to be a good host. Once a camping spot was found for the evening in a small copse and a fire was lit, Simon and Jenkins were allowed to leave the waggon and stretch their legs, although a man with a rifle walked with them. Then they were called to the fire and sat, with heads bowed, as Schmidt delivered a lengthy prayer in Afrikaans. Cups of water and plates of meat stew – they had shot a gazelle earlier in the day, the leader explained – were set before them, with chunks of unleavened bread.

Pipes were lit and Schmidt approached and sat cross-legged alongside. The big bearded man who had apprehended them at the donga sat next to him, his rifle at his side. Of Hardy there was no sign.

'Now,' said Schmidt, 'I am a veldt kornet in the Transvaal militia, and as you will have been told by Mr Hardy, if you did not know already, the Transvaal has declared its independence.' His blue eyes smiled affably enough in the firelight. 'You British have achieved the impossible: you have united us. We have established a new capital at Heidelberg and elected a triumvirate of our own people – Paul Kruger, Piet Joubert and Marthinus Pretorious – to lead us. By now, all your garrisons at Pretoria, Potchefstroom, Standerton, Lydenburg, Rustenburg, Marabastad and Wakkerstroom will have been surrounded and most of them will have surrendered.'

Simon interrupted. 'Ambushing a British column before war was declared does not sound an honourable thing to do.'

Schmidt blinked for a moment. 'I was there,' he said coldly. 'They were informed of the position and told that continuing their march towards Pretoria would be an act of war. They had the choice and they chose to fight. They had to accept the consequences.'

'Oh come now, Kornet Schmidt. You know that that colonel had no choice. As a soldier, he could not surrender. But he and most of his men were shot down from cover before they could lift a rifle.'

The Boer on Schmidt's right snorted but the leader remained silent for a moment. Then he said, 'I don't think you realise your position, Mr . . . er . . . Fonthill. We have found you near our southern border, armed with the latest British rifles. We understand from two farmers near here that you have visited them, clearly attempting to ascertain the temper of our people in the event of war. You say that you are making for Kimberley, but you are heading in the wrong direction. We believe that you are British scouts, preparing the way for an invasion. You are not in uniform but you look to me like soldiers. We have the right to hang you.'

Simon made to speak but Schmidt held up his hand to silence him. 'Our people does not have a standing army with generals and such. I only command here with the agreement of these men. We take our major decisions by voting. Now, you have heard what I believe. I wish to hear what you have to say. Then we shall take a vote.'

'Bloody 'ell, man,' exploded Jenkins. 'That's a bit rough, that is. Where were you when we was fighting the Zulus – your enemy, eh? You left us to do your dirty work for you then, bach, didn't you? Now you want to 'ang us. That don't seem fair, now does it?'

Simon realised with a sinking heart that Jenkins had revealed their past links with the army, but the point seemed to have been missed by the Boer, who kept his eyes on Simon, waiting for his reply.

He gulped. 'We are not spies and we are not in the army,' he said, 'although, as Mr Jenkins has said, we did serve in the 24th Regiment of Foot and fought at Isandlwana and Rorke's Drift. We left the service at the end of the war and are looking to find a new life here. We had heard of the opportunities at Kimberley and were on our way there. We may well be off course, but people who do not know the veldt find that easy to do. You are welcome to search our belongings to find evidence of links with the army. You will find nothing.' He took a breath.

'As for the rifles, they are our old army issue. We were allowed to buy them for hunting when we left the service.' His voice rose slightly now and he emphasised each word. 'If you hang us on this so-called evidence, you will be committing an act of murder and consequently would have no right to call yourselves Christians. The world would hear of it and you and your countrymen would be rightly condemned. We entered what you now call your country when it was under British jurisdiction, having been annexed by us three years ago with the complete agreement of your then government. When we crossed the border you had not then declared your independence. Indeed, we knew nothing of this until Mr Hardy told us. We were therefore not – I repeat not – entering foreign, let alone enemy territory.'

A silence fell on those nearby. Simon realised that they must have been listening and he wondered how many had understood.

Schmidt heard him expressionlessly. Then he nodded in acknowledgement and gave a curt order. Immediately Simon and Jenkins found their hands being tied behind their backs. The Boer said, 'I shall put what you have said to my people. For the moment, I am afraid you must stay bound.' Then he clapped his hands to gain attention from his men and walked away, to be in a better position to address them.

Simon was suddenly aware that Al had appeared and was sitting silently behind them, but his attention was now focused on Schmidt. The Boer spoke slowly, with little emphasis, only an occasional nod towards the two of them. It seemed that his was the only address to be made, so Simon presumed he was presenting the case for both prosecution and defence. The man guarding them had moved slightly forward, the better to hear the speaker, although he retained his rifle.

' 'Ere, bach.' It was a mark of Jenkins's distress that he had dropped the 'sir'. 'We can't be 'ung like common criminals, can we? That's not right.'

Simon licked his lips, now as dry and hard as old leather, but could think of nothing in reply. Then he felt a pressure from behind on his wrists, and realised that someone – Al, of course – was sawing away at his bonds with a knife. In a moment his hands were free and the American was working on the rope that bound Jenkins. 'Keep your hands together behind your backs, as though you're still tied,' he whispered to them both. 'If the vote goes agin' ya, then I'll try 'n' get the rifle off that chile there.'

Simon nodded in relief. It was a chance, a faint chance, but better than being strung up without a fight.

Eventually Schmidt stopped speaking and quietly Al eased along the ground on his bottom so that he was almost alongside the man with the rifle who was guarding them. Simon saw that the American had a big Bowie knife in his hand.

Now the Boer leader turned his head round the circle, lit sporadically as the fire flared intermittently. He seemed to look at each sombre, bearded face in turn and Simon felt a stab of fear run through him. It was a frightening scene, as though the devil was casting flickering shadows around an inquisitorial woodland court. It was also, he realised, the moment of truth for them both. Schmidt spoke one word. He was putting their lives to the vote.

Six hands rose from the circle of twenty or so men around the fire.

They included, Simon noted, those of the three men who had arrested them at the donga. Another word was uttered and it elicited double the response. Simon exchanged a glance of horror with Jenkins. Which way had the vote gone?

Schmidt nodded and walked back to them. 'You won't hang,' he said. 'Your argument won the day.'

Simon tried to keep his face as immobile as possible, though he was forced to let a gasp of air escape. He realised that he had been holding his breath but he would not give this cold man the pleasure of realising that he was relieved or of thanking him.

'So,' he said. 'What happens now? You will release us, of course?'

'No.' Schmidt's face remained impassive – did the man never show emotion? 'You should thank the Lord that we are reasonable and merciful men. But I remain convinced that you are British scouts and therefore I cannot let you go to tell your general in Natal of our presence here just across the border. So you will remain with us as prisoners, and when we have completed our mission, we will take you back to Heidelberg, where you will be detained as prisoners of war. Now you will not be treated badly, of course, and I am prepared to free your hands and allow you movement within our camp if I have your word that you will not attempt to escape.'

Simon did not hesitate. 'Thank you for the offer, but the answer is no. You have no right to detain non-combatants and we retain the right to attempt to escape.'

'Very well.' The Boer smiled, but without humour. 'That is just the response I would have expected from a British officer. You will remain bound except for meals and you will stay within the waggon on the march and at all other times. You will be under surveillance and I must warn you that you will be shot if you attempt to leave the waggon.' He looked down at the American. 'I do not think it wise to allow Mr Hardy to stay with you, so he can sleep under the stars, like the rest of us.'

Hardy's eyes twinkled. 'Sure appreciate that, Mr Smith. Hope it don't rain, though.'

At a curt command, Simon and Jenkins were escorted back to the waggon. They took care to wind the loose ends of the cords around their wrists so that they seemed still to be bound. At the cannon they saw that their horses had not been put with the Boer ponies but were tethered to graze at the rear of the camp, close by the waggon, their saddles on the ground near them. Their bedrolls were thrown into the waggon and Hardy's was handed out to him from the waggon's interior.

In the minor bustle that ensued, Hardy managed a quiet word in Simon's ear. 'Ah'll come 'bout two hours afore sun-up.'

Simon could not help wondering at the tall Texan's assurance, but the man was as good as his word. The two prisoners were lying in a fretful doze when a scuffling at the canvas opening at the rear of the waggon woke them.

'Just you git inside now, ma chile, an' you won't git hurt.' Hardy was pushing forward the guard who had been left by the horses to watch over them and the prisoners. The Texan was levelling one of his long-barrelled Colts at the man's head. 'Now just sit down there, sonny.' He nodded. 'You fellers bind him nice an' tight with your cords and stuff a handkerchief in his mouth and keep it in place with that neckerchief o' his. Don't want to disturb everyone's well-earned sleep.'

'Blimey, bach,' said Jenkins, happily transferring his own bindings to the wrists of the Boer, 'you don't 'alf work fast.'

'Waal,' responded Hardy, flashing his teeth in the gloom, 'when a man's gotta go, he might as well just git an' go, that's what ah've always said.'

Simon tightened a knot behind the Boer's head, returning the man's indignant glare with a smile of his own. 'How the hell did you get your revolvers back, Al?'

'While the captain was doin' his judgement stuff and his troops was all a-listenin' to his words, ah just stole off and had a look in mah saddle pack. Ah thought ah'd seen the handle of one of mah Colts peepin' out, and sure enough, that's where they'd put 'em fer safe keepin', good as their word. Fine fellers fer keepin' their word, these Boers. Mind you,' he flashed his smile, 'could've hanged you as easy as splittin' peas, ah'm thinkin'.'

'That's true. Now. What sort of guard is being kept?'

The Texan scratched his head. 'Waal, to tell you the truth, not much of one, as far as ah can see. These heah Boers are good shots right 'nuff, but they ain't proper soldiers, that's fer sure. Apart from this feller heah, they don't seem to have posted proper sentries. Custer wouldn't have allowed that.'

'Good. Jenkins, please tie the legs and feet of our friend here. We don't want him hopping around. Now, let me take a look.'

Simon eased his way through the waggon opening and slipped to the ground. Cautiously he crept underneath the waggon and surveyed the camp. The big fire had burned low but there was enough light from the embers to see the rolled forms of the Boer party, stretched out around the fire like spokes in a wheel. The shadows between the trees surrounding the camp could have concealed a guard, but although he stared into the woods and focused hard for at least a minute, he could see no signs of movement. As Al had said, the Boers might be damned fine fighters but they lacked the elementary discipline of trained soldiers. They probably felt that they were far enough from the border to do without such conventional precautions. Nevertheless, saddling the horses without waking anyone would be a problem.

He put his head back within the waggon. 'All right,' he whispered. 'Come on. The horses are nearby, thank goodness, so you two must saddle up without making a sound. Then we will lead them back to the north, away from the camp, and wheel round behind this copse before we mount. There doesn't appear to be a guard, but these Boers sleep with one ear open, so we mustn't make a sound.'

As the others worked on the horses, patting them and whispering reassuringly, Simon struggled to free the bolt linking the cannon to the waggon, finally wrenching it free and throwing it into the woods. The barrel tilted up and he scooped up handfuls of dust and stones of all sizes and tipped them down the muzzle. Jenkins, tightening cinches, nodded approvingly. Then, treading gingerly, the three led the horses away from the camp through the trees until they met the trail. There they turned south, and after three minutes or so mounted and put their horses first into a trot and then to the gallop.

'Waal, bless ma soul,' chortled Al as he sat erect on his

magnificent Custer, his Stetson hanging down his back on a neck cord, 'that was just too damned easy.'

They had been riding for about an hour, at walking pace now to spare their horses, when the sun began to send cartwheels of golden rays into the darkness from the tips of the Drakensbergs ahead and to their left. Unseen, but from all sides, dozens of birds broke into song to welcome the new day. Overhead, a steppe buzzard wheeled low. The flat veldt had already been left behind and they could just perceive the terrain now undulating before them, breaking out here and there into distinctive flat-topped outcrops of rock, like miniature forms of the Table Mountain that Simon had climbed in Cape Town.

'Reminds me of Utah,' said Hardy. 'Just like the buttes there.'

Simon shot him a quick look and wondered for a moment. 'Hmm,' he said. 'You really have been everywhere, haven't you?'

But it was Jenkins who threw up his hand. 'Shush,' he ordered. He slipped off his horse and fell to the ground, pressing his ear to the stunted brown grass. 'Horsemen,' he cried. 'Not far away. Probably behind us.'

'Waal.' Hardy nodded in approval. 'Just like an Injun tracker. Ah'm impressed.'

Jenkins grinned. 'Saw a black feller do this in Zululand,' he said. 'Only trouble is . . .' he put a forefinger into his ear, 'you end up with an earwig in your ear'ole, see.'

Simon stood in the stirrups and looked behind them, but it was still too dark to see their pursuers. 'I reckon the border is about thirty-five miles or so,' he said. 'Too far to out-gallop them, I'd say, but we don't have too much artillery to fight them off.' Having forsaken their Martini-Henrys, they had taken the Boer guard's Westley Richards rifle and his bandolier, but then it would be down to Hardy's Winchester – a short-range weapon – and his two handguns, which, of course, carried over an even shorter distance. 'Let's see if we can shake 'em off.' Simon pointed to the south-west. 'Get off this trail and make for the rocky ground leading up to that kopje. On the hard stuff they might find it difficult to track us.'

They hauled their horses' heads round and set off, as fast as the broken ground could take them, towards a stubby rock of a hill that loomed off to their right. As the ground sloped upwards to give birth to the kopje, it revealed outcrops of ironstone that broke up into gullies, wide enough to take their horses. It was not the best defensive position in the world, but it was shelter of sorts. They dismounted, hitched the horses in the deepest gully to a grizzled stump of karoo shrub and crouched around a cleft in a rock, watching the trail to the north in the growing light.

They did not have long to wait. The Boers were riding hard – Simon presumed that they must have been covering the ground in spells of galloping and cantering – and there were seven of them, following a leader who was leaning low over his mount's neck, studying the track as he galloped. They sped past the point where the three had branched off on to the stony ground and Simon heaved a sigh of relief. Then, however, he bit his lip as the leader of the horsemen threw up his hand to halt the party. The sun had now cleared the peak to the east and it flooded the plain with light. By its rays they could see that the Boers had clearly lost their trail and were debating which direction to follow to pick it up again.

'They must be damn fine trackers,' said Simon.

As they watched, the leader stood in his stirrups and pointed first to the kopje where they were hiding and then to a more distant hill to the east. Immediately the party split into two groups and began trotting, their eyes scanning the ground, in diametrically opposed directions, the first group of four heading towards the kopje.

'Well, look you,' said Jenkins, his eyes narrowed. 'Seems we're goin' to 'ave to fight after all.'

'Yes,' replied Simon, 'but these chaps have eyes like hawks. Keep down under cover. At least we've made them split their forces. Three against four is better odds.'

'Yes, bach sir, until the other lot comes up, that is.'

The tall Texan said nothing but he eased the long Colts in their holsters.

'You take the Westley Richards, 352,' said Simon. 'Al, do you want the Winchester?'

'Nope. Reckon ah'm better with mah pearl-handled babies, iffen it's all the same to you.'

'Fine. I will take your rifle. Now, this is what we do. We are going to have to fight, so we must fight to kill. We have the advantage of surprise.' He swallowed because he felt far less confident than he sounded. 'They can't be sure that we are here and they will know that if we are not, they will have to make up lost time to catch us up down the trail. So they will have half a mind on that problem.'

He took a quick look through the crevice. The four horsemen were about three hundred yards away now, approaching the kopje, their rifles held across their saddles.

Simon turned back. 'As soon as we shoot, of course, the others will come back to attack us. So we must kill these four before they have time to find cover. This means . . .' he wiped a bead of perspiration from his brow, 'this means that we don't shoot until the last minute, at such short range that we can't miss. Now, 352, you take the man on the right of the four, I will take the next man along and Al, you take the third. Whoever can reload quickest takes the last one. Don't shoot until I tell you. Understood?'

The two nodded. Simon decided that the hunting party would be too close for him to take another look, so he mouthed, 'I'll count to ten and then we fire. Starting now: one, two . . .'

But he got no further. For some reason – perhaps a snake in the gully or because he scented the approach of other horses – one of their mounts chose just that moment to whinny. Immediately, Simon shouted, 'Fire!' and sprang around the side of the rock, the Winchester stock at his shoulder.

The resulting action was not at all what he had planned or expected. As though in slow motion, he saw his target raise his head in surprise and struggle with his horse, which had reared at Simon's sudden appearance. Simon's shot missed both horse and rider and whistled out over the veldt. He heard a click as Jenkin's rifle misfired and then the Welshman's cry of fury. The four horsemen wheeled their mounts around to bring their rifles into play.

At that point, the Texan stepped from behind the rocks into full view of the Boers. Simon saw with horror that his Colts were still in their holsters and that although his hands were hovering over their pearl handles, Hardy seemed to be making no effort to draw them, almost offering himself as a target. Instinctively, Simon shouted, 'Al!' For a microsecond his cry diverted the Boers and suddenly the American's hands became a blur of action. A Colt appeared in his right hand and with his left he began fanning the cocking hammer – Simon learned later that the guns were single action – as four shots sounded, almost as one. Slowly, all four Boers, their rifles in mid air, bent over and slid to the ground, blood oozing from wounds in their chests. Hardy watched them for a moment, then replaced the pistol in its holster.

'Good God,' breathed Simon, his tongue running over his lips.

'Bloody 'ell,' said Jenkins.

'Reckon them others will be over here afore you can say shortnin' bread,' murmured Hardy. 'Better pick up their rifles, ah guess, eh, Simon?' The tall Texan displayed no obvious emotion, but Simon noted that his hands were shaking and his face perspiring.

'Are they all dead?' asked Simon, moving towards the first man.

'Ah guess so.' Hardy's face was taut and his jaw clenched. He stood staring at the dead men.

Jenkins whistled. 'Blimey, Ally. I've never seen anythin' like that. You ought to be in a fairground, see.'

Simon gazed across the plain. The other three Boers were galloping towards them and would be upon the kopje within about ten minutes. There was no time to run – and this time there would be no surprise.

'Yes, let's gather the rifles and their bandoliers,' he said, feeling distinctly superfluous. 'Let's hope they don't all misfire this time. And let's bring their horses into the gully. Quickly now.'

This done, Simon and Jenkins quickly examined the Westley Richards rifles, the latter with a faint air of disgust. They were the same calibre as the British Martinis, but they required the fitting of percussion caps as well as the use of paper-wrapped cartridges. 'No wonder the bloody thing wouldn't fire,' muttered an aggrieved Jenkins.

'Should've told you,' Hardy said quietly. 'Mah Winchester fires to the right. You need to compensate it a touch.'

'Thank you,' said Simon. But his eyes and his mind were now on the three figures approaching them across the veldt. They would now be able to see their four comrades lying in front of the kopje. How would they attack? From what Simon had heard, the Boers preferred to use their hunting skills to take advantage of the terrain and fire from cover. So there would be no storming of the position and making easy targets this time. These three could afford to pin down their prey and wait until the main party arrived – with the cannon? Frightening thought. Simon concentrated.

'Look,' he said. 'It's three against three and they could hold us here. I don't want to be still around when the rest of them arrive with that cannon. We must outmanoeuvre them somehow.'

The Texan's blue eyes looked doubtful. 'Don't see much hope of that on this plain,' he said.

'What do you 'ave in mind, bach sir?' asked Jenkins.

Simon made his decision quickly. 'Right. Jenkins, can you quickly climb . . . no, sorry, you don't like heights. I had forgotten. Al, do you think that you could take your Winchester up to the top of this kopje? That should give you a chance of shooting down on these people even when they've taken cover.'

The tall thin man nodded. 'Reckon so. Better be goin' now so as ah'm ready to receive 'em.' He slipped away down the gully and they could hear him scrambling up the rock on the Boers' blind side.

'What do you want me to do, then?' asked Jenkins, a note of anxiety creeping into his voice. 'Better I stay with you, bach, eh?'

'No.' Simon squinted at the approaching Boers. 'We haven't got much time. I don't know how big this kopje is round the base, but I'm gambling it's not too far. Can you get across to the flank of the damned thing and get into a position where you can enfilade these chaps? I'll set up three rifles along here and shoot from all three in turn, so that the Boers will think we're staying put to shoot it out. All right? Good. Get going.'

'But you'll never 'it a bleedin' thing.'

'Off you go, or it will be too late. Now. Go.'

Jenkins sucked in his moustache, scowled but took off, rifle in hand, scrambling among the rocks, and was soon out of sight.

92

Simon picked up three of the Westleys, saw that they were properly loaded and laid them along the gully, a handful of caps and paper-wrapped cartridges at the side of each. Then he settled down to wait.

The Boers came up at the canter. Just out of range, they dismounted, and while one led their ponies away out of sight, the other two crouched and, spreading out, began crawling to gain vantage points to fire on Simon's position from different angles. The third then appeared and as quickly disappeared as he sought cover. Simon had to admit that the Boers' fieldcraft was impeccable. He had no idea where they had crawled to until, far to his left, a rifle cracked and a bullet hit the rock behind his head. He carefully noted the position and then waited. It wasn't long before two more reports came from different directions. Again he noted them, then crawled to the rifle on his left and, fervently wishing he was a better shot, delivered a retort to the first marksman. He scrambled along the line and fired shots from the other two Westleys, taking a heavy kick in the shoulder each time but noticing that the power of the South African rifles was heavy, for a great shower of rock sprang from his third bullet, hitting surprisingly near to his intended target. Good, although accuracy was not the most desired feature at the moment – he wanted firepower, to delay the Boer assault until Jenkins and Hardy could come into play.

The trouble was that they did *not* come into play. For at least ten minutes Simon scrambled amongst the rocks firing at puffs of smoke that seemed to change their positions all the time and, indeed, to get nearer. Without an elbow or an ankle to be seen, the Boers were somehow wriggling across this open ground towards him and becoming more accurate in their fire. As he sighted along the barrel of one of the Westleys, a bullet crashed into the rock about three inches from his face, sending a sliver of ironstone into his cheek and tearing it open, so that blood poured into his mouth and down his chin. Spitting, he withdrew the rifle and, moving to the other side of the rock which sheltered him, took a hurried shot at a fragmented view of a shoulder which appeared to be frighteningly close to him – perhaps only one hundred yards away. Where the hell were Al and Jenkins? If they did not open fire soon, the three Boers would be upon him and then he would stand no chance at all.

Despite his anxiety and the speed with which he was forced to crawl between the three positions, Simon became aware that the Boer marksman to his left had fallen silent. There had been no puff of smoke from his position for at least three minutes. Simon did not flatter himself that his own shooting had found its target, and certainly there had been no other fire to threaten him. The answer was clear: the man was stalking him across the broken ground to the left, either to rush him from the flank or crawl behind and deliver a fatal shot into his back. A shaft of fear ran through Simon. Now he knew how a gazelle must feel, sensing that a lion was out there somewhere in the long grass but not knowing which way to run. Why were Jenkins and Al not shooting?

Simon dispatched two hurried valedictory bullets from the two Westleys to his right, then, withdrawing the third rifle, he ducked down into the gully behind him that now sheltered not only their own horses but also those of the dead Boers. Seven horses, then, were milling about in the narrow space, wide-eyed at the shooting and pulling at the reins that tethered them to the karoo bush. They offered the only cover, for the gully was open at both ends, so, murmuring words of comfort to the horses, Simon slipped between his own mount and the giant chestnut, which seemed the quietest of the animals. Kneeling there, he swung his head continually to look at both ends of the gully. From which direction would the final assault come? He licked dry lips and gripped his rifle. He would have time for only one shot . . .

Then, blessedly, he heard two loud reports, one from directly above him and the other from round the kopje to his right. Had Al and Jenkins been able to join the battle at last? He had hardly had time to sense relief when a shower of stones to his left made him spin round to see a large bearded Boer – undoubtedly the man who had first crept up on them in the donga yesterday – slip down the slope into the end of the gully. He had seen the horses, of course, but not Simon bent down in their midst, for he was now creeping along the bed of the gully, putting one foot before the other with great care as, with rifle at the ready, he approached the little opening halfway along the gully wall through which Simon had entered. Simon was close enough to see every strand of his long greasy hair hanging down from his broken-brimmed hat and hear his breathing – close enough, indeed, to kill him, for he was clearly still unobserved.

Slowly Simon raised his rifle and, peering from below the belly of the chestnut, sighted it on the big man's chest. The range was short enough so that even he could not miss, but as his finger tightened on the trigger, he found that, somehow, he could not pull it. It was not a matter of reason, rather of sensitivity. He was *too* close. It would have been assassination rather than killing, murder rather than self-protection. He stayed kneeling, impotently sighting along the barrel, quite unable to fire at the Boer.

And then the big man saw him. For what seemed to Simon like all eternity, the two stared at each other across the underbelly of the horse. Then the Afrikaner swung his rifle round and fired. Miraculously, in that confined space, the bullet missed both man and horses and crashed into the rock face behind Simon. But the noise of the shot and its proximity sent the horses rearing, wide-eyed. The Boer ducked protectively and shied away, but one of the chestnut's hooves caught him fully on the side of the head so that he crashed against the wall of the gully and then slumped to the ground, quite unconscious. Simon, fearing for his own life, standing as he was in the middle of the plunging, rearing horses, sought to soothe them with his voice and hands, and eventually he did so, so that they stood shivering, their nostrils flared.

Simon suddenly realised that he had heard no further firing after the shots from, hopefully, the guns of Jenkins and Hardy. Had they found their targets, or were they still trying to discover their positions? And were the two remaining Boers now virtually the other side of the gully, with their rifles aimed ready to put a bullet through his forehead as soon as he showed his nose round that opening? He wiped the blood from his chin and the perspiration from his forehead and took a deep breath. His rifle levelled from the hip, he sprang into the gap – and found himself looking into the startled face of Jenkins.

'Good God,' said Simon, sinking on to his haunches. 'Where the hell have you been?'

'Been?' Jenkins puffed out his cheeks indignantly. 'Been? I've been runnin' round this bleedin' piece of rock like you told me to till me shirt's wringin' wet with sweat, see. I only just arrived in time to pot that feller out there who was about to crawl into the gully, look you. This bloody koppee, or whatever you call it, is miles round, so it is.'

'Sorry, old chap. I've had a bit of a hectic time.'

'Hey, bach sir, you're bleedin'. Did they wing you?'

'No. Looks worse than it is. Just a chip of stone. Where's Al?'

'Oh, 'e got the other one out there. But I think 'e's still tryin' to climb down this bloody mountain. Where's the third man, then?'

Simon nodded. 'In the gully. He got kicked by Al's horse. We'd better see if he's all right.'

They found the Boer with blood trickling from a wound in his head, but his eyes were open and he was stirring, trying to regain his feet. Simon removed his rifle, as Hardy appeared, blowing and looking distinctively dishevelled.

'Did you get your man, Al?' asked Simon. The tall man nodded – it was now clear that he rarely spoke if there was nothing to say. 'Right, would you please lead the horses away and give them water. We want to mount soon.' He turned to Jenkins. 'Three five two, did you kill the other one?'

The Welshman shook his head. 'Only got 'im through the shoulder, look you, but I took away 'is rifle on the way 'ere an 'e looked as though 'e wasn't goin' anywhere.'

'Right. See how he is and then would you please get a shirt off one of the dead men – pick the cleanest – and bring it here.'

Jenkins's eyebrows shot up. 'Blimey, we're not goin' to dress up like Boers, now are we?'

'No. But we're going to need cloth for bandages and, by the sound of your man, a sling too, and I don't fancy ripping up our shirts. Now get a move on. We haven't got much time.'

The Boer had slumped down again, his hand to his head, after vainly trying to get to his feet. Simon now cradled his head and put his water bottle to the wounded man's mouth and watched him swallow in great gulps. Then he shook out a clean handkerchief from his pocket, soaked it from the bottle and began cleaning the wound. The big man winced but said nothing.

'Well,' said Simon, having staunched the flow of blood, 'it's a nasty cut with a swelling to match and you're going to have a headache. But it seems to me that there's no fracture of the skull, so you'll be all right.'

The man's black eyes regarded him with suspicion. 'Why didn't you kill me when you had the chance?'

Simon shrugged. 'Don't really know. I probably should have done, because I saw you vote to have us hanged. To be honest, I'm not much of a killer and I think I'd had enough.'

'Ach. What will you do with me now?'

'Bandage you up – and your comrade who was wounded by one of us – and sit you down here to wait for your own people. I presume that they are on their way?'

'Ja. We had a little trouble limbering up our cannon, but they should be here soon. You should go.'

'I intend to.'

'What is your name, English?'

'Simon Fonthill. What is yours?'

'Gideon ter Haar.'

'Sounds very Dutch.'

'Ja. I will remember you.' The bearded face broke into a smile. 'I owe you a favour – just the one. I will repay it before I try and kill you when next we meet.'

'Thanks very much. Very kind of you.'

They were interrupted by the arrival of Jenkins, carrying a bloodstained shirt. 'Best I could do,' he said. Simon tore it into strips and, wringing out his bloody handkerchief, soaked it in fresh water before applying it to the bearded Boer's head.

'Here,' he said to Jenkins, 'tie this in place with one of these strips. And keep an eye on this chap. He's still big enough to cause trouble. I'll see what I can do with the man you hit.'

Seeing the position of the man Jenkins had wounded, Simon realised that the Welshman had intervened only just in time, for the

97

Boer was about to crawl into the gully from the other end. Attacked from both sides, Simon would not have stood a chance. He gulped as he knelt by the injured man. Jenkins's bullet had entered through the man's right shoulder blade and emerged through the shoulder. The bone had been splintered but at least the slug did not remain within the wound. Simon did what he could to ease the man's pain, put his injured arm into a sling and left him in the shade with a water bottle.

Hardy had now watered all of the horses and tied the Boer mounts on to a leading rein behind Custer. They were ready to go – and not a moment too soon, because Simon could see what looked like a dust cloud on the trail to the north. He mounted and called to the bearded Dutchman, now kneeling by the side of his wounded comrade.

'Mr ter Haar, tell your people that we are sorry that there was no time to bury the dead. It's something they will have to do, I am afraid. And tell them that there is no point in pursuing us. We have fresh horses that we can ride in rotation and we shall be across the border in a couple of hours. I hope your comrade recovers.'

'Thank you, English. God go with you.'

Simon pulled on the rein and the little cavalcade set off at a brisk trot towards the south, where the dark blue outline of the Drakensbergs marked the skyline like a jagged set of dentures. They rode, trotting and cantering, for about an hour, keeping a sharp eye behind them to the north. But there was no apparent sign of them being followed and Simon presumed that Kornet Schmidt would have his hands too full now to contemplate further pursuit.

His thoughts now turned to his report to General Colley. Well, the general would already know that he was well and truly at war, for the news of the Boers' declaration of independence and their obliteration of the British column at Bronkhorstspruit would surely have reached him. At least, Simon reflected, he was returning with seven sturdy Boer ponies, and with good horses selling at thirty pounds a head in Natal, they would be welcome. But there was also much to tell Colley, for the general would certainly want to send troops into the Transvaal as soon as possible to relieve his beleaguered garrisons and Simon had already plotted the best route, together with notes about the obvious places where the Boers would try and attack him. And it looked as though they planned to do so from forward positions in the Transvaal, otherwise why would Schmidt be sent down to the border? How long, he wondered, would it take Colley to mount a viable invasion? Did he have the troops and the weapons available to him in a Natal denuded of both since the end of the Zulu War?

The thought of weapons reminded him vividly of Hardy, and he dropped to the rear to ride alongside the Texan.

'Tell me, Al,' he asked, 'why did you take such a terrible risk by stepping out in front of the Boers like that and giving them a chance to kill you before you drew that great pistol of yours?'

For the second time since their meeting, the American showed signs of discomfort. He sniffed and looked up at the sky, now a bright blue and where, behind them, vultures were wheeling – it was just as well that Schmidt's burial party had arrived in time. Then he examined his richly worked boots for a moment. 'Waal,' he ventured at last, 'ah guess ah just had somethin' to prove.'

He wrinkled his eyes and stared straight ahead at the distant mountains, now looming a little nearer. He offered no further comment, so Simon decided not to pursue the matter. There was obviously much still to be learned about this tall, slender man with the fast hands and the ability to kill so quickly.

Chapter 5

The three riders pressed on through that hot day, changing their horses twice to maintain the pace. Simon was not now worried that Schmidt and his party might overtake them but rather that they might meet other bands of armed Boer militia ahead of them, reconnoitring the border. He was in no mood for a further fight and it seemed that this was true of Hardy also, if his continued silence was any yard-stick. But it was impossible to remain morose for long in Jenkins's company, and shortly after they crossed the border and slipped under the looming presence of the Majuba mountain, the Texan's slow smile began to respond to the Welshman's chatter.

It was dusk before they reached the little town of Newcastle, some thirty-five miles deep into Natal, where Simon had been told before they set out that he would find General Pomeroy-Colley. Originally known as Post Halt Two, and little more than a village, it had been a popular stopover for waggons journeying between the old Port Natal – Durban – and the high veldt of the Transvaal. Now, as the three tired men rode in from the north, it became clear to them that Colley was establishing Newcastle as the springboard for the invasion.

On a bluff overlooking the motley collection of corrugated-iron stores, canvas tents and adobe buildings that made up the township stood Fort Amiel, erected some three years before as a defensive measure in case the annexation of the Transvaal turned sour. It had also been used as a convalescent station for General Wood's column during the Zulu War. It consisted now of little more than a ditch, a rampart and a low stone wall, enclosing a brick-built hospital and rows of army tents. To Simon's weary eye, it would not form a serious deterrent to a determined artillery-based Boer attack, but, despite the

101

late hour, there was much military bustle in the town itself, with limbers being pulled through the streets, mounted horsemen riding by in a wide variety of jackets, ranging in colour from scarlet to khaki, and individual infantrymen lounging on the sidewalks in uniforms that had – only just – survived the Zulu and Sekukuni campaigns.

More importantly, Newcastle possessed two hotels, the smaller of which offered them what they were assured was the last available room in town. Luxurious it was not, but it did contain three beds, chamber pots and a marble-topped washstand. They accepted it with relief and Simon decided that reporting to the Commander-in-Chief could wait until the next morning. After eating the best meal the hotel could provide and drinking seven bottles of Bass between them – Jenkins consumed four – the three retired early to their beds. As they did so, a heavy thunder crash broke over the town, lightning illuminated their dusty window and heavy rain began to fall. The Natal–Transvaal summer – the rainy season – had begun.

The headquarters of Major General Sir George Pomeroy-Colley was, in fact, in the larger hotel next door, but even so Simon was drenched by the time he presented himself to the general the following evening.

'Good lord,' said Colley, striding forward with hand outstretched. 'My dear fellow – you've been wounded.'

Simon grinned inwardly and thought how very different this caring man was to Roberts and Wolseley, the other two prickly, driving generals he had served. 'It's nothing, sir,' he said, dabbing at the still open wound on his cheek. 'Just a scratch from a sliver of stone.'

'Well you look as though you n-n-need a stitch or two in that. First tell me how it happened before you give me the rest of your news. I see, by the way, that you have returned almost exactly six weeks after your departure.' He smiled. 'I d-d-do like a man who keeps his word.'

Simon took a deep breath and related how, after their uneventful reconnaissance through the Drakensbergs and into the Transvaal, they had had their brush with Kornet Schmidt's troop and met Hardy.

102

'A field gun, you say,' mused the general. 'If it was merely a border patrol they wouldn't want to be burdened with that.'

Simon leaned forward. 'Precisely, sir. It is my belief that they were a forward party, sent down hurriedly to establish the best position near the border for the Boers to concentrate their troops to forestall your own invasion. In my opinion, they won't want you to debouch on to the Transvaal veldt and will stop you by advancing themselves into Natal to take you on just north of here.'

Colley pulled a face. 'The Transvaalers *invading Natal*! D-d-doesn't sound their style at all. My view is that they'll wait until we actually invade and then take us on on the plain . . . defending their homeland on their own soil in the full view of the world and all that sort of tosh.'

'No, sir. They won't invade as such; merely advance across the border to fight us on the best defensive position for miles around.' He pulled a map across the general's desk. 'May I?'

'Of course.'

'You can only take your column into the Transvaal along the main route north here.' He traced his finger up from Newcastle. 'Everything narrows down here: you've got the Drakensbergs on the left and the Buffalo river on your right, and it's the only way an army can get through. But about five miles south of the border on our side is the narrowest part of all, with only about a mile or two between the mountains and the river at a place called Laing's Nek. The Boers will take you there, sir, and as soon as they have gathered their forces on their side of the border, say about here, at Volkrust, they will move down and take up their positions and wait for you. The question is, can you get there and move through before they can establish themselves?'

A silence fell on the room as Colley concentrated on the map. At length he nodded. 'I know where you're t-t-talking about. I have had no time at all to look up there myself because I've had so much to do trying to gather some sort of column together. Anyway,' he smiled, 'that's why I sent you north. To be m-m-my eyes.

'To answer your question, I don't know how fast the Boers can move but I certainly can't advance for about a month yet. I am

103

working as d-d-damned hard as I can to put some sort of force together to relieve all my garrisons, which are now, as I suspected, under siege. I don't have the luxury of waiting for troops to come from India again so I have to use the men I've got here already to cobble something together quickly. B-b-but it can't be until mid to late January. Will the Boers be in position before then, do you think?'

Simon sighed. ' 'Fraid so, sir. As you know, they don't have a standing army as such, but from what I've been able to learn, they can call up about seven thousand men. All able-bodied males between the ages of sixteen and sixty will have been mustered by now. Each man is a self-contained unit, arriving on horseback with rifle, bandolier full of ammunition and several days' worth of rations, which will have been packed by his wife. So you see, sir, the entire nation becomes an army and the army is the entire nation. What's more, they are all cavalry so they can move incredibly quickly. I would think that the slopes of Laing's Nek will be occupied by Boers within a week.'

'Artillery?'

'I don't know about that, but' – his thoughts flashed back to time spent in the Transvaal the year before – 'I know that the Transvaalers are close to the Germans, and I have seen German pieces of ordnance in the north. That light cannon being brought down here was new and almost certainly German. But they will rely on their rifles more than artillery. You know, sir, they really are magnificent marksmen – our poor chaps at Bronkhorstspruit died with several bullets each in the head. And they know how to make good use of ground.'

Both men had been standing, but now Colley gestured to Simon to sit and regarded him steadily for a moment with his soft brown eyes. Then he smiled. 'My dear boy, I do think that you are being just a bit too pessimistic, you know. The B-B-Boers may be good hit-and-run fighters, or fine at laying an ambush, as at Bronkhorstspruit. But they will lack discipline. Up against professional troops they will break.'

He held up his hand as Simon moved to interrupt. 'If proper precautions had been taken by the 94th on the march at Bronkhorstspruit then that tragedy would never have happened. I do have respect for the Boers and, indeed, understand their desire to free their homeland, as they see it. I do not wish this war to become a race struggle between the Dutch and the English throughout the colony, and indeed, Fonthill, I have refused offers of assistance from elsewhere in South Africa which might in the long term extend the struggle and array the civil population of the country against one another.' The warm, confiding smile returned. 'B-b-but I must carry out my duty and relieve our forces in those garrisons as quickly as possible. I won't have the largest or best army in the world with which to advance on the Transvaal, but I think it will be sufficient for the job in hand.

'However, F-F-Fonthill,' he turned his head to the window and looked out at the rain, much lighter now, and spoke quietly, as though half to himself, 'I am issuing a general order to try and check the violent vengeful feeling which, unfortunately, is almost sure to spring up in such a war.' He turned back and smiled again. 'I know that war cannot be made with rosewater and I am not much troubled with sentiment when the safety of the troops is at stake, but I hate this "atrocity manufacturing" and its effects on the men, tending to make them either cowards or butchers.

'Now.' He leaned his chair back. 'I am grateful for all that you have done and for the advice that you have given me. I was told that you were shrewd m-m-militarily far beyond your age and rank, and you seem to have lived up to that commendation. Your brush with that Boer party is indicative of that. So . . .' he let the chair fall forwards with a crash, 'I have another rather difficult and delicate job for you.'

'Sir?'

'More of that tomorrow. I have much on my hands at the moment and I have a very important letter to draft. Please come and see me at eight a.m. tomorrow and I can brief you fully. Oh, and this work can involve not only the famous 352 but this Buffalo Bill chappie, if you wish. Now, Fonthill, please excuse me.'

'Of course, sir.'

'Ah. Fonthill . . .'

'Sir?'

'Happy Christmas.'

'Good lord. What date is it?'

'December the twenty-third. Tomorrow is Christmas Eve. After I have seen you, I leave for 'Maritzburg to gather what men I can – and to see my wife. Are you married, my boy?'

'No, sir.' Simon's reply was quick and emphatic. For a moment it nonplussed the general.

'Well, I recommend it. Good morning.'

Simon was a trifle early for his appointment the next day and so he was kept waiting. He noticed now that both hotels had hung coloured bunting around their public rooms and had put sprigs of evergreen behind the pictures on the walls. He also realised that the military presence he had observed on riding in was, in fact, quite modest. Indeed, a quick strike by the Boers down through the pass in the Drakensbergs now would probably meet with little resistance. Nevertheless, he felt that that would be unlikely. The general was right: the Afrikaners were not offensive fighters and they would not easily give up the chance of tackling Colley from a defensive position at Laing's Nek.

At 8.20 he was ushered in to see the general, who was signing a document. He was waved to a seat as Colley carefully put the letter into an envelope, deposited a little sealing wax made pliable by a candle and then stamped it heavily with his seal.

He held up the envelope. 'Now, Fonthill, I want you to take this yourself to Jan Hendrik Brand, the p-p-president of the Orange Free State, at his capital in Bloemfontein. I am very sorry to have to ask this of you, but I believe it important that he receives it as soon as possible, so I must ask you to set out immediately.' He pulled at his beard and gave his sad smile. 'It means you missing whatever Christmas f-f-festivities Newcastle can offer, I'm afraid. You will need to prepare for the journey, of course. Can you start this afternoon?'

'Of course, sir.' Simon had been dreading the thought of a synthetic Christmas in the hotel next door: the drinking, the toasting, the inevitable singing of carols, the false jollity – while back home in England, Alice would be spending her first Christmas with her new husband . . . Hell! The need to ride somewhere, anywhere, urgently would be a welcome diversion.

'Do sit down, Fonthill.' As Simon perched on the edge of the button-backed chair facing the desk, Colley stood and began walking round the room as he spoke, so that Simon was forced to turn his head to follow him.

'Now, you may wonder why I am not sending this letter through the normal channels. The reason is that it is an important message, of some sophistication, and I want to send it to Brand via special messenger to underline its importance. I am writing to the president, you see, in my c-c-capacity not only as Commander-in-Chief of South-East Africa but also as High Commissioner. This letter, then, concerns diplomatic matters as well as military. Do you follow?'

'So far so good, sir.'

'Good.' Colley carefully adjusted the Ashanti War painting behind his desk. 'I am requesting the president to send an answer back to me with you, so you w-w-will wait there until it is prepared and given to you. Then make all haste to return here to give it to me. I may be here or further to the north. But find me with it. Is that clear?'

'Yes, sir.'

'I need not burden you with the full content of the letter, but I think you should be aware of the main thrust of it. The p-p-position is this.' The general, dressed for his journey south in light khaki drill devoid of badges of rank but wearing puttees and large boots, perched somewhat incongruously on the corner of the desk and leaned down to speak earnestly to the young man facing him.

'I did not want this war, but we have it now and it has to be fought. It would be disastrous, however – both politically back home and militarily here – if it escalated into a full-scale conflict between the Boers of South Africa and the imperial forces. The people of the Orange Free State are key to this and it is vital that they do not join with their brothers in the north to fight against us. This is therefore a personal plea from me to the president to stay out of the war. I am even asking for his advice on what I can do to assist him in this endeavour and, indeed, to mitigate the conflict in the Transvaal. At the same time, however, I am explaining to him the hopelessness of the Transvaalers' cause. I have explained that, in addition to the forces I have here, there are two cavalry regiments, two infantry regiments and two batteries of artillery on their way to reinforce me, and twice that number more would reach me within a month if I telegraph home the wish.' Colley smiled. 'Just a touch – in the lightest possible way – of the heavy hand there, Fonthill, you understand.'

Simon nodded, but his mind was full of questions.

'In my letter I have introduced you as a young but important member of my civil staff in Natal, who, although he has now left the army, had a b-b-brilliant record in terms of fighting not only at Isandlwana and Rorke's Drift but also in Afghanistan and the recent Sekukuni campaign. I have informed the president that you know the territory in the north, that you are c-c-currently quite au fait with the situation in the Transvaal and that you have my complete confidence.'

The general's eyes were now almost a-twinkle. Was there some mischief afoot? Simon intervened before Colley could continue. 'I am more than happy, of course, sir, to undertake this mission,' he said, 'and I realise its importance. In fact that is the point. I hope that you don't think I am reflecting either self-doubt or impertinence in suggesting that perhaps you should have someone of – what shall I say? – more seniority undertaking it.'

'Ah, Fonthill, the question does you c-c-credit!' Colley was now positively beaming. 'To be frank, the answer is no. Oh, I have senior officers here who are fine soldiers who would seem to fit the bill. But their role is fighting and I do not have complete confidence in their ability to be diplomatic.' The general's expression now softened and the brown eyes assumed an almost apologetic air. 'What was it the great Duke of Wellington said – "There is n-n-nothing so stupid as a gallant British officer"? I am exaggerating, of course, to make the point, but anyway, I need every senior officer I have at the moment to train and drill this rather rag-tag army with which I shall have to confront these will-o'-the-wisp marksmen of yours.'

Simon frowned. 'I see that, sir, but surely I shall be nothing more than a messenger?'

'Not quite – and this is the point.' The general eased himself off the corner of the desk and resumed his seat. He picked up his pen and tapped it idly against his thumbnail. 'I don't know Brand, but I am informed that he is a balanced individual, unlike some of his more volatile colleagues in the Transvaal, and that he is very shrewd. I can quite see, therefore, that he might think that my references to the strength of my army here are rather over-egged, to impress.' The gentle smile returned. 'As, indeed, they are.

'In the circumstances, then, he might well subject you to a gentle inquisition about the real strength of my forces here.' Colley leaned forward. 'Such a questioning directed at a b-b-bluff colonel would elicit loyal support of my claims. You would not expect such an experienced soldier to express even a twinge of doubt about our strength here. However,' the general leaned back, 'Brand might well attempt to take advantage of your obvious youth and seeming lack of experience to elicit a truthful and ingenuous indiscretion which would reveal that we are not as strong as my letter claims. D' you follow, Fonthill?'

Simon blew out his cheeks. 'Bit of a double bluff, eh?'

'Exactly. Look, my boy, it may seem that I am playing games, but I promise you I am not. I have eighteen hundred British troops completely trapped and besieged in Transvaal garrisons. Whatever the ambivalence displayed by our Liberal government – and I expect p-p-plenty of that – I know that public opinion back home will demand that I march north as quickly as possible to raise those sieges. I probably have insufficient quality and quantity of men to do that with complete confidence, but I can't afford to wait. Given my strength, I must play every c-c-card I can to ensure that this war does not escalate to include the Free Staters. I am sure you understand.'

Simon slowly nodded his head. He understood all right, but the task ahead of him sounded delicate, if not downright awkward. Not exactly scouting for an army in the field. 'Of course, sir,' he said, trying to sound confident.

'Now,' Colley continued, 'Sir Garnet Wolseley tells me that you have ability and common sense and I am sure that is t-t-true. If Brand does question you along these lines, then convey that I am building a formidable force that is almost ready to march. He won't expect you to give him chapter and verse, of course, but you might perhaps drop in the fact that you believe there is a naval contingent in Cape Town p-p-preparing to join the column.' He chuckled. 'The power of our navy always frightened foreigners. But above all, try and sound open and frank – and *completely confident*. Do I make myself clear?'

'Quite clear, sir.'

'Good. One more thing. The Free State is, of course, independent, but I have no reason to think that Brand will be unsympathetic. In fact, I understand that the Transvaalers accuse him of being too English. B-b-but he could well be under some sort of pressure from other European powers to throw in his lot with the Transvaal. I hear from London that Leon Gambetta, the president of the French Assembly, has said that the British are "ignoble" in fighting the Boers, and Bismarck has informed Viscount Goschen that we ought to have done anything rather than fight the white man in South Africa.' The general's mellifluous voice took on a note of gentle indignation. 'You see, the Empire has c-c-critics everywhere. I imagine it is the price of success.'

'But how might this affect my task in Bloemfontein?' asked Simon.

'Well, I hope it won't. But you might find that there are representatives of, say, Germany, at Brand's court, so to speak. If you do, tread with care. We do not, of course, want an international incident.'

Simon gulped. 'Tread with care. Yes, of course, sir.'

'Now,' Colley stood and his voice became stronger, 'I am not sending an army escort with you, because I do not want r-r-redcoats being flaunted in the Orange Free State at this moment, for obvious reasons. I do not anticipate that your journey will be interrupted at all – I have today telegraphed the president, telling him to expect you. But you will need some sort of protection on the way and it seems to me that your m-m-man Jenkins and even this strange American, if he wishes to accompany you, will fulfil this task quite well.' He offered Simon the letter and a small piece of paper with it. 'This is a chit to the quartermaster. He will provide new Martini-Henrys and whatever other small arms you need, and also . . .' he paused and smiled, 'a suit of tails and white tie for you. Strangely enough, the QM tells me that he can manage this.'

'Good lord.' Simon's jaw dropped for a moment.

'You are entering diplomatic territory now, Fonthill, so you must look the part if called upon to do a little formal representation. Sorry we can't give you the rank of ambassador. Now be on your way, and good luck.'

Simon stood and shook the general's hand, his head buzzing. 'Thank you, Sir George,' he said.

Chapter 6

Simon felt ridiculous asking Jenkins to pack white tie and tails into a special flat pack that would hang behind his saddle roll, and the Welshman put on his particularly lugubrious face at the request. 'Where do I put the dancin' shoes, then?' he asked.

'Damn,' said Simon. 'Good point. I can't go to a reception – even in Bloemfontein – in riding boots.' And he rushed to the only outfitters in Newcastle and bought a pair of black shoes, not exactly suitable for evening wear but, with a little elbow grease from Jenkins to bequeath polish, able to pass muster.

The Welshman did not take easily to the news that they would set off that afternoon, in the light rain that was falling, and so miss the Christmas Eve festivities in the hotel and the feasting that was set to follow the next day. But Simon was adamant. He had promised Colley that they would be on their way as soon as possible, and anyway, he had no desire to celebrate Christmas.

He approached Al Hardy with some reticence. The tall Texan had stayed strangely quiet since their arrival in Newcastle, spending the two days mainly engrossed in endless games of cards with Jenkins, to whom he taught poker. On their brief acquaintance, Simon had grown to like the man, and he and 352 seemed to have become bosom friends. Yet there was undoubtedly something bizarre about him – after all, what was an American frontiersman, clearly a gunman, doing wandering around South Africa? Was he, could he be on the run from the law? But if so, why run so far? Canada, for goodness' sake, would be an equally secure refuge and a damn site nearer.

Certainly Hardy seemed to have no financial worries. Although he spent little on himself (he made no attempt to match Jenkins's consumption of liquor), he was meticulous in his attention to Custer, turning down Simon's offer of finding army stabling and putting the big chestnut in the most expensive livery stable in town. In terms of approaching the Texan to accompany them, Simon was rather ambivalent. On the one hand, the man was so damned conspicuous, with his buckskins and big Stetson (Simon had managed to persuade him to leave his gun belt in the bottom of the chest of drawers in their room during their stay in Newcastle); perhaps not the most ideal companion for a diplomatic mission. Yet he matched Jenkins in his courage and marksmanship and one couldn't wish for a better man to have at one's side in a tight corner. It was with some diffidence, then, that Simon asked if he wished to travel with them to Bloemfontein.

'Waal, sonny,' said the tall man, hitching up his tight trousers. 'Ah don't much fancy ridin' out in this rain an' all. But ah guess ah ain't got much else to do in this one-horse town, so ah might as well come along to keep you outta trouble, if you want me, that is.'

'Oh, very much so, although I'm afraid there will be no pay in it.'

'Ah've got enough to get by.'

'Good. We will ride out at four o'clock.'

The rain, in fact, had stopped by the time they walked their horses out of Newcastle, leading a packhorse behind them. Simon had contemplated taking a Cape cart with them but had decided against it. Although the Free State was completely independent and he was not anticipating trouble on the way, he wanted to be able to move quickly if need be, and a cart would slow them down. As it was, they made slow enough progress, for the heavy overnight rain had turned the previously dusty track into muddy ruts, and the dongas that it seemed had carried no water for decades had turned momentarily into rushing torrents. They climbed high through a pass in the northern fringe of the Drakensbergs and descended again to flat, rolling veldt lands broken by ironstone kopjes. They camped by a small river bed just before dark, digging a channel around their tent to prevent themselves being swamped by another sudden storm.

Eighteen days later, they reined in their tired horses on one of four low hills surrounding Bloemfontein and looked down on the little town. Their journey had been uneventful and, indeed, not uncomfortable. The summer, although hot, was not advanced, the rain had kept off and the three men had been able to find overnight lodgings at several Boer farms on the way, taking advantage of the old Roman Dutch law that ruled that folk should not be allowed to go hungry if there was food nearby and they had the means to pay. In other words, the Boers were under an obligation to sell food and offer shelter if they had it – and they did so, although their prices, felt Simon, were unreasonably high. The farmers were uncommunicative and often surly, and in many ways it was a relief to reach the small and unpretentious capital of the Free State.

Shimmering now in the summer sun but fanned by a fresh breeze, it presented a fair picture, nestling in the hollow between the northern and southern hills. The three travellers gazed down on a succession of small houses with galvanised-iron roofs, interspersed with a delightful mixture of green trees: cypress, blue gums and, near a central lake retained by a dam, weeping willows. In the centre they could make out a large square where, it seemed, a market was being held. A citadel, composed of a loose stone wall with what looked like two old smooth-bore 24-pounder cannon on top, dominated the main east-to-west road that ran through the centre of the town, and by the lake, a fountain twinkled in the sunlight. Bloemfontein beckoned enticingly.

The three rode down the slope and through to the centre of the town. 'Looks just like Omaha, Texas,' murmured Hardy.

Simon thought for a moment. He had read the Lewis and Clarke diaries of their great expedition up the Missouri and knew a little about the West. 'I thought Omaha was in Nebraska,' he said.

'What? Oh yeah. The one I had in mind is smaller, in Texas.'

'Ah.'

Simon felt that it would be right to deliver his letter the moment they reached the capital, so he was directed to the House of Assembly, a seemingly new, rather grand building erected next to the dam. While the others waited, he entered and handed the letter to a clerk, who seemed suitably impressed.

'Please tell the president,' Simon said, 'that I have delivered this

115

letter the moment I arrived in town. I shall now find lodgings and will call later to make an appointment to pay my respects to Mr Brand.'

The clerk suggested that they might all be best suited at a medium-sized hotel just off the main square, and there, indeed, they found the luxury of three rooms, although the price seemed extortionate to Simon. In fact, it did not take them long to discover that all prices were high in Bloemfontein: five shillings for a bottle of Bass and one shilling for a slice of bread and butter and a cup of tea. On complaining, they were told that the capital had more than doubled in size over the last ten years and that business was booming. Simon knew that the Free State had finally settled its long war with the Basutos, who had ceded to the state a hundred-mile stretch of land, high in the Maluti Mountains, that had proved to be one of the richest corn-growing territories in South Africa. The diamond fields to the west of the state were providing a ready market for its meat and other agricultural products, and diamonds had also been discovered at Jagersfontein. Unlike the Transvaal, the economy of Mr Brand's little republic, roughly the size of Great Britain, was obviously burgeoning.

Simon was luxuriating in a hot bath when a messenger arrived to say that the president would receive him at four p.m. He put on a change of clothes – the tails hung, ludicrously irrelevant, in an unpainted wooden cupboard – and hurried round to the House of Assembly, the venue for the meetings of the Volksraad and the office of the President of the Free State.

He was received courteously by a small, bearded man with upright posture and kindly eyes, who was wearing a well-cut suit of trad- itional broadcloth, heavy enough in the heat of this early summer.

'Captain Fonthill,' said Brand, 'come here and sit beside me. It's good of you to come straight round after your long ride. Won't you take a cup of tea?'

'Thank you, sir.' Simon regarded the man with interest. In the few moments he had had to spare at Newcastle before leaving, he had pumped Colley's ADC for background on the president. What he had learned showed that in the turbulent waters of South African politics, Brand stood out as a stable rock. A lawyer from the Cape who had been called to the bar in London, Jan Brand had been appointed president of the new state sixteen years before, in 1864, ten years after the British Government had been quite happy to cede sovereignty back to the farmers north of the Orange River. Since then, he had carefully maintained good terms with both his Boer brothers north of the Vaal and the British in the Cape. He had also, however, showed courage by conducting a long and, in the end, successful campaign against his Basuto neighbours. The little lawyer, then, was a man of parts. War against the British Empire, however, was a different matter. Could he afford to stay on the sidelines now that the Transvaal had opened hostilities against the British? He would be under strong pressure from his people to establish a common Boer front against the colonial powers in the south. Which way would he jump?

Whatever the pressures, they seemed to sit easily on the president. 'Now,' he enquired, 'how was the journey? Did our people offer you food and shelter on the way?'

Simon munched a biscuit. 'Indeed they did, sir. I have every cause, both here and in the Transvaal, to be grateful for Boer hospitality.'

'Ah yes. Sir George mentioned in his letter that you had been involved in the late campaign against Sekukuni's people. I must congratulate you on that. Our folk there made a hash of trying to put him down. General Wolseley showed how it should be done. Most impressive.'

Simon made a mental note of the phrase 'our folk'. The Transvaal was a different country, but Brand obviously still regarded them as kith and kin. The president continued to make polite conversation.

'If I may say so, Captain Fonthill, you are remarkably young to have seen so much active service in such a short time. The Zulu War, the business in Afghanistan and, lastly, the bePedi campaign. You are quite a veteran.'

'Yes, Mr President, I have been lucky. Many of my contemporaries have been forced to kick their heels doing guard duties back home. But I am out of the army now.'

Brand nodded. 'So I understand. Do take another biscuit. What, then, do you think of this present mess?'

Simon swallowed. Ah, the first test! He selected another oatmeal biscuit, such a delicious delicacy after so much biltong on the long ride from Newcastle. 'Well, sir, that's what it is, really, a mess. There is so much to do in terms of developing the territories here. We should not be wasting time and money and spilling blood in this way.'

'I quite agree.' The president sighed. 'I have already written to Sir George suggesting that he should send Sir Henry de Villiers, First Justice of the Cape Colony, to Pretoria to make a study of the Transvaal's grievances on the spot and put forward a plan for a solution. But the outbreak of war makes that quite irrelevant, of course.'

Simon felt this was the moment to take the initiative.

'May I ask you, sir, whether you will stay out of it?'

Brand shot him a quick glance. 'As you probably know, Sir George has asked me the same question. He has also requested that I send a reply back to him with you as soon as possible. Well now,' he dusted biscuit crumbs from his suit, 'answering such a question requires a lot of thought. My position here is difficult, you know, Fonthill. There are already quite a few Free Staters in the north who have crossed the Vaal to join the Transvaalers in what they consider to be their struggle for liberty. It is all right for us. We have had the luxury of possessing our own independence for over twenty-five years now. We can well understand that our brothers to the north would like to be in a similar position.'

Simon shifted on the sofa. 'I understand that, sir, and it must be a difficult problem for you. But I presume that you would not wish this conflict to escalate into an Anglo-Boer war?'

'Quite so.' The president smiled. 'But perhaps it will be all over quite quickly. The general must have strong forces he is gathering in the Cape, surely?'

Ah, the gentle inquisition by the ex-lawyer! Simon thought quickly. As an ex-Cape Colony man, Brand would certainly have his own sources in Cape Town who would keep him au fait with the comparative paucity of Colley's resources. It would not do to bluster falsely.

'As you probably know, sir,' he said, 'the end of the Zulu War has meant that many of the seasoned troops that the general would have wished to have at his command have been sent home. But what is left will provide a hard core of professionals around which the general is building quickly. From what I have seen, I know that by now he will have sufficient troops to form a column capable of invading the Transvaal and relieving the garrisons there. And, of course, there are other detachments on the high seas on their way to reinforce him.'

Simon smiled. 'I have great respect for the fighting abilities of the Boer people,' he went on. 'They are probably the best marksmen and, indeed, light cavalry in the world. Sometimes, the British Army can seem to plod rather – I was at Isandlwana, remember – and lose the first battle. But we usually win the last battle and the war. Think of Waterloo.'

'Ah,' replied Brand, 'think also of Saratoga. You lost all your colonies in the Americas.' He held up his hand as Simon began to reply. 'But I do not wish to waste your time in debate, stimulating as it is. You have put your point of view very well and I must not detain you longer.' They both stood, and the president continued, 'As I have said, I wish to consider my reply to Sir George very carefully, and that includes consulting my colleagues, some of whom are away. The need for haste, in any case, is not now apparent, given that hostilities have commenced. I am afraid that one letter from me will not stop this war overnight. So, shall we say that I will give you my reply to General Colley in four days' time? Can you remain with us for that time?'

'Of course, sir, although I would not wish to stay longer.'

'I understand. Now,' the president's expression softened, 'it is my turn to ask something of you. My wife and I are holding a ball in three days' time.' He gave his gentle smile, so reminiscent of Colley's. 'We have to do something, you know, to relieve the monotony of life here on the veldt. It will not match the splendour of your London gatherings but we do have guests here from other nations and I must offer them entertainment. We are very short of presentable young men and I would be most grateful, Captain Fonthill, if you would be our guest.'

Simon bowed. 'Of course, sir, you are very kind, although I must warn you that I have yet to master this new style of Viennese waltzing, or whatever they call it.'

'Dash it, so have I. We may be forced to dance together, my boy.'

They both laughed at the jest, and Brand took Simon's arm and gently ushered him to the door. 'One more favour, I fear,' he said. 'My wife is holding a small dinner party tomorrow evening, in honour of two German guests we have here.' His eyes twinkled. 'I think it would be a jolly good thing if the British Empire was represented at the table. It is really quite informal, so I don't want to involve your diplomatic people here, although . . .' His voice tailed away. 'It is dress, I am afraid. I don't suppose you have . . .?'

Simon drew himself up in mock indignation. 'I do hope, Mr President,' he said, 'that you would not imagine for a moment that an English gentleman would cross three hundred and fifty miles of veldt without taking white tie and tails with him?'

Brand threw back his head and roared with laughter. 'Ah, you English,' he said. 'Where in the world would we be without you?'

Back in the hotel, Simon found that Jenkins and Hardy were absent, presumably exploring the pleasures of Bloemfontein, and he lay back on his bed for a while, his hands behind his head. The gentle sparring with Brand had proved inconclusive but he did not see what more he could do to bring the president down on the side of non-intervention. After all, the man was a shrewd politician and he would do what was right for his people – the role he had been fulfilling successfully now for more than sixteen years. What was rather more daunting, however, was the prospect of the dinner party.

Germans? He knew enough about foreign affairs to realise that Bismarck, the German chancellor, was the greatest opponent Britain and its empire faced on the continent of Europe. Throughout the world, the old Prussian was working to build an empire of Germany's own: a 'place in the sun', particularly in Africa and usually to Britain's detriment. The two Germans at the dinner party were probably members of the German diplomatic corps, sent here from Berlin to persuade – bribe? – Brand to throw in his lot with the

Transvaal. If so, where were the British diplomats? Surely the British Empire was represented in the Orange Free State capital? Simon frowned. It was all very well Brand saying that it was an informal dinner party. Politics and the war were bound to be discussed and Simon felt himself ill-equipped to represent his country at this highly skilled game – and he certainly did not fancy extending his fledgling diplomatic career at this level.

Nor, for that matter, did he look forward with relish to attending the ball. He hated small talk and he was a hopeless dancer. When was the last time he had danced? Of course, with Alice . . . Alice! Damn it all to hell and blazes! He sprang to his feet, found the bar, sank two large whiskies very quickly and went to bed early.

The next morning, Simon gave his companions a rough outline of his conversation with Brand and they seemed happy enough to wait in this pleasant town for four days before setting out on the long journey back to Natal. The three tended their mounts in the livery stable and then a grumpy Jenkins was put to finding an iron with which to press Simon's tails, while the other two walked through the town. Hardy was strangely reticent with Simon, although he had made a firm friend of Jenkins, and Simon, resolved to take his mind off the prospect of a difficult evening, decided to take advantage of their time together to find out a little more about the tall Texan. They found a bar and leaned on it to drink two very expensive pints of beer.

'Hey,' said Hardy. 'Is 352 really your *servant*?'

Simon nodded. 'He was my batman in the army, and when I came out he wanted to stay with me, so I bought him out.' He smiled, half apologetically. 'I know it sounds terribly stuffy, but an English gentleman is supposed to have a servant, you know.'

Hardy supped his beer. 'Yup,' he said, 'sounds stuffy all right.'

'Well, it's not as bad as it seems. I have to pay Jenkins, of course, because he must be independent and that means he has to do some work for the money. That's the way he wants it. As a matter of fact, there is very little to do because, as you can see, we live a rough sort of life. Actually, he is my best friend. He has saved my life about half a dozen times since we first met in the army depot at Brecon back

121

home, and I have managed to get him out of trouble a few times too. It's a partnership, really.'

'Waal,' the Texan drawled. 'Seems to work beautifully, ah'll allow that.'

'What about you, Al? Were you born in Texas?'

Hardy's eyes seemed to glaze over and he looked away. 'Yup.'

'Anywhere I'd know?'

'Doubt it. Little bitty town.'

Simon sipped his own beer. 'Where on earth did you learn to shoot with those pistols like that? It was breathtaking.'

A slow grin came over the American's face. 'Took mah breath away a bit too, ah can tell ya. Thought ah was jest a bit too late a-drawin'.'

'Yes, but where did you learn to shoot like that?'

Hardy shrugged his shoulders. 'Yah had to learn to shoot when ah was a kid, just to survive. The Injuns were all around us in them days. It was rough. Mah daddy was scalped.'

'Good lord, how terrible. What tribe?'

'What?' The pale blue eyes swung round on Simon, almost accusingly.

'Er . . . what tribe was it? I've always been interested in the American West, you see.'

A cloud seemed to descend on Hardy's face. He pulled on his neat little beard for a moment. 'Cain't quite remember,' he said distantly. 'Sioux, Cheyenne. Somethin' like that.'

Simon drew a breath but then thought better of pursuing the conversation. It seemed clear that Hardy did not want to talk about his past. They finished their beer in silence and walked back to the hotel.

Six hours later, Simon struggled into his white tie and tails, with a little help from Jenkins. The shoes were far from being patent leather and they had resisted much of the little man's attempt to buff them into some sort of gleam. In addition, the shirt was a little too big and the cuff links provided by the quartermaster in Newcastle were made of some sort of alloy stamped with a rather vulgar reproduction of the 58th Regiment's numerals. Nevertheless, said Jenkins, standing back to take in the general impression, 'You look good enough to sit next to the Queen.'

There were eight for dinner: the Brands; a rather elderly Afrikaner lady whose name Simon never did catch but who it seemed had recently been widowed and was a friend of the Brands; a stout German whose name Simon *did* retain – Borkenhagen – who had settled in Bloemfontein and was editor of *The Bloemfontein Express*, with his wife; and two German visitors who seemed to be the centre of attention.

They were introduced as Baron Wilhelm von Bethman and his 'business associate' Countess Anna Scheel. The baron was small, slim and elegant, with a clipped black moustache, cold grey eyes and a scar that ran from his cheekbone to the corner of his moustache. He wore his white tie and tails as though born to them and spoke with confidence in almost unaccented English – the adopted language, it seemed, of the gathering. The baron was clearly a man of the world. Yet there was something disturbing, even threatening, about his manner. He stood braced, legs well apart, with his chin thrust forward. He rarely smiled, and when he did, the smile never travelled as far as his eyes, which remained expressionless. On introduction, those eyes took Simon in slowly, almost insolently, as they travelled the length of his ill-fitting tails. He nodded without bowing, briefly shook hands, held Simon's gaze for a moment with those dark grey eyes and then turned away without a word. It was as though an unspoken warning had been given, or territory had been marked. Simon felt cold suddenly and turned with relief to meet the baron's companion.

He was rewarded. The countess too was dark, with hair as black as a raven's wing that gleamed richly in the gaslight and that had been arranged high on her head in lustrous waves above a diamond tiara. Her eyes were doe-like brown and set wide apart under arched brows. She had dressed for the heat of the summer and her silk gown was cut very low to reveal skin whose ivory texture was set off impeccably by a brilliant diamond necklace. Her cheekbones were high, her hands were small and she was quite the most beautiful thing that Simon had ever seen. In contrast to her companion, she smiled warmly on introduction and began chatting in equally faultless English. The fact that she was probably three or four years older than Simon – perhaps thirty years of age? – made her only more intriguing.

The eight exchanged slightly awkward conversation while drinking champagne and Simon realised that he had been invited, of course, to partner the Boer widow, a role he felt handicapped to play because, for the life of him, he could not remember her name. His embarrassment was heightened when they were called to dinner because, of course, he was placed next to her. On his right, however, was the countess – a fact that both delighted and daunted him. Simon became acutely aware of both her haunting perfume and his own gauche cuff links. He felt like a stevedore at a Palace garden party and he compensated for his awkwardness by engaging the Afrikaner lady in desperate conversation.

After a while, this was interrupted by a delicate touch on his arm. He took a deep breath and turned. 'Captain,' the countess said, with a look of histrionic reproach on her face, 'I do believe you are neglecting me.' He realised that her English did, in fact, carry the slightest of accents, but the pouting reproach was immediately replaced by a warm smile.

'I, ah, do beg your pardon, Countess,' he mumbled.

'No, no. None of this countess nonsense here. After all, we are not in stuffy Europe now.' Her smile widened to reveal, of course, perfect teeth. 'We are in wonderful, exciting Africa. You must call me Anna and I shall call you Simon.'

'Very well, er, Anna. Of course. Yes.' Sitting just a few inches away from this ravishing woman, who was clearly quite happy to put herself out to charm him, despite his badly fitted shirt and the awful cuff links, Simon felt a surging wave of physical attraction. For a brief moment he caught a glimpse of himself in the candle-framed mirror on the wall opposite. The reflection showed a face, tanned and hawk-like with its broken nose, sitting incongruously atop the starched white collar and grinning – a great schoolboy grin. He tried to gather his composure. 'Um . . . what brings you to wonderful, exciting Bloemfontein, then, Anna?'

'What brings me? Ah. Business. Dull, fusty old business, Simon.

Yes, yes, I know. Women are not supposed to be involved in such things, but I have inherited some shareholdings and I refuse to let other people tell me what to do with them. So I am involved with the business.' She held up her hand. 'No. I am not going to tell you what it is – that is much too boring.'

'Very well. Then tell me what part of Germany is your home?'

'Essen. Again, not exciting, I am afraid. A dull industrial city.'

'Ah, yes. Just north of Cologne, if I remember.'

'You have been there?'

'Well, very near there. In my last year at Sandhurst – that's our officers' school. Some of us were invited to go to Germany to watch the manoeuvres of your army. It was very impressive.'

'*Sprechen Sie Deutsch?*'

'*Ein Bisschen. Ich habe es in der . . . er . . . Schule gerlernt, aber leider habe ich viel vergessen.*'

'Well, that was said very fluently. You will soon pick it up again. I must teach you.' This last sentence was said as the countess leaned towards him slightly, touching his arm. Her perfume met Simon's nostrils again and set his heart pounding anew.

He attempted to clear his throat. 'Your English is excellent, Coun . . . Anna. You put me to shame. Where did you learn it?'

'At school in England.' She lowered her head slightly and looked up at him through her lashes. 'Oh, I learned so many things there that I enjoyed, you know. I learned how to hunt, do embroidery, act in Shakespeare, play bridge and . . . yes, even play cricket. Do you know, I was the best off-break bowler in the school. Do you know how to bowl an off-break, Simon?'

He shook his head, thinking that she could talk to him about Polynesian postage stamps for the rest of the evening for all he cared, as long as he could sit close to her, looking into her deep brown eyes.

'Tut, tut. And you an Englishman. Look.' She leaned forward and seized an orange. 'Now, observe closely. You grasp the ball so and curl the forefinger – this finger – around just the other side of where the seam should be, and as you let it go, you twist the wrist like this and spin the ball with the forefinger across the seam, so . . .' and she demonstrated with the orange, her head close to his. The action

125

attracted the attention of the rest of the diners, who watched her in silence for a moment.

'Ah,' said the countess, looking up. 'I was just demonstrating to Captain Fonthill how to bowl an off-break at cricket. He does not know, so he has no right to call himself an Englishman. Don't you agree, Wilhelm?'

The baron did not smile but stared at Simon briefly. 'Cricket? Something I know nothing about. Nor do I wish to learn.'

The awkward silence that followed was broken by Mrs Brand. A stoutish, motherly woman, she chose this moment to rise. 'I think, ladies,' she said, 'it is time we retired to leave the gentlemen to do whatever it is they do when ladies retire. I shall send in the liqueurs and cigars, Jan. Now don't be too long. We shall expect you in the drawing room in about thirty minutes.' She smiled around the table and the ladies dutifully rose, gathered their long skirts about them and left the room in a swish of silk and taffeta. Almost immediately, a black servant entered carrying a tray with decanters of cognac and port and a large box of cigars.

Small talk ensued as the drinks were passed around and cigars selected, and then Borkenhagen, the newspaper editor, thrust out his legs and addressed Brand, although, of course, the gathering was now intimate enough for everyone to hear. 'What are you going to do about the Transvaal, Jan?' He spoke in an accent that combined the guttural sonority of both the German and the Taal tongues.

Brand shot a quick glance that embraced Simon and von Bethman and smiled. 'Ach, everyone's asking me that. Dammit all, man, there's not much I can do now. The war has started; it will probably have to run its course.'

Borkenhagen, a big man with heavy side-whiskers, persisted. 'You know what I mean, Mr President,' he growled. 'Don't you think we should support our brothers across the Vaal, *ja*?'

Brand sighed. 'I've read all your leaders in the *Express* and I know your views. You want a bond – a union of all Afrikaners within South Africa. Well, I see your point and it may happen one day, but I remain unconvinced that our interests are the same as those of the Transvaal. We have our freedom and it has been carefully maintained for sixteen years now. I don't want to do anything that might compromise that.'

The journalist gave a less than gracious nod to Simon. 'With due respect to this young man here,' he said, 'it will only be a question of time before the British annex us again. Then we shall have to fight anyway. Let's do it now, while we have support.'

Brand smiled across the table at Simon. 'I am sorry, Captain Fonthill,' he said, 'but we Afrikaners do speak bluntly – particularly the German ones.' He frowned at Borkenhagen. 'I don't think that we should discuss these local and difficult political matters at the dinner table. Let us enjoy our brandy and speak of world affairs.'

The baron leaned forward, blue cigar smoke curling up around his startlingly grey eyes. 'But Herr President,' he said, 'these are matters which concern the world. I can assure you, having recently come from Berlin, that all eyes in Europe – and probably those in America too – are on what happens here now. The British should give the Transvaal its independence. The British have a big enough empire already. They are too greedy. They cannot lift their noses from the trough. They should not fight the Boers.'

The eyes of the three men turned to Simon. Earlier, Simon had resolved that he would not enter into a political debate. He lacked the experience to hold his own in the cut and thrust of this sort of argument, and anyway, with Brand poised to jump down from the fence one way or the other, it could be dangerous. But the cool stare of the two Afrikaners and the provocative language of Bethman – what the hell was his exact relationship with Anna anyway? – were too much.

He took a mouthful of cognac. 'I agree that we should not fight the Transvaalers,' he said, as steadily as he could, 'but I do take exception to your language in describing my country, Baron. We have recently successfully fought lifelong enemies of the Boers in the Zulus and the bePedi tribe of Sekukuni, so removing threats from the people of the Transvaal and the Orange Free State and allowing them to get on with their pastoral lifestyles. An army that does that certainly would not wish to turn its rifles on the very people it has been protecting. No, the first shots in this miserable business were fired by the Transvaalers. A British column was ambushed and given

127

very little chance of defending itself. Whatever the political background, it was the wrong thing to do. No country – certainly not yours, Baron – would allow that sort of action to go without response.'

The German lifted his left eyebrow and directed a look of cool contempt at Simon. 'It was not an ambush. The British colonel was given the opportunity of laying down his arms.'

'Were you at Bronkhorstspruit, sir?'

'*Nein*. But I was nearby in Heidelberg – that is the new capital of the Transvaal – and heard all about it.'

'Allow me to correct you, Baron. Pretoria remains the capital of the Transvaal, where a British garrison is in place. I was not at the ambush either but I have interviewed a man who was there – a neutral who has therefore no irons in this particular fire – and he tells me that no honourable man could have surrendered immediately like that. The British had no time to even level their rifles before, standing in the open as they were, they were gunned down.' Simon made an effort to maintain an even tone. 'One hundred and twenty of our men were killed. They were shot at point-blank range and I understand that many of them had as many as four or five bullet holes in their heads. That was an act of aggression, and as a result, General Colley is now forced to march into the Transvaal.'

'Where he will lose all his men,' Borkenhagen growled through a fog of cigar smoke.

'That remains to be seen,' said Simon coolly.

'Despite what you have said, young man,' said the baron, 'white man should not fight white man in Africa.'

'To repeat, sir, I agree with you. But I can only point out that you should say that to your friends in Heidelberg who opened the hostilities.'

Brand, who had been listening to the exchanges keenly, coughed. 'I think, gentlemen,' he said, 'that we have taken that discussion as far as it can go.' What could have been described as a mischievous twinkle came into his eye as he turned to Bethman. 'Did you have a successful mission in Heidelberg, then, Baron?'

The German shot a very quick glance at Simon before replying.

'*Ja*, thank you, Mr President. Very successful, in fact.' He smiled, his face giving the impression that it was unused to relaxing in this way. 'Perhaps rather more successful than my visit here, eh?' The smile gave way to a staccato laugh.

Brand returned the smile, then looked over his shoulder. 'I think, gentlemen, that the ladies will be becoming a little restive.' He stood. 'Shall we join them?'

The men entered the small salon trailing clouds of cigar smoke behind them. Anna Scheel caught Simon's eye immediately and patted the space on the small chaise-longue next to her. Trying not to seem too eager, Simon slightly lengthened his stride and joined her. Mrs Brand was speaking in her open, disingenuous way.

'It is very difficult for us to maintain style here, you know,' she said, waving her fan to show the homespun but, to Simon's eye, perfectly acceptable furnishings in the room. 'Jan's salary is only five thousand pounds a year and that does not leave us very much room to entertain in a manner which befits the president of a republic.'

Brand coughed, perhaps to hide some embarrassment. 'Come, my dear, you make the Orange Free State sound like America or France. We are a small state that some fifty years ago only existed in a few covered wagons. We are making our own way very well, slowly but surely. We don't need or desire all the trappings of a large, settled country.'

'Mr President,' Frau Borkenhagen's voice was an echo of her husband's in its pitch and tone, 'you entertain very well, and those of us who are lucky enough to have experienced your hospitality are all most grateful.' She looked around the room for approval. 'I am sure that we are all looking forward to the ball the day after tomorrow.'

There was a low murmur of 'Hear, hear.'

'Ah, the ball.' The countess spoke in low tones directly to Simon. 'Are you to be there, Simon?'

'Only if you are, ma'am.'

She laughed. 'Ah, you are learning the gallant ways of the *salon* very quickly. So,' she tapped him on the arm with her fan, 'will you dance with me, then?'

'Of course. But you may regret it, because I am very clumsy.'

'We will manage, you and I.' Her smiling eyes held his, perhaps a moment longer than propriety allowed, and Simon felt his cheeks redden.

She lowered her gaze and Simon looked across the room. Baron von Bethman was regarding him steadily, a look of undisguised malevolence on his face. Simon's first instinct was to drop his eyes, as conventional politeness would dictate. But he did not. He stayed holding the other's gaze, keeping his face as coolly expressionless as the baron's was openly malignant. Was the man jealous or just expressing his ethnic prejudice? Simon decided that he didn't care but was not going to be intimidated by this Teutonic bully, so he kept his gaze locked on to those icy grey eyes across the room. The two must have stayed that way for all of thirty seconds, like matador and bull sizing each other up for the battle to come. Then, at last, the baron looked away. First blood to me, thought Simon. Then, some vestige of diplomatic conscience stirred within him and struggled through the champagne haze that was beginning to cloud his head, and he felt ashamed – ashamed of this macho posturing, this game-playing with a man who could be dangerous and even harmful to his country's cause.

He shook his head in a brief moment of self-rebuke and felt a gentle pressure on his arm. Anna was looking at him with a half-smile on her lips but a puzzled, questioning look in her eyes. In a split second, Simon gave way to temptation.

'Would you care to come riding with me tomorrow?' he asked. 'The weather seems to be clement and I understand that the countryside around here, although rather flat, can be quite interesting and good for riding.'

Her reaction was immediate. The half-smile turned into a beam revealing those delicious white teeth. 'What a good idea,' she said. 'Meet me by the citadel at two thirty. Would that be convenient?'

Simon swallowed. 'Most convenient,' he said.

The gathering broke up shortly afterwards and Simon walked back to his hotel, his heart singing and his head, if not in a whirl, then certainly buzzing with desire and fascination. He had not, he realised, ever before looked forward with such pleasurable anticipation to riding a horse. Jenkins would be amazed. Yet as he walked in the warm air along the tree-lined avenues, his mind could not help but dwell on the reason for the presence of the two Germans in Bloemfontein. They had clearly travelled to the Free State capital from the Transvaal – presuming, that is, they had travelled together. Were they lovers? Simon's jaw clenched at the thought. Surely not, given Anna's warmth towards him. He sighed. What a beautiful, desirable woman . . . but what the hell was such a sophisticated creature doing in the land of the dour, earthy Boers? And what the hell was she doing, for that matter, with the surly baron?

He wandered on, past his hotel, his white tie and tails attracting enquiring looks from the few people, white and black, who still walked the streets. He found himself at the citadel and stood for a moment, looking up at the old cannon perched on top of the loose stones of the wall. Yes, they were indeed 24-pounders. He examined the guns for a moment, his hands deep in his pockets, his brain trying to pin down something elusive . . . some link. Cannon. Germans. Anna. Essen. Ah, he had it! Essen, Anna's home town in Germany, was also the home of the giant armaments factory Krupp, the largest manufacturer of weapons in the world. So that was it. Anna had said she was a shareholder in a company. Was she in South Africa selling guns to the Boers? It seemed inconceivable that such a young, delicate and beautiful woman could be involved in such a sordid business. Von Bethman, yes. But not Anna, surely? Yet presumably she was travelling with the baron and he had smirked that he had had a successful visit to Heidelberg, the new Boer capital of the Transvaal – and there would be no other town in the world where the demand for sophisticated weaponry would be higher. Von Bethman had also referred ruefully to his comparative lack of success here, in the Free State. That would be because Brand was not in the business of going to war, or at least not yet.

A warning note echoed deep in Simon's brain as he turned back to the hotel. These were deep waters. What was it that Colley had said? 'Tread with care.' He shook his head in frustration. Surely there couldn't be any harm in riding with the woman? And anyway, perhaps he could learn something about the presence of these two exotic creatures in this dour backwater of Africa?

The next morning a beaming Jenkins came to pick up Simon's dress shirt to wash and iron it anew in readiness for the following evening's entertainment. 'I've found some starch in this funny little place,' he announced triumphantly, 'so I can make you look beautiful for the ball an' all, Cinderella. An' give me those shoes, see, and I'll try an' make 'em gleam.

'Sorry I've been neglecting you two,' said Simon. 'What have you been up to?'

Jenkins's beam turned into a wicked grin. 'Ally's been teachin' the locals 'ow to play poker. We've made a fortune, look you.'

'What? You as well?'

'Ooh yes. When 'e's taught 'em, see, they want to play. It's natural, isn't it? So we play 'em as a team – and we win. We're doin' nicely, see. I must say, bach sir, I quite like this postin'. I'd be 'appy to stay 'ere for a while, so I would.'

Simon sighed. 'Oh lord. Do be careful. I somehow never thought that the Boers would gamble.'

'Ooh no. It's not them. There's a funny collection of fellers that get in the bars 'ere: English, but Germans an' Dutch too. They can't resist a flutter, see.'

'Right. But don't get into a fight, because we are skating on thin ice here. And anyway, it looks as though we will be leaving the day after tomorrow.'

Jenkins pulled a face. 'Ah. Right you are then.'

Slightly concerned what Jenkins would say about him actually riding for pleasure, Simon groomed his horse himself that morning, rubbing a little wax into the leathers and polishing, as best he could, the harness. If the beast looked smart, he reasoned, perhaps Anna wouldn't notice the inadequacy of the horseman.

Early as he was, Anna was waiting for him at the citadel. Predictably, she was mounted on a well-bred mare whose coat shone in the afternoon sun and who pranced in anticipation as he cantered up. She was riding side-saddle, wearing a long black skirt that draped one side of her mount, a crisp white blouse buttoned at throat and wrist and a saucy narrow-brimmed straw hat kept in place by a green scarf tied under her chin. Damn! Apple green. Alice's favourite colour. He shook his head to remove the vision and took off his hat and swept it low in a gallant gesture.

'You look an absolute picture, Countess,' he smiled. 'I wish I had a rose garden I could take you to so that the blossoms could see you.'

She smiled reciprocally. 'Now please be careful. I am not used to such flowery compliments in southern Africa. They might go to my head.'

'Oh, I do hope so.'

They sat grinning at each other like children in the warm sun and Simon felt that he had known her for months, instead of hours. He dug in his heels and led the way out of the centre, up to where the circle of hills looked down on the little town.

'Do you like riding?' she asked.

Simon decided not to dissemble. 'As a matter of fact, no,' he said. 'I am not a good horseman, and although I've spent hours in the saddle in this country, I just know I would be unseated if I had to take a fence even now. It's a terrible admission for a soldier . . .' he corrected himself quickly, 'an ex-soldier, that is, to make, but there it is. Thank God I was never a cavalryman.'

She flashed him a smile, almost, it seemed, of relief. 'Well, do you know, Simon, I feel exactly the same. Fashion dictates that I must ride side-saddle but I always feel so precarious in this ridiculous posture. I am not allowed to put on breeches and ride astride as a proper horsewoman should. What is it you say? It's not the done thing. But I am so happy to be with you out here in this fresh clear air, so I don't mind. Nevertheless . . .' she turned and fumbled with the strap of a saddle bag behind her, 'I have taken the liberty of packing us a picnic. Let us find somewhere congenial and take some refreshment. Yes?'

'Yes indeed. What a resourceful woman you are.'

They found welcome shade in a hollow where blue gum and willow trees – the latter showing that water was near – spread a broken canopy above them. From a roll tied behind her saddle Anna shook out a plaid blanket that she spread on the coarse grass, while Simon unloaded the contents of her bags and carefully deposited delicate sandwiches, several pastries, yellow custards, a little fruit and even a bottle of yellow-glinting wine.

'I hope you don't mind, Simon,' she said. 'I know I should have brought tea, but even in my boarding school in Kent I could never acquire the taste. So we have a little wine. Scandalous at tea-time, I know, but let us be daring.'

'*Very* scandalous, but let's.'

They half sat, half lay on the blanket, eating the delicacies and drinking the surprisingly good wine – from the vineyards of the Cape, explained Anna. After the initial flirting exchanges, Simon had begun to feel slightly uncomfortable. He had never formally courted anyone in his life. Alice and he had been thrown together by the exigencies of war, at first in Zululand and then in Afghanistan, and his love for her had owed nothing to the elaborate exchanges of gentle innuendo and compliments that attended the forming of amorous relationships back home. He lacked the will or the ability to exchange small talk, and now he lay propped on one elbow munching a sandwich in silence, stealing a gaze at his companion from the corner of his eye. Part of the problem was that she was so staggeringly beautiful. She had taken off her straw hat and sat now, quite at ease, her knees drawn up to reveal shiny, very feminine riding boots and just a glimpse of a frothy underskirt. One arm was tucked around her knees while she held up her glass with her other hand and sipped the wine, looking out across the veldt from a dip in the hollow's edge, without, it seemed, a care in the world. Simon noted the whiteness of her throat and the way her bosom curved out her white blouse, and he felt a surge of desire run through his body and his mind, starved as they had been over the last few months of anything but male company, danger and hard exercise.

She turned. 'Do tell me, Simon,' she said, 'what exactly are you doing here?'

Ah, the gentle interrogation! Simon sat up and tried to regain his composure. After all, it was probably a genuine question, born of polite interest and even, perhaps, of some care for him and his career. But best be careful.

He coughed on the sandwich. 'Oh, I'm just a messenger really. I've brought along a letter for the president. Not all that important really, otherwise they would have sent a colonel or the Brigade of Guards with it.'

She threw back her head and laughed. 'You do put yourself down, you know. I would have thought there was a perfectly good telegraph service between Newcastle and Bloemfontein that would have served better – and quicker – than taking out at the beginning of war a brilliant young officer who had fought with distinction at Isandlwana, Rorke's Drift, Kabul and Kandahar and using him as a simple postman.'

Simon's jaw dropped. 'How did you know about my background? And that I had come from Newcastle?'

Quite unfazed, she gave him a pretty pout. 'Oh come now, Simon. This is a small place and you know what women are like about gossip. You are the talk of the town, my boy. Quite a desirable catch too, I would say.' She lowered her head and looked up at him through her eyelashes. 'Do be careful, my dear. There will be hordes of eligible young Boer maidens after you N and all of them anxious to know what President Brand will say in reply to General Colley.'

Simon jerked his head up at her directness and stared at her. But Anna remained smiling and held his gaze innocently: a pretty woman – no, a beautiful woman – engaging in mildly flirtatious word-play and hoping to impress with her scrap of knowledge of the masculine world, probably picked up from dinner-table gossip. A series of warnings, thoughts, emotions flashed through Simon's brain as he looked into those delightful, guileless brown eyes. Was she trying to elicit information from him, and if so, why? What good would it be to her? And why did he have to sit here gently sparring with her when he could be kissing her . . . He cleared his throat.

'What nonsense you do talk, Anna. But tell me then. What exactly are *you* doing in Bloemfontein?'

She tossed her head. 'Oh, it's no secret, Simon. We – that is, Wilhelm and I – are trying to sell good German arms to the Boers of the Orange Free State. We did quite well in the Transvaal, as you can imagine, but the worthy President Brand is being a little less co-operative.' She smiled again. 'You will remember that I told you I was a shareholder in a German company. Well, I am a working woman also and I am here to do a job.'

'Krupps, of course.'

She nodded her head but her smile had now disappeared. 'Full marks.'

'It is strange work for a woman.'

'Is it?' She frowned for a moment. '*Ja*, I suppose it is. But . . .' She paused for a moment and looked out across the veldt. 'There were, what shall I say . . . unusual circumstances about it all.' She levelled a direct gaze at him, shorn of all coquettishness. 'Perhaps one day I will tell you all about it. But for now,' she held up her glass, 'let us drink a little more wine and not talk about such things. This day is too fine for that.'

They drank their wine and finished the picnic and talked of this and that in a desultory way, but somehow the spark, the frisson that had marked their first few minutes had slipped away, and eventually they packed up their detritus and made no more of their ride than simply ambling back down the hillside into Bloemfontein. They parted at the citadel, however, companionably enough and Anna held Simon's hand rather longer than necessary as they said goodbye.

'Remember,' she said, 'you will dance with me tomorrow night.'

The touch of her hand renewed Simon's desire for a moment and he put her fingers to his lips in an uncharacteristically Latin gesture. 'How could I forget?' he said. 'Although you may regret it. As I said, I am rather clumsy.'

She did not smile, but held his gaze. 'I don't think I will regret it. Goodbye, Simon.'

The next day came and Simon, Jenkins and Hardy spent the morning getting in provisions for their departure on the morrow. In truth, however, Simon's mind was far more occupied with the ball to come and the thought of seeing Anna – the enigmatic, strange, beautiful Anna – that evening. He wished that he could somehow metamorphose into an elegant sophisticate who could dance, talk of worldly things with beautiful women and be at ease in that foreign cocoon that seemed to surround Anna when she was on parade on social occasions. Ah well, he would just have to do his best.

As a result, he took special care with his toilet that evening, leaving his shave until an hour before the ball was due to commence. He had to admit that Jenkins had done wonders with his shoes, which now gleamed like a guardsman's boots. The Welshman helped Simon dress, showing all the care of a debutante's mother preparing her offspring for her first outing of the season. And he revealed another hidden skill: looping Simon's white tie with assurance and producing from somewhere a white rose for his buttonhole.

'Now, bach sir,' said the little man, stepping back and regarding Simon with approval, 'go an' enjoy yourself and dance with all the pretty girls. But don't be too late comin' 'ome, mind you.'

'Oh do shut up.' But Simon stepped out with rather more confidence than he had possessed when facing Brand's dinner party.

It seemed, from the carriages that were queuing to drop their passengers outside the new House of Assembly, that Bloemfontein's world and his wife were attending the president's ball. Seeing the elegant tail coats and ballgowns of the guests stepping down, Simon was reminded that the little town was the epicentre of an expanding economy, and also that it was the capital of the state. Tiaras and carefully brushed silver hair marked out the diplomatic representatives from countries far and near. The Orange Free State was still an unsophisticated farming country, but the glitter on display tonight reflected respect for Brand and his stewardship. As Simon handed in his gilt-edged invitation card at the door, he could not help wondering if this would be the swansong for the republic – the Boer version of the Brussels Ball before Waterloo.

Once inside, Simon's eye sought Anna. She was with von Bethman, of course, but also a small gathering of heavily moustached men and stout women, perhaps from the German embassy or consulate. Of course she outshone them all, in a white dress nipped in tightly at the waist and then elegantly expanding to sweep the floor. Some sort of blue sash or order featuring a large glittering star at the bosom was arranged to fall from her shoulder to her hip, and diamonds were on display again, sparkling from tiara and necklace.

Immediately Simon felt gauche and clumsy, but she caught his eye and, without interrupting her conversation, smiled at him and held up her dance card. It seemed that she was waving it to make a point to her listeners, but Simon knew it was a reminder and an invitation and he felt himself flush like a schoolboy.

As soon as she was free of her tight circle of companions for a moment, he strode towards her. 'May I?' he asked, taking her card.

The white teeth flashed. 'Ah, Simon. You're too late. Look.' She opened her card and, yes, every dance was taken. Simon felt his heart plummet like a stone.

'Oh. I am sorry.' He bowed and made to turn away.

'Wait,' she said. 'Look.' She pointed. 'You were a little late, so I filled in this dance here in your name. I do hope that I have spelled it right.' She glanced up at him with that well-remembered look through her eyelashes. 'It's the last dance before the interval, so that means we can take our glasses into the garden.'

Simon swallowed. 'What a damned good idea,' he grinned.

'Yes, isn't it? Now do excuse me, my dear, but I must go back to my boring German friends.'

Walking away on air, Simon immediately marked the card of his Afrikaner widow of the previous evening and also that of Mrs Brand. Paying his respects to her husband inevitably led to his introduction to a tall, grey-haired man wearing a monocle and a row of miniature medal ribbons on his lapel. Colonel Ralph Bentley, it seemed, was the newly appointed British diplomatic representative in the Free State capital, and he shook Simon's hand affably enough and then led him away to a quiet corner in the teeming reception area.

'Only arrived yesterday, Fonthill,' he said, half apologetically, 'otherwise I suppose Colley would have asked you to give the letter to me so that I could have delivered it via the normal channels, so to speak.'

'Quite so, sir,' said Simon. 'I had wondered why I had not been instructed accordingly.' He felt it better not to inform the colonel about the full extent of his orders.

'Know what's in it, of course,' the colonel went on. 'Don't expect that Brand will give much away, but he's a man of his word and he won't lie. Whatever promise he makes he will stick to. His answer will be important. I presume that you have not had a reply yet?'

'No, sir. Probably tomorrow.'

'Well, no doubt the president will give me a copy.' He shot a keen glance at Simon. 'That's the way it's done, yer know.'

'Quite so, sir.'

The colonel bestowed an amused eye on Anna Scheel across the room. 'Beautiful woman, my boy. You seem to know her.'

'Not very well, Colonel. I met her via the president the other evening.'

'Did you now?' The tall man smiled.

'As a matter of fact . . .' Simon began, and then paused, wondering how to frame the question. 'I wondered . . . er . . . about her background. I understand that she is a businesswoman.'

The colonel threw back his head in a silent guffaw. 'Oh, she's that all right. Inherited about twenty thousand shares in Krupps, the munitions people, from her uncle, don't yer know. I understand that she knows the business very well and can discuss the relative merits of a Mauser and a Martini-Henry rifle with the best of 'em. But she's a bit of an enigma.'

'What do you mean, sir?'

'She seems to know everyone and have the most remarkably . . . ah . . . eclectic circle of friends. Probably harmless but could be dangerous. I should be a bit careful. Damned fine woman, though.'

'And Baron von Bethman?'

'Oh he's probably even more dangerous, my boy. He's virtually Krupp's highest-level salesman – government to government and all that sort of thing. He has the reputation of being a very nasty piece of work.'

'In what way?'

The colonel allowed his monocle to drop on to his chest on its black cord and leaned forward conspiratorially. 'Bit of a killer, actually. What I mean is that he is a most accomplished duellist, pistols or swords. Killed a fellow student at Heidelberg – you're only supposed to slash the cheek or something, y' know, but he went the whole hog. And I understand that he has contrived to set up duels with two other men and killed 'em too. Not a feller to be crossed, Fonthill. Keep away from 'em all, I'd say.'

'Is he . . . er . . . married to the countess?'

'No. You will have noted they carry different titles and are introduced accordingly. But I should think that there's something going on there, wouldn't you? Eh? Eh?'

'Well yes, I suppose so, sir.'

The colonel nodded and ambled away, leaving Simon with more than a little to think about. The band striking up reminded him of his duty, and he found his Boer widow and, grimly concentrating on the steps, moved her into a quadrille. He survived it somehow, returned his charge to her chair and then found a glass of champagne and downed it in one gulp. Oh lord! What had he got himself into? What sort of web of high-level affairs did the countess and the baron spin as they travelled the world? How many pies did they dip their elegant fingers into? Well. He shrugged. He would be very small fry to them. He had no influence and represented no danger. Nevertheless, he resolved to be careful and to act with great restraint.

Then Anna swept by in the arms of an elegant man with a stern grey beard. She caught Simon's eye and raised her eyebrow. As she turned in the waltz she held his gaze and her eyebrow fell, and for one brief moment the tip of her tongue protruded from her lips. Then she was swept away. It was a message of intimacy that made Simon feel weak at the knees. He quickly downed another glass of champagne, all thoughts of restraint banished.

He honoured his commitment to Mrs Brand and found himself enjoying her company, not least because, like him, she was a poor dancer and was happy to jog along, ignoring the intricacies of the steps but chatting away. Reluctantly, Simon felt he should make the most of his opportunity.

'Mrs Brand,' he asked, sounding as innocent as he could, 'will the people of the Free State do what the president and the Volksraad recommend? I am talking about the Transvaal war, of course.'

'Only if they like the decision. The Boers are very independent, you know, but in matters of state they are also very lazy. Jan is extremely shrewd and he will only lead if he knows they will follow.'

'And will he lead them into war against the British?'

She smiled up at him. 'Ah, for the answer to that question, Captain Fonthill, you must wait until my husband gives you his letter.'

As Simon returned Mrs Brand to the little group of Afrikaner matrons from which he had claimed her for his dance, the president clutched his arm. 'I should be able to give you your letter by about eleven o'clock tomorrow morning, Fonthill,' he said. 'Can you call at my office at that time?'

'Of course, sir.'

Damn! Simon had half hoped that he would be granted at least another day in Bloemfontein to give him the chance of seeing Anna. He stole a quick glance at her amongst the dancers in the crowded ballroom. She was partnering an elderly man, who, from his ill-fitting evening dress, his untrimmed beard and his heavy eyebrows, was probably a member of the Volksraad. They were both laughing. What an open, gregarious person she was! She carried laughter with her wherever she went. There seemed no dissembling or deceit in her manner with anyone.

Feeling a little better, he waited impatiently until his programme told him that the last dance before the interval had arrived. Blast! It was a polka, which, to Simon, was a quite unmanageable series of hops and jumps. Nevertheless, he strode across to where Anna was laughing with her German colleagues and bowed. She made a quick pretence of consulting her card, then smiled, curtsied and gave Simon her hand. He led her away under the cold eye of Baron von Bethman.

As the music began, Simon said: 'Anna, if I tried to dance this with you, I should tread all over you and make a complete fool of myself. May I get you a glass of champagne or punch and take you into the garden? It is a beautiful evening.'

She cocked her head on one side coquettishly. 'Simon, I can't imagine anything nicer. Champagne, please. You will find me by the big blue gum tree at the end of the garden.'

At first he could not see her, for the sun had gone down and a milky moon was hidden by clouds. Then he caught a flash of white from the dark foliage in the distance, away from the path. He found her leaning against the far side of the tree and he silently offered her the champagne. She took it, and as she lowered her head to sip, looked up at him. There seemed to be no evidence of the coquette in the glance, no teasing, no smile – just a look of open directness, perhaps questioning.

Simon felt a pulse begin to beat in his forehead. Slowly he bent and put his glass on the grass and gently took hers from her hand and put it down also. Then he took her into his arms. She offered no resistance but came to him willingly, slipping both arms around his neck, running the fingers of her right hand through the hair at the back of his head and responding to his kiss ardently.

For Simon, all the hardship and frustration of the past months – the agony of his rejection by Alice, the discomfort of the days in the desert, the threat of death in the Boer camp – slipped away as he held this beautiful woman to him in the warmth of the evening. Desire exploded within him in resistance to the enforced celibacy of his lifestyle. Her perfume seemed to consume him as he kissed her neck and shoulders.

Anna pulled away from him for a moment and cupped his face in her hand. '*Mein lieber lieber Junge*,' she murmured.

Simon clutched the hand and brought it to his mouth. 'Anna,' he said, 'I desire you. You must know that. I . . . I . . . I can't help myself.'

She kissed him again, this time softly and with great tenderness, and then withdrew again, shaking her head slowly. She had tears in her eyes. 'It is not possible, Simon,' she whispered. 'There is too much . . . too much . . .'

'Too much what? You are not married, are you?'

She shook her head again, and this time the tears were rolling down her cheeks. Simon held her close again and began kissing away the tears, murmuring into her ear.

They were still locked in this embrace when Simon felt a hand seize his arm. Von Bethman's eyes were blazing. 'Get away from her,' he snarled. 'How dare you assault my cousin, you barbarian? *Englische Schweinhund.*'

Anna put a hand to her mouth. '*Nein, Wilhelm. Nein . . .*'

Instinctively Simon swung his fist. The blow was too hurried and missed the chin, catching the baron high on the cheekbone. But it was strong enough to send the German crashing to the turf. He lay there for a moment, his hand to his face. Then he rose and confronted Simon.

'You have laid your hands on a member of my family and you have struck me,' he said, almost in a whisper. Simon noticed that the scar on his face now seemed blue in the moonlight. 'I demand satisfaction. You are clearly no gentleman, in that you fight with your fists. But, because I have issued you the challenge, you may choose your weapons. Do so now, for we must fight in the morning.'

Anna drew in her breath and stepped between the two men. She began talking to von Bethman in German, speaking urgently and, it was clear, pleadingly. In supplication, she clutched at the lapel of his coat. He removed her hand and shook his head. 'I and our family have been insulted,' he said. 'We duel in the morning.'

The countess turned her tear-stained face to Simon and began talking to him in German for a moment before, realising her mistake, she changed to English. 'Simon, don't do this stupid, awful thing. I have told him that this was just a matter of the moment. I have explained that I . . . I led you on. Now please apologise and nothing will come of this.'

Simon regarded her with horror. 'It was *not* a matter of the moment,' he said slowly. 'If you are not married or betrothed, then I have every right to kiss you, if you were willing. And dammit, Anna, you were.'

She smiled sadly. 'Yes, I was.' Then, as though recovering, she shook her head fiercely and her voice dropped to a whisper. 'No, Simon. Please, please apologise. He . . . he will kill you. He is a famous duellist. He does not wound, he kills. Please, please . . .'

Simon turned to the baron. 'I am at your service, sir,' he said.

Von Bethman gave a stiff bow. 'Very well. Your weapons? Pistols or swords?'

Simon's mind was in a turmoil, but he forced himself to think rationally. If von Bethman was determined to kill him, then pistols would be the easiest way, particularly as Simon was such a poor shot. Just one bullet would do it . . . He might stand a better chance with swords. He regarded the baron critically. Small physique, no doubt light on his feet. Not foils or épées, then.

143

'Swords,' he said, realising his voice sounded hoarse. 'Sabres.'

For a moment the baron looked disconcerted. 'Sabres? We might have difficulty in finding them here. I'

'Sabres. If duelling sabres are not available, then cavalry sabres. There should be plenty of them about.'

'Very well. I will consult with my colleagues and we will find the weapons to match your choice and also suggest the venue. You are happy that I do that?'

'Of course.'

'You will need a second. My second will call on him to arrange the details. Can you nominate him now or do you need time?' There was an undoubted sneer in the German's voice.

'Of course not. His name is Jenkins and we are both staying at the Voertrekker Hotel.'

'Very well. We should fight early but we need time to arrange everything. Shall we say ten o'clock tomorrow? Good. My man will call on yours at eight-thirty.'

He took a step nearer and put his face so close to Simon's that the latter could detect a faint trace of garlic on the German's breath. His eyes were cold still, but now gleaming with a kind of suppressed pleasure. 'Now, my friend,' he murmured, so that Anna standing nearby, her hand to her mouth, could not hear. 'No man has ever struck me and lived. Tomorrow, I will kill you. Be sure that you say your prayers tonight, Englishman.'

Then he turned. 'Now, Anna. Wipe your face and come.' He took the countess's arm, and with one anguished look over her shoulder, she and her protector were gone.

Chapter 7

'You're doing what?' Jenkins sat on the edge of his bed in his underdrawers, his mouth open and his eyes popping.

'I'm fighting a duel at ten o'clock tomorrow morning,' repeated Simon, trying to keep his voice matter-of-fact. 'I want you be my second.'

They were talking in Jenkins's room at the hotel, a little before eleven p.m., after Simon's return from the ball. He had sought to follow Anna, but she had been swept away by von Bethman and the German contingent, and after staying a while in desultory conversation with Colonel Bentley to preserve appearances – Simon could not remember a word they exchanged – he too had made his excuses and left.

Walking back to the hotel, Simon's thoughts had whirled around in his head to produce a conclusion as sour as the aftertaste of the champagne. He was almost certainly going to be killed in the morning. His opponent was a skilled swordsman – that scar on his face was obviously a relic of a previous encounter – and if by some miracle he escaped, he was bound to be disgraced. Duelling was illegal in England, and although there had probably been no necessity to pass the same law in the Free State, he had seriously compromised his position by provoking a challenge from a German nobleman in the president's garden. Once again he recalled Colley's stricture to 'tread with care' and he groaned inwardly. What a mess! It had been with nothing but despair in his mind, then, that he had knocked on Jenkins's door.

'I'll be your third or fourth if you like, bach sir,' said the Welshman. 'But tell me about it. Who are you fightin', why are you

145

fightin' 'im and what do I 'ave to do? Is it like bein' second in a boxin' match, then?'

'More or less. I don't know much about it. I've never fought a duel before.' Simon sighed, sat on the edge of Jenkins's bed and related the story, stumbling a little as he spoke of Anna and his feelings for her.

The little Welshman sat up, tugging at his moustache. 'Well, I must say,' he said eventually, 'this is a bit of a pickle, isn't it? I don't know what Miss Alice would say about it, I really don't.'

'Alice Griffith is married by now and out of my life,' hissed Simon, glad of a chance to vent his anger and despair. 'Don't mention her again.'

Jenkins held up his hand. 'All right, all right. It's not my fault, now is it? We've got to think about this. Mind you,' his face descended into lugubrious folds, 'you run the thinkin' department, so I don't really see what I can do, short of shootin' the bloke. Can you fence, then?'

'A bit. I was quite good at sabres at Sandhurst. That's why I chose them. You know I'm not much good at shooting.'

'Well there's a bit of relief, isn't it? Let's get old Ally out of bed and see what he can suggest.'

'No.' Simon stood. 'There's no need to involve him. I'll just have to get on with it. Look, the German's second will come around to see you at about nine tomorrow to inform you of the venue and whatever other details are necessary. That's the way it's done, it seems. Be honest with him and explain that you don't know much about this business and he will tell you the rules.'

Simon walked to the door, paused and turned. 'There's one other important thing. I am supposed to be calling on President Brand at eleven tomorrow, to pick up his reply to General Colley. If . . . if . . . I am unable to see him, I would like you to find Colonel Bentley, who is the British diplomatic representative here – they will tell you at the House of Assembly where he is to be found – explain that I am . . . er . . . indisposed and ask him to collect the letter himself. I have a couple of letters I must write myself tonight which perhaps you would post for me tomorrow if, ah, things go wrong.'

Jenkins's face was now so crestfallen that Simon was forced to laugh. 'Cheer up,' he said. 'He's only a little fellow and we all know that little chaps can't fight. Look at you. I'll cut his head off. Now get some sleep. You have some hard seconding to do tomorrow.'

The jocularity disappeared immediately Simon returned to his own room. He pulled a rather curled sheet of the hotel's plain notepaper towards him, dipped a pen into the inkwell and wrote a short letter to his parents, at home in Brecon. He avoided giving them too many details, merely explaining that it was a matter of honour and expressing his love and thanks to them for their support of him during his upbringing. His letter to Anna Scheel was even shorter. He thought for a moment of writing to Alice Griffith but decided against it. She had now left his life and there would be no point. She would discover his fate soon enough.

Lying in bed, he desperately tried to recall the fundamentals of fencing. He had received some training in it as a sport and he dimly recalled something about not attacking when one's opponent was on the offensive; one had to wait one's turn, so to speak. He remembered a series of stamping forays and then retreats along a defined area. It all seemed so much nonsense now. Much of the instruction at Sandhurst had centred on fighting from horseback: using the point, the slash, and the reverse swing on poor natives or infantrymen on the run. He had never been trained to duel. After all, that was what Prussians did. Perhaps von Bethman would let him bring his horse? What the hell! He eventually found escape in sleep.

Rising early, Simon packed his belongings and dressed simply in riding boots, corduroy breeches and open-necked white shirt. He had no appetite and took only a cup of tea. There was no sign of either Jenkins or Hardy, so he wandered into the small tree-shaded garden at the rear of the hotel, found a heavy stick and spent some minutes swinging it and then simulating lunges and parries. He felt vaguely ridiculous but it loosened his muscles. He looked up through the tracery of the willow tree's branches to the blue sky above. This waiting was awful, but at least it was a fine morning on which to die.

It was nearly 9.45 before a perspiring Jenkins returned to the hotel. 'I was getting worried,' said Simon. 'Where have you been?'

'I've been chattin' to the bleedin' enemy, surveyin' the battlefield and inspectin' the weapons. Now listen, bach sir. We've only got a few minutes.' He motioned to the ground and they sat cross-legged together in the garden.

'First of all,' said Jenkins, 'they're a lot of bloody toffs an' they don't think much of you for 'avin' me as a second.'

Simon found it within himself to grin. 'No, I didn't think they would. The trouble was I couldn't get the Prince of Wales at such short notice.'

'Quite so, indeed, an' all that stuff. Second thing is, I've caught a glimpse of the opponent an 'e's a cocky little shit. Now listen, bach sir.' He gave Simon a meaningful stare. 'You know I've fought all me life – all kinds of blokes, see, with all kinds of weapons: me fists, shovels, pickaxes, bricklayer's 'ods, knives an' bayonets. Well, I've always won an' I've always felt good when the other bugger felt cocky to begin with. I think 'e will come straight at you from the word go, so be prepared for that and if you can let 'im blow 'imself out a bit. 'E's a lot older than you and less fit.'

Simon nodded and quickly reflected that a man could have a far worse second than Jenkins when fighting for his life, despite his inexperience of the etiquette of duelling.

'Now,' continued the little man, 'third thing is, these sabres are bloody 'eavy things. Von something or other – the other bloke's second – tells me that they couldn't find proper fencin' things, so you are using cavalry sabres. They've sharpened them up but they still feel like a ton o' bricks. This is in your favour because the other bugger is only a little chap. Now I'm only a little chap but I'm strong, see. For all 'is prancin' about, look you, I reckon that this baron bloke ain't all that strong. So when you get the chance, swing the bloody sabre at 'im 'ard. 'E won't be used to that sort of stuff. 'E'll be used to them thin, pointed things.'

'You mean foils or épées?'

'Don't know what they're called, but even though I can't speak German, I knew that none of 'em were 'appy with fighting with these bloody great meat cleavers. So that's again in your favour, see.'

'Yes, thank you, 352. Hadn't we better be going?'

'Last thing. You've gotta toss for choice of ends. I think you'll be allowed to call because – what do they call it? – you are the challenged one, see. All right then. I shall be providin' the coin, or rather Ally is though I've got it in my pocket, so make sure you call tails. Right? And then you must face the sun.'

'Surely not! That will be a disadvantage, won't it? The sun will be in my eyes.'

'Not this mornin' it won't. Trust me. Now. Come on or we shall be late.'

'Where are we fighting?'

'In the garden of the Germans' place – embassy or whatever you call it. Off we go. It's only round the corner. There's plenty of bloody rules about this business but I've already forgotten 'em. They'll explain.'

They rose to their feet and set off, Jenkins wiping the perspiration from his forehead, for the sun was strong. Simon's mouth was dry but he felt immensely comforted by the little man's participation. He no longer felt vulnerably alone. He had a sudden thought. 'Where's Al?'

'Never you mind about 'im, bach sir. 'E's around somewhere. Just you keep your mind on the job in 'and and we'll wipe the floor with 'em, you'll see.'

The German Embassy was an unimpressive wooden house with the customary galvanised-iron roof, although the building was a little larger than usual. At its rear, it boasted a square garden protected by a green wall of bushes and trees. More importantly, the garden was laid to well-watered lawn and it was quite flat.

The scene that met Simon's eye made him gulp involuntarily. By the entrance to the garden, a scrubbed table was set with a bowl of steaming water, various coloured bottles and a gruesome display of surgeon's instruments. A man wearing a rubber apron stood by its side. On the lawn, white tapes had been laid to create a rectangle some twenty metres by six in area. Outside it stood half a dozen men, two of them in the grey uniforms of German officers, tightly buttoned to the neck despite the heat. Von Bethman stood a little to one side. He looked slim and neat in black riding breeches, soft rubber-soled shoes and a white shirt, open to the waist. He stared at Simon expressionlessly. Of Anna, of course, there was no sign.

One of the uniformed officers approached Simon and Jenkins, clicked his heels and bowed to each in turn. His monocle glinted in the morning sun. 'Good morning,' he said and then addressed Simon in heavily accented English. 'Captain, your second appeared to be unfamiliar with the rules for duelling. If you are in agreement, then, I suggest that we roughly follow those established in Germany for the *Mensuren* events in Heidelberg.'

'By all means,' said Simon. He had no idea what that meant, but he was grateful and surprised to find that his voice was not croaking.

'Good. We cannot follow them closely, of course, because we do not duel in the right conditions, but permit me to explain the basics in English for you both.'

'Very well.'

'Now, gentlemen,' he said, calling von Bethman over. The two combatants regarded each other. Simon kept his face expressionless but his eyes remained firmly fixed on those of the baron. The latter allowed his lip to curl in a faint smile as he took in Simon's scuffed riding boots and wrinkled shirt.

The second began. 'Myself and the English second will mark with our swords,' he handed Jenkins a German dress sword, 'the standing positions for the combatants in the middle of the duelling area. This will leave a distance of approximately half a metre between the points of your weapons, arms extended.' His voice was high-pitched and unmodulated, as though he was issuing parade-ground instructions but in conversational tones. 'You will not step outside the area which has been marked with the tape. Duellists will not ward off their opponent's blade with their unarmed hand. Sabre rules will be followed, which means that the target area is above the waist only. The legs are not targets. Seconds will intervene the moment the rules are contravened.'

Simon looked around. The duelling area was, in effect, a long strip along which virtually the only movement possible was forwards or back. There could be little chance of sideways evasive action. He licked his lips and, for the first time, felt real fear.

The officer was droning on. 'You are allowed to stoop, rise, vault to the right or left or turn around each other, as long as you stay within the prescribed area. When one of the parties concedes he is hurt or a wound is noticed by his second, the second will raise his sword, while the opposing second cries out, "Strike up the blades." Then both combatants take a step back, although remaining *en garde*. Understood, *ja?*'

Simon and Jenkins nodded.

The second's voice dropped for a moment and seemed to Simon to take on a more sinister note. 'You will fence on, without interruption – there will be no separate rounds – until a conclusive wound is delivered, or until one or the other withdraws. Remember, you may cut and slash as well as lunge with the point. Now, please choose your weapons.'

The second of the uniformed officers stepped forward, clicked his heels and presented two sabres, hilts first, across his forearm. The German second announced, with a touch of annoyance, as though it was something he had omitted to say: 'They have been measured and weighed and are of equal length and weight.'

With hardly a glance at it, Simon took a sabre. It truly was a brutish instrument. The blade was slightly curved and was a little under a metre in length, and the tip and the edge had been freshly ground so that the serrations glittered in the morning sun. He weighed it for a moment and then, dimly remembering instructions in technique, whirled it from the elbow, keeping the wrist locked. It was heavy all right, but he felt he could handle it. Now that the moment of truth had approached, he felt strangely calm. In fact, it was Jenkins who now appeared to be on edge, looking around him at the trees as though expecting divine intervention at the last minute.

'Please hand your sabres to the doctor for disinfecting with carbolic acid.'

God, thought Simon, how long do these opening rituals take? Let's just get on with it! But the preparations were still not quite complete. He and the baron were asked to open their shirts to the waist to ensure that they were not wearing protective padding, and then a silk handkerchief was tied around their sword-arm wrists.

'What's this for?' Simon demanded of the doctor.

'To protect the arteries,' he replied. 'They are particularly vulnerable here.' And he tapped Simon's wrist.

'Now, gentlemen,' the second was back in command again, 'I will toss a coin – ah, thank you.' Jenkins had handed him a sovereign. 'And Captain Fonthill will call heads or tails for the opening position. I do it now.' Up went the coin.

'Tails,' called Simon.

'*Ja*. It is tails.'

'Thank you very much, bach,' said Jenkins, rather anxiously it seemed, seizing the coin and putting it into his trouser pocket. Simon looked up. True enough, the fencing strip seemed to stretch east to west. As instructed, he chose to face east, although the sun had not appeared through the tracery of leaves and branches and there seemed no advantage at all in having choice of opening position.

'Now, gentlemen.' The uniformed second took up his position in the centre of the strip and slightly to one side – would he be able to keep his monocle in position all through the duel? – with his sword pointing due south. With an irritated gesture, he indicated that Jenkins should do the same on the other side, so that their swords were touching. '*En garde*.'

With practised ease, von Bethman slipped into place, his feet angled at ninety degrees to each other, his legs agonisingly bent, his left hand held high behind him, with the wrist dangling foppishly, and his sword held out towards Simon, horizontal to the ground and about a foot from those of the seconds. Simon attempted to adopt the same posture and immediately felt ridiculous, so he relaxed into an easier if less formal position, standing side on to his opponent, his knees slightly bent, his own sword extended a foot short of the seconds' swords.

'Good luck, boyo,' breathed Jenkins. 'I'll kill the bastard if you don't.'

'*Allez!*' shrieked the monocled German – and they were off.

As Jenkins had predicted, the baron immediately attacked. After the briefest of preparatory touches to Simon's blade, he feinted to the body and then lunged to the face, his right leg stretched to its limit, his left bent at right angles. Somehow, Simon fended off the attack –

it was too clumsy a movement to be called a parry – and then caught the tip of von Bethman's blade on his hand-guard as the German elegantly switched his attack to the body again. The baron, completely in control of his movements, stepped back for a moment and then, in a flurry of lunges, attacked once more, his blade seeming to Simon to move like the tongue of a snake as it thrust forward at him in fluid movements of flickering silver. This time Simon gave way, stamping back in his riding boots and flailing – there was no other word for it – with his sabre to protect himself.

The baron's strategy undoubtedly was one of all-out attack, and yet it was clear that he was attempting to fence as though he had a lightweight épée in his hand, instead of the heavy, sharp-edged sabre. He was eschewing – perhaps arrogantly? – the use of slash or swing in favour of the thrust with the point. Yet the curved, cutlass-like sabre was not suited to these quicksilver tactics. The weight of the weapon was pulling at his wrist and forecasting his moves, so that Simon was able to parry, albeit at the last minute. Nevertheless, it was already clear that the German was by far the better swordsman and that it would not be long before he drew blood.

They broke for a second or two as von Bethman walked back contemptuously to his mark, and Simon recalled Jenkins's advice to 'let 'im blow 'imself out a bit'. God, he thought. If only I get the chance!

Then, this time without warning, the baron was back. Simon was aware of a sharp pain in his forearm, and suddenly his sabre had been twisted from his grasp and sailed high into the air before falling, point down, to quiver in the grass.

'Oi, or whatever it is,' he heard Jenkins cry. ' 'Ang on, 'e's 'urt.'

A murmur of admiration for the skill of the move rose from the group of watching Germans, then, from the German second: 'Strike up the blades. Herr Doctor . . .'

The medico came running forward, his rubber apron slapping against his thighs, but Simon thrust him aside. 'It is nothing,' he said.

'Do you concede?' asked von Bethman's second.

Simon looked for a brief moment at the sneer on the baron's face. He was obviously congratulating himself on the thrust that had disarmed his opponent. But there was also perspiration beading his forehead.

'Good God, no,' said Simon. 'We said we would fight until a conclusive wound. This is only a scratch. My sword, please.'

The point of his sabre was carefully cleaned with a cloth, disinfected again and then handed back to him.

'*En garde encore*, gentlemen,' cried the second, and once more they touched swords in the centre.

The baron spoke for the first time. 'Don't worry, I have decided not to kill you, pretty boy,' he growled. 'But I am going to cut your face to pieces so that no woman will ever look at you again.'

'Really?' gasped Simon. The slash to his forearm was now beginning to burn. 'What? Make me as ugly as you?'

'No speaking during the combat, gentlemen,' warned the German second in his parade-ground monotone. And then his high-pitched '*Allez!*'

Immediately the baron came forward once more, lunging and feinting, the deliberate thrusts always now directed at Simon's face. The attacks were skilful and lightning quick, but Simon's height gave him a slight advantage in reach and the German's targeting of the face seemed to be proving counterproductive, in that Simon was able to tilt his head back and parry, albeit clumsily.

Nevertheless, von Bethman's lunges were getting nearer and Simon's defensive moves ever more maladroit. One thrust, to the right eye, ended in an upward flick of the blade's sharp tip which cut through Simon's eyebrow, sending blood trickling down into his eye and on to his cheek. Closing the eye, Simon had a momentary, squinted close-up glimpse of the German's look of savage exhilaration at the pain he had caused. The bastard was trying to blind him!

Simon realised that with one eye closed by the blood from the cut brow, he was virtually finished. His only hope was to counterattack. But how could he get round that flashing blade, always darting towards his face? Then, as their blades clashed and stayed crossed above the hand-guards for a second, he sensed the first moment of weakness in the German. Von Bethman's blade moved down and to the right as Simon pressed hard on it. Was he becoming tired? Into Simon's head for a second flashed a picture from six years ago – the image of his sabre instructor at Sandhurst, twirling his weapon from the elbow in quick, circular motions and saying, 'Of course, if you are the stronger, the Hungarian technique can be effective . . .'

Suddenly, fired by rage, frustration and the pain from his cut forearm and eyebrow, Simon whirled into the attack. For a moment, the baron was nonplussed by the strange, circular movement of his opponent's blade and Simon saw, for the first time, a look of apprehension come into his eyes. Then the German was defending himself desperately as Simon dropped all pretence at swordsmanship and began slashing and cutting at him with the edge, rather than the point, of the sabre. The attack was almost barbaric in its pace and power, and its very primitiveness suddenly gave Simon the advantage, for von Bethman had learned no formal moves at Heidelberg to counter this kind of onslaught. He fell back defensively for the first time, desperately parrying the mighty blows which drove his blade back on to him, at one time causing it to kiss his face, so strong was the slash.

'Yes, yes,' cried Jenkins. 'Go for 'im, bach!'

'Silence,' shouted the opposing second.

Neither the attack nor the defence could be maintained at this level of ferocity for long, but it was the German who gave way. His elegant rubber pump slipped slightly on the grass as he stepped back in retreat and his blade swung away weakly for a second. It gave Simon a brief opening and his sabre came down in a brutal arc, cutting deeply into the German's sword arm, above the wrist, and sending a fountain of blood curling up and then down on to the grass.

This was no scratch, and a cry of agony came from the baron as he dropped his sword to clutch at the deep gash, blood oozing through his fingers.

'What you'd call a conclusive wound, I think,' gasped Simon.

'Strike up the whatsits,' shouted Jenkins belatedly, his face beaming with joy.

The doctor rushed forward and bent to the side of the baron, who was now kneeling on the grass, his face contorted in pain. They spoke in German and the doctor gestured to the monocled second, who also knelt at von Bethman's side. Eventually, the latter looked up and addressed Simon. 'The duel is yours, sir,' he said. 'The baron's sword arm is now useless and he is unable to continue.'

'Thank you,' gasped Simon, still trying to regain his breath. 'Then if you gentlemen will excuse me, I will say good morning. I have an appointment to keep.'

'Fonthill.' The cry came from von Bethman. His voice had descended into little more than a whisper. 'You fought like a peasant.'

'No. I fought like a soldier. *You* fought like a prancing courtesan.'

The baron's features were screwed into an expression of pure hatred. 'I shall kill you the next time we meet,' he said through clenched teeth. 'Be sure of that.'

'I shall look forward to it,' said Simon. He threw down his sabre and walked away. At the entrance to the garden he stopped and looked back. The baron, still lying on the ground, was regarding him with a look of pure malevolence. For a second, a shudder of apprehension flashed through Simon's body. It was clear that he had made a lifelong enemy of this cruel, bitter man. This was an untamed, violent country. Would the German find an opportunity of taking his revenge? A phrase from Sandhurst days came back to him: 'Watch your back, soldier . . .' He sighed, shook his head and walked through the gate.

'Good day, all,' said Jenkins cheerily and followed suit. They left behind a silent group of Germans huddled around the kneeling figure of Baron Wilhelm von Bethman.

Once outside the embassy, Simon leaned against the fence, his whole body trembling and his face white beneath the blood now pouring down his cheek.

' 'Ere,' said Jenkins. He produced a grubby handkerchief and began dabbing gently at the wound. 'Ah, it's not too bad. Bit of cold water on it and a bandage or somethin' an' you'll be fine. I'll see to that gash in your arm as well.'

Simon sucked in breath. 'God, 352,' he said, 'I thought I was done for. He was all over me at the beginning. But you were right. He did run out of puff first and it was lucky I was able to hang on. But for goodness' sake don't let me go duelling again. I'm no bloody good at it.'

Jenkins stopped his ministrations and grabbed Simon's hand. 'Oh sorry, bach sir,' he said as Simon winced. 'No bloody good, my arse. By golly, you did well. I thought you was a goner, at first, as well, I really did. 'E was prancin' about all over the place, look you. But it was all right when you lost your temper, see. Bloody 'ell, man, you nearly killed 'im. We didn't need old . . .' He paused.

'Didn't need old who?'

'Oh, nothin'. It was just a little plan I 'ad, but it didn't seem to work anyway. Never mind. We won.'

Simon lifted his good eyebrow and glared at Jenkins, his head on one side. 'That reminds me, show me that sovereign.'

'Ooh, that's Ally's. I wouldn't want to 'and it over, see.'

'Yes you would. Come on.'

Reluctantly, Jenkins dug into his pocket and gave Simon the sovereign.

'I thought so,' said Simon, examining it. 'Just as well I called tails, wasn't it, because there's no side with heads on it.'

'Well,' said Jenkins scratching his chin. ''E's a bit of a lad, is old Ally. You know, bach sir, I think 'e cheats at cards, too.'

The American chose just that moment to join them. His normally immaculate buckskins were stained green and his beautifully worked leather boots were scuffed. He looked at the pair of them ruefully. 'Sorry,' he said to Jenkins. 'Ah couldn't climb the dang blasted tree. So ah couldn't work this.' He handed a small hand mirror to the Welshman and beamed at Simon. 'But ah just managed to get up on to a lower branch in time to see you give that German feller a real roastin'. Sonny, this chile was real proud of you.'

Simon shook his head, half in amusement and half in anger. 'It was going to be shining the reflected light of the sun into his eyes, was it?'

'Well,' Jenkins wiped his moustache and gave a shamefaced grin, 'it was all I could think of, look you. If this bloody American 'ad moved 'is arse a bit faster up that tree, it could 'ave worked and saved you gettin' those cuts, see.'

157

Simon extended his hand to both of them. 'Gentlemen,' he said, 'I am grateful for your loyalty. But thank God I didn't need your help in the end. Now, come on and let's get out of here. I've got to get patched up and then see the president.'

In the hotel there was little time to do other than bathe Simon's wounds, bandage his forearm and apply a little cooking oil from the kitchen to his eyebrow to seal the cut. Then, in riding clothes but with his shirtsleeve buttoned down to cover the bandage, he strode off to the House of Assembly to keep his appointment.

As he walked, Simon rationalised his situation. It was unlikely that news of the duel would have leaked out. Other than he and Jenkins, all those attending the clash were Germans, even the doctor. These stiffly buttoned Prussians were unlikely, he reasoned, to leak the story of the defeat of their champion – and the baron would certainly never tell anyone how he had been beaten by a novice English swordsman. But Anna would know. Anna – ah, Anna! He realised with a start that he had hardly thought of her since rising to meet his destiny at the embassy. What was that strange power that von Bethman seemed to exercise over her? What did he call her? His cousin. Hmm. It was with a sense of shame that Simon became aware that his ardour for the beautiful countess had diminished overnight. And yet . . . He recalled the softness of her skin and the delicate arch of her eyebrows; the way she looked up at him through her eyelashes. Oh, Lord! At that point, walking under the blue African sky, having fought his first duel and narrowly escaped with his life, Simon just didn't know what to think.

Brand was in a jovial mood as he received Simon. The ball had obviously been a great success and he thanked his visitor for attending. 'You did your duty on the dance floor very well, Fonthill,' he smiled. 'Damned sight better than I did.'

'Sorry, sir, but I had to opt out of the polka. Bit like dancing to Morse code, I thought.'

'Quite right. Good gracious. That's a nasty cut. How did that happen?'

'Just a slight argument with a door post. It's nothing really, sir.'

'Right. Now. Glad to see that you are dressed for the journey and are ready to go. But let me detain you just for a moment. Sit down.' The president took up a stout buff-coloured envelope from his desk and handed it to Simon. 'There's the reply to General Colley. No news had yet come through to me from Natal about troop movements, so as far as I know, the general has made no advance yet. But I flatter myself that he will be interested in what I have to say, so you should make haste to take it to him as fast as you can.

'Now, it wouldn't be right for me to give you a copy of what I have said to Colley, because of course it is confidential. But you should know the gist of it, in case,' he gestured to the envelope, 'something should happen to the document en route.

'I have told the general that my colleagues – at least the majority of them that matter – on the Volksraad and I have no intention at this point of entering the war on the side of the Transvaal against the British.'

'That's good news, sir.'

'Yes, but wait a moment. We would only do so if we came under so much pressure from our people in the Free State that we had no choice but to bend to their will. Personally, I doubt if that will happen, because, as I have often said,' and he smiled, 'we Boers are an easy-going people and we are happy to continue our peaceful ways if we are left alone. However, we could be roused if the war is conducted in such a way – excessive cruelty or reprisals against the civilian population, for instance – that it seems only right that we should go to the aid of our brothers in the north. I am sure you understand.'

'Yes, Mr President. I understand.'

'Very well.' Brand rose and extended his hand. 'Now make all haste with my letter.' They shook hands and then the president put a restraining hand on Simon's arm. 'One more thing. In view of what I have said, you may just feel that it would be wise or expedient to convey the contents of my letter to Colonel Bentley here in Bloemfontein so that he can telegraph them ahead of you to Colley. Please do not do so. I would not like my opinions to leak out here, and putting them on the open telegraph would be one sure way of doing that – even if you people have some sort of code you can use. Do you understand?'

'Of course, sir. You have my word.'

'Then be on your way, and God's speed.'

As Simon reached the door, Brand called out: 'I do hope that you have found your brief stay in our town diverting, Fonthill.'

Simon smiled. 'In every way, sir. In every way.'

Outside the assembly building, Simon stood for a moment in indecision. Then, thrusting the envelope inside his jacket, he made his way to the best hotel in town, where he knew that the baron and the countess were staying. At the reception desk he asked to see Anna, and was asked to wait while his message was taken to her room. He had no idea what he would say to her, but he knew that he had to see her again, to test his feelings and to gain some sort of understanding of her relationship with von Bethman. It was an uneasy wait, for he had no desire to encounter the baron, but not a long one. Within three minutes a terse message was delivered to say that the countess was not receiving callers.

Simon shrugged and made his way back to his own hotel, where he found Jenkins and a spruced-up Al loading the packhorse. He went to his room and tore up the letters he had written the previous evening. As he did so, something evocative but elusive about the place made him sit back, nostrils twitching, and look around him closely. Nothing seemed to have been disturbed and the door had been locked. What, then, was it? On an impulse he went to the shabby chest of drawers where his change of socks, his underpants and his meagre supply of three shirts were kept. There was something wrong . . . yes, they had been rearranged. Subtly but unmistakably, because, for all his servanting skills, Jenkins could not fold a shirt correctly and Simon had refolded them with the sleeves on the outside. Now, in conventional style, the sleeves had been tucked inside the fold of the shirt, as a wife or maidservant might do. Someone had been rifling through his drawers! Nothing else seemed to have been disturbed. Whoever had visited him had been looking for something he might have hidden there. Something easy to hide among shirts. Something small and flat . . . of course! Brand's letter! Involuntarily, he touched the fat envelope inside his jacket for reassurance. Then he sat back in the chair and looked around and tried to concentrate.

What had alerted him? Something elusive which did not fit easily into this Spartan room. Then he recognised it: it was perfume, the perfume that he would remember for the rest of his life. Anna had been in his room.

He rushed down the stairs to the young Afrikaner behind the reception desk.

'Has anyone been in my room this morning?'

'Only the maid, sir.'

'Anyone else?'

'No. You did have a visitor about an hour ago, but she did not go upstairs – well, at least as far as I know. And your key has always been here. The lady left this for you. I did not see you return or I would have given it to you then.'

Simon nodded slowly, took the slim envelope handed to him and returned to his room. Sitting, he held the envelope to his nostrils for a moment and confirmed that heady and erotic perfume. Then he tore it open and read:

My dear, dear Simon,

I cannot tell you the relief with which I have just heard that you have survived the duel and, indeed, inflicted a wound on Wilhelm von Bethman – although I take no satisfaction in this last thing. I am experiencing only shame and guilt that my irresponsible actions led you into this awful situation in the first place and so endangered your life. If you had died, part of me would have died also.

I am glad and grateful to have earned your affection (please forgive me if I do not express myself well, but my English lessons in Kent did not prepare me to write this sort of letter). I can only say that we must not see each other again, for reasons which are complicated and which perhaps one day I might have the opportunity of explaining to you.

Please do not try and find me, but STAY SAFE and please, please remember me with affection.

Yours most sincerely,

Anna

Simon threw down the letter, walked round the room, then picked it up, sat down on the edge of the bed and slowly read it again. *Reasons which are complicated* ... What did that mean? Was she secretly married to von Bethman, or more to the point, was she in the employ of the German Government and – he must face it – a spy, working for Bismarck? Perhaps the two together? That would explain her coming to his room to look for Brand's letter. Or, and his heart lifted for a moment, was she seeking some kind of keepsake to remember him by? Eventually Simon folded the letter, held it to his nostrils again, closed his eyes and sighed. No use pursuing it – he had a job to do. He carefully put the folded sheet away in the breast pocket of his shirt, stood and took a deep breath.

Down below, the other two were waiting. Without a word, Simon mounted his horse, pulled its head around and headed the little party away east out of Bloemfontein, towards Natal and the war that awaited them.

Chapter 8

At first Simon set a blistering pace, his mind far away and consumed by memories of ivory-skinned décolletage, soft brown eyes and a perfume which even now was fading from the letter at his breast. It was the gentle-voiced Hardy who protested. The American rarely cared for his personal comfort but he was ever vigilant about the health of his horse.

'Hey, Simon,' he called from the rear. 'Ah'm thinkin' that old Custer ain't likin' this hoss race you've entered him for. Cain't we slow up a mite?'

'Oh, sorry, Al. Certainly. I'm afraid I was far away.'

'In bloody Germany,' murmured Jenkins in a stage whisper.

Simon glared at him but said nothing. In truth, once the pace had been slowed it was not unpleasant riding across the undulating veldt, with a wind softening the rays of the early summer sun, although the nearer they came to the Natal border, the more frequent became the sudden and torrential rain showers that flooded the dongas and turned the trail into red mud.

They found that Hardy had acquired some knowledge of the local flora and fauna. A strange bird flew low over the grass, its gossamer-like tail floating behind it. 'That's a long-tailed widder bird,' drawled the American. 'Loses its tail in the winter.' He also pointed out, high above them, the white-backed Cape vulture. 'They can see for miles,' he said, 'an' once they see one of their kind circling far away, they know it's feedin' time and they all hop over fast as a prairie dawg after a rattler.'

A new ritual had entered into the journey. If they were camping out on the plain, away from a Boer farm, Al would practise drawing his revolver from its holster and shooting at some target, a rock or a stunted piece of bush. It was clear that the amazing speed and accuracy he had displayed in killing the Boer horsemen was no fluke. Invariably he hit his selected target, sometimes drawing with his back to it and shooting on the turn.

' 'Ere,' said Jenkins one morning as they were saddling up after witnessing another display of virtuoso marksmanship, 'you must 'ave been in old Buffalo Bill's circus, eh, Ally?'

'Nope,' said Hardy.

'Well then, 'ow many men 'ave you killed with those bloody things?'

The American shrugged. 'Cain't remember.'

'Blimey. All right then. Don't tell us your life story. See if I care, bach.'

In fact, the journey had cemented the Welshman and the American's friendship, with Hardy's monosyllabic personality happily complementing Jenkins's garrulousness. Every evening before turning in they played cards together. Yet after his initial openness, the Texan had certainly retreated into his shell and there were no more references to General Custer, the Little Bighorn or, indeed, life on the great plains of America. Simon had long ago come to the conclusion that Hardy had run into some sort of trouble and been forced to flee the North American continent. Gambling, perhaps? But he resolved not to pry. It was comforting enough having the genial, quietly spoken gunman with them without demanding his curriculum vitae.

A little over two weeks after leaving Bloemfontein, the trio walked their horses into Newcastle. They had been away more than a month and it was clear that General Colley had begun his advance and that they had just missed his departure. The tracks around Fort Amiel, above the town, were deep in mud and rutted from the wheels of hundreds of waggons and the passage of a small army.

Simon called at the general's old headquarters and met Lieutenant Elwes, one of Colley's young ADCs, who was, he said, clearing up after the departure of the column. They recognised each other from Simon's visits to the general.

164

'What sort of column is it?' asked Simon.

'Bit of a ragbag really,' said the young man in tones redolent of Eton College. 'But the general felt he'd just got to get on with it and relieve those garrisons in the Transvaal. The press at home and all that.'

'What's he got?'

'Just under fifteen hundred men in all.'

Simon sighed. 'Not enough,' he said. 'The Boers could have twice that many marksmen up on the Nek by now. What is the strength?'

Elwes pulled a well-thumbed sheet of paper towards him. 'The column is called the Natal Field Force,' he said. 'The guts of it are five companies of the 58th Regiment and five companies of the 3/60th Rifles. But no real cavalry, just mounted infantry – a squadron of a hundred and thirty men, sixty-one from the Natal Mounted Police and a naval brigade of a hundred and twenty-seven men from a ship at the Cape.'

'Artillery?'

'Not too bad. There are four nine-pounder guns, two seven-pounders, two Gatling guns with the naval lads and three twenty-four-pounder rocket tubes.'

Simon registered a sad smile at the mention of the rockets. He remembered watching a battery of the things doing nothing whatever to deter the Zulus as they poured across the plain towards the encampment at Isandlwana. 'When did the column leave?' he asked.

'Only yesterday. If I were you I would bed down for the night here and leave tomorrow. You will catch them easily.' Elwes pushed his hand through tousled hair. 'The bloody column is not exactly speeding along. it's taken us a month to get here from the coast. Rain and mud most of the time. We had to manhandle the waggons and the guns most of the way. The general intends to make his forward camp at Mount Prospect, a sort of flat hill about twenty-two miles north of here, then he's going to invade the Transvaal through the gap in the hills at Laing's Nek.'

'Where the Boers will be waiting for him.'

'What?'

165

'Never mind. What's this?' Simon pointed to a single sheet of paper.

'It's a copy of Sir George's general order to the troops.'

'May I?'

'Of course.'

Simon read it quickly. It was of the 'England expects' kind of exhortation, but towards the end it included words typical of Colley's gentle broad-mindedness but also of his strength of purpose. Referring to the Boers, he had written, 'They are in the main a brave and high-spirited people, actuated by feelings entitled to our respect. However, I am determined that the stain cast on our arms must be quickly effaced and the rebellion put down . . .'

Simon turned back to the subaltern. 'How are things in the Transvaal?'

The young man made a face. 'Bloody awful. Our troops there are still holed up in the garrison towns and, by the look of it, terrified to come out. All formal government is suspended. You know, Fonthill, that's why the old man has to go. He knows he hasn't got much of a column. The regulars are tired after the Zulu and Sekukuni campaigns and their uniforms are threadbare. But he can't stand by and wait until he gets reinforcements because he will be criticised back home and he is worried that the Free Staters might come in.'

'What about reinforcements?'

'Should be landing at the Cape about now. I'm not privy to the strength but I gather that they are from India and Afghanistan.' The young man gave a rueful smile. 'Shame he couldn't wait for them. But he couldn't, you see.'

'Yes. I know. Thanks for the background. I should be able to catch up with the column tomorrow.'

'Yes, I'm following soon. Get up there as soon as you can. Sir George hasn't got any scouts who he feels he can really rely on.'

Simon, Jenkins and Hardy were up, saddled and mounted before dawn the next day. Once again Simon had given the American the chance of slipping away – it was not, after all, his war. But Hardy shook his head. 'No, sonny,' he said. 'This chile has quite enjoyed ridin' with you fellers and ah still ain't forgiven them Boers fer shuttin' me up in a waggon. P'raps the general could do with another scout.'

Simon grinned at the prospect of this buckskinned figure, with his wide Stetson and pearl-handled Colts, riding scout for the gentle-voiced Colley, a conservative general if ever there was one. But if Hardy could scout as well as he could shoot – and it seemed that Custer had trusted him – then all would be well. And he enlivened the scene anyway.

The weather was foul, with driving rain suddenly springing up from behind the mountains to the north and equally quickly dying away again, leaving inches of water and red mud everywhere. It was not difficult to follow the column, for the road north was now heavily rutted and the grass completely beaten down for yards either side of the track. The three men could see where the sodden clay had been scoured out as carts and guns had had to be manhandled into the drifts and up out of them again. It was heavy going, and the rain was compounded by the sweltering heat and humidity, but Simon pressed on for he was anxious to relieve Colley of the threat – or at least the immediate threat – of the Free State Boers joining in with the men of the Transvaal.

It was dusk and, inevitably, raining again when the three finally caught up with the column just as it was outspanning at the place the general had decided to make his headquarters for the final invasion of the Transvaal. Mount Prospect was more a hill than a mountain, but it was high enough and flat enough to allow the column to camp there securely and to have some sort of view through the trees of the surrounding countryside and the road north. With the purple clouds hanging low over the tent tops, that view provided a grim prospect. The way for the advance could be seen to climb steadily towards the distant ridge of Laing's Nek, which lay in the centre of a rough crescent of stony black hills, the ends of the semicircle pointing to the south and Newcastle. To the left, looming over the road, was the strange, flat-topped cone of Mount Majuba, meaning 'dove' in Zulu and named allegedly by the great Zulu chief Shaka after the doves he found there.

167

Colley was busy laagering his wagons – he was the kind of general who attended to detail – but Simon sought him out and delivered his letter from President Brand.

'Good man, Fonthill,' said Colley, shaking the rain from his beard. 'Here, let's get out of this d-d-damned rain.'

Together they climbed into a waggon, where Colley's ADC lit a lantern and the general slit open the envelope and read its contents, squinting through his spectacles.

He put down the two sheets of paper and took off his glasses. 'You know the contents?'

'Roughly, sir, yes. President Brand told me.'

'Well, this is a b-b-blessed relief. It means that my left flank is more or less secure anyway, and as I have no intention of murdering civilians or anything of that kind, it should stay that way. Now, my boy, did you have t-t-time enough at Bloemfontein to pick up the attitude of the Boers there, or any other background?'

Simon wrinkled his nose. 'Not quite, sir. I only had four days. But I must say that the president seemed a straight sort of chap. I should think you could rely on his word. There is one other thing, though . . .'

'Yes.' Colley spoke eagerly and leaned forward. Simon realised how vulnerable the general must feel, eight thousand miles from his superiors, cut off from his main troops in the north and with little intelligence to inform his actions.

'You were right when you said that there could be Germans talking to Brand in his capital.'

'Ah.'

'Yes. There seems quite a strong sort of permanent delegation at Bloemfontein anyway, in the Prussian Embassy. But while I was there there was also a Baron von Bethman. I believe that he represents Krupps, the big German armament manufacturers at Essen, and that he had arrived in the Free State only a little time before me from Heidelberg in the Transvaal.'

'Ah, the new so-called Boer capital.'

'Precisely. From one or two hints that I picked up, it seemed as though he had done very satisfactory business in Heidelberg but less so in Bloemfontein. In other words, he is supplying weapons to the Transvaal but not to the Free State.'

'Damn.' Colley pulled at his beard. 'Not good news, not g-g-good news at all.' He spoke now as though half to himself. 'We know that the Boers can shoot, but they can't if they haven't got ammunition – and without an effective arms manufacturing capacity of their own, they could soon run out. B-b-but not if the Germans are supplying them. All the more reason for me to invade as soon as possible. Now, I am sorry to ask you this, after your long ride from the Free State and then straight up here, but I want you to g-g-get out tomorrow up to the Nek and scout the enemy's position. Can you do that?'

'Of course, sir. Do you have any information at all about their disposition?'

'Not a sausage.' The soft eyes twinkled for a moment. 'Shows how strong we are in the scouting department, my boy – and how much we need you. Trouble is, you see, I've no decent cavalry, let alone scouts. No. From what you told me earlier, it seems that it will be the Nek where the Boers will stand and fight. If I can clear them out of there – and I am sure I can, cavalry or no cavalry – then I am through into the Transvaal. So get up there and nose about. Give me some idea of where they are and how many. Do you still have your Welshman with you?'

Simon took the opportunity to confirm not only Jenkins's worth but also to request that Hardy be put on the payroll too.

'A scout for Custer, you say?' The soft smile came back. 'Goodness, I hope he doesn't lead me into the same mess that he took that gallant soldier into. But of course we need every man who can ride well and analyse what he sees. Count him in and on the payroll – but only as a private, I fear. I'll scribble an order.'

'Thank you, sir. We will leave at daybreak.'

Simon found that his partners had set up their three tiny bivouac tents under a large cypress tree out of the rain and he informed them of the general's orders.

'You're on the payroll now, Al,' he told the Texan. 'Scout first class, seconded from the US 7th Cavalry – or something like that.'

'Don't need the money, Simon.'

'Ooh, good,' grinned Jenkins. 'I'll 'ave it then. Better still, you keep it and I'll take if off you at poker, see.' The grin disappeared and was replaced by a frown. 'Except that I never win, do I? Ah well . . .'

The rain had stopped as the three scouts set off before daybreak and a glow behind the hills to the east bespoke a fine day. Simon cursed. As he remembered the terrain, there was not much cover leading up to the Nek, and rain would, at least, have kept the Boers' heads down for a while. They would have to approach the ridge with great care.

The heights which barred the way to the Transvaal looked menacing as the three men neared them, the sunlight slipping like rapier thrusts through the scudding clouds to illuminate parts of the swelling green and brown hills ahead. No trees were evident, but little lines of brushwood marked the lines of ravines that streaked the southern slopes facing them.

On their way south from the Transvaal a few weeks before, Simon had not studied the terrain closely, making only a few notes of the main geographical features and so confirming that crossing the Nek would be the general's only viable route to the rebel state in the north. Now, however, he could see more clearly the semicircular nature of the ridge ahead, with its two horns running southwards, overlooking a plateau which in turn formed a kind of amphitheatre through which wound the road to the north. The lowest part of the ridge lay directly ahead. It was a broad saddle rising some five hundred feet from the plain – Laing's Nek, so named after a farmer whose house, or its remains, could be seen standing below the crest. The road ran over the saddle and was completely dominated by the heights on either side.

About a mile from the Nek, as the soggy track began to climb more steeply, Simon called a halt and pointed up ahead. Immediately facing them, the road curled away to the right and then back again to the left, bending out of sight as it cut between the hills on either side. To the left, Majuba curled up some 1,250 feet directly from the Nek, forming the left horn. The right horn was formed by lower, more undulating hills but Simon recalled that behind them, to the east, lay the steep gorge of the Buffalo river.

'By now,' he said, 'I should think that the Boers will be installed – and probably dug in – on either side of the road, looking down on it. The general can't get round to the left there because of the mountain, so he will probably have to attack up the Nek on the right, where it is less steep, though,' he mused, hand partly covering his mouth, 'still bloody difficult.

'I know that there is no hope of outflanking the Boer positions, what with the mountain on the left and the gorge to the right. So our job is to find out exactly where the enemy is entrenched, and get some idea of their strength and the best approach for the attack. Understood?'

'Oh, is that all?' muttered Jenkins, his eyes wide. ' 'Ow are we goin' to find all that out – just stroll up and ask 'em?'

'Something like that. Now, Al,' Simon turned to the American, 'you take the western side. Make sure that there really is no way through there and get some idea of the Boer strength.'

For the first time since their meeting, the tall American looked disconcerted. 'Umm,' he pondered, looking ahead. 'Western side. Now exactly which way would that be, sonny?' He grinned apologetically. 'Ah find this southern hemisphere stuff just a tad confusin', yah know.'

'What?' Simon was equally disconcerted. 'But the points of the compass remain the same whether we're in the northern or southern hemisphere. Surely you know that?'

'Ah, sure. So . . .' the Texan paused for a moment, looking ahead, 'so you want me to go that side of the road an' scout a bit, huh?' And he pointed to the right.

'No. The other side. To the left. The mountain side.' Simon sighed. 'Look. You will need to be careful, because the Boers will be watching the road. So, a few hundred yards ahead, cut off left and start to climb. After a while I guess you will have to leave Custer and scramble up the mountain so that you can see where the road climbs the Nek. If you get high enough, you should be able to look down on the Boer positions if, as I suspect, they have dug in on that side of the road, as well as the eastern side. Try and get some idea of how many there might be and what their field of fire is. Is that understood?'

171

'Sure is, sonny. Leave it to me.'

'Al . . .'

'Yup?'

'When you start your scrambling, it would be as well to remove your white hat. You will be seen for miles if you don't.'

'Gosh, yes. Sure 'nuff.'

'Good. We'll meet back here in five hours. Don't get into a fight, just run if you have to.' Simon looked at Al keenly. 'Will you be able to find your way back? Would you like to borrow my compass?'

'Gee, no. Ah'll just take mah position from the sun if ah have to.'

'Right. Off you go then. Jenkins and I will scout this side of the road. If you hear shots, just get out of here. We shall be running too.'

The American nodded to Simon and then to Jenkins, kicked in his heels and rode away, looking every inch a horseman and scout as he gently rose to the rhythm of Custer's canter.

Simon's eyes narrowed as he watched him go. 'How can a scout not know the difference between east and west?' he murmured.

Jenkins shrugged his shoulders. 'Dunno. But as you well know, bach sir, I can't tell the damned difference either.'

'Yes, but you weren't a scout for Custer. Ah well, come on. Let's try and climb as high as we can before we dismount.'

The terrain was not quite so unhelpful to scouting as it appeared at first. Despite the absence of trees, the rain had stimulated grass to grow and the slopes leading up to the Nek were fissured by ravines. After about a quarter of a mile they found a gully where they were able to tether their horses out of sight of all but the closest observation. Then they began their final advance on foot, climbing gently the while and always keeping a careful lookout towards the top of the low ridge.

Even so, they were almost surprised by a pair of Boer horsemen who materialised from a line of brushwood to their right and above them. Simon and Jenkins flattened themselves in a declivity in the ground as the Boers walked their horses and paused about fifty yards above them. In that still morning it was possible to hear every word they said – but not possible to comprehend it, for they spoke in Taal. Nevertheless, looking up through the tall tangle of grass, Simon could see that the Boers were looking through field glasses south, towards Mount Pleasant. A third horseman appeared and produced an old-fashioned telescope that he too levelled towards the south.

All three were dressed almost identically: heavy serge jackets from under which, despite the heat, peeped waistcoats; dirty corduroy trousers; scuffed boots; and wide-brimmed, high-crowned felt hats. They carried rifles and each wore a bandolier of cartridges across his breast. Each face was heavily bearded but it was the third man who attracted Simon's attention. His lanky black hair was balanced by a severe spade beard and his nose was long and splayed at the nostrils. He exuded an air of authority, confirmed when one of the others addressed him as 'Commandant General'. The man replied monosyllabically, not taking his eyes from his glasses. They spoke further, and Blackbeard was addressed by the second man as 'Commandant Joubert'. From the tone, it was obvious that the man was held in some respect. They all stayed for perhaps three minutes before Joubert pulled on his reins and rode away, leading the others back up to the low ridge.

'Phew!' Jenkins wiped his brow. 'They were lookin' right over us. Thank God they didn't look down, eh?'

'Yes.' Simon was frowning, trying to recall the name he had heard. 'Joubert,' he mused. 'Commandant General Joubert. Where have I heard that name before. Joubert . . . Yes. I've got it!' He turned to Jenkins. 'He's Piet Joubert, one of the triumvirate who are leading the new republic. Gosh. If they have sent one of the top three men down here they must mean business. He will have a reasonable force at his command. Come on, let's see if we can get some idea of the size of it.'

'Oh blimey.' Jenkins scrambled up after him, shaking his head and muttering. ' 'Ere we go again, back puttin' our 'eads into the bleedin' lion's mouth.'

Crouching low and holding their rifles at the trail, the two part crawled, part walked up to their right, towards the top of the first of what appeared to be two separate low hills which merged into the

Nek and commanded the road below. Some hundred feet from the rounded summit, Jenkins pulled at Simon's shirtsleeve.

'Enemy's just up there,' he whispered. 'See 'is 'at, look.'

Squinting upwards through the scrub, Simon concentrated and eventually saw the outline of a slouch hat. Then, to the left, another and another. 'Trenches,' he hissed. 'They're dug in all along the top, blast it. That's as far as we can go.'

Beckoning Jenkins to follow, Simon slithered down the side of the hill and then turned and began crawling along its gentle face, parallel with the road and towards the Nek.

'Where are we goin' then?' hissed Jenkins.

Simon paused and nodded towards where the Nek rose, carrying the road with it. He gestured to the second hill ahead and to the right of them. It was marginally higher than the first. 'I want to see if Joubert has dug in along the top there as well,' he whispered. 'If he hasn't, then Colley might be able to take these first entrenchments. But if the Boers have further trenches on this second hill, then they have a considerable force here and Colley will have a hell of a problem on his hands to break through. It will mean that the Nek is defended in depth and I'm not sure that the general can take it with the force he has. Come on and keep your head down.'

The two continued their cautious progress, and eventually Simon found a lone cedar tree, some sixty feet high.

'Right,' he said. 'You stay here. There looks enough cover for me to climb up here and get some sort of view ahead. Here. Give me a bunk-up.'

Jenkins made a back, and, balancing on it, Simon was just able to grasp a sturdy branch and haul himself up. As the Welshman watched anxiously, he made his way about two thirds up the height of the tree, where he produced his telescope and levelled it. After five minutes, he lowered himself down again.

'Now don't tell me we've got to keep goin' up to that Nek place,' Jenkins implored.

Simon lay down on the grass for a moment to get his breath back and made a negative face. 'No,' he said. 'I've seen enough. There are lines of trenches all along up there, not only facing down to the road but also stretching along the top, commanding the southern approaches. They are well dug in and I could see the tops of a hell of a lot of tents behind. Joubert has a small army here. Time to go back and pick up Al.'

Now steering well away from the fortified tops of the hills, the two made their way back parallel to the road and eventually found their horses. Mounting, they rode back to the rendezvous point. There was no sign of Al.

Simon consulted his timepiece. 'We've been away about four hours,' he said. 'I said five, so we can give him about an hour and a half.'

Jenkins wrinkled his face in disagreement. 'Oh no, bach sir,' he said. 'Give 'im a couple of hours. Don't forget, 'e gets confused in the southern hemisphere, like.'

'Confused my foot.' Simon glowered. 'A scout is supposed to be able to find his way around, whatever the terrain or the bloody hemisphere. But all right. Two hours it is. Then we must go or we shall be caught after dark.'

They settled down to wait, but not for long. After only about thirty-five minutes the tall Texan came trotting down the trail, his white Stetson hanging down his neck at the back by its cord and Custer prancing as though he was performing before royalty.

'Howdy,' he acknowledged them, with a shy grin.

'What luck, A1?' enquired Simon.

'Bin up and down that danged mountain, Simon, an' ah don't recommend doin' that in mah fine Texas boots, ah'll tell yah.'

'No, I can quite imagine. But what about the Boers? Are they on that side of the road?'

'Sure 'nuff. The mountain rises a bit steep there, straight up, in fact. But these fellers are dug in, facin' this way, in a single line of trenches. Ground's hard there, so they're more like scooped-out lines, an' not offerin' much cover, ah'd say. But they've heaped up rocks and they're there all right. An' they can shoot down on anyone comin' up at 'em or along the road.'

'How many?'

'Couldn't exactly count 'em, but maybe three hundred or so. It's steep there an' it would be danged difficult, ah'd say, to go straight up at 'em. Even General Custer wouldn't do it.'

'Hmm. No way through there for the main force, then. Good work, Al. Let's get back and report.'

Once again the heavens opened as they rode back to Mount Prospect and they were drenched and bedraggled by the time they reached the British lines. Jenkins and Hardy went to their tents to dry out but Simon reported directly to Colley.

'My dear fellow, you're soaked,' said the general. 'Here, dry yourself off,' and he threw a towel to Simon.

'Thank you, sir.' As he rubbed his hair, Simon reflected again how easy it was to see why Colley's men loved him.

'Right,' said the general. 'Have some coffee and then tell me all you know. I am anxious to get m-m-moving as soon as this weather clears. Tomorrow, if possible.'

Simon accepted the cup gratefully. 'Well, Sir George, it's your decision, of course. But you may feel that that would be inadvisable. Let me sketch the Boers' position for you, as best as the three of us could define it.'

Colley frowned at Simon's negative tone, but he threw him a pencil and a sheet of paper and Simon drew a rough map. 'You will see, then, that the Boers are entrenched on both sides of the road. So you will be unable to push through and over the Nek without clearing the enemy positions that command the road. On the left here, on the lower slopes of Majuba, there are fewer of them – Hardy, our American, reckons maybe about three hundred or so. They are not particularly well entrenched because they are on stony ground, but they have thrown up a line of rocks – I think they call them *sangers* in Afrikaans – and the slope is so bad that you would have difficulty getting through up there anyway, even without being under heavy fire from above.'

'Artillery should shift them.'

'I doubt it, sir. As I say, you couldn't take the whole column up and over that way, waggons and all, anyway, and you would be under fire from the Boer positions on the other side of the road as well as from the trenches above.'

176

He pointed with his pencil at the first hill. 'This is slightly the lower of the two on the eastern side of the road, but it is still a stiffish climb and the enemy is well entrenched along the top, looking down at the road. I should think that it could be vulnerable – I couldn't get close enough to see how many men are dug in there – but if you take this hill, then you still have to advance up this slope to the next one, where there are even more of the Boers entrenched and they would have a clear field of fire on anyone advancing on them.'

Colley examined the drawing and stroked his beard. Then he looked up and smiled at Simon. 'I know that you have a high opinion of Boer marksmanship, Fonthill, but I have to repeat that these people are not trained soldiers. I cannot escape the feeling that, honest patriots as they are, they will break and run when they are put under a bombardment and face a disciplined charge by regular soldiers. Our chaps with bayonets should clear them.

Simon forced a return smile. 'Well, sir, as I say, it is your decision, but there are another couple of factors you should take account of.'

'Very well.'

'Firstly, sir, I believe that the Boers are under the personal command of Commandant General Piet Joubert, one of the triumvirate who have been elected to run the new Transvaal republic. I have no idea how good a soldier he is, but if Heidelberg has sent one of the top men down here to fight you, they really must mean business. It could even be that, having seen you off, so to speak, Joubert will lead his force down to invade Natal.'

Colley frowned in disagreement. 'Doubt it. I very much doubt it. As I've said before, the Boers are not invaders. Anyway, would they have enough men?'

'This is the second point. I climbed a tree to get a better view of the positions on the second hill. Beyond the trenches I could see line after line of tents, obviously stretching back behind the hill. I should say that Joubert has probably got as many as two thousand burghers up there, so that he outnumbers you.'

'Hmm.' Silence fell inside the tent. The two ADCs standing

deferentially behind the general – Simon recognised young Elwes – fidgeted. Simon took a deep breath and made one last attempt to sway the general.

'Sir,' he said, 'I promise you that the Boers have shrewdly placed themselves in a very sound defensive position. Even though they are not regular soldiers, somebody in command there – presumably Joubert – knows what he is doing. In addition, I believe that they outnumber you. Surely it would be better to wait until your reinforcements now at the Cape are able to get up here? Then you could attack with far more confidence.'

Colley gave his sad smile. 'My dear Fonthill, I do not lack confidence. I believe that, outnumbered or not, British soldiers can defeat an army of farmers, good shots though they may be.'

A murmur of 'Hear, hear' came from the ADCs at the rear.

'In any case,' the general continued, 'I don't really have a choice, you see. If I don't advance into the Transvaal soon, I believe that our besieged garrisons in places like Potchefstroom will have to surrender.'

He put a kindly hand on Simon's shoulder. 'I appreciate your advice and your good scouting work. In an ideal world perhaps one should wait. But I have often said that you may class most men, soldiers especially, as those who see the difficulty of a thing and why it cannot be done, and those who see the way of overcoming difficulties and doing it – and I have always aimed at belonging to the latter class. Now do go and get some rest. I intend to move up to attack in the morning, unless this damned rain makes it completely impossible. I would like you and your two men to attach yourselves to my headquarters staff, so report to me soon after dawn.'

'Very good, sir.' Simon nodded to the ADCs and stooped out of the tent. He found that Jenkins and Hardy had pitched their three small tents to form a semicircle and suspended a tarpaulin over their openings, under which they had somehow managed to light a fire. The rain had eased somewhat but a thick mist had descended.

'So,' said Jenkins. 'Attack at dawn, is it?'

'Something like that.'

'Well I'll be danged,' murmured Hardy. 'Could just be another

Little Bighorn. Even ah can see that them fellers are in a well-defended position.'

'I agree. I tried to argue, but the general feels he can show the Boers the bayonet and make them run. He could be right, but it could also be nasty. We'll have to see.'

Chapter 9

The three rose well before dawn to find that the rain had completely lifted. The camp was abustle. Tents were being struck, fires were being doused and it was clear that the column was going to advance. Simon noticed that the red-coated infantrymen had dyed their once white helmets and cross belts brown with cow dung and coffee grounds but the officers stood out conspicuously with their brightly polished brasses and gleaming sword scabbards. Simon shook his head. They were obvious targets for the Boer marksmen.

The three scouts joined Colley's small headquarters staff, which was busy allocating about two hundred men and two Gatlings to stay and guard the camp and baggage. The rest moved forward, the men singing the latest song from back home, 'Grandfather's Clock', accompanied by a score of penny whistles. Simon made a quick estimate of the force: there were just under nine hundred infantrymen and about a hundred and eighty mounted soldiers, a great many of whom were sitting their horses with undoubted trepidation. Simon felt a pang of sympathy for them. Accompanying the troops were six cannon and three rocket tubes, but the core of the force consisted of five companies of the 58th Regiment of Foot and an equal number of the 3/60th Rifles, all wearing sun-bleached and patched uniforms of thick serge and carrying full packs in the sun. They looked less than smart and, after their long and hard march from the south, gave out an air of resigned fatigue. Simon remembered that these were the men who had been left behind at the end of the Zulu and Sekukuni campaigns to be garrison troops in South Africa, after their comrades had returned home. They had not been expected to go into action.

The men sweated copiously in their broadcloth and under their

181

packs but they were glad to be marching in sunlight instead of rain, and despite its fatigue the column made good time. It was not long before Colley was able to draw up his force across a grassy plateau and a slight ridge under and about two thousand yards from the Boer positions. The general rode forward and, Simon's sketch in one hand, spent some time scanning the looming hills with his binoculars. Then he returned and summoned his senior officers. Simon was invited to join the circle.

Colley spoke quietly and exuded an air of complete confidence. The aim, he explained, was to clear the Boers from the two main hills on the right side of the road, since the entrenchments on the slopes of Majuba Hill on the left could only be reached by a precipitous climb. The Boers were spread over a wide area and therefore he intended to mask his intentions – and keep the enemy widely deployed until the last minute – by advancing up the road towards the Nek and then suddenly attacking the second and highest hill, immediately overlooking the Nek, which he considered to be the key position in the Boer defences. Not only did it command the main advance along the road from the south and, to a large extent, the first hill, but it also had a field of fire beyond Majuba to the north and on to the Boers in the entrenchments on the mountain's slopes.

At this, Simon drew in his breath. Surely it would be better to clear the first and easiest of the hilltop positions, even if it did allow the enemy to deploy? Once the first hill was taken there was a gentler slope up which to attack the main entrenchments on the second, and, of course, there would be no flanking fire to contend with from the men on that first hill. But the general was continuing.

'Before we make the attack,' he said, 'the artillery and rockets will direct their fire on the Boer emplacements on the Nek and the main hill. We will allow about fifteen minutes for the bombardment before attacking.' He smiled. 'We may well find that the cannonade will do the trick for us. I doubt very much whether the Boers are accustomed to artillery fire. They could well break and run after a few minutes' pounding.'

The officers allowed themselves a few polite chuckles.

'Now, Deane.' The general turned to the colonel who was in

nominal command of the Natal Field Force. 'You will lead the 58th in the attack on the main hill.'

'Honoured, sir,' said Deane.

'You will be covered, of course, by continued artillery fire until you reach the summit. You will also be protected from flanking fire from the first hill by the mounted squadron at your rear, who, at the first sign of concentrated fire on you, will attack the first hill and clear it. Right, Brownlow?'

'Delighted, sir,' acknowledged the young major of the King's Dragoon Guards in charge of the mounted infantry.

'I shall push the rockets up as far towards the Nek as I can. I can see a wall from some old farm there that will give them good protection and they should be able to direct fire on the Boers from a different angle. A company of the Rifles and the Naval Brigade will go with them. The rest of the Rifles and the Mounted Police will stay in reserve with me. Understood?'

There was a murmur of acquiescence and, indeed, approval from the circle of officers and the meeting broke up. Colley beckoned Simon towards him.

'Stay with me until we have launched the attack,' he said, 'just in case I need you. Then you may care to join the fun with the 58th when they advance. I am allowing the staff to go forward.'

'Thank you, sir.' Simon swallowed. He was not too sure that the opportunity of climbing that hillside into a wall of Boer fire was something for which to thank anyone. But, of course, there was no choice. 'We will certainly do so.'

The general laid his hand on Simon's arm and a twinkle came into his eye. 'One thing, though, my boy,' he said. 'Tell that Texan chap to take his white hat off. When they see it, the Boers might think I'm surrendering.'

'Very good, sir. We'll bury it if necessary.'

From the top of the ridge, Simon and his companions watched as the Natal Field Force made its advance. First the artillery deployed down the ridge and then opened fire. As it did so, the rockets, with their protective force of rifles and Mounted Police, galloped up the road and quickly set up behind the distant wall. The hiss and sparks of the rockets were soon joining in with the brutal cacophony of the cannon, and fragments of rock could be seen splintering up from the Nek directly ahead and on the crest of the main hill. Under cover of the bombardment, the main force – no singing now and no penny whistles in evidence – marched up the gently rising road into the valley formed by the mountain on the left and the low hills on the right.

'A fine sight, eh, gentlemen?' murmured Colley, his field binoculars scanning the tops of the two hills.

There was a low mumble of agreement from the ADCs and runners, but Simon remained silent. His own telescope was focused on the hill crests. From the position on the ridge, it should have been possible to see some signs, at least, of the evacuation of the Boer trenches if the artillery fire was having its expected effect. But there was no movement at all.

'It looks to me, sir,' he said, 'as if the Boers are not being affected by the bombardment. I think that they are staying in their trenches and keeping their heads down.'

'Humph.' Then, 'Ah. Now we should see some results. Deane has let his men off their straps and up the hill.'

It was true. The infantrymen of the 58th had turned to their right and were beginning the ascent of the main hill.

'But they're in close order!' Simon could not but expostulate as he saw the redcoats begin their climb in a tightly packed column of companies, four abreast. They would present a solid target block to the men in the trenches once they reached the summit.

'Yes. Well. The shells will keep the Boers' heads down and then Deane will be upon 'em before they can level their rifles.' But Colley did not sound completely convinced.

In fact, there was no fire on the climbing men from the crest above them, only desultory sniping from Boer skirmishers on the slopes of the first hill, firing at their flank. At a range of about nine hundred yards it was largely ineffective, but its effect on Brownlow was immediate. The men of the 58th had hardly begun their scramble upwards before he pulled his first troop to the right, and without, it seemed, pausing to find the best route to the top, set it and the second

184

troop behind him to gallop straight up the hill by the steepest gradient.

'By jove, that's a bit premature,' murmured Colley, 'and they're going up the hardest way.'

'Permission to join the 58th, sir?' The request came from Lieutenant Elwes, his voice sounding high-pitched against the crack of the cannon.

'What? Oh, yes. Off you go. And you too, Fonthill, with your chaps. Good luck and good hunting. Runners, stay with me.'

With Elwes and three other members of Colley's staff, Simon, Jenkins and Hardy galloped down the ridge and advanced along the road. Pulling his horse back to a canter, Simon watched the development of the attack up the hill on his right. Despite the gradient, Brownlow and his first troop now seemed to be on the crest of the hill, although it was clear that their horses were blown and their swaying, inexperienced riders, swords in hand, had been able to do very little to guide them up the steep climb. Once on the flat summit, however, the folly of setting cavalry – and untrained cavalry at that – to attack well-entrenched riflemen became apparent. Simon pulled his horse to a halt and focused his telescope. He sucked in his breath with a hiss as he heard, even above the cannonade, the sharp rattle of musketry and then saw the leading file of horsemen go down under that first volley. In a second, the hilltop was a mêlée of prancing riderless horses as a second volley followed the first. Then he saw the second troop wheel round and turn back well below the summit and, in ragged disorder, plunge down the hill the way it had come, white-faced riders desperately trying to retain their seats as their mounts hurtled down. Within minutes, the Mounted Squadron's attack on the first hill had disintegrated into a rout and the 58th's right flank had become exposed.

'Bloody 'ell!' Jenkins and Hardy had appeared at Simon's side. 'They were bloody fools, look you, to go up that way in the first place. They stood no chance. No chance at all.'

As if to emphasise Jenkins's words, a whiff of white gun smoke floated down from the crest and, once again, the smell of cordite – the acrid perfume of battle – touched their nostrils. Simon gulped.

'Come on,' he said. 'We'd better go and catch up the others. The 58th are going to need all the help they can get now.'

The redcoats were still under no direct fire as they slipped and slithered in the wet grass that covered the bottom of the slope of the second hill, for the artillery continued to lay down its curtain of shot along the ridge of the hill and the Nek itself. And indeed, the slope was dead ground. As the three scouts and the others dismounted and tethered their horses to a scrubby bush, however, Simon could see that the Boers on the first hill, having seen off the pathetic charge of Brownlow's cavalry, were already slipping down from their crest to spread along the upper slopes, the better to direct fire on the 58th.

The gradient that the infantry were climbing was about one in fifteen – not as bad as that tackled so peremptorily by Brownlow – but looking up, Simon was amazed to see that all the officers of the 58th remained mounted, their horses somehow climbing up in a sequence of leaps and bounds and the officers leaning forward, their backs splendidly hollowed in parade-ground fashion, urging their beasts on as though in some three-day event in the Home Counties.

Simon began a mad scramble to reach Colonel Deane, who was in the lead and was barking at his men to retain their dressing as they climbed. Panting after his exertion, Simon eventually caught up with him and pointed to the right and to the rear, where dun-coloured figures could be seen slipping down from the summit of the first hill.

'Colonel,' he gasped, 'the cavalry attack on that hill has completely failed. This has freed the Boers up there to take up positions to fire on you. You will need to detach at least a platoon to face them and keep their heads down.'

'What? Ah, you're the scout feller. Right. Thank you. I've got it. Major Essex, send out a platoon to stop those snipers from getting near us. Now come on, men. Onwards and upwards. Keep your lines now. Keep your bearing.'

Simon sank down on to the wet grass and shook his head. As he did so, the labouring infantrymen struggled around him, their red faces exuding perspiration as they dug the butts of their rifles into the ground to help their climb. He noticed sadly that some of them had noses redder than their faded coats, still peeling from the hot sun that had interspersed the rain bursts on their long treks up from Cape Town and Durban. Brave men, climbing upwards in close-order formation, keeping their line and keeping their bearing.

Jenkins and Hardy joined him as the sudden cessation of the artillery cannonade showed that the first line of troops were nearing the summit. Simon noted with relief that the Texan had left his white Stetson down below with his horse and his normally spotless buckskins were now soiled from the climb so that he merged more happily into the landscape. Even so, he attracted amused stares from the sweating soldiers as they stepped around the squatting trio.

One grinning Yorkshireman called out: 'Eeh, lad, we'm fightin' Bo-ars, not bloody Indians.'

Hardy was not fazed. He grinned and called back in impeccable moorland dialect: 'Reet, lad. Ah'll remember that.'

'Blimey, Al,' said Jenkins. 'That sounded real Yorkshire, like.'

The Texan looked embarrassed for a moment. 'Met a Yorkshireman on the boat comin' over,' he confided. 'Funny ol' talkin' they do.' Then he cocked a slightly anxious eyebrow towards the summit. 'Up to the top with the rest of 'em, Simon?' he asked.

'I'm afraid so, Al. I'm sorry. It's not your war.'

A slow smile spread across the American's face. 'Waal,' he drawled, 'ah guess it is now. Come on then. Let's git up there and go an' win it.'

The three got to their feet and easily overtook the labouring infantrymen ahead of them, so that they were just behind the first company of the 58th, who, led by Colonel Deane still on his splendid horse, were now cresting the brow of the hill. Among their number were two young subalterns, one carrying the regimental colours and the other with the Queen's colour. Just behind Simon and his companions, down the hill, a loud chattering revealed the presence of Lieutenant Elwes and his fellow Old Etonian, Lieutenant Monck.

Simon hauled himself over the brow of the hill to gaze on a strangely tranquil tableau as the leading companies of the 58th, still in close order, stood to regain their breath after the climb. The end of the bombardment had produced a surreal silence, broken only by the panting of the exhausted men and, overhead, the cry of a solitary reed cormorant which had risen from the river below. Ahead, Colonel Deane stood in his stirrups to get a better view of the Boer positions. It was as though the gods had cried 'Halt!' and the actors in the tragedy had been frozen in their positions for a few seconds, the better to appreciate what was to come.

A glacis-like slope led up to the trenches only a hundred and fifty yards away. The British, on completely open ground, were staring down the barrels of at least five hundred rifles and Simon could clearly see the beards on the faces of the riflemen as they squinted through the sights of their weapons.

Too late Deane realised the trap into which he had led his men. Turning in his saddle, his sword raised, he screamed, 'Open order. To the right and left. Fix bay—' But before he could complete the order, his body and that of his horse were riddled with bullets as the line of trenches belched fire and smoke. As Deane had turned, Simon had yelled, 'Down, for God's sake,' and pushed Jenkins and Hardy back over the edge of the ridge, falling to the earth himself as he heard the Boer signal to fire.

In fact, the men of the 58th, lined up ahead of him, acted as a protective screen as the Boer bullets cut through them, scything them to the ground like corn collapsing to the reapers. Lifting his head as the Boers reloaded and the gun smoke partially cleared, Simon saw that every one of the officers who had urged their horses over the brow of the hill and offered so enticing a target, with their glittering scabbards and pristine scarlet coats, had perished. Now their horses were plunging, wide-eyed, across the little plateau. Amazingly, some infantrymen had somehow survived that first searing volley and were kneeling in the open and attempting to exchange fire with the entrenched Boers. Rather more had managed to spread out across the plateau to find individual cover of sorts behind rocks and in shallow depressions, and they too were returning the Boers' fire. Some had even managed to approach as near as forty yards to the Boer trenches. For tired garrison troops, they were showing remarkable resilience and bravery.

Below him, Simon heard Elwes cry out, 'Come along, Monck. *Floreat Etona!* We must be in the front rank.' Before he could stop him, the young lieutenant had scrambled up over the edge, only immediately to topple backwards over it again with two black bullet holes in his forehead. Simon, his heart thumping, lay with his cheek pressed into the rough sand at the edge of the plateau as he heard bullets hiss across the grass and thud into the body of a young infantryman lying before him. Slowly he edged backwards and was able to slip down over the brow of the hill and join Jenkins and Hardy crouched on the slope. Below them, the rest of the 58th were still climbing.

'Bloody 'ell, bach sir,' muttered Jenkins, blowing out his cheeks. 'That was a bit 'ot. There's no way I'm goin' back up there, see.'

Simon nodded. He ran his tongue over parched lips and realised that he was trembling. He pointed to the right. 'Let's edge along there,' he said. He was aware that his voice sounded quite hoarse. 'There's a kind of rock formation over the top which should provide a bit of cover. We might be able to crawl up behind it and give some sort of covering fire to the poor bastards still caught on the top. Come on.'

The three scouts moved along the slope just below the edge. As they did so, they could hear the ping of bullets ricocheting off stone just above their heads and whining out across the valley. Below them, in the dead ground, the infantrymen had paused in their climb, bewildered and leaderless.

Simon halted at where he guessed the rock outcrop was positioned over the lip and cautiously raised his head. He had guessed correctly, and gesturing the others to follow, he scrambled over the edge. There was just room for them on a flat terrace behind the rocky knoll which projected forward on to the plateau. Pathetically, some of the 58th had charged the Boer lines and now lay before them, their bodies inert. Others had managed to find sufficient cover on the plateau to offer resistance and a lively musketry duel had ensued. Even so, it was a contest that could have only one ending, for the Boers – the better shots anyway – were firing from stable, well-protected positions in their trenches and the soldiers were unable to offer concentrated fire from their individual points of refuge.

To Simon's right, he could define four redcoats sprawled out making the most of a declivity in the ground and offering spirited fire. Further along, two more soldiers were shooting from behind another outcrop of rock. He turned to his companions.

'Somehow,' he said, 'we've got to set up sufficient covering fire to enable some of the fellows out on the plateau to crawl back over the edge.'

Jenkins sucked in his moustache. 'Only three of us, bach sir. I don't think we've got enough firepower.'

'I know we haven't, but we can try. It's the only way those chaps out there will get back. Let me see if I can get these others to help.'

He called out to the redcoats to his right. 'You men.' His voice retained the tone of command and they looked round in surprise. 'Cease firing. Tell those other two on your right as well. Then, when I give the order, fire on the trenches as fast as you can to give some of the others the chance to retire. Understood?'

'Er . . . very good, sir.'

Simon sucked in a deep breath. Then, at the top of his voice, he shouted: 'Men of the 58th out there. Retire when I give the order. We will mount covering fire.' He turned to his companions. 'Ready?'

Jenkins had laid a row of cartridges ready to slip into his Martini-Henry, and Al, his eyes wide, was snuggling the stock of his Winchester into his shoulder. They both gave him a quick nod.

Taking in another breath, Simon stood for a moment, revealing himself above the rock. 'Rapid fire,' he screamed, 'COMMENCE. Fifty-eighth, double back NOW.'

The resulting fusillade from the nine men was not the heaviest seen on the field of battle, but at least it was concentrated. Simon was aware that Hardy, in particular, was able to get off shot after shot in rapid sequence from his Winchester repeater, and a number of slouch hats above the Boer trenches slipped out of view and, for a brief moment, the enemy fire perceptibly slackened. As it did so, red-coated figures began doubling back and flinging themselves over the edge of the plateau.

But the covering fire offered by the nine rifles was too weak to give anything but the briefest respite, and within seconds the Boer firing recommenced with even more intensity. A dozen of the fleeing soldiers, those who had paused for a moment before running back, were caught, throwing up their rifles and collapsing as the Boer shots took them in the back.

At this point, however, Simon became aware of a third factor. From the edge of the hill the distinctive crack of Martini-Henry rifle fire began to grow louder, and as he looked, he saw that the second line of companies of the 58th were crawling on to the plateau and beginning to set up a disciplined fire. Scrambling back to the edge of the ridge and looking down, Simon saw that the remainder of the infantrymen were being ordered to climb the last few yards in open order and to spread around the perimeter.

A major from the staff had taken charge and he climbed up to Simon and extended his hand. 'Essex,' he said. 'I'm about the only senior man left.' He was still short of breath from his climb. 'Just caught up in time to take charge. Heard you shout and gathered what you were up to. Capital thing. I know you're a scout. Ex-army?'

Simon nodded. 'Fonthill. Late of the 24th Foot and of the Queen's Own Corps of Guides, India.'

'Ah, yes. Now I've placed you. I was at Isandlwana too. Good man. Now, we've got to get out of here. The Boers are far too well entrenched and there are too many of 'em to charge, and besides,' he shot a sad glance at the bodies around them and bit his grizzled moustache, 'these Dutchmen are damned good shots. We have enough rifles to keep the so and sos in their trenches for a bit, but once we start to withdraw, they'll be out of there, over here and shooting down at us before you can say God Save the Queen. Can you send one of your scouts down to the general and ask him to lay down an artillery barrage on the top here again as we retreat down this damned hill? Also get him to put forward some of the rifles of the 3/60th to stop the Boers coming at us from the left on the Nek.'

'Of course.' Simon thought quickly. Jenkins would never find the general. The little Welshman, brave as a lion and a superb shot and horseman, completely lacked a sense of direction. He would be as likely to wander into the Boer camp as find Colley down below. 'I'll send my American,' he said.

Hardy was briefed and, without a word, began loping down the

191

slope of the hillside like a Cheyenne warrior. Simon took the major's arm as he was about to move away. 'The artillery – what about the wounded lying up on the plateau?' he asked. 'And the poor devils who are out there still trying to shoot? They could be blown to pieces.'

Essex's face remained impassive, although his grey eyes flickered for a moment. 'Can't be helped, old boy,' he murmured. 'For the greater good and all that, don't you know. But I'm going to try and get some of 'em back now, if we can lay down enough rifle fire – as you tried to do a minute ago. Should stand a better chance now that the extra companies are up. We've got to retreat in good order.'

He slipped away and Simon and Jenkins exchanged half-smiles. 'Good order' was ever important to the British Army, but in this case it was vital to prevent a rout, a helter-skelter tumble down the hill with the Boers picking off the scramblers from the brow of the hill.

Somehow Essex had managed to get the remaining five companies of the 58th over the brow of the hill and, lying flat behind whatever cover they could find, directing continuous fire on the Boer trenches. The enemy were too well protected for the fire to cause many casualties, but it served to disrupt the Boers' aim for a while. Then a bugle sounded the retreat and those out on the plateau who could move ran like hares for the security of the lip. As before, some of them were caught as the riflemen in the trenches belatedly realised what was happening, but enough made the edge to cause Essex to order the withdrawal of his three companies on the right of his front. As they did so, and hearing the bugle call, a number of Boers rose from behind their cover to effect a pursuit, but the remaining two companies, firing in ordered volleys, sent them ducking down again behind their sangars.

Simon scrambled back to the edge of the ridge and looked down. Essex had stopped the five retreating companies about two hundred yards down the slope, so that they stood in open order, their rifles pointing upwards to the lip, waiting to cover the retreat of their brothers left behind.

'Time to go, 352,' said Simon. Together, the two slipped over the edge and stumbled down the hill to join the line of waiting riflemen. The bugle sounded again and the remaining two companies appeared over the brow and came running down the slope, through the lines, to form their own firing line further down the hill. As they did so, the crest became occupied by Boers, who were immediately sent diving back for cover as a volley from the first three companies crashed out. Then the exercise was repeated as the companies exchanged positions. The boom of cannon from down below and the scream of shells overhead showed that the bombardment had recommenced to cover the retreat. Hardy had got through.

It was a classical 'retreat in good order', with the artillery cannonade and the disciplined rifle fire preventing harassment and pursuit of the troops as they fell back. Simon and Jenkins, falling into line with the first three companies and firing and moving when they did, could not but feel stirred at the way it was managed. After the débâcle of Brownlow's charge and the suicidal attack on the trenches, it was a relief to witness these tired infantrymen – 'only garrison troops' – retreating with perfect discipline in the face of a determined and well-armed enemy.

As Essex had predicted, the Boers entrenched lower down on the Nek on the enemy's right had left their trenches and advanced in an attempt to harass the retreating 58th from the flank. But Colley had ordered forward strong detachments of the Rifles and the Naval Brigade from his reserve and they were driving the dun-coloured figures back up the slope.

At the bottom they met Al Hardy, his white Stetson now firmly back in place. He nodded to them. 'Looks as though we've got them bits o' flags back too,' he drawled, indicating the regimental colours and the Queen's standard, now in the care of a sergeant.

Jenkins grinned. 'Important that, Al,' he said. 'British Army never leaves its colours behind.'

'Nope. Ah guess so. Only the poor fellers who carry them in, eh?' It was true. There was no sign of the two subalterns who had taken the colours up the hill.

Simon and Jenkins slumped down on the grass at the bottom of the hill as the remainder of the 58th formed up and began marching up the road in perfect order, as though on parade, back to where they had originally formed up only a couple of hours ago. The midday sun beat down on them with little pity, and Simon wiped his brow.

'I wouldn't want to go through that again,' he said.

Hardy screwed up his eyes and looked up at the hill crest. 'Better 'n Little Bighorn anyways,' he murmured. 'At least your general got most of his men back agin. Custer never did.'

Simon addressed the ground. 'Maybe, but too many men were left up there.' He looked up. 'Come on. Better get our horses and see if the general has got anything for us to do on the retreat.'

They found Colley by the side of the road, standing quietly and watching the men of the 58th march past. His face was set in grim lines but he occasionally called out, 'Well done, men. I am proud of you. Well done.'

Simon felt sympathy well up within him. Colley had been defeated, there was no doubt about that, and news of defeat was not something that the British public back home was used to receiving from the borders of its empire. Now the British Army had suffered two setbacks within two years: firstly from spear-carrying Zulus at Isandlwana and now from these amateur soldiers from the farms of the Transvaal. It was true that this battle was no massacre, that Colley had been able to withdraw the majority of his troops safely and that he had probably been facing superior numbers. But he had been dealt a bloody nose and his invasion of the Transvaal would now probably have to await the arrival of reinforcements. Meanwhile, his garrisons in the north remained under siege, and, without a doubt, the press at home would be on his back.

'Anything we can do, sir?' enquired Simon.

'What?' Colley's eyes looked tired. 'Oh, Fonthill. Thank you. I hear you and your chaps behaved gallantly. I am falling back to Mount Prospect, of course. I would be delighted if the Boers would attack me there but I doubt very much if they would be so stupid.' He smiled. 'I am putting back a strong rearguard and I wouldn't think for a moment that the Boers would leave their emplacements and try and fight us in the open. But I would be grateful if you and your men would scout behind the rearguard and make sure that we are not

194

being followed in force. I don't have much cavalry left – at least not in good shape.'

'Very good, sir.'

'Oh, and Fonthill.'

'Sir?'

'You were quite right about the strength of the Boers.'

'I take no consolation from that, sir. But thank you.'

'Yes, well. We shall have another go at them, of course. And the next time I shall win.'

'Of course, sir.'

'Well done, Fonthill. Please convey my thanks to your other two scouts.'

'I will, sir. Thank you.'

The retreat back to Mount Pleasant was uneventful, if dreary. As predicted by Colley, the Boers did not venture down from their hilltop emplacements to force another encounter. In fact, as Simon, Jenkins and Hardy ranged behind the rearguard of the column, it seemed that the enemy had not even sent out scouts to observe the retreat.

That evening, behind hastily reinforced entrenchments at his encampment, Colley addressed his force. Typically, he personally accepted the blame for the repulse at Laing's Nek and totally exonerated the 58th for failing to clear the second hill. There was no mention of Brownlow's blunder at the first. He concluded: 'We certainly shall take possession of those hills eventually and I sincerely hope that all those men who have so nobly done their duty today will be with me then.'

'So,' asked Jenkins as they walked away from the gathering, 'what's 'e goin' to do now, then?'

'He won't want to have another go at Laing's Nek without new troops, particularly proper cavalry,' said Simon. 'I guess he will just wait here, making sure that the Boers don't even think about invading Natal, until he can get his reinforcements up from the south. By the look of it, he will certainly want a new intake of officers – including senior ones, at that.'

'Oh, bloody 'ell. Don't start volunteerin'.'

'No fear of that.'

Later, Simon walked over to Colley's headquarters. There, he learned that the day had cost the loss of seven officers and seventy-seven men killed, three officers and a hundred and ten men wounded, and two prisoners. The general's staff, whom he had allowed to join the assault, had been almost completely wiped out. But it was the 58th which had borne the brunt of the casualties: seventy-four killed and a hundred and one wounded, thirty-five per cent of its total strength. And the Boers? No one knew but they were likely to have sustained very few casualties.

That night, Simon lay in his bedroll, the smell of wood smoke from the dying fire outside pervading his bivouac tent. But it was cordite, the aroma of warfare, of death and of killing, which lingered in his nostrils. He had escaped death again and he wondered how much longer he could ride his luck. Inconsequentially, he thought of Anna, and then of Alice. Would he see either of them again? Almost certainly not. But what the hell did it matter? He rolled over and sought sleep.

Chapter 10

Despite the setback at Laing's Nek and the losses suffered by the 58th, the mood in the camp at Mount Prospect was not one of dejection. After his tragic charge up the first hill and the shameful rout of his second troop, Brownlow had refused to speak to his men, but Colley had not rebuked him. Word had filtered down that General Sir Evelyn Wood, a much-respected hero of the Zulu campaign, was on his way out to Cape Town to become the general's second in command. Wood was senior in both rank and experience as a fighting soldier to Sir George, but such was the popularity of Colley within the army that Wood, it was said, had unselfishly agreed to accept the post. The first of the reinforcements had already arrived in the south from India – the 2/60th Rifles, the 15th Hussars (*real* cavalry at last!) and an artillery battery – and the 83rd and 92nd regiments and a second Naval Brigade of fifty-eight men with two nine-pounder guns were expected any day. The feeling in the camp was that with these reinforcements and with his hard-won knowledge of the terrain, the kind but shrewd Colley would be able to sweep the Boers from the hills and march over the Nek into the Transvaal and then on to relieve his besieged garrisons in the state.

Simon knew that Colley had briefly considered falling back to Newcastle, some twenty miles to the south. But the general had resolved to deny the enemy the psychological victory of seeing him retreat, and except for sending back the Natal Mounted Police to bolster the garrison at Newcastle, he had maintained his force and his position at Mount Prospect. He was, however, concerned about his lines of communication to the south.

Two days after the battle, Simon was summoned to the general's tent. He was welcomed with a smile and gestured to sit on a camp stool.

'These farmers fought a p-p-pretty good defensive battle,' Colley began, 'but I wish that they'd be a bit more ambitious and attack me here. What do you think of the chances of that happening, Fonthill?'

Simon had noticed that, since the death of Deane and the loss of virtually all his senior staff officers, the general had taken to using his scout as a kind of sounding board, sometimes murmuring his thoughts aloud as though Simon was not there, at others, as today, asking his advice directly.

'Bit unlikely I should say, sir.' Simon's thoughts returned to President Brand's delicate balancing act. 'It's one thing to defend one's homeland but quite another to invade Natal. I think Joubert and his colleagues will always have one eye on world opinion and would be reluctant to lose approval by crossing the border aggressively. As you said yourself, the Boers are not really invaders. They will certainly have come to have a look at you here and will have seen how strong this position is. They won't want to risk losing what they won at the Nek.'

'Quite so. But they could well try and cut me off here by b-b-breaking my line of communications to Newcastle.'

'Indeed, sir. But I doubt whether they have either the will or sufficient numbers of men to hole you up here, particularly with reinforcements on the way.'

Colley ran his fingers through his beard. 'You've said that the Boers are pretty mobile, yes?'

Simon nodded. 'Very. I'd say that they are among the best light cavalry in the world.'

'Right. I want you and your two scouts to patrol the road back down to Newcastle. Native carriers are taking the mail back and forth, but until I am sure that the Boers have no intention of attacking me here, I d-d-don't want to detach forces to keep the road open, so you must be my eyes along that w-w-way. Don't engage, of course, but I want to know the instant the Boers come out in any sort of force. I don't want them to block the road to Newcastle. Understood?'

'Understood, sir.'

The twenty miles of well-beaten track that led back to Newcastle was reasonably open country, less mountainous than the terrain north of Mount Prospect, although the *kloofs* of the Drakensbergs skirted the track to the west. This time of the summer rainy season, however, found the road at its worst. The track itself was only a succession of shallow fords, mud holes and boulders of rock, and at roughly the halfway point between Prospect and Newcastle, it crossed the Ingogo river at a drift which was normally only about two feet deep at low water, but which could become a dangerous crossing after heavy rain.

Simon divided the road between the three of them into three beats of just over six miles, with each man exchanging his beat through the day to ensure that familiarity did not breed complacency. But it was boring work. There was no sign of Boer activity and the intermittent rain and the muddy, broken track made the riding difficult and uncomfortable.

It was with relief, then, that Simon, having ended the day at the end of the line at Newcastle and been last man back at Prospect, saw Jenkins waving an envelope at him as he rode in. A letter from home! Something to relieve the monotony of this tedious picket duty. He took the envelope with alacrity but his pleasure receded immediately when he recognised his mother's strong, sloping hand. He knew that, inevitably, the letter would contain an account of Alice's wedding to Covington and he certainly did not want to read about that.

He tucked the envelope under his waterproof and led his mare away to the lines, where rough canvas shelters had been erected, unsaddled her and rubbed her down. Later, as he sipped a mug of tea in his bivouac tent he sighed, frowned, slit open the envelope and began reading. He could not refrain from smiling, however, as he immediately encountered his mother's familiar direct style.

My dear Simon,

Why on earth don't you write more often!!?? Really, my boy, you are a great trial to us and you must try and be more, well, filial! You have been away from home now for so long. It really does seem as though you are deliberately chasing trouble – and yet you are no longer even in the army! One letter from you, my dear, in the last two months is simply not enough. I sometimes wonder if this strange manservant of yours is a bad influence on you. It does not do, Simon, to get too close to the working classes. It is healthy and RIGHT to maintain a distance between you and these sort of people, however worthy they may seem.

Now, as soon as you can, please do write and tell us what is happening to you. We informed General Wolseley, of course, that you were in Cairo and we received your scribbled one-page note from wherever it was in South Africa. But it told us very little. I expect to hear from you now by return.

Your father and I are very well, although it is proving a bad winter and the major spends far too much time with Llewellyn out in the cold, ditching and hedging on the edges of the estate. I worry constantly about him coming down with a chill, but he pays no heed to my chiding.

Alice had a simply splendid wedding three weeks ago in the village church at Chilwood. It was a very fine occasion with lots of people from the regiment attending, of course. Quite like old times for your father! Alice looked lovely in a cream confection – strange she did not wear white! – although she seemed perhaps just a little peaky, if you know what I mean. Probably the strain of it all . . .

Simon put down the letter and closed his eyes for a moment. Then, pinching the bridge of his nose with finger and thumb, he continued reading.

Covington looked very dashing in his colonel's uniform with all his medals. His face is terribly scarred, of course, and he wears a black patch to cover his sightless eye. They have fitted some hook contraption to cover the loss of his hand. It is quite amazing what they can do these days to alleviate the effect of these dreadful wounds. They are going to live on his estate in

Norfolk, *although I did hear that he is hoping to rejoin the army once Alice is settled in there. It seems most unlikely to me that he could play a full part in the regiment again, but I believe he has influence.*

Brigadier Griffith, of course, feels that his daughter has made a good match, although your father and I still believe that Covington is rather too old for Alice. There was a time, you know, when the major and I had hopes that you and she might . . . but that is all water under the bridge now, of course.

My dear, even if you don't write to us — and you jolly well must — you certainly must write to Alice. She asked after you of course — a trifle wistfully, I felt. Anyway, her address is as follows: Blackdown Hall, Frettenham, near Norwich, Norfolk.

Simon put down the letter again and stared at the canvas above his head. Then he carefully tore out the address and put it into his wallet. The letter concluded with a brief sentence from his father, warm but anodyne in content, and Simon tossed the pages on to the top of his haversack. But the reference to Alice's wedding brought back the agony of his love for her. It was a feeling which had been sublimated for a while by the potent physical presence of Anna Scheel, so perhaps this meant that he *could* find someone else one day. Even so, the thought of Alice in her cream wedding dress set his mind racing. Later, Jenkins and Hardy were amazed when he insisted on joining them in a hand of poker. He lost, of course, but he didn't seem to mind. Jenkins accused him of not concentrating.

The next day's patrolling was equally uneventful, although for once there was no sign of rain. The sky was clear and the sun seemed unusually large and hung like an incandescent fireball, causing wisps of steam to rise from the puddles and mini-drifts along the track. On his return, however, Simon found a summons from the general awaiting him.

'You have obviously seen no sign of Boer m-m-movement along the track to Newcastle?' he was asked as soon as he entered Colley's tent.

'No, sir.'

'Well, I feel in my bones that Johnny Boer will make an attempt now to cut off my lines of c-c-communication back to Natal, now that the weather has lifted for a moment. I therefore intend to make a reconnaissance in force along the road and am writing the orders now. But a mail detachment is leaving before dawn tomorrow and I want to t-t-test the water, so to speak. I want you and your two chaps to go with it. Any sign of interference, bring 'em back straight away. Right?'

'Right, sir.'

The mail detachment was small, two Zulu carriers mounted on ponies and carrying the post in large canvas bags slung around their necks, with an escort of three mounted infantrymen plus Simon, Jenkins and Hardy. They set off in the pre-dawn darkness, splashing through the puddles, Simon leading the way well ahead of the little party and Jenkins and Hardy – the better horsemen – well spaced out on the flanks. One of the mounted infantrymen hung back behind to give warning of a possible attack from that quarter.

The sun had risen by the time the little party reached the double drift just above the confluence of the Ingogo and Harte rivers, some five miles south of Mount Prospect. The water, ochre-coloured from particles of dolarite stone, had risen since Simon's last patrol and it reached the haunches of the scouts' horses as they waded in. The three had joined together to make the crossing, and Al nodded upstream to where a bird had noisily entered the water.

'That, mah friends, was the long-beaked darter,' he drawled. 'Only bird equipped to eat fish under water.'

Jenkins shook his head. 'Sometimes, Al,' he said, 'I think you make this stuff up.'

'Nossir. Just interested in flora an' fauna, is all.'

As the three urged their horses up a steepish rise to reach a stony plateau above the crossing, Al pointed to the right. 'See that water buck, with that white ring on its rump—'

He was interrupted by the *ping* of a bullet that seemed to whistle between the three of them. Three further shots rang out and Jenkins's horse reared and then toppled over, bleeding from the shoulder, throwing the Welshman clear. Within seconds, Hardy's

Colt had appeared in his hand and he fired twice at horsemen who now appeared over a low rise to their left. Jenkins scrambled to his feet and Simon bent down from the saddle, grabbed his outstretched hand and somehow hauled him up behind him on to his mount's rump. Hardy now had both Colts in his hands and was slowly urging Custer forward with his knees towards the advancing horsemen, taking cool aim and firing sequentially. Two of the Boers fell from their saddles and the others paused for a moment, clearly surprised at Hardy's advance and the accurate fire from the American's pistols.

'Quick,' shouted Simon. 'Back to the drift. The others won't have crossed yet. We must save the mail.'

The two horses and their three riders turned and galloped back down the slope, in time to see the mail detachment cantering towards them on the other side of the ford.

'Enemy ahead,' shouted Simon, as his horse splashed into the first drift, Jenkins hanging on with both arms locked round his waist. 'Couriers turn back to the camp. Escort dismount and give us covering fire.'

As the Zulus turned their ponies round and urged them back up the track, the three mounted infantrymen, acting with commendable alacrity, flung themselves from their horses, knelt and opened rapid, if inaccurate, fire from their carbines at the Boers as they crested the rise above the first of the two drifts. It was enough to halt the pursuit, and the Boers dismounted and began returning the fire.

The covering fire was light but sufficient to deter the usually accurate Boer shooting, and Simon, Al and Jenkins were able to cross both drifts, dismount at the far side and add their own fire to that of the infantrymen. The duel that followed was inconsequential, but it was clear that there were insufficient Boers to ford the drifts in the face of the rifles opposing them, and there was no other crossing for miles.

'Right,' said Simon. He nodded to the infantrymen. 'You three take Jenkins here and catch up with the mail. I doubt if the Boers are this side of the Ingogo, so hurry them along back to Mount Prospect. Al and I will stay long enough to deter pursuit.'

Jenkins opened his mouth to argue, but Simon shook his head. 'Off you go and take charge. We will follow in a few minutes.'

In fact, Simon was not at all sure that there were no Boers between the river and the camp, but the risk had to be taken. In the event, however, he was proved right. After levelling a fusillade of fire at the ridge top, he and the American mounted their horses and spurred them away back up the broken track. It was half an hour before they caught up with Jenkins and the mail detachment, but they were not pursued and soon the little party rode into Mount Prospect.

Simon immediately reported to the general

Colley put down his pen and listened with care. 'You d-d-did well to save the mail. That settles it. I can't have them cutting off the road. I shall leave early tomorrow with three hundred men and we shall escort a c-c-convoy of supplies back from Newcastle. I shall want you to scout ahead. We march at eight a.m.'

Chapter 11

The day dawned brightly and a warm sun welcomed Colley's force as it mustered within the camp's earthworks. The column consisted of five companies of the 60th Rifles, thirty-eight mounted infantry and four horse-drawn guns, and as Simon and his two comrades rode out ahead – Jenkins was now re-horsed, of course – the men were laughing and joking and calling to each other in the sunlight as they fell into line. They were equipped to travel light, for the general hoped to be back in the camp by early afternoon, but Simon shook his head as he noted that they carried little food or water. It was clear that if a Boer commando lay ahead, Colley expected to brush it aside like a fly. It was as though the battle of Laing's Nek had not taken place.

The three scouts again spread out, a little more widely this time and riding more slowly. Simon felt sure that the column would be attacked. The question was, where?

Their journey was uneventful, however, until they came to the double drift at the Ingogo and Harte rivers. On the other side the track ran upwards to the stony plateau where they had been attacked the day before. Simon was still unsure how they could have been ambushed on what seemed to be a flat plain. It was obvious, however, that the rolling grassland, made green by the recent rains, must conceal declivities and fissures which could hide horsemen. This was dangerous territory and the obvious place for a second ambush. He decided to wait for the main force before crossing.

He rode to meet Colley and pointed across the river. 'This is where we were attacked yesterday, sir. That plateau seems able to conceal horsemen.'

'Hmm.' The general consulted his map. 'Seems to be called Schuin's Hoogte, if I've pronounced it r-r-right. Looks innocent enough to me.'

'Quite so, General. But you might consider it prudent to put some men and, say, a couple of guns up on that point to the right,' Simon gestured to a spur on the north side of the crossing, 'to command the drifts in case you need to cross back in a hurry.'

Colley shot him a keen glance. 'I don't anticipate c-c-crossing back in a hurry, Fonthill.' He spoke with a smile that disarmed the sharpness of the retort. 'But you are probably right.' A company of the Rifles and two of the guns were marched up the spur while the remainder of the column rested. Simon, Jenkins and Hardy splashed across the drifts and fanned out, and minutes later the main crossing began.

The three scouts had cantered cautiously past the place of the previous day's ambuscade when a whistle from Al made Simon halt. There, some thousand yards to the right, about one hundred Boer horsemen sat watching them. They made no attempt to ride forward. It was as though they were waiting for the main column to appear. Simon immediately told Hardy to ride back and warn the general while he and Jenkins waited and watched in turn.

Clearly the news had not daunted or delayed Colley, for the leading files of the column breasted the rise on to the plateau very soon afterwards. The general rode forward to join Simon and examined the Boers through his field glasses. The Boers, still immobile, seemed to be reined in on an open slope beyond a small ravine. It was a tempting sight.

'Guns forward and unlimber,' barked the general. The two nine-pounders were wheeled round in the centre of the plateau while the column waited expectantly. So too did the Boers, who made no attempt to move.

'Cheeky blighters,' murmured Colley, his glasses to his eyes. 'Right. Send 'em packing with a few shells in their middle.'

A murmur of expectation rose from the watching infantrymen, for whom nothing was more satisfying than seeing artillery disperse cavalry. The guns were loaded and the first sent its shell screaming high over the horsemen to burst some distance away on the slope beyond. It was, in fact, a poor opening shot, but then the unexpected happened. Instead of wheeling away in consternation, the Boer horsemen calmly rode forward and reached the cover of the ravine. There, they dismounted and ranged along its lip to open fierce and accurate rifle fire on the stationary column exposed in the centre of the plateau. What was more, Simon realised that a contingent of Boers were pushing around the column's right flank to envelop the plateau. From being in command of the situation, Colley was now under attack, and within seconds the initiative had been stolen from him.

Before the trap could be closed, the general sent two horsemen galloping back to Mount Prospect with orders for three companies of the 58th to reinforce the Rifles covering the drift. Then he ordered his troops to disperse along the edge of the plateau to take what cover could be found behind the individual sandstone rocks that littered the rolling ground. Simon, Jenkins and Hardy crawled away to find what shelter they could.

No stone, however, was big enough to give cover to the guns. They remained in the centre of the plateau, completely exposed. Simon, lying spread-eagled, his belly pressed to the earth, watched with growing dismay as, one by one, the men servicing the guns were picked off by the Boers, now almost invisible, firing as they were from the cover of the long *tombookie* grass. Volunteers were called from the infantry to man the nine-pounders, and brave men stepped forward. But as soon as they bent to lift a shell or lay the barrel, they were jerked upright and collapsed to the ground, riddled by bullets. Eventually the guns stood untended. If it were not for the red-coated bodies lying around them, they could have been gaunt sculptures, erected in the centre of the plateau to mark a cause lost many years before.

The sun was now high overhead, and cries of 'Anybody got water?' came from various parts of the baking field. Simon crawled to where Jenkins and Hardy were lying behind a large yellow rock, coolly firing either side of it.

'This is another mess, look you,' said Jenkins, perspiration trickling down his sunburned face. 'If they get all around us then I'd say we're done for, because there's not enough cover to face every bleedin' way. If they keep inchin' round, see, we shall 'ave bullets up the arse as well as in the 'ead.'

Simon nodded. The plateau was about four acres in extent and triangular in shape. In its centre it was fairly level, although studded with outcrops of rock, but it fell away at the edges and the Boers were successfully inching their way around the British in an attempt to surround them completely. Would Colley set up a bayonet charge to stop the encirclement?

He did not – perhaps remembering the gallant efforts that had miscarried so tragically at Laing's Nek. Instead, he retrieved another failed gambit from the Nek, and Brownlow – still in charge of the handful of mounted infantry – was directed to lead a cavalry charge on the Boers' flank. It proved equally disastrous, as the burghers' relentless fire cut down horses by the dozen and sent wounded animals, wide-eyed with pain and fear, plunging around the battlefield, trampling on the wounded, the dead and the living alike. Simon shook his head in despair as the shrieks of the beasts added to the crackle of musketry and the cries of the wounded.

'They're goin' to kill Custer,' shouted Hardy, looking to where they had left their horses in the centre of this cauldron.

'No,' said Simon. 'They're only bringing down the cavalry mounts attacking them. Horses are currency to the Boers. They won't kill them randomly. They will hope to finish us and capture them to use themselves. Don't worry.'

He looked hard at Al. The American hardly ever expressed emotion, unless something threatened his magnificent horse. This was not his war, but here he was, mollified now by Simon's reassurance, carefully sighting along the barrel of his Winchester, picking his target and firing methodically. Did he take joy in trying to kill the enemy? Did he feel fear? The answer to both questions seemed to be no. Certainly neither emotion seemed to possess Jenkins, now doing what he did best, coolly firing and reloading, firing and reloading, quite expressionless. They made a fine pair of fighting men, one from the plains of Texas, the other from the hills and valleys of north Wales. Separated at birth by some six thousand miles, but now joined together in combat – and perhaps in death.

Simon sighed and licked his lips. He looked up into a sky that seemed completely blue and benevolent. To the north, the slopes of Majuba seemed more gentle from this aspect and the undulating, mountainous skyline promised grassland walks and bucolic views. Yet here, on the unpronounceable Schuin's Hoogte, the acrid taste of cordite was once again drying his mouth and sickening his stomach. What a place to die!

The battle had settled down into a musketry duel, the Martini-Henry versus the Westley Richards, and clouds of smoke, constantly replenished from six hundred rifle barrels, drifted across the plateau. The redcoats had found what cover they could and were directing strong, if erratic, fire at their half-hidden assailants. Yet it was not a stalemate, for the Boers could be seen still moving to the east to complete their encirclement of the British.

Simon glanced across to where Colley was crouching behind the dubious cover of a dead horse. Digging in his elbows and keeping his head down – the Boers, it seemed, always went for the head if they could, and they were good enough to find it nine times out of ten – he crawled across to the general.

'I'm sure you know, sir,' he said, 'that they are still trying to get round us. With respect, do you think, perhaps, a bayonet charge . . .?'

'No. Suicide.' Colley's tone was curt, but it was clear that he was aware of the danger – not least because of the increasingly odoriferous presence of Brownlow's dead horses, reminders of the last attempt to roll up the enemy's flank.

The general lifted his head and called to where his depleted staff were crouching. 'Mac,' he bellowed.

Captain MacGregor, a well-moustached and highly regarded young officer, crawled across to join the general. 'Sir.'

Colley gestured to an outcrop of rock some six hundred yards away across open ground to the east, untenanted by either attackers or defenders, but only about sixty yards from the nearest Boers. 'Do you think you can get across there with about seventy rifles and stop these d-d-damned farmers from encroaching further along that way to take us from the rear? It's clear ground so you'll lose men, but we've got to stop 'em.'

MacGregor's moustache quivered for a fraction of a second. 'Of course, sir. Give me a minute.'

'Fonthill,' said Colley. 'You've got g-g-good shooters. Take your chaps with Mac.'

Simon gulped. How could anyone survive running across that open ground commanded by the most accurate marksmen in the world? For a brief moment he thought of arguing. What was the difference between a bayonet charge and sending riflemen to take up a position? And what the hell, he wasn't in the army. He didn't have to obey senseless, hopeless orders! He tried to clear his throat. 'Very good, sir,' he croaked.

He waved to Jenkins and Hardy and the three of them ran at the crouch to where MacGregor was mustering a group of rifles. Somehow there seemed to be a brief lull in the firing. Were the Boers aware of this desperate ploy and just waiting to cut them down as they ran across the grass?

'Right,' said MacGregor. 'Run like hell.'

Heads down, as though their helmets could protect them from bullets, the seventy men ran for their lives into a maelstrom of fire. Incredibly, MacGregor had retrieved his horse and, mounted, led the charge from the front. Inevitably the animal was shot from under him, but somehow he survived, regained his feet and, revolver in hand, continued to lead his men. Simon, Jenkins and Al were wedged into the middle of the charging contingent and this must have served as a protective screen, for the burghers unleashed a curtain of bullets that brought down soldiers all around the three scouts. At one stage Al slipped and measured his full length in a puddle halfway across. Jenkins and Simon immediately dragged him to his feet and the three resumed their desperate dash for the outcrop of rock, jumping over the fallen bodies of riflemen as they ran.

Exhausted, the survivors collapsed behind the safety of the rock as bullets ricocheted from its edges. Simon panted to regain his breath and looked around. No more than twenty of the seventy riflemen had reached the outcrop, and a trail of bodies stretching across the open ground showed the way they had come and the price that had been paid. Yet it was clear that it was a decisive position on the open ground of the plateau. It commanded the downward sloping edge, otherwise protected from the British fire from in the centre and along which the Boers would have to advance if they were to complete the encirclement. The burghers were near, damned near, but to take the rock they too would have to charge across the sixty yards of open ground. Would they do it? Simon sucked in his breath.

MacGregor seemed to read his thoughts. 'Boers don't have bayonets and they don't like charging,' he growled, brushing up the ends of his moustache. 'We're a bit close, but my bet is that they won't come at us.' He turned to the rest of his depleted band. 'Now, all of you deploy around this damned mountain and find protected positions. Keep your heads down but keep shooting to show these farmers that we're in position here. You five,' he indicated a group of riflemen, their cheeks blown out as they tried to regain their breath, 'keep to the side here and train your rifles on the slope below. If the enemy gets by there I'll have you court-martialled for dereliction of duty.' He grinned momentarily 'On second thoughts, no I won't, because we shall all be dead.'

The riflemen grinned back, and one called out, 'I'd rather be court-martialled if it's all the same to you, sir.' Simon felt a sudden surge of emotion at the resilient cheerfulness of the rank-and-file British soldier. Many of the 60th Rifles, unlike the 58th, were old hands and they would know that their position, forced out on the plateau in a position suicidally close to the enemy, was comparatively hopeless. Yet here they were, under a blazing sun without food or water, joking with their officer as they settled down, nuzzling their rifles into their cheeks. There was no hint of resentment towards the general who had led them into this trap.

'Gaaddamn. Just look at this.' Al indicated the brown slime that covered the length of his fine buckskins. 'How the hell can a feller fight a war lookin' like this? Ah'll never git this suit cleaned out heah in this gaadforsaken hole, now will ah?'

Jenkins called down from the position he had taken high up the rock. 'Don't worry, bach. Where we're goin' there'll be plenty of 'eat

211

to dry it out, and then you can just borrow a trident thing to brush it clean like, can't you?'

Simon allowed himself a smile and then scrambled to where MacGregor was sitting, his back to the rock. 'What do you think our chances are, Mac?' he asked.

'Well, if they don't rush us – and as I've said, it would be out of character – we could sit here all day, I would think. They can't get round us, but without food or water we won't last through tomorrow, that's a certainty, old boy.'

Simon looked up at the sky. It was still brazen blue overhead but to the south a sullen grey weather front was building. He indicated it. 'That could play a part. I can't see the Boers staying out in the open in a storm, somehow. But it could also lead the Ingogo to flood and cut off our retreat.'

MacGregor grinned. 'Bit buggered all round, old thing, aren't we?'

'Looks like it.'

'Ah well. That's the army for you.'

'Mac, could I ask you something?'

'Anything you like, old fruit.'

'Why on earth did you mount your charger to lead the dash to this damned rock?'

MacGregor frowned. 'Can't quite see the point of the question, old boy.'

'Well, you must have known that you present a prime target. You know the Boers go for the officers first. And you must also have known that your horse would be killed. I can't quite—'

MacGregor lifted his eyebrows. 'You must have gone a bit native since you left the 24th, old lad. You know the men like to be led by an officer on horseback. Sets us apart and also sets an example, don't you know. Sorry about the nag. But we got here, didn't we?'

Simon smiled. 'I suppose we did. Some of us, anyway.' He shook his head, only half concealing his wonderment, and crawled back to his firing position. *Had* he gone native? Probably. Certainly he found himself questioning more and more the entrenched habits – the inculcated *stupidity* – of the British officer class. He slotted his rifle through a niche in the rock and took a quick potshot at a slouch hat peeping above the rim of the ravine ahead of him. It helped to relieve his irritation.

Through the long afternoon the firing continued, with the British, behind their poor cover, getting the worst of the exchange. Several attempts were made by the Boers to push around below the eastern end of the perimeter, but the fire of the small party manning the rocky spur provoked their retreat. A kind of bloody stalemate descended upon Schuin's Hoogte. And then, towards sundown, the heavens opened.

Simon took advantage of the downpour and the growing darkness to worm his way along the ground towards the Boer positions. Taking precious cover from a small rock, he watched as the rain thundered down and saw much activity as sodden-hatted men carefully carried long bundles to the rear. It was a moment or two before he realised what was happening: the Boers were carrying their dead and wounded off the battlefield. But did this presage the retirement of the whole force? A bullet hit his rock and sent splinters into his hair, and he decided he was too close to stay longer.

Back at the outpost, he consulted MacGregor. 'Do you think they're getting out of here?'

The young man wrinkled his face. 'Shouldn't think so. They've got us on toast and they know it. If they are anything like proper soldiers they will stay overnight and starve us out tomorrow. We can't hold on much longer and they probably know that.'

Simon frowned. 'Yes. But they're *not* proper soldiers. Good fighters but not conventional soldiers. Farmers don't like staying out all night in the rain. I'm going to see the general.'

'Very well, but let me have a look first . . .' MacGregor lifted his head for a moment. A rifle shot rang out and the young captain jerked back and slithered down the rock. Simon pulled him over and saw a small black hole just beneath his helmet. MacGregor's eyes, wide open, stared back at him, as though in surprise. Simon closed his own eyes for a second, shook his head slowly and then pulled down the dead man's eyelids.

In the downpour, it was easier to make his way to where Colley still sat, now a forlorn, bedraggled figure. 'I'm afraid MacGregor's dead, sir. But the enemy are removing their dead and wounded and I have a feeling that they are preparing to pull out,' he reported.

Colley sighed. 'Too many good men . . . too many . . .' He shook his head, then: 'I doubt if the Boers are pulling out. If they are, then they're damned fools. Very well, Fonthill. Tell the senior officers to join me here – and when you've b-b-brought 'em, you stay too.'

It was a small group of eight officers who gathered round the general, hunching their shoulders against the driving rain but holding out their helmets and drinking the precious liquid gathered there.

'Gentlemen,' said Colley, 'Fonthill here believes that the enemy may be retiring. If this p-p-proves to be true, we have two choices. We can stay here and throw up earthworks under cover of darkness and fight it out with the Boers – who will surely be reinforced – in the morning. This rain will ease our water shortage and help the wounded, but we have no rations, of course. Or we can try and slip away ourselves. The Ingogo c-c-crossing will be sure to be guarded, but we can attempt to force our passage and get back to Mount Prospect. This will be rough work and an alert enemy could cut us to pieces during the withdrawal. And the two r-r-rivers may be so swollen that the drifts are unfordable. Difficulties f-f-face us either way, but I would value your opinions before making up my own mind.' The general's tone was gentle and even, and it was as though he was posing a hypothetical problem to a class of officer cadets at Sandhurst, yet the sun-blackened, rain-streaked faces that regarded him reflected the tension that hung over the gathering.

'Stay here and fight it out in the morning,' offered a major of the Rifles. 'Give 'em a bayonet charge at dawn.'

Colley smiled. 'Across open ground, against some of the best marksmen in the world?' he enquired.

'But the Boers could decimate us as we cross the two rivers,' said a lieutenant colonel. 'We would be completely at their mercy – even if we could find our way in the darkness. And the rivers will be swollen.'

Simon intervened. 'Let me and my two scouts go down there, General. At least we should be able to find out how heavily the crossings are defended and where the Boers are situated. In retreat, you could perhaps surprise and overwhelm the enemy posts – and don't forget, you have placed guns and infantry on that knoll on the far side to cover our crossing.'

'Thank you, Fonthill, that is exactly what I had in mind.' Colley shot him a quick glance of gratitude. 'You see, gentlemen, I fear that without what is left of our force, Mount Prospect would not be able to withstand an attack in force by the Boer army from Laing's Nek. I cannot take the risk that we would be starved out tomorrow or the day after and be forced to surrender. We must fight our way back to Prospect. Go when you are ready, Fonthill.'

Jenkins was less than impressed by the task confronting them. 'What,' he expostulated, 'go down to the river in this pitch black and explain to the Boers that we're comin' and would they kindly stand aside? The general must be barmy. But 'e's already shown that, 'asn't 'e? Oh, sorry, bach sir. No disrespect intended. But we shall be drowned either one way or the bloody other, you must admit that.'

'Nonsense. It's less than two miles to the crossings. Come on. We're supposed to be scouts after all. Al, get the horses and make sure they're all right. Three five two, check the rifle mechanisms and see if you can dry 'em and oil 'em. We may have to fight our way back.'

Within thirty minutes it was completely dark and the three men set out. The rain was still falling and the track was a quagmire, but the passage of the column was still clearly marked, and the three of them spread out in their familiar arrowhead formation, hunched low in their saddles and with rifles at the ready, and began making their way back to the drifts. Simon chose not to take the most direct route, for this must surely be guarded, but instead slipped away from the plateau where the encircling ring had not been completed and then, working on a compass bearing, planned to swing round to pick up the track later. It was nerve-racking work, with a Boer challenge or a bullet expected at any minute as their horses picked their way fastidiously across the terrain that sloped gently down to the rivers.

After some thirty minutes Simon found the well-beaten track again, and shortly afterwards they all heard rather than saw the rivers. It was clear that the larger Ingogo and even the small Harte

215

were in spate. In the darkness, the now khaki-coloured waters were tumbling between the banks, tossing small tree branches in the strong current, while a fierce hissing showed that shingle was being forced downstream on the river bed. The good news, however, was that there was no sign of Boer guards or patrols, although it was clear that a large force had gathered at the crossing recently.

'Sorry, bach sir,' said Jenkins, 'but I can't swim. You'll never get me goin' across that lot.'

'No,' responded Simon. 'We must test the depth. I'll go. You two stay here.'

'No, suh.' Hardy urged his giant horse towards the water's edge. 'Ol' Custer heah is bigger 'n your two horses and I'll back him to get across. Now.' He unhitched a rope lariat and gave an end to Simon, tying the other to the pommel of his high saddle. 'Just you two hold on to this an' pull me out if ah gits into trouble. If ah jerk, it means ah'm across, so let go.'

'Thanks, Al,' said Simon. 'But don't take risks. When you get across, ride up to the spur and see if that contingent of the 58th is still there. But be cautious. It may be, judging from these tracks here, that the Boers have crossed in force and overwhelmed the post. And for God's sake take off that blasted Stetson. It positively glows in the dark.'

Hardy, however, paid no attention, and carefully letting out the rope, he urged Custer into the swollen river. At first the big chestnut was wide-eyed and fearful, but he braced his hooves on the bottom and began to make his way across the torrent. It was not, in fact, as deep as it looked and the waters came only up to the horse's belly.

' 'E won't like that,' murmured Jenkins. 'Now 'e's gettin' 'is fancy pants wet again. That won't be popular.'

The tall American quickly disappeared into the gloom and eventually they felt a tug on the rope and let it go, watching it bounce along the top of the surging water as it was retrieved from the other side. Then they were left to wait, listening to the roar and hiss of the torrent.

It was, perhaps, half an hour later when they saw the white

216

Stetson loom out of the darkness. Thankfully, the rain had eased, although the water remained high.

Hardy squeezed the water from his beard. 'It's clear, both waters,' he reported. 'Ah reckon that, with arms linked, the column could cross right 'nuff, though it won't be easy. It'll be slow, an' if them Boers do come back they could pick us off nice 'n' easy. But there ain't no sign of 'em.'

'What about the 58th on the spur?'

'They're still there, sure 'nuff, an' about an hour an' a half ago they fought off a large party of Boers who tried to cross from just about heah. They stopped 'em from crossin', so hopefully there ain't none o' the enemy on the other side between us and Mount Prospect.'

'I'm not sure about that, but thanks, Al. That was good work. I'm amazed that the Boers have left the crossing unguarded. Absolutely amazed.'

Jenkins sniffed and removed a large dewdrop hanging from his nose. 'Very sensible, if you ask me. This ain't no night for goin' poncin' about crossing rivers, look you.'

Emboldened by the absence of the Boers, the little party followed the track directly back to the plateau and reported to an anxious Colley.

'What, nobody at all?'

'Not a sausage, sir.'

'Could be a t-t-trap, of course.'

'Possibly. But don't forget, sir, that, wonderful fighters as they are, the Boers are not a conventionally disciplined army. They are a civilian militia and the burghers would not fancy sitting out all night in this storm. Also, they have no way of knowing that the column has no food and water, so I think they are expecting you to fight it out tomorrow and will have left only the lightest guard to keep an eye on you before mopping you up after daybreak. If you want to move, I recommend you go right away, General.'

The reference to the column's lack of supplies brought the faintest of winces to Colley's face, but, polite as ever, he nodded. 'Thank you, Fonthill. Excellent work as usual. I shall take your advice. We will move out as soon as we are formed up.'

217

The rain had returned but the noise of the storm muffled the column's preparations to move out. The men were quietly withdrawn from the perimeter and formed up into a hollow square, with the remaining horses harnessed to the two guns in the centre. The wounded were made as comfortable as possible in the driving rain, but they had to be left behind and their protesting cries mingled with the creak of harnesses as the column pulled out.

The three scouts fanned out ahead of the troops in the lead and Simon thought it wise to eschew the track and make their way to the drifts once again by the convoluted route they had taken earlier. The column halted about half a mile from the two rivers while the scouts went on ahead to ensure that no vedettes had been posted by the Boers during their absence. Again, they found the crossings undefended, although the swirling waters seemed higher.

In the pitch darkness and driving rain the rivers now presented a real danger. Orders were given for the men to link arms and the leading files edged into the swollen torrent. The water came up to their armpits and two men were immediately swept away to be lost into the night. But the gaps were closed, and somehow, inch by inch, the leaders reached the other side and scrambled up the far bank. The guns, virtually submerged, were pulled across by the horses and eventually the whole column had crossed. A total of seven men, however, had been drowned and the general made no attempt in the atrocious conditions to contact his detachment on the spur. The column had to reach Mount Prospect before dawn or offer easy pickings to the Boer marksmen.

Scouting out ahead of the van, Simon and his companions were spared the horrors of that night march back to the camp. Roughly halfway along the five-mile route, the horses could no longer pull the guns unaided and men had to manhandle the cannon the rest of the way. At about four a.m., the bedraggled and exhausted column arrived at Mount Prospect. It had been a miraculous escape and, in its way, a kind of triumph, for the Boers, sheltering from the storm, had allowed Colley and his men to slip away without a shot being fired. Yet nearly half of the three hundred men who had marched out of the camp so happily twenty-four hours earlier had been lost. The guns had been saved but the dead had been left unburied and most of the wounded remained behind.

Like the rest of the returned troops, Simon, Jenkins and Hardy crawled gratefully into their bedrolls as the rain continued to beat on their tent canvas. They were roused some five hours later to ride back to Schuin's Hoogte under a flag of truce with a major and a burial party to bring back the wounded and inter the dead. The final twist to the tragedy of the 'reconnaissance in force', however, occurred two days later when it was revealed that the officers killed had been buried with the other ranks. Colley, it seemed, was unhappy at this solecism, which was very much against the custom of the day, and Simon shook his head in disbelief when he heard that a second party had been sent out to disinter the officers and bring them back to Mount Prospect for burial in the sheltered little cemetery there, reserved for those of commissioned rank.

'Ah thought that all dead were as one in the eyes of the Lord,' observed Hardy.

Simon could think of nothing to say.

Chapter 12

Sir George Colley displayed his best qualities in the days following the battle of Ingogo. The men and the guns left on the spur overlooking the drifts had ridden in unscathed the following day, pleased at having repulsed the attack made on them by the Boers during the storm, and he himself referred to the extrication of his column from Schuin's Hoogte as a triumph and bustled about the camp beaming and smiling as though a great victory had been achieved. He spoke of the fine quality of Wood's reinforcements now nearing Newcastle, and although he demurred at marching out in strength to meet them, he expressed no doubt that they would fight their way through if they were attacked. Yet behind the happy countenance his eyes looked tired, and it was notable that his stammer had become worse. He was still in telegraphic communication with Newcastle, and therefore with London, for the Boers had not cut the lines, and it was obvious that a great deal of activity at government level was in progress, for the general was to be seen in his tent every night working far into the early hours by the light of an oil lamp. In these matters he had little help, because his staff had been reduced now to one staff officer and one very young ADC.

The cutting of the telegraph link with the south three days later, therefore, was particularly inconvenient, and Colley mustered his three scouts and a troop of mounted infantry and attempted to slip through the Boer ring by night and ride to Newcastle. Simon, leading the party, hoped that a fog that had sprung up would cloak their passage as they crossed the Buffalo river at the rear of the camp at Mount Prospect. But the mist had cleared when they reached the lower ground of the Buffalo valley, and with a bright moon rising,

Simon felt it unsafe to continue. Three days later, however, the party tried again and this time the mist hung low through the night. As a result, Simon, Jenkins and Hardy once again found themselves riding into a Newcastle bursting at the seams with newly arrived troops from the south.

Just under eight hundred men had marched up from the coast, representing the first contingent of Colley's reinforcements, all of them from India. The main elements consisted of five hundred and eighteen men of the 58th Highlanders, veterans of the recent successful Afghan campaign, among whose officers Simon recognised some familiar faces; a hundred and three horsemen of the 15th Hussars; and, this time, a more substantial Naval Brigade of fifty-eight bluejackets. To Simon and Jenkins the Highlanders presented a strange appearance, for this was the first time that British troops had gone into action wearing the new khaki tunics in place of the traditional red coats, while all their officers sported the new Sam Browne cross belts.

'Blimey,' said Jenkins. 'Put 'em into the desert country and you won't see 'em.'

'I think that's the idea,' replied Simon.

With the troops rode General Sir Evelyn Wood, bluff and hearty, wearing the ribbon of the Victoria Cross he had won against the Zulus. The two generals were closeted together for two days. During this time the three scouts were forced to kick their heels in the little town, and Simon took the opportunity to attempt to pen a letter to Alice. He wanted to write warmly – though not too warmly – but conventionally, telling her that he had heard that her wedding had been a great occasion and wishing her well in her new life. Yet every word he conjured up seemed trite, anodyne and quite unrepresentative of what he really wanted to say. But what *did* he want to say? That he loved her still and always would? He could not write that to a married woman. So what was the point? He thought of his desire – no, his *lust* – for Anna Scheel and realised that he was unworthy anyway to write to Alice Griffith . . . Alice Covington. Ah, the very name seemed to wring his heart! Swearing, he tore up his efforts and gave up the attempt.

It was clear, from the buzzing of clerks around Colley's headquarters in the main hotel, that the general was back in full contact with his masters in London's Whitehall. It was also clear that, from the darkening of his usually genial countenance, this long-distance relationship was not going as smoothly as it might. Only five days after his arrival at Newcastle, General Wood was dispatched back to Pietermaritzburg to hasten the arrival of more reinforcements to Newcastle. Simon, an interested observer of the activity, could not help but wonder why a general was needed for this task. Was a rift developing between the two? He could well imagine that the presence of his deputy – a man senior to him in rank anyway – could possibly be proving irksome to Colley. Wood had won his spurs, not to mention his VC, many times over in combat. His superior had commanded only twice in the field – and both times he had been defeated. It would be understandable if even the equable Colley was beginning to show signs of strain.

The general marched back to Camp Prospect, this time at the head of a force too strong for the Boers to attack, and the following day Simon was summoned to his tent. The call was a relief, for now perhaps he could gain some idea of what was happening.

'Got a job for you.' Colley's smile was as genuine as ever, although Simon noticed that a nerve was now twitching just below the general's right eye.

'Thank goodness for that, sir,' said Simon. 'I was beginning to feel that I ought to hand back my pay.'

Colley's smile widened. 'Goodness, don't do that. The Horse Guards would accept it in a flash.' They both grinned and then the bearded man's expression darkened.

'I don't mind confessing to you, Fonthill,' he said, 'that I am not at all happy with the way our masters back home are b-b-behaving. Here we are, now happily reinforced and for the first time able to advance through into the Transvaal with real c-c-confidence to relieve our people besieged up there, yet the government is negotiating with the Boers and, by the look of it, offering to appease them. Just when we are ready to go.'

'Good lord. It's not as though you have suffered two overwhelming defeats, sir.' Simon felt a twinge of conscience at offering such an ingratiating comment, but his liking for Colley and his desire to give him some scrap of comfort overrode his respect for the truth. And Ingogo, anyway, could count as some sort of draw.

'Quite so.' The general shot him a grateful glance. 'Well, we might still have a chance of having a go at them, although I doubt it. For the moment I have been instructed to offer the so-called B-B-Boer government terms for a suspension of hostilities.'

Colley looked down at the document on his table for a moment and silence ensued. Simon felt a sudden surge of sympathy for the general. Here was a man whose path to the top of his career had been almost uneventfully smooth. Until now, every task he had been offered he had accomplished with elan – district magistrate in South Africa, hard-working subaltern at the sacking of the Summer Palace in the China War of 1860, organiser of Wolseley's transport and logistics in the Ashanti War, writer of the chapter on the British Army for the ninth edition of the *Encyclopaedia Britannica*, and private secretary and chief adviser to the Viceroy of India. Now that the longed-for first command of an army in the field had arrived, he had sustained two setbacks but, it seemed, was not to be allowed the opportunity to reverse them. It was a cruel and even puzzling intervention by Gladstone's government, particularly so after it had expended so much time and money on providing him with the means of achieving a final career-saving victory.

Colley was now gazing unseeingly out of the tent opening and Simon felt it unwise to interrupt. Eventually, the general looked back and smiled at him. 'Your f-f-friend Brand of the Orange Free State has been working away between London and Heidelberg attempting to broker an agreement, and our government has floated some sort of proposal to divide the Transvaal into two, r-r-restoring independence to the purely Dutch districts while retaining our sovereignty over the native b-b-border districts. Of course, I have advised strongly against that. But amazingly, Kruger, on behalf of the Triumvirate, has now written to me out of the b-b-blue offering to withdraw from Natal and s-s-submit the Boers' case to a Royal Commission of Inquiry, if we too withdraw our t-t-troops from the Transvaal.'

Simon's eyebrows lifted. 'So the war could be over?'

'Perhaps, but it's not quite as s-s-simple as that. I have been instructed to agree to the setting up of a Royal Commission, if the Boers now in arms cease their opposition. I have also been instructed to set a r-r-reasonable timetable for the Boers' reply to this offer. I have asked for their agreement within forty-eight hours.' He held up the document. 'This letter says all that. You know I always believe in telling the messenger the content of the message he is carrying. I want you to take this letter through to the Boer commander on Laing's Nek. I think it better that a civilian takes it, rather than an officer in bright brass and a red coat. Makes it seem rather more Colonial Office than Horse Guards – and so it jolly well is, because I know that the army would never bend the knee in these circumstances. Take your two scouts with you as escorts.'

Colley stood and gave Simon the envelope. 'I also know, Fonthill, that I can trust you to do the job well. The letter is addressed to Vice President Kruger, but I understand that General Nicholas Smit – he's the chap who attacked us at the Ingogo plain – is now in command at the Nek. He has already proven himself to be an honourable and fine man, by the way – over the burials and so on. Hand the letter to him personally and no one else.'

Simon's mind raced. The importance of the letter put a heavy responsibility on his shoulders, although there should be no real difficulty about delivering it under the protection of a flag of truce. But it also gave him entry to the Boers' position on Laing's Nek, with the consequent chance of assessing their positions.

He gulped. 'Sir, would you wish me to wait the forty-eight hours within the Boer camp and bring back the reply?'

Colley shook his head. 'No. Tell them to send their own messenger back to me at Prospect.' A wintry smile stole across his face for a brief moment but it did not reach his eyes. 'If they can give me a reply within forty-eight hours, that is. Now, off you go.'

Simon felt uneasy as, flanked by Jenkins and Hardy, he rode along the familiar track towards Laing's Nek, carrying a borrowed cavalryman's lance to which was fixed a white pennant. He had insisted that the three of them should look their best as emissaries of the British Government, so they had all put on their best clothes. Somehow Al had scrubbed clean his buckskins and, with Stetson and goatee, looked the epitome of the Western frontiersman; Jenkins, his hair brushed flat as it ever could be, had found clean shirts for himself and Simon. Even so, none of the trio was comfortable as they approached the valley leading up to the Nek. They had left their weapons behind and it seemed incongruous to ride towards two thousand hostile rifles with only a scrap of white cotton as protection.

As they neared the brooding presence of Majuba, Simon examined it again with interest. It was known locally as a hill, but it was more of a small mountain, standing more than six thousand feet above sea level and climbing well over a thousand feet from the western end of the Nek. The summer's wet weather had left a cap of white cloud clinging to its truncated peak, but below that the mountain's slopes were clearly marked by parallel strata of sandstone and shale, breaking into giant stairways of terraces and cliffs. Simon mused that if troops could be placed on the summit – particularly with artillery – then the Boers' positions on the Nek and the hills opposite would be made completely untenable. But could it be climbed?

His thoughts were interrupted by the approach of a group of about half a dozen horsemen, riding towards them down the slope from the Nek. Their leader, a heavy man with a beard larger than those of the others (did the Boers use facial hair as a badge of rank? mused Simon), held up his hand and greeted them with a grin.

'Good day, English,' he said. 'Have you come to surrender already?'

Simon grinned back. 'No, but we are quite prepared to take your surrender if you wish. I have a letter from Major General Sir George Pomeroy-Colley to Vice President Kruger. I am instructed to hand it personally to General Nicholas Smit. Can you please take us to him?'

The big man rode around the trio and noted that they carried no weapons. 'Is this the end of the war then, man?'

'I wouldn't know. I am only the messenger. But I don't think we should delay.'

'*Ja*. Follow us.'

He turned and the little party cantered up the rise towards the trenches on the Nek, which could now be clearly seen. Simon noted that the Boer fortifications had been extended further up the slopes of Majuba and that they now appeared to be more sophisticated, with walls of rock emplacements stretching to either side.

'Durned sight more of the varmints now than when we last came,' murmured Al.

'Aye,' agreed Jenkins. 'I do 'ope the general 'as given up any idea of 'avin' another go straight at 'em, like, up these slopes. We wouldn't stand a chance.'

Simon nodded agreement, looking around him with interest. The network of sangars stretched back behind the crest, offering protection for support riflemen away from artillery shell bursts, and the whole camp was thronged with bandoliered burghers, smoking pipes, cleaning rifles, walking their ponies back to the horse lines behind, or simply lying down sleeping, their hats tipped over their faces. It was clear that the whole position had been strengthened since the engagement. The Boers, it seemed, were here to stay.

Then he stiffened in the saddle. To his right, high on a rock, watching him intently, stood a small, slim man carrying his right arm lightly in a sling. He stood out from the Boers in that he was dressed in smart riding breeches and a spotless white shirt. Baron Wilhelm von Bethman had lost none of his elegance since last they had met. Simon had not thought for a moment that the German would have accompanied the Boers on their 'invasion' of Natal and had presumed that he and Anna would have taken ship home to Germany by now. What was he doing in the Boer stronghold? And if *he* was here, would Anna be also? His heart quickened for a moment, then he frowned and dismissed the thought with a toss of his head. This was no place for a woman, and beside, she had gone from his life. He gave the baron no sign of recognition and received none in return.

Nevertheless, he looked around him with unusual care as they were taken to a cluster of tents at the rear of the Nek and gestured to dismount at one no more pretentious than the rest. 'Please wait here,' said their guide, who then disappeared inside the tent.

They stayed there for only a brief time but Simon was aware how conspicuous Hardy was in that encampment where every man dressed the same: dirty lace-up boots, shapeless jackets, corduroy trousers, unkempt beards under broad-brimmed hats. Here, the Texan looked like some showpiece in his yellow buckskins, finely worked riding boots, white hat and beautifully trimmed Vandyke beard. Yet he showed no sign of discomfort as Boers gathered round him and regarded him with open-mouthed astonishment. He merely stood, thumbs hooked into his belt from which hung the two empty holsters, and gazed into infinity, a faint smile on his face.

'Blimey,' confided Jenkins to Simon from the corner of his mouth, ' 'e's lovin' every minute of this. We could 'ave taken an admission charge, look you.'

They were received inside the tent by a tall man in, unusually, a white jacket but sporting the conventional long beard. His forehead was large and his brown eyes smiled kindly as he extended his hand.

'Welcome, gentlemen,' he said. 'My name is Nicholas Smit. Please sit down and take some tea with us.'

'Thank you, sir. I am Simon Fonthill, late captain in the 24th Regiment of Foot and the Queen's Own Corps of Guards. This is ex-Sergeant Jenkins, of the same regiments, and Mr Al Hardy, formerly of the American army.'

'Ah yes. I have heard of you and, indeed, saw you at our recent little brush on Schuin's Hoogte.' He gestured again for them to sit. 'I understand that Mr Hardy, in particular, is renowed as a shootist with his pistols, but I cannot help wondering why an American should be fighting with the British Army . . .?'

He left the question hanging, rather like a gentle rebuke, and Hardy coloured slightly.

'Waal, General,' he said, shifting in his seat. 'Ah was arrested by your people up in the north, though ah was only mindin' mah own business. Ah was thrown into a waggon an' kept a prisoner and didn't take kindly to that. So I escaped with the captain and the sergeant heah and ah've bin helpin' out with 'em. Scoutin' and such.'

Smit nodded gravely. 'I see. Well, I apologise to you if you felt that you were mistreated. These are strange times for us, as you can see.'

His face softened slightly. 'But we seem to have suffered as a result of making an enemy of you. You shoot very well, I understand.'

Simon felt it time to intervene. Smit seemed genial enough, but the story of their fracas in south Transvaal seemed to have spread through the Boer ranks. It could be harmful to revive the details. 'I have a letter for you, sir,' he said. 'At least, it is for Vice President Kruger, and Major General Colley would be grateful if you could convey it to him.' He handed over the envelope.

The big man took it, removed a hunting knife from his belt and began slitting it open. 'I will read it if you will allow,' he said. 'Perhaps it may need a rapid response, and the vice president, of course, is not here.'

He wound the endpieces of a pair of wire-rimmed spectacles around his ears, pursed his lips and, frowning, began reading aloud, slowly, as though the English words were difficult:

' "Sir, I have the honour to acknowledge the receipt of your letter of the twelfth instant . . ." '

He paused, glanced at the date at the top of the letter and looked at Simon over the top of his spectacles. 'But this letter is dated the twenty-first, and today, I believe, is the twenty-fourth. There seems to have been no urgency in replying to the vice president's letter, nor, indeed, in conveying the reply to us here.'

Simon swallowed. 'I am sorry, sir. I would imagine that the general had to confer with London. Certainly, I was handed this letter only today to bring to you.'

Smit nodded and continued reading aloud: ' "In reply, I am to inform you that on the Boers now in arms against Her Majesty's authority ceasing armed opposition, Her Majesty's Government will be ready to appoint a commission with large powers who may develop the scheme referred to in Lord Kimberley's . . ." '

The Boer looked up at Simon again. 'I think he is the minister for colonies, is he not?'

'The Colonial Secretary, sir, yes.'

Smit continued reading: ' ". . . Lord Kimberley's telegram of the eighth instant, communicated to you through His Honour, President Brand. I am to add that upon this proposal being accepted within forty-eight hours, I have the authority to agree a suspension of hostilities on our part." '

Smit removed his spectacles but his frown had deepened. 'I shall, of course, relay this letter immediately to Vice President Kruger in the north. But I must say that, given the distances involved, forty-eight hours leaves us very little time to reply. I am not sure of the exact whereabouts of Mr Kruger, but as I say, this important message will be sent to him without delay. I would be grateful if you would explain this to Major General Colley, Mr Fonthill.'

'Of course I will, sir.'

'Good. Now – how do you take your tea?'

'General Smit.' The voice came from behind Simon's head, from the entrance to the tent. Von Bethman stood outlined against the light of the entrance, dramatically pointing one finger at Simon. 'This man is a British spy and should be arrested and hanged immediately.'

'Baron.' Smit rose slowly from his seat. 'Ach, I think you are mistaken. Captain Fonthill is indeed from the British camp, but he comes here under a flag of truce to bring a message from the British commander-in-chief to Vice President Kruger. I do not see how he can be on a spying mission, for I have the letter here and it is in answer to one sent earlier. Now, do come in. Won't you join us in a cup of tea?'

The general's tone was mild, and if it was not for the fact that he spoke in the guttural tones of an Afrikaner, he could have been a British clergyman welcoming an unexpected parishioner.

Von Bethman strode forward. 'Herr General, I know this man. He was arrested by your men as he was skulking behind your lines in the Transvaal, preparing for an invasion by the British, but he escaped, killing as he went. Then I met him in Bloemfontein, wheedling away at President Brand to persuade him not to support you and your brothers. There he insulted me and the Countess Scheel but fled before I could exact a proper price for his insolence.' The German's eyes were no longer cold but glowing with hatred, and he had withdrawn his right hand from its sling to emphasise his points. But he spoke evenly and clinically, like an attorney presenting a prosecution's case. 'He may well have brought a letter for you, but his real purpose will be to spy out your positions before the British attack again. I tell you, the man is dangerous and should be executed before he does further damage to your cause.'

Smit frowned. 'There can be no question of that, Baron. Whether what you say is true or not, Captain Fonthill and his companions are protected by a flag of truce. I know nothing of the captain's activities in the Free State, although I was aware that they had been apprehended by us earlier and had somehow ridden away. But these things happen in war.'

His voice softened and he turned to Simon. 'War is a terrible thing, Mr Fonthill. Let us end it as soon as possible. Tell General Colley that I will convey his letter to Mr Kruger with all haste. Now, when you have finished your tea, I will ask you to return to your camp. However . . .' He paused for a moment, his finger to his lips, his brow furrowed. 'The baron is an honoured guest here and has already proved his friendship towards our cause. In view of what he has said, I fear I must have you all blindfolded as you ride through our lines. I will send an escort with you, and the blindfolds will be removed, of course, as soon as you are well clear of the Nek.'

Simon put down his cup. 'Thank you, sir. We will leave immediately then.' He directed a cool gaze at von Bethman. 'I will merely say that we are not spies and have done nothing dishonourable. We are not members of the British Army, that is true, but we are scouts who ride ahead of the regular forces, as scouts have always done, in the service of our country. That is all. The baron hates the British and his views are unbalanced. Thank you for your courtesy, sir, and good morning.'

As he turned on his heel, Simon heard the baron speak quickly and loudly in German, but then he was through the tent opening, followed quickly by Jenkins and Hardy. There they were stopped and led to their horses and bandannas were tied around their eyes, though not before Simon had taken a last look around him.

They rode in silence and semi-darkness before, after about twenty minutes, the blindfolds were removed and they were sent on their way with a courteous salute from the large bearded man in charge of the escort.

'It's mah opinion,' said Hardy after a while, 'that you've upset that German chile just a touch. I guess he could be a real dangerous critter. Simon, you should watch your back.' He spoke with a half-grin on his lips, but his eyes were serious.

Jenkins let out a snort. ''E's a nasty piece of work, all right. But 'e's only a little feller an' everyone knows that little fellers are no danger to anyone.' He grinned to underline the jest.

Simon reined in his horse and turned it to look back one more time at the Nek. 'I'm not worried about him,' he said. 'But I would like to know quite what he's doing with the Boers. It looks as though the German government is really putting some weight behind the Afrikaner wheel.' He shielded his eyes to inspect more closely the hilltops they had just vacated. 'I'm glad, though, that they didn't put the blindfolds on until the return journey. I think I've seen enough to help the general.'

He pulled his mount's head round and they resumed their amble towards the British camp. But Simon was not thinking about the Boer defences. His mind was now consumed with thoughts of Anna Scheel. If von Bethman was embedded in the Boer headquarters, then he must have some official status representing the German government. And that must surely mean that Anna *had* acted as a spy, attempting to charm Simon – seduce him, even – sufficiently to learn the contents of Brand's reply to Colley, to the point where she had gained entry to his room to steal or read the letter. He ran his tongue over dry lips. This meant, of course, that she had never cared for him at all . . . But if her mission was one of seduction, then surely the baron would have been a party to it and would not have intervened on that moonlit evening in Bloemfontein? Unless, perhaps, the German had become genuinely jealous and overstepped the mark. Simon shrugged his shoulders. It didn't matter a damn now either way. And yet he could not erase from his mind the touch of his lips on her soft skin and the erotic fragrance of her perfume. Damn and blast the woman!

They had walked their horses for a further thirty minutes or so when they became aware that, far behind them, a horseman was galloping towards them from the direction of the Nek. Unarmed as they were, Simon felt vulnerable and immediately reinstated the white flag on the cavalry lance he still carried, as they urged their horses into a canter.

'I think we should wait, bach sir,' said Jenkins evenly. 'It looks to me, see, as though it's a woman ridin' after us.'

'What?' Simon swung round and pulled out his field glasses. The lenses showed that their pursuer was, indeed, riding side-saddle, although she was maintaining her seat effortlessly, despite the speed at which she was moving. As Simon focused, the rider came into view more clearly. Anna Scheel was dressed as though for a morning's canter on London's Rotten Row: black riding boots, beautifully cut full skirt, and, despite the sun, matching jacket. He could just make out that a saucy top hat was pinned to her hair and a smart veil was tied under her chin. She was urging her steed on, although it was clear that she had been seen and the three were waiting for her.

'Watch out, bach sir,' said Jenkins. 'It could be a trap.'

'I don't think so,' said Simon, ranging his field glasses slightly to left and right of the rider. 'It seems that she is alone. We must wait for her.' He found that his heart was pounding.

The countess reined in some two hundred yards from them and allowed her horse to walk towards them as she untied her veil for a moment, wiping her brow and cheeks with a small handkerchief before retying the veil beneath her chin. It was clear that she was perturbed and was anxious to regain her composure before facing the three men.

'I am so glad to have caught you, gentlemen,' she said as she joined them. 'I only heard that you had been in the Boer camp after you had left, and I had to ride hard.' She looked at Simon with an expression he had not seen on her face before – part anxiety, part supplication and completely alien to the air of self-possession she had worn in Bloemfontein. 'Good afternoon, Simon,' she said.

'Good afternoon, Countess.' His voice was cold and she half flinched at its tone.

She turned in the saddle quickly to look behind her before facing back to address Simon. 'Would it be possible, Simon, for you to spare me a moment . . . er . . . in private. I am afraid that I am in some distress and I have no one else to turn to. I would be grateful for your help.'

Simon's first instinct was to dismiss her with polite irony. After all, it seemed clear now that she was an agent of a foreign and unfriendly power – why else was she in the Boer camp? – and quite capable of enmeshing him in a web of further deceit. Yet there was something heartfelt in her appeal, a directness and air of ingenuousness in her voice that made him think again. And she was looking quite, quite beautiful, the gallop having brought colour to her cheeks and a glisten of moisture to her eyes – or was that an incipient tear? He made up his mind.

'Careful, bach,' he heard Jenkins murmur.

'You two ride on back to the camp,' he said. 'It's only about another four miles and I will follow directly.'

Jenkins gave a distinct hiss as he turned his horse's head around but the two walked their animals away without further complaint. Simon took up Anna's rein and led her to a cleft in a nearby sandstone rock, which remained open to the distant Nek but provided some cover. He slid from his horse and held up his arms to help her dismount. He closed his eyes and gritted his teeth for a moment as he smelt the familiar fragrance, then he led the horses into the cleft and found a grassy mound for Anna and himself to sit on, half out of the cleft so that they could command its approach. They sat for a moment, side by side, in silence.

'How can I help you, Anna?'

She turned to him, as though in relief.

'Oh thank you, Simon.' She paused and then looked up at him in that familiar way through her eyelashes. For a moment it seemed that the coquette was back. 'I have no right to ask you, but I must.'

Simon steeled his heart. 'What can I do?'

'Please, you can . . . you can . . . take me to the British camp and give me refuge there.'

His eyes widened. 'Refuge? From whom?'

'From von Bethman, my brother-in-law.'

'Brother-in-law! I thought you were cousins. You *are* married, then?'

'No, although I was. He is my late husband's stepbrother.'

Simon sighed. 'You had better tell me what has happened, although I am not sure that I can guarantee you entry to the British camp.' He thought of adding, 'as an agent of the German government' but thought better of it.

'Yes, yes, of course. It must seem strange to you.' She was nodding now, her eyes widened, all traces of the coquette departed. 'Let me tell you what has happened and then,' it was her turn to sigh, 'I must tell you my background. After that perhaps you will understand.'

She untied the veil at her throat and took off the absurd hat, shaking her head so that the lustrous coils of her hair loosened somewhat and gleamed in the afternoon sun.

'I had been riding – to the north of the Boer camp – for exercise and returned to find the camp agog with the fact that you had just departed. My servant described you and I realised immediately who it was. And Simon,' she looked up at him again through her lashes, 'my heart leapt a little.'

Simon disregarded this. 'What the hell were you doing in the Boer camp anyway? A foreign army in the field, fighting a war, is no place for a German countess, I would have thought.'

'I was with Wilhelm, of course.'

'Ah yes, your cousin – or brother-in-law, or whatever.'

'Brother-in-law. I don't know why he calls me his cousin when we meet strangers.' She shrugged. 'Perhaps it is because he wants to disabuse them of the idea that we are . . . are . . . closer than we are. In Prussia, you see – sorry, we must call it Germany now – marriages between first cousins are frowned upon.'

'Go on with your story.'

'When I returned to hear that you had just left, my first reaction was to ride after you. Then,' she hesitated, 'I realised that I could not. I had vowed never to see you again. Then Wilhelm strode up. He was incredibly angry, having just left you, and he accused me of riding off on some assignation to meet you. He is incredibly jealous, you see, Simon.'

'Does he have reason to be? Are you lovers?'

'No, no, never. In fact, I hate him.' The look on her face was

235

beyond dissembling, and despite himself, Simon was stirred. He laid a hand on her arm and, immediately and with relief, she covered it with her own. 'And never more so than now. He seized my riding crop and whipped my leg, so – look.' She pulled up her riding habit and underskirt and revealed two red weals on her knee, just above the boot. 'Of course, this frightened the horse and she bolted, and then and there I decided to keep on riding and find you.'

'Good God! The swine!' Simon shook his head in disbelief. 'But why do you stay with him if you hate him so? What sort of hold does he have on you?'

'Ah, yes. Time to tell you all, I think, my dear.' She cast an anxious eye over the hills to their right. 'But I must be quick. It could be that Wilhelm has ridden after me and we must be careful.'

'I will keep watch. Tell me your story.'

'Very well. My mother was English and my father was Prussian; they are both dead now. Our home was in Essen, and ten years ago, after my childhood at school in Kent, I returned there and, under pressure from my parents, married a friend of theirs, Ernst Scheel. He was much older than me and a childless widower, but I grew to love him for his gentleness and kindness.'

For a moment her voice fell away. Then she cleared her throat and continued. 'We were happy. Ernst was a member of the Krupps family and served on the board. We lived well because the company was flourishing, particularly after the war with France and Bismarck's terrible policy of "blood and iron".' Her quick glance to Simon now was one almost of apology. 'I was able to dress well and I suppose you could say that I was spoilt. We tried for children but were unsuccessful. Then, in an act of stupidity and selfishness, I ruined our happiness.'

Simon gripped her hand. 'Look, Anna, you don't have to tell me all of this.'

She smiled through the tears that were now in her eyes. 'Ach, but I do, Simon,' she said, and he realised that this was the first time he had heard her voice betray her Teutonic origins. 'What is it that they say – that confession is good for the soul. So let me confess to you.

'About seven years ago I met a young English officer. He was very like you – younger than me, handsome and impulsive. I loved Ernst, but even so, I succumbed to this young man.' She looked Simon fully in the face. 'When I first met you I thought that, somehow, he had returned, at least in spirit. That is why . . . but never mind that. I became pregnant by him. My young man then disappeared very quickly.'

'The bounder!'

Anna shook her head. 'No. I don't blame him. He had no money and was trying to make his way in the British Army. A scandal would have finished his career. I don't blame him, but it was very sad for me at the time.'

'What happened? Was there . . . was there . . . an abortion?'

'No. I confessed to Ernst, but he insisted that the baby was a love child and demanded life. He forgave me and said that the child should be brought up as his own – the baby we had long wanted. He was a very fine man.'

A silence fell between them. The sun had long slipped away behind the Drakensbergs to the west and long shadows were falling over the plain. Somewhere the haw-di-haw bird uttered its eponymous cry.

Simon coughed. 'A fine man indeed. How did he die?'

'He suffered a heart attack shortly after my son was born. He was only forty-nine. I named the boy Ernst, after him.'

'Was this, er, public knowledge, or at least within the family?'

'No. Ernst's family are – what is the English phrase – very strait-laced, I think you say. He felt that they should not know, in case, once he had gone, it affected their attitude to the boy. The money, you see, came from the family business and could have been withdrawn and we would have been penniless. So everybody believed that Ernst was the father. Except . . .'

'Von Bethman?'

'To this day I do not know how he found out. We were never close, but a little time after Ernst's death, he confronted me – he even knew the name of the father. He threatened to tell the family, which would have meant our ruin.'

'The bastard!'

Anna smiled through her tears. 'Ah, Simon, you do so remind me of . . . of . . . no, never mind. I always knew that Wilhelm desired me and I expected that he would demand that we should marry. But to my surprise, he did not do so.'

Simon swung his head as, out of the corner of his eye, he thought he saw a flash of light reflected high on the hillside to his right. A harness buckle, perhaps? But he could see nothing move. He asked, 'But he made some conditions, eh?'

'Oh yes. He insisted that the boy should remain in Germany and he also said that he wanted me to take up Ernst's seat on the board of Krupps – he has some influence there, you know – and travel with him on his sales expeditions around the world.'

'What a strange thing to demand. Why would he do that?'

'I think there were two reasons. First, he realised that I needed some role to fulfil me and he knew that I possessed some – what shall I call them? – social skills that would help him in his work. Second, I believe that he hoped that working with him might make me think more highly of him, so that when he did propose, I would accept.'

'And did it?'

'No. He is a mean, manipulative man and very cruel. That is why I was so fearful for you in that duel. He is jealous, and that is why I have never encouraged any man, because I was afraid that Wilhelm would try to take little Ernst away from me.'

Simon raised an eyebrow. 'No encouragement? What about that evening in Bloemfontein?'

She had the grace to blush. 'Ah, Simon, you are right to rebuke me. You so reminded me of . . . Let us say you slipped under my guard. I fear that I was not made to be chaste all my life, and . . .'

Suddenly she threw her arms around him and kissed him fully on the lips. He responded ardently for a brief moment then, slowly, he untangled her arms, held both of her hands in his and spoke to her slowly, his face a few inches away from hers.

'Anna, I think you were trying to seduce me so that you could discover what exactly I was doing in Bloemfontein.'

She shook her head vigorously. 'No, no, Simon. I knew what you were doing there – that charming old English gentleman with the monocle – Colonel somebody or other – told me all about it when he danced with me.'

Simon sighed. So much for Bentley's warning about Anna being a dangerous woman! He tried again. 'But Anna, I know that you came into my room at Bloemfontein and went through my clothes, looking for Brand's letter to Colley.'

Her eyes widened. 'Yes, that's true. How clever of you to know! Wilhelm made me do it – he has often forced me to do little things like that. He is very close to Bismarck, you see, and likes to please him by sending titbits back to him in Berlin. But they have all seemed rather harmless to me – not state secrets or anything like that. I never expected for a minute that I would find that letter, but it did give me a chance of leaving you *my* letter. I am not really a spy, some sort of femme fatale.' She drew away from him and a look of disdain distorted her features. 'And I would never use my body for that purpose.'

Then she leaned across to him again and took his hand. 'Simon, please believe me.'

Simon looked deeply into her eyes. They were wide and innocent and lovely. He swallowed and forced his brain to work.

'What do you hope to do in the British camp? Surely by riding away you are deserting your child back in Essen?'

She frowned and nodded. 'Yes. This terrifies me. Wilhelm has never hit me before but I can see now that he is close to the edge and will force himself upon me. I realise that I cannot stay with him. You see,' she kissed him artlessly, quite chastely, on the cheek, 'I have been worried about him for some time – since your duel, in fact. So I have made a contingency, I think you call it. I have been able to put some money into a bank account in London and I have arranged with my nanny looking after Ernst in Essen,' she grinned, 'she is Scottish and big, to take the boy quickly away to London when she receives a cable from me. I hope that General Colley will give me shelter and allow me to cable back to her. I could not do that, of course, from the Boer camp with Wilhelm there.'

They sat in silence for a while. Then Anna began to speak again, her eyes downcast. 'Simon, I need you to intercede for me with the general. I will make no further demands on you. I am thirty-two years old now with a child – far too old for you, even if you ... ah ... desired me – which I am sure you do not now. So I can make my own way and you must not feel sorry for me. But ...' she looked up at him through her eyelashes in that familiar, heart-dropping way, 'I will always, always be grateful to you.'

Slowly, ignoring the messages his brain was trying to send him, Simon bent his head to kiss her, just as the first bullet cracked into the rock above his head, sending splinters flying and making the horses rear. The second caught the sleeve of his jacket and he sprang to his feet, swinging Anna away and attempting to push her behind the rock, but as he caught her arm, the third round took her fully in the breast, knocking her over so that she sprawled backwards on to the grass, a red stain spreading quickly across her blouse.

'Anna!' He threw himself upon her as a fourth bullet tore into the grass near his shoulder. Whoever was shooting had a quick-loading rifle and a keen eye. Simon desperately splayed his feet to gain a footing in the loose sand and grass and, still lying on top of Anna to protect her, somehow managed to haul her around the corner of the rock, further into the crevice out of the line of fire. He cradled her in his arms and held her close, so that her blood spread across his own shirt. He inhaled the fragrance of her perfume and slapped her face gently as he looked into her eyes. But they were sightless. She was quite dead.

For a moment he rocked her gently. Then he became aware that there had been no more shots for nearly a minute. Had the sniper gone? No. More likely he was manoeuvring to gain a sight line into the crevice – or advancing now to complete the kill. Simon looked towards his horse, but the rifle holster was empty and he remembered that, of course, he and the others had ridden to the Boer camp unarmed. He was quite defenceless against this unknown, unseen marksman. Gently, he lowered Anna to the ground, and picked up the cavalry lance, with its white flag still attached. At least, perhaps he could throw the damned thing at the killer as he advanced. Then, with great caution, he poked his head over the rock and slowly raised his field glasses to his eye. Yes. There he was, a horseman picking his way carefully down the hillside opposite; coming towards him, white shirt quite conspicuous, rifle athwart the saddle. Von Bethman advancing to complete the execution.

Simon looked around him in desperation. The rock above him offered little protection and he could easily be picked off as he climbed higher. If he mounted now and fled he could possibly outride the German, but . . . He glanced down at Anna, all colour gone from her cheeks as she lay crumpled on the ground, her blouse now completely scarlet. He felt he could not leave her like that. Perhaps . . . He chewed his lip and thought hard. He would wait hidden until the last minute, then stampede the horses into von Bethman and charge him with the lance. A hundred to one chance, but better than nothing.

He eased the field glasses above the rock again and focused on the figure now trotting leisurely across the flat valley, in no hurry to complete his kill, for they were alone in this wild landscape.

As he watched, he saw the German rein in, stand in his stirrups with some hesitation and raise his hand to shield his eyes as he stared to the south-east, around the rock to Simon's right. Then Simon heard the thud of hooves and heard Jenkins's cry, 'There's the bastard, over there, look you,' as his two companions rounded the rock and pulled up their horses.

'Quick,' shouted Simon. 'Help me with her – on my horse. I'm afraid she's dead, but I want to take her.' He mounted and Hardy picked up the lifeless form and unceremoniously bundled it across the saddle in front of Simon. 'Ride for your life,' screamed Simon. 'He will remember that we are unarmed. Go now, now.'

Heads down, the three dug in their heels, and their wide-eyed mounts, followed by Anna's riderless horse, thundered around the rock and set off at full gallop back towards Mount Prospect. Two rifle reports followed them as von Bethman belatedly recognised the unarmed rescuers, but it was too late. They were away and safe.

Chapter 13

Eventually they allowed their panting horses to slow to a walk and crossed the lines of the laagered waggons at Mount Prospect without further incident. As they rode, Simon cushioned Anna's head and attempted to answer his companions' questions. At the instigation of a suspicious Jenkins, they had, it seemed pulled up only half a mile along the track to wait for Simon and had galloped back on hearing the first shot. But Simon was in no mood to recount Anna's story. At first he was unsure whether von Bethman had shot at him or deliberately at Anna. Then he realised that the German had obviously been aiming for him, desperate to kill the man who seemed to be taking away his love, and that Anna had intercepted the shot.

Once again Simon's brain began to swim as he attempted, within his sullen silence, to make sense of it all. Had he loved Anna? He gave an almost imperceptible shake of the head. No. Not love. It was Alice that he loved and always would. And yet . . . what would have happened had he taken Anna back to camp and interceded on her behalf with the general? Would he have been able to resist her? Probably not. He looked down and touched her cold cheek – and then another thought struck him. Had this all been a great subterfuge to enable her to penetrate the British headquarters and report back to the Boers? Again, no. She would have been so shrouded with suspicion that it would have been impossible for her to have carried out any sort of spying mission, and in any case the war was almost over, wasn't it? And why would von Bethman have intervened if she was successfully spinning her web of deception? He remembered the utter conviction with which she had told him her story. Anna Scheel had not been lying. She had become just another victim of this war and of one man's black jealousy. Simon's thoughts turned finally to Anna's child. Little Ernst would now quite probably be brought up under the close supervision of von Bethman, his mother's killer and a man who could not possibly bear any love for the child. Simon's mouth set in a hard line. There was only one solution to that problem. He decided then and there that he would have to kill von Bethman.

His immediate problem, however, was what to tell Colley. As the three crossed the lines, he directed Jenkins and Hardy to take Anna's body to the sick bay while he peeled off to report to the general. He paused for a moment outside the C-in-C's tent while he rehearsed what to say. He had to confess that the story sounded less than credible, but decided to tell Colley everything, except the events leading up to the duel, and the duel itself.

The general listened with rapt attention. At Anna's death he threw up his hands. 'How tragic. It is terrible enough to have brave young soldiers killed in this terrible conflict, but for it to happen to a woman . . . it beggars belief, Fonthill. That man must be a monster!' He took off his spectacles and thought for a moment. 'But what on earth was he doing in the Boer headquarters, eh? And how was it that you so outraged the man?'

'I have no idea, sir,' lied Simon. 'He is a very Prussian Prussian, so to speak, and I think that he just hates the British and everything to do with the British Empire. He was clearly trying to kill me when he hit the countess, as she was pleading with me to bring her here.'

Colley sucked the endpiece of his spectacles. 'You say she said he was close to B-B-Bismarck. Hmmm. I don't like that, Fonthill. I don't like that at all.' It was clear that, caring man though he was, the general was now becoming more perturbed to hear of the German's presence in the Boer headquarters and the influence he seemed to exert there, than of the death of an unknown German noblewoman. To Colley, bedevilled by the prevarications of the Gladstone cabinet in London, the possible ramifications of von Bethman's activities was one more unwelcome factor in the political quagmire in which he was becoming embroiled.

He frowned and shot a keen and not altogether approving look at

Simon. 'You realise that this could involve the Foreign Office and g-g-goodness knows who else? Less significant events have started European wars. You must write me a full r-r-report, Fonthill, and I will consider whether I need to send it to London. As she is – was – a lady of noble birth, we may have to make a full explanation to Berlin. Perhaps not. I will think about it. Of course, the countess will have a full Christian burial here – with the officers, of course. I will see to that. Now, t-t-tell me about the Boer camp. You delivered the letter to Smit, of course?'

'Yes, sir. General Smit asked me to tell you that he would convey your letter to Vice President Kruger as soon as possible but that Kruger was away from Heidelberg and it might take a little time for the letter to reach him. I, er, got the impression that he felt that forty-eight hours was a rather tight timetable within which to expect a reply.'

Colley snorted. 'That's their problem, not mine.' He stared out of the tent unseeingly and a heavy silence ensued before Simon broke it.

'I should tell you, sir, that the Boers have dug many more trenches, put up stone emplacements and extended along the Nek up the lower slopes of Majuba. I would say that they have also received many reinforcements. All in all, sir, it seems to me that the Nek would now be a very tough nut indeed to crack.'

'Improved their lines, eh?' The general seemed surprised and even annoyed. Simon couldn't think why. It seemed the obvious thing for the Boers to do, for they would know of the arrival of British reinforcements. 'Well,' continued Colley, 'I don't intend to sit here like a wet lettuce while the Boers make up their minds about our offer. Tomorrow I shall make a d-d-detailed reconnaissance around the back of the Boer lines, round their extreme left flank, across the Buffalo into the Transvaal. I want to look at the options open to me, if a direct attack on the Nek is out of the question. I shall take a small escort of Hussars and I shall want you and your scouts to guide us. We will leave shortly after dawn.'

'Very good, sir.'

Simon hurried to the sick bay and found that Anna, in an isolation tent, had already been sewn up in a shroud. He stood looking down at the pitiable bundle, remembering the gown she had worn at Brand's ball, her vibrancy that evening, the curve of her cheek and . . .

'How did it happen?' An army surgeon had crept up behind him.

'What? Oh, sniper's bullet. Think it was meant for me.'

'Really?' The doctor, blue eyes deep in a seamed face, were looking at him quizzically. 'Damned fine woman. What the hell was she—'

'Sorry,' said Simon hurriedly. 'I must go. When will she be . . . er . . .?'

'Within about an hour. Doesn't do to hang about in this climate. Burial party's on its way.'

'Thank you. Now please excuse me.'

Simon set out to look for Jenkins and Hardy. He found them on the edge of the camp, under the shade of a large cypress tree. There, reunited with his Colts, Hardy was once again practising his marksmanship, but this time he was performing before an admiring audience of Gordon Highlanders. As they watched, he stood with his back to his target – two beer bottles perched on a wall overlooking the empty veldt – and, at a shouted command, whirled, drew his revolver and shattered both bottles. The demonstration was repeated seven times and only once did the Texan miss. At first Simon was indignant that Anna's death should have had so little effect on his companions. Then he too became entranced by Hardy's skill.

'Hey, laddie,' shouted a kilted Scot, 'can ye do that when yer pissed?'

'Only when ah *am* pissed, sonny,' drawled Hardy.

'Where did ye learn it, then?'

'Shootin' Injuns an' moose on mah daddy's ranch in Texas.'

One bearded sergeant reacted to this. 'Och, surely the moose are further north, up in Canada? I served there fer a time wi' General Wolseley on the Red River Expedition. You no have them in Texas, I'm thinkin'.'

Hardy spat. 'Had 'em where *ah* was growin' up, that's fer sure.'

The Texan rejected further calls to show off his skills, pleading wastage of cartridges, and as from the fringe of the dispersing crowd Simon watched Hardy phlegmatically reloading his pistol, he wondered anew about this strange creature who had attached himself to them. The man seemed to have become even more withdrawn and monosyllabic since the Ingogo battle, hardly ever speaking unless drawn into conversation by the garrulous Jenkins. Yet there was much that was likeable about the lanky American. He rarely ventured an opinion but was always happy to do what was asked. His love of the outdoors was palpable and his equable nature and occasional shafts of wit made him an ideal companion. Simon realised that when the frontiersman eventually left to go his own way, as was inevitable, he would miss his company – and his air of mystery.

In this context, and freeing his thoughts for a moment from the memory of Anna, he put a companionable arm through that of the Texan as they walked to their tents and said, 'Now come on, Al. Even I know that moose are never found as far south as Texas. Were you pulling his leg?'

The tall man was unfazed. 'Sure 'nuff,' he said. 'Gotta keep puttin' these smartasses down – particularly the Jocks.'

'You know, Al bach,' said Jenkins, walking with them, 'you're wastin' your time doin' all that shootin' for nothin'. You could be chargin' for the entertainment, like in a circus, see.' He turned to Simon. 'If I got in a bit of trainin', I could be as good as old Al 'ere, but with me rifle, look you. Probably shootin' backwards from between me legs. And I could charge a dram for every shot. Now *that* would be sensible.'

Hardy just grinned and chewed his tobacco.

Simon left them and made his way to the little compound where lay the officers' burial ground. It was a peaceful spot, from where a clear view could be had of the looming figure of Majuba, with the Nek below it. He was just in time to see the shroud being lowered into the ground by four Zulus, under the supervision of a rather worried-looking padre.

'Ah, young man,' said the padre, 'do you know anything about this lady? I know only her name, and it would be Christian to be able to say just a little more in laying her to rest.'

Simon nodded, not trusting himself to speak. Eventually he cleared his throat and said: 'She was a German countess and a widow and a loving mother. She was also very brave and died brutally a long way from her home. I am sure, Padre, that you will find something appropriate from the scriptures to say. I will stay.'

After the brief service, he gathered together a few drooping wild veldt flowers and put them on the mound of earth. He attempted his own prayer but could think of nothing to say. He did, however, detain a corporal of the 58th who was passing and pressed a half-sovereign into his hand. 'Can you make a good wooden cross?' he asked.

'O' course, sir, yessir.'

'Good. Make the best you can and put it at the head of this grave. Carve this into the crosspiece.' He scribbled on a scrap of paper. 'Anna Scheel, killed in action, 17/2/1881. RIP.' 'Can you do that? I am away tomorrow but I will return the day afterwards.'

Later, as they sat round a spluttering, dampish fire drinking tea, Simon told Jenkins and Hardy of their assignment for the next morning. As usual, Jenkins was puzzled.

'Now this bloody war is supposed to be almost over, isn't it? I thought that the letter we took today agreed to a cestation . . . cissisation . . . ending of 'ostilities for a bit. Why does the general want to go prowlin' about round the back of the enemy, like? If 'e's caught by 'em, there'd be a bit of a row back 'ome, wouldn't there?'

Simon nodded. 'Probably. The trouble is, you see, I think he's been getting a bit of a bad press both here and at home. It's rather unfair in a way, because although he lost a lot of men on the Nek and the Ingogo, he did not have to sacrifice ground or a good tactical position and he withdrew his troops more or less in good order from both encounters. His very presence here has drawn south a large contingent of the Boer army and so relieved pressure on our besieged garrisons in the Transvaal. Having said that, he has not been able to have a definitive set-to with the Boers and – equally importantly – he has not been able to dislodge them from British territory in Natal.' He prodded the ground gloomily with a stick. 'I would say that General Colley is itching to retrieve his reputation and also to find some way of getting the Boers to retreat, but London won't let him. So he's poking around to find a route out of the impasse.'

Jenkins sniffed. 'Well, beggin' your pardon, bach sir, but I don't much fancy goin' with him tomorrow. This bloke 'as a nasty 'abit of leadin' us right into the mire, if you ask me.'

Hardy stood, threw away the dregs of his tea and stretched. 'This chile is hittin' the hay, if we're ridin' at dawn. Good night, boys.'

The others nodded to him, and when the tall figure had slipped away from the firelit circle, Jenkins leaned across and put a hand on Simon's knee. 'Sorry about the German lady, bach,' he said. 'I could see that you was upset like, but you know, it's probably all for the best. It wouldn't 'ave worked, would it?'

Simon frowned. 'What the hell are you talking about?'

'Well – you and 'er. I wouldn't 'ave thought she was your cup o' tea, so to speak. Now, Miss Alice—'

'Miss Alice is bloody well married and is probably already pregnant with Covington's child. So that's that.' He scowled and rose. 'No point in talking about it further. Early start tomorrow. Good night, 352.'

Jenkins watched him go. 'Ah well,' he murmured. 'I'm glad, at least. Wouldn't have wanted to live in bloody Germany . . .'

The serrations of the hills to the east stood in purple silhouette against the rays of the hidden sun as the general and his escort rode out the next morning. With the three scouts in the lead in their familiar arrowhead formation, the party headed south and crossed the Buffalo some miles behind Mount Prospect, climbed the Transvaal shore of the river and wheeled to the north until they were to the rear of the Boers' position on Laing's Nek. Colley gestured to a high spot and they climbed to it and reined in. Following the arrival of the reinforcements from the south, the general had gained a new chief of staff, Lieutenant Colonel Herbert Stewart, to replace the dead Colonel Deane, and the two men now rode forward and studied the northern prospect of Mount Majuba intensely through their field glasses. They sat apart for at least an hour examining the mountain and the surrounding country, their heads together in earnest conversation, then ordered the return to Mount Prospect.

'What was all that about then?' asked Jenkins as they rode ahead of the returning party.

'I'm not sure,' said Simon. 'But I don't like the smell of it.'

The next day Simon settled down to write his report about Anna. After two pages he screwed them up and threw them away. He would await events before perjuring himself on paper. In the mean time, the general would have enough to do. Later he saw Colley and his chief of staff once again in deep conversation at the northern edge of the camp. At one point a native who lived in one of the neighbouring farms was summoned and was closely cross-questioned by the two men. During the interrogation the black man lifted his arm and pointed towards Majuba, but the general quickly pulled the man's arm down again. Simon, watching unseen from under a tree, blew out his cheeks. It was clear that what he had feared was about to happen. Colley intended to do the impossible: he was going to try and take Majuba!

Simon retreated to his tent to pick up his own field glasses and covertly examined the mountain ahead. Its every detail was now visible in the clear air of that South African summer, and the morning sun defined its ravines, cloofs, ridges and contours through the magnification of the binoculars as though they were less than a quarter of a mile away, instead of four. From this southerly aspect it could be seen that a lower hill or small mountain, the Nkwelo, was connected to the westerly slopes of Majuba by a nek or saddle, and to Simon this seemed to present the best approach. But the path to Majuba's summit from the nek looked to be a difficult climb – as, indeed, did all the approaches facing south. The flat-topped mountain seemed to hunch itself upwards at the last in an almost vertical ring of rough, fissured rock. And from what Simon could remember of the view from the north, the same gaunt necklace ringed the throat of the mountain at that side too. Surely, whatever the approach used, no column of troops carrying full equipment could climb that?

Which begged the question, of course, whether they would be forced to do so under fire. Simon focused his lenses on the table at the summit of the mountain. It was well known to all of Colley's force that the Boers had placed a small piquet on the summit as observers. There they were now – seemingly just one or two familiarly hatted burghers strolling along in silhouette against the blue sky. But was that all there were? And were they withdrawn at night?

The last question made Simon lower his glasses. Surely Colley would not attempt a night ascent? The risk of crossing four miles – probably six if the attempt was made via the north or even the nearest route via the Nkwelo saddle – of hostile open territory in the dark and then scaling a seemingly unclimbable mountain without knowing if it was defended must be too great to be contemplated, even by a general desperate to redeem himself. Wolfe had done something similar at Quebec, but Simon could not recall from his knowledge of recent military history another instance of a night attack being successful in these conditions. He did, however, remember the chaos of night manoeuvres on the Brecon Beacons, with whole companies losing themselves on those hills – gentle and unchallenging compared with the unknown ravines and rocky fissures of Majuba. Then a further, more pleasurable thought struck him. Chaos? If it was like that – and it almost certainly would be – could there be an opportunity of slipping away, down to the Nek below, and finding von Bethman?

The idea prompted a grim smile and he walked back to his tent in deep contemplation.

That evening he was summoned to Colley's tent. Inside, flanking the general, were Lieutenant Colonel Stewart and a Major Fraser of the Royal Engineers, another newly joined member of the staff. They all wore expressions of suppressed excitement, like boys about to break out of boarding school to raid a tuck shop. After effecting the introductions, Colley lowered his voice and said: 'I am leading a column this evening after d-d-dark to take possession of Majuba.'

Simon nodded and then remembered to be surprised. 'Really, sir? Won't that be interpreted by the Boers and even the people back home as an offensive move during what is virtually a ceasefire?'

Colley glowered and Simon realised that now that the general had a full staff again, his scout no longer possessed the privilege of offering advice inherited from the massacre of the staff at the Nek.

'Certainly not,' snapped Colley. 'The Boers have a p-p-piquet up on the mountain that the local Zulus reliably inform me is withdrawn at night. I am therefore merely taking unoccupied Natal territory which belongs to Her Majesty. And anyway, that is none of your business. What *will* be your business, Fonthill, is to go ahead of the column, with your scouts and two local Kaffirs who know the mountain well. You will guide us in. We will c-c-climb the mountain via the Nkwelo hill and scale Majuba proper along the nek that connects the two of them. I am informed that the top of Majuba consists of a saucer-like depression ringed by boulders and that water can be found not far below the surface.'

His expression softened. 'Now, I understand your anxiety, my boy. You have had experience of the Boers' obduracy at first hand. But this move c-c-cannot be interpreted as being aggressive, for if we are right that the piquets are removed at night – and it will be part of your job to ascertain this before we crest the summit – then we can occupy the d-d-damned thing without bloodshed. It will just be a troop movement.' He chuckled. 'Of course, I will then be able to look down over the Boer defences on Laing's Nek and command the approaches to it from the Natal side as well, and this will make 'em feel dashed uncomfortable. It might even persuade them to pull out of Natal and await developments on the political front.'

Simon nodded. 'I see the point, sir. When do you intend to march?'

'At ten p.m. The force will not be large – only approximately six hundred men. No one outside this tent knows of my intentions at the moment because I want this move to be carried out in the utmost secrecy. We shall b-b-begin marshalling the troops at about eight thirty, but until then keep this under your hat. We shall march without lights and I understand that it is likely to be a dark evening . . .'

Simon groaned inwardly.

'It is vital, therefore, that the column does not become broken up during the hours of darkness. The two Zulus are waiting outside. You know the country, but talk to them about the route – they speak good English – and scan it carefully as discreetly as you can from the camp. No p-p-pointing to the mountain, now. I want the full column to be on top of Majuba by dawn, looking down on Johnny Boer when he wakes up. Come back to me when you have d-d-d-decided exactly which way we go. Understood, Fonthill?'

'Understood, sir.'

'Any questions?'

'Do you intend to try and put guns up on the summit, General?'

'Not tonight. Nor Gatling guns either. It will be difficult enough trying to get six hundred fully equipped men up there in the darkness as it is. But it will do the Boers no harm t-t-to think that we might have cannon up there commanding their camp. And, in the light of events, we might try and hoist a few mountain guns up later. All right?'

'Quite clear, sir.'

Colley extended a placatory hand and smiled. 'Jolly good, Fonthill. My two staff officers here and I will be in the van of the column and we shall therefore be right behind you. Good luck. We shall d-d-depend on you.'

'Thank you, sir.'

Outside the tent, Simon found the two Zulu trackers squatting on their haunches, clenching assegais in their right hands, their faces completely expressionless. For a brief moment his stomach dropped as he looked again at the razor-sharp tips of their spears – the *iklwas*, so-called by the Zulus after the sound they made as they were twisted and removed from the flesh of their victims. His mind went back to Isandlwana and Rorke's Drift, where he had warded off thrust after thrust from assegais like these until his tired arms threatened to drop his rifle and bayonet. Then he took a deep breath and beckoned to the Zulus to accompany him to his tent. They loped behind him as he retrieved his binoculars and then squatted with him under the cypress tree looking out towards Majuba.

The Zulus explained with a touch of proprietorial pride that although the Boers called the mountain Spitskop, it had been named Amajuba, 'the Hill of the Doves', by the great King Shaka when he had passed this way some fifty years before after returning from one of his punitive expeditions against a neighbouring tribe. Shaka had felt that the slabs of rock that encircled the summit made it look from a distance like a native dovecote. It was, they said, not as difficult to climb as it looked and the easiest route was certainly via Imquala. But the problem would arise when a plateau halfway up the first hill had been reached, for the troops would then have to head north and follow a track along the side of Imquala only wide enough for men to walk in single file, with a steep drop to one side. The path would lead to another open plateau at the northern end of Imquala and from there the route lay along the wide ridge which was the saddle and which led to Majuba itself and the final climb. From the foothills of Imquala to the summit of Majuba was just under three miles.

Simon frowned and bit his lip. Not difficult for the Zulus. But could six hundred troops, in full battle order, find their way in darkness up one and a half mountains? And would the Boers be waiting for them if they did reach the summit? He pressed the question again on the Zulus, but they assured him that the Boer piquet always left the mountain at dusk. He nodded. Farmers again. Magnificent horsemen, fine marksmen, but not *real* soldiers – not disciplined enough to stay the night on an open mountaintop. At least, that was the hope!

The Zulus confirmed that the easiest way to approach the mountain was to advance along the main road towards the Nek and then, once in the horseshoe embrace of the hills on either side, turn off to the left and begin the climb of Imquala. But Simon felt that this was to take the column far too close to the Boer lines and that it would be best to take a more circuitous route and turn off earlier. Colley agreed when he made his recommendation.

As lights-out sounded at 8.30 and the men prepared to retire for the night, a sudden flurry of activity broke out around the staff tents. Subalterns ran to senior officers and orders were issued for the chosen troops to prepare for the night march.

After alerting Jenkins and Hardy about the task ahead and briefing them as best he could, Simon cornered a young lieutenant and questioned him about the strength of the column. He learned that the force was to consist of two companies of the 58th Regiment of Foot, two companies of the 3/60th Rifles, three companies of the 92nd Highlanders, a company-strength Naval Brigade and specialist odds and ends from other units. Each man was to carry his rifle, seventy rounds of ammunition, a greatcoat, a waterproof sheet, and rations for three days – a total weight of fifty-eight pounds. In addition, each company was to take four picks and six shovels. Heavy loads all right. But why such an eclectic selection of men from different units? There would be no homogeneity, no familiar hierarchy of officers down which command could be passed in the event of casualties and, indeed, no one familiar regimental commander around whom troops could rally – Colley himself was not instantly recognisable to the rank and file. Why throw together such an odd mixture of riflemen, sailors and Highlanders to carry out a night operation of great complexity?

Simon put the question to the subaltern. The young man pulled at his moustache. 'I think the old man wants to share around the glory a bit,' he confided. 'Give the chaps of the 58th a chance to have another go, so to speak, and the new boys a bite of the cherry too. Not a bad idea, don't you know.'

But Simon shook his head as he walked away. It sounded amateurish to him. His apprehension grew as the bustle of the preparations consumed about one third of the camp. Those left behind were openly envious of the men now so quickly preparing to march through the night. The destination remained a secret but it was generally presumed along the lines that the general was going to make some sort of direct attack on the Boers again, probably against the enemy entrenched along the Nek. Spirits were high. It was a relief that part of Colley's command at least was going into action.

Simon found himself thinking again about Hardy. It was, after all, not his war and he felt guilty that the American was to be drawn once more into a highly dangerous situation. After the Little Bighorn, Laing's Nek and the Ingogo, the Texan must surely think that all generals were incompetent! He put it to Hardy that this was one engagement that he might care to miss.

Jenkins added his own voice to the argument. 'Yes, Ally,' he said. 'Go an' find your own war, killin' Red Indians an' that. This is really our little battle, see. Stay 'ere an' try an' improve your poker. You're fallin' away a bit. I only owe you somethin' like twenty thousand pounds now.'

The American's response was the same as before. He gave them his laconic smile. 'Met a Yorkshireman once. He used to say, "In for a penny, in for a pound." Ah guess that's me now. Ah'll just jog along as usual behind you two fellers.'

Promptly at ten o'clock, Simon, Jenkins and Hardy followed closely behind the two Zulu trackers at the head of the column. Simon had decided that they should leave their horses behind so as to match the pace of the marching men, even though the officers behind them, of course, were mounted. Colley had ordered that the 'Lights Out' bugle should be sounded from the north of the camp so that it could clearly be heard in the Boer entrenchments and all fires and lights had been promptly put out at the same time. Enemy observers would be in no doubt that the English had retired for the night. It was to the accompaniment of only a very muffled cheer from the troops remaining, then, that the vanguard wound its way between the waggons and began the march on Majuba.

Apart from the occasional creak of webbing and the soft thud from the hooves of the officers' chargers, it was a silent column. The redcoats of the 58th – the survivors of the first attack on Laing's Nek – were given the honour of leading. Behind them marched the Rifles, themselves the veterans of the Ingogo battle; followed by the kilted and khaki-coated Gordon Highlanders, new to South Africa but covered with honours from Roberts's recent campaign in Afghanistan; while bringing up the rear trudged the blue jackets of the Naval Brigade. The night was not as dark as had been predicted, and although the sky was moonless, the bulk of Majuba could clearly be seen ahead, looming large and menacing against the lighter blue of the heavens. Looking back, Simon sensed an air of excitement pervading the thin column of figures winding behind him. Whatever was going to happen – and the troops and their junior officers had still not been told their destination – the marching men sensed that revenge against the Boers was within their reach.

'I 'ope these black lads know where the 'ell we're goin', because I don't,' confided Jenkins. But the Zulus padded along confidently enough and gestured to Simon when the time came to turn off the track and begin the ascent of Imquala. He turned to Colley and pointed to the left, and the general nodded.

As the Zulus had predicted, the initial stages were not difficult and the whole column was able to reach the first plateau halfway up Imquala without incident. Here, Colley directed that the two companies of the Rifles should be left to protect his line of communications and to send a vedette to the top of Imquala in the morning. Then Simon followed the receding figures of the Zulus along the thin single track that skirted the side of the mountain. Here he knew he would have trouble with Jenkins. This most courageous of warriors secretly nurtured two great fears: the sea and heights. Luckily, the night was dark enough for no one to see the sheer drop to their right, but even so, the Welshman clung to the rock face to his left.

'Sorry, bach sir,' he whispered. 'Just tell everyone to step around me. I'll catch you all up later when I've 'ad a bit of a breather, like.'

'No,' hissed Simon, his face so close to that of his comrade that he could smell the perspiration and the fear. 'You could be shot for cowardice and that would be inconvenient, to say the least. Who would do my washing? Now come on, 352. Hold on to my belt and tread in my footsteps. This bit's not long. The general's riding his bloody horse along this path and he's not fazed. Come on now. Al, help him.'

The American slipped off his belt and offered the end to Jenkins. From behind came an urgent whisper from Colley. 'Everything all right, Fonthill?'

'Perfectly all right, sir.'

Clasping Simon's belt with one hand and the end of Hardy's with the other, Jenkins – stirred by the patrician tones behind him – began to inch his way along the track, his face to the wall. Simon had lost the Zulus ahead of him but that was not a problem. There was only one way they could go. He was conscious that Jenkins's terror would hold up the whole column, but the pace of the advance would have been slowed considerably by the need to advance in single file anyway. It just couldn't be helped.

At last the rock face fell away and the ground opened out, and here the Zulus were waiting for them. 'Well done, 352,' said Simon, and the broad little man collapsed to the ground in relief.

'Glad we got here,' murmured Hardy. 'Mah pants were comin' down.'

Colley called a brief halt to allow the column to re-form before tackling the saddle that now led upwards to Majuba itself. Here the wind whistled from the veldt to the north and dogs could be heard barking down below, setting everyone's nerves on edge. Simon looked at his watch: one a.m. They had reached, he estimated, the probable halfway point of the march. Now, slightly round the bluff shoulder of Majuba and directly down below, the Boers lay sleeping. A missed step here, sending a man and his equipment bouncing down the slope, would waken the whole camp.

The column plodded on until it reached the second plateau, which marked the end of the saddle and the beginning of the last, steepest climb to the summit of Majuba. At the end of the plateau, before the path petered out to an intermittent track and the semi-vertical haul began, Colley called another halt and it became immediately apparent that the column had lost its line and several sections had somehow strayed. What Simon had feared had now materialised.

'Get back, Fonthill,' ordered the general, 'and be sheepdog. Round the blasted stragglers up in double-quick time. If we're caught strung out on this mountainside when dawn breaks everything is lost. Use your men as markers.'

Simon thought it wiser to leave Jenkins sheltering behind a rock, but took Hardy and the two Zulus with him to spread out along the plateau and bring in the errant groups of men, allowing himself leave to curse their young officers for allowing them to blunder off. 'There's only one bloody way to go, and that's up,' he hissed to them.

It took a full hour for all the stragglers to be brought in, but eventually the column was formed up again to the general's satisfaction. Here, before the last section was attempted, Colley left behind the officers' chargers, and a company of Highlanders were detached to stay on the spur to dig in 'as far as possible' and form a post capable of providing cover for the horses and receiving ammunition and reinforcements the next day from Mount Prospect. From here, roughly an hour behind schedule and with the fear that dawn would find them exposed and clinging like flies to the mountainside, the final scramble up to the summit of Majuba began.

It was, of course, by far the most difficult and dangerous part of

258

the whole venture. The path had virtually disappeared and the climbing men had to negotiate gullies, sharp rocky buttresses and deep re-entrants covered in thorny brushwood. Increasingly Simon, now in the lead with Major Fraser, had to pull himself upwards on his hands and knees with tufts of grass to make any progress at all. He gasped in great lungfuls of thin air as he climbed – a reminder that they were now dragging themselves upwards at an altitude of well over six thousand feet.

Impelled by the need to maintain his role as scout at the head of the column, Simon had long since had to relinquish his personal care of the vertigo-ridden Jenkins. Looking down now, however, he was relieved and amazed to see the Welshman, shoulder to shoulder with Hardy, gradually inching up the mountain not far below. Just able to catch his eye in the poor light, the perspiring Jenkins mouthed, 'Bloody 'ell,' before pressing his face back to the slope.

It was now virtually impossible to preserve silence, and slipping and sliding men were clanking their water bottles and bayonet scabbards against the rocks and cursing softly as they grappled with the face of the mountain. These noises, hastily suppressed by NCOs and officers, sent hearts racing as the men looked upwards. For added to the immense difficulties presented by the terrain and altitude was now the fear that up there, behind where the lip of the summit presented a black line against the stars, might be lying a line of the best marksmen in the world, just waiting for the order to emerge from hiding, present their rifles and fire down on them. If the summit was manned, the exhausted climbers would stand no chance of defending themselves. It would be a massacre, and Simon's tongue, dry enough as it was already, cleaved to the roof of his mouth at the thought. The darkness and the strange silhouettes presented by the boulders and crags added to the fear.

From out of the semi-darkness, the two Zulus had now reappeared to join Fraser and Simon just below the lip of the rim of the summit. With immense care, the four men spread out and slowly lifted their heads above the rocky rim. No bearded, bandoliered, slouch-hatted figures met their gaze. The summit – or at least what they could see of it – seemed empty of life. They hauled themselves over the edge and Fraser silently indicated for the natives to go to right and left and reconnoitre the rim. Within seconds, it seemed, they reappeared. 'Nobody, baas,' said the elder of the two. The summit of Majuba was unoccupied. Grinning at each other, Fraser and Simon shook hands. Simon looked at his watch: it was just after four a.m.

Hardly had he done so when Colley himself, incongruous in a pair of white tennis shoes into which he had changed after dismounting from his horse, appeared over the edge.

'It seems, sir,' said Fraser, 'that we have the mountain to ourselves.'

'Splendid. But we must make sure. Deploy the men around the edge. No noise, now.'

As the breathless soldiers began arriving on the summit, Colley himself helped Fraser and Stewart to spread the men around the edge of the mountaintop. Simon pulled Jenkins up, as Hardy pushed from below, and the three scouts fell on to the rough grass, each trying to regain his breath. 'No problem at all, really, look you,' eventually confided Jenkins. 'It's just a question of not lookin' down, see. Anybody can do it.'

The sky had hardly lightened, but up there, where it seemed possible to reach upwards and grab a handful of stars in each hand, the geography of the summit could be more or less made out. Simon realised that the mountaintop was, indeed, a saucer-like depression, roughly triangular in shape and measuring about three quarters of a mile in circumference and perhaps ten acres in extent, with the grassy floor of the basin falling to between ten and forty feet from the enclosing rim and strewn with boulders and smaller rocks. The saucer was roughly bisected by a low ridge running more or less parallel to the north-eastern face of the triangle. It joined two kopjes which rose opposite each other on the rim and which the Zulus told Simon were known to them as Majuba's Breasts, though the troops soon named these hillocks after the officers commanding the troops allocated to them. So the western breast, conical in shape and the highest point of the mountain, was called Macdonald's Kopje and the other, which only just rose above the rim, was dubbed Hay's Kopje.

The general and Stewart busied themselves distributing each contingent of breathless men around the rim as they arrived. No thought was given to incorporating the strengths and weaknesses of the position into the distribution: the men were set down equally around the edge, some twelve paces between each of them. There was no concentration at the most vulnerable points of the perimeter.

As the last man came on to the mountaintop, the promise of a rosy dawn began to show over the hills on the Buffalo river side. Colley had executed his night march and captured on time the key point of Majuba Hill, overlooking the Boer positions, without losing a single man. He had achieved the near impossible.

Simon realised that he had not given a thought to von Bethman during the climb. Well, the swine would just have to wait.

Chapter 14

Once the men had been positioned, Colley ordered a signal to be made to Mount Prospect, from a position out of sight of the Boers, reporting the success of the march. Then, as the officers began sorting out the men into their respective units, the general, accompanied by Colonel Stewart, Major Fraser and the naval officer commanding the bluejackets, Commander Romilly, began a closer inspection of the position. The sun was now just beginning to climb beyond the eastern peaks and it was pleasant in the half-light to be high on the mountaintop on that Sunday morning of 27 February 1881. As the four men picked their way along the springy grass between the rocks, they came upon Simon and Hardy preparing coffee, with Jenkins stretched at their side, fast asleep.

'Well d-d-done, Fonthill,' said Colley, nodding also to Hardy. 'You got us here, and on time too. First class.'

'Thank you, sir.'

'We're taking a look around,' continued Colley. 'Come along and see what we've got up here. You c-c-come too, General Custer.'

The general was obviously in a high, happy mood after the successful conclusion to the night march, and although Simon was tired and wished nothing more than to finish his coffee and stretch out on the turf beside Jenkins, he felt it would be ill-mannered to refuse. 'Thank you, General,' he said, rising to his feet. Hardy followed suit, rather more languorously.

In the improving light, the details of the site could be distinguished more clearly. The ascent had been made up the mountain's south-west shoulder, and it could now be seen how difficult had been the approach. Looking down, Simon could pick out the terraces and ravines and the rocky escarpment studded with stunted bushes and trees. It seemed almost impossible that troops so heavily laden could have ascended this way in the darkness. But he also noted that the lowest slopes were concealed from view from the summit. An attacking force could gather there without being seen from the top.

The north-eastern face overlooked the Boer positions on Laing's Nek, and the breakfast fires of the enemy way down below could clearly be seen, pricking the deep purple of the valley like hundreds of fireflies. It was the morning of the Sabbath, and Simon reflected that the Boers would not be looking to take arms on the holy day. They would consider it a sin for any Christian to have aggressive thoughts on a Sunday. Did this mean that they would not fight to regain the mountain if their leaders demanded it? Simon sighed. Who was to know? More significant to the moment, perhaps, was the fact that the mountain sloped quite gently here away from the summit to a brow beneath and seemed more easily climbed. Beyond and beneath the brow, in turn, a wide, flat terrace stretched before ending in a further drop. From the lip of the summit a distinctive knoll projected from its northern point. It was joined to the summit by a narrow saddle less than seventy yards long and standing only just a little lower than the rim. It commanded the last hundred feet or so of the ascent to the summit from this side, and the general directed that a handful of Highlanders, under the command of a subaltern, should be posted on the knoll to defend it and command the final approach to the top. This was immediately dubbed 'the Gordons' Knoll'.

The positioning of the defenders of Majuba – if it needed to be defended, for who would dare to attack it? – was now more or less complete. The northern half of the mountaintop was allocated to the Gordons, the 58th were posted along the southern face, and the sailors manned the southern angle of the triangle, including a little projecting knoll there which became 'Sailors' Knoll', of course. Colley had made his headquarters in the lowest, central portion of the saucer, under the protection of the bisecting ridge. The hollow was about two hundred yards long and sixty yards wide, and here he had decided to place his reserve of three companies. Two doctors were now setting up a makeshift hospital there and wells were being dug for water.

General Colley looked around with some satisfaction. He turned to Simon. 'We could stay here for ever,' he said.

'Quite so, sir.' But what was the point? 'May I ask, General, what is your intention?'

Colley shot him a quick glance. 'All I ask of the men is that they hold this hill for three d-d-days.' He turned to Stewart and the naval commander. 'I intend to order up reinforcements from Newcastle – the Hussars and the 60th Rifles – immediately. Once everything is settled up here later today, I shall return to Prospect and leave you, Romilly, in t-t-temporary command here until I return.'

Simon caught Hardy's eye. At last he began to understand. It would take about three days before the reinforcements could come up from Newcastle. Colley would probably haul up mountain guns to the summit tomorrow, and when his fresh troops arrived, he would lead a direct attack on Laing's Nek, supported by the artillery on Majuba. Caught between two fires, the Boers would break and retreat and be vulnerable to pursuit by the cavalry. But perhaps, faced with being commanded from Majuba's top, they would withdraw back into the Transvaal before a shot was fired anyway? That would be a triumph politically for Colley, though less impressive militarily.

A shot and then laughter from the north-eastern perimeter ended Simon's musing. A group of Highlanders were standing on the lip in the now strong morning sunlight, looking down on the Boer positions far below and jeering. One of them was gesturing with the smoking barrel of his rifle. 'Come on up, yer boogers,' he shouted.

Colley was unamused. 'Go and s-s-stop that, Stewart,' he ordered. 'I do not want to provoke the enemy unnecessarily.'

The colonel strode away and Fraser, frowning, turned to the General. 'Sir George, given the amount of dead ground that we can't command from the top here, don't you think it would be wise to dig some trenches across the saucer as a defensive resort?'

Colley looked around, wrinkling his eyes against the newly risen sun. 'Oh, I don't think so, Fraser. If they do get up, they won't have artillery, only r-r rifles, and it won't be necessary.'

Simon sucked in his breath. With 'only rifles', the Boers had already inflicted two near defeats on Colley already. Would he never learn?

But Fraser persisted. 'Very well, sir, but I do feel that we should have fall-back redoubts placed strategically. We can build them easily enough from the rocks lying about the place. I would suggest that we place one here, to overlook the approach of reinforcements from Mount Prospect, another one on Macdonald's Kopje and a third on the eastern corner, overlooking the Nek.'

Colley sighed. 'Oh, very well,' he said, as though placating an insistent child. 'But the men have had a long march and a difficult climb and they are t-t-tired. Don't start the work now. Let them rest. There is no hurry.'

'Very good, sir.'

The general turned to his scouts. 'As a matter of fact, I think we could all do with some rest. I suggest you f-f-fellows get some while you can. I shall probably want you to come back with me later in the day, Fonthill. Now good morning to you.'

'Good morning, sir.'

Simon and Hardy returned to find a tousle-haired Jenkins frying bacon on a small fire. The smell was delicious and the three breakfasted heartily, but Simon was withdrawn. He had seen enough of the defences around the perimeter not to share the general's sanguinity about their position on the mountaintop. It was true that two of the three faces of Majuba looked unscalable in the face of determined fire from the defenders on the summit, but the third approach, that from the Boer lines on Laing's Nek below, appeared to offer an easier way to the top. The point was that, as Fraser had explained, the climb offered plenty of dead ground that was beneficial to attackers – in other words, much of their approach would not be seen by the defenders on the lip. It offered no field of fire. It was terrain in which climbers could bunch and mount an attack from quite close to the summit. The general did not seem to realise this, for he was making no attempt to deploy his troops to counter the threat. But would the Boers attack? Good fighters as they were, would they have the stomach for this kind of dangerous, physically daunting climb? Trained soldiers might take it on – the British Tommy certainly would, because he always obeyed orders – but would these farmers, these independent, mercurial burghers do so?

Simon's thoughts were interrupted by a cry, again from the north-eastern lip of the crater. A Jock was standing there, looking down on the Boer positions, his kilt swirling in the morning breeze, his new-style khaki jacket unbuttoned. 'Hey,' he shouted, pointing down, 'the boogers are pullin' oot. They're pullin' oot, ah tell ye.'

Simon threw down his plate and joined others running to the edge. It was true, or seemed to be. Far below, the Boers – little more than black dots – were driving in their oxen and inspanning their waggons, and the plain was dotted with horsemen. A cheer broke out from the men on the rim. Simon, however, remained silent. He could see that, from the apparent confusion of the camps below, bodies of horsemen were emerging to ride towards the lower spurs of the mountain, disappearing from view as they closed in on it directly below him. The Boers now clearly realised that the British were in possession of Majuba. Was this the beginning of an attempt to retake the mountain?

Simon reported accordingly to the general. But Colley, busily writing, seemed to attach no significance to the development. With his usual courtesy, he thanked Simon without additional comment and continued to write his dispatch.

Thoughtfully, Simon strode back to the edge. The view was magnificent. The great brown and green grass uplands of the veldt stretched far away to the north like a roughly woven carpet, broken by the deep cut of the Buffalo as it curved away into Zululand to the east and dotted with those distinctive table-topped peaks that rose from the plain as though a giant had plucked them up with his fingertips and then tried to press them flat with his thumb. The air was clean, fresh and clear, and looking in every direction, Simon could see no sign of human habitation. Yet here, in this corner of this beautiful, vast, comparatively empty land, the people of two minority white races had chosen to try and kill each other. He sighed and looked again down at Laing's Nek. Was von Bethman still there, among the Boer encampments? And would the subsequent battle – if there was to be one – allow him to get close enough to settle his debt with the German?

The question caused Simon to take in a deep breath. Kill him? How? Would he steal up on him – God knows how in the midst of the enemy – and simply shoot him down? No. He could never kill a man in cold blood. How then? Another duel? Simon smiled. He had had luck on his side the last time and he doubted if he could survive another display of swordsmanship from this master duellist, even if his sword arm had not quite recovered. Pistols, then? He sighed. His skills in revolver shooting at Sandhurst had earned derision from all his peers. Perhaps he would simply have to break von Bethman's neck. Not gentlemanly, but par for the course, probably, in this grim, primitive land. He stiffened and took a deep draught of the crisp air. One thing was certain. His resolve to kill von Bethman had not weakened. He owed it to Anna. He *would* kill the bastard!

Simon walked slowly back to the centre of the hollow and climbed a rock so that he could gain some sort of general view of the defences. He reckoned that, after leaving behind the companies to protect his route to and from the mountain, Colley had just under four hundred men on Majuba. Surely enough to defend the perimeter? His eye followed the rim around. The men were lying in the now warm sun, most of them sleeping following the exigencies of the night, some of them smoking and chatting in a desultory way, others playing cards. The atmosphere was superficially soporific, yet underneath he sensed a tension, a hidden disquiet, an undercurrent of apprehension. The last time he had experienced that feeling of unease was in a British camp, out on a plain in Zululand beneath a giant rock called Isandlwana. He swallowed. It was the waiting, of course, the frustration of not knowing what was going to happen.

He decided that he would walk around the rim in the hope that the exercise would dispel the gloom. Jenkins and Hardy fell into step beside him, the latter, of course, once again attracting questioning looks and the odd whistle. The American took not the slightest notice, slowly striding along, one thumb hooked into his belt, the heel of the other resting on the pearl handle of one of his Colts.

'It's all a bit strange, then, isn't it?' said Jenkins. 'What are all these chaps up 'ere *for* exactly? It's nice for a picnic, I'll grant you, but what are we goin' to *do*? Sit on the edge an' fart down on 'em? I don't understand, see.'

Simon grinned. 'I'm not sure I do, either. I think the idea is to bring up some guns tomorrow – if the Boers let us, that is – and either scare them off with the threat of bombarding them from up here, or bring up troops and attack them frontally down there under cover of the guns.'

'And are those gennulmen down there just goin' to let us stay up heah?'

Simon thought – not for the first time – that on the rare occasions that he spoke, Al usually hit the nail on the head. 'That,' he replied, 'we'll just have to wait and see.'

The three walked on in silence. One of the riflemen, seeing in Simon's bearing something of the officer, called: 'What's going to happen, sir? What are we going to do up here?'

Simon tried to be reassuring. 'We're occupying a key position, commanding the Boer lines. They will probably withdraw as a result.'

'Umph!' Jenkins rolled his eyes and then, when out of earshot of the soldier, 'An' pigs will fly an' all.'

A scattered, distant outbreak of firing from below the northwestern face brought an instant response from some of the Highlanders lining the rim on that side, and the three scouts hurried over to investigate. So too did a young Scottish subaltern.

'Don't waste your ammunition, dammit,' the lieutenant shouted at his men. 'You are way out of range and so are they.'

But further sporadic firing followed from the general direction of the Boer lines – or was it nearer and higher up the mountain slopes? Could this be the beginning of the battle? wondered Simon.

'Well, it shows that the Boers know we are here all right,' he murmured. 'But does it mean that they intend to attack us, or are they just letting off a bit of steam before they pull out? Hard to tell really.' He peered over the lip but could see no telltale wisp of gun smoke or sign of movement among the stunted trees and rocks down below. He shrugged, and the three continued their perambulations around the edge of the saucer.

He noticed with approval that some bluejackets on the southern tip, just above where the troops had first clambered on to the summit, were using stones to build some sort of fortification. Whether this was a piece of local initiative or on direction he could not tell, for no officer was in attendance. Elsewhere, on the Rifles' section, some primitive low walls of stones had been put together but Simon doubted their efficacy. Given the Boers' accuracy, and the loose construction of the wall, there would be more damage caused by flying stone chips than bullets. But he held back his criticism. Hell – he wasn't in the army now! Certainly no work had yet started on the three redoubts suggested by Fraser.

Boer fire had now become more persistent, although it was proving harmless. Some of the snipers had obviously wormed their way up the mountainside, but their rounds were either flattening themselves against the vertical rock walls just below the summit or wailing way overhead. None of the defenders had yet been hit. Perhaps Majuba *was* the defensive fortress that Colley obviously presumed it to be.

Looking back, Simon saw that the general and Commander Romilly were standing near the Naval Brigade's position to the east of the southern point of the perimeter, in a hollow that extended to the edge, so lowering the rim of the saucer at that point. Perhaps they were discussing how the redoubt should be built there, for the commander was pointing. Then, suddenly, a shot echoed from down below and Romilly spun around and slumped to the ground. With a cry, Colley knelt by his side and Simon and Hardy – Jenkins had dropped behind to talk to an infantryman – sprinted towards them.

They found Romilly murmuring, 'I'm all right.' But it was clear that he was not, for blood was spreading quickly from a wound in his stomach and also oozing from a corner of his mouth.

Colley rose and cupped his hand to his mouth. 'Stretcher-bearers here, quickly,' he shouted. He knelt again and took Romilly's hand, and then looked up at Simon. 'Most amazing thing,' he said. 'I saw them, two of them, down there, with their r-r-rifles. They will never reach us, I said. It's all of nine hundred yards. Then they shot. Amazing.'

The stretcher-bearers took the commander back to the little hollow in the middle of the depression where the medics had mounted their grim paraphernalia and the general returned to his command post nearby and, without a word, curled up and closed his eyes. There was no attempt to issue further orders directing the building of the redoubts. This air of lassitude seemed to be reflected by the soldiers lining the perimeter. Several amused themselves by making an occasional reply to the scattered shots that came from below, but most of them lay at their posts waiting. Waiting for what, though? From the general downwards, the British officers seemed to evince no expectation of an attack. And certainly there was little evidence so far that the Boers were making any preparation to climb the mountain in force. The firing that came from the slopes below showed that they had not retreated back into the Transvaal as, no doubt, Colley expected, but it was spasmodic and, seemingly, lacked direction or disciplined control.

Simon and his two companions, still partly numbed by the sudden shooting down of the commander at such a distance, could not avoid being tainted by the torpor that pervaded the mountaintop. They returned to the ashes of their fire and sprawled at its edge. Hardy immediately fell asleep.

'I can't help thinking of home,' murmured Simon. 'Perhaps it's time to go back.'

Jenkins looked around him and sniffed. 'When will that be, then?'

'As soon as we get off this accursed mountain. One way or another, this campaign is over, and I can't see any point in continuing to serve Colley. And anyway, I have a job to do.'

Jenkins frowned. 'I know what you're thinkin', but I don't see what you can do about that. The bloke's probably gone back to Germany by now anyway. And if 'e's not, you can't just walk up to 'im and shoot 'im, now can you? Even in this place there must be laws about that sort o' thing.'

'Well he shot her, didn't he?'

'Yes, well . . . oh, I don't know. But just be careful, bach sir. You're good at doin' the thinkin' bit. With respect, you're not good at the killin' part – though you've done your share, I must say. But think now, eh?'

Simon nodded absently. 'I know what you mean, but to tell you the truth, 352, I'm getting a bit tired of all this killing. It seems so damned pointless.'

'Yes, well, don't worry about tryin' to kill this baron bloke then. After all, it was a family matter as far as I can understand it.'

Simon shook his head. 'No. He was trying to kill me. The swine was jealous, that's all. She didn't deserve that kind of death. He was a malicious bastard and I am worried that he will take over her child. Anna would have hated that. I owe it to her to stop him doing that.'

The fusillade of shooting from below them on the northern side of Majuba now seemed more concentrated and made them both lift their heads.

'What's goin' to 'appen then, d'you think?' asked Jenkins. 'There's not much point in us sittin' up 'ere doin' nothin', is there?'

'No.' Simon scrambled to his feet. 'What's worrying me is that the general doesn't seem to have properly reconnoitred the perimeter. Certainly he hasn't posted vedettes down the slopes and there's a lot of dead ground there. I hope we're not going to be taken by surprise, though we ought to be all right. There are men posted on those kopjes jutting out on our flanks and they should command the last approaches to the top.'

As though on cue, a strong rattle of rifle fire broke out from the northern sector, where the Gordon Highlanders were posted. This time, however, it was sustained and came, it seemed, not from further down the mountainside but from just under the lip. Simon shook Hardy awake and the three of them grabbed their rifles and sprinted to what appeared to be the threatened sector. Running towards them was a young subaltern from the Gordons, Ian Hamilton, who had been put in charge of the Highlanders out on the isolated Gordons' Knoll. Simon noted that he had bullet holes in his kilt.

'They seem to have gathered just underneath us,' he shouted as he ran past. 'Can't really see them, but they're making us keep our heads down with some damned fine shooting. I've asked for reinforcements twice. No one seems interested. I'm trying again now.'

The three ran to the brow of the hill on the northern point of the perimeter, where they could look down the narrow saddle which connected Gordons' Knoll to the main defences on the mountaintop. The handful of Highlanders holding the isolated knoll, who could see further down the mountainside, of course, than the defenders on the top, were obviously being subjected to concentrated rifle fire from, it seemed, the edge of the terrace some hundred and fifty feet below them. The knoll was just a mound of earth-covered rock jutting out from the thin saddle and its little garrison had nothing to protect them from this kind of heavy fire. Four of the Gordons were already lying inert by its edge, but the remainder were doing their best to reply, even though it meant exposing themselves. The Highlanders on the perimeter above could do nothing to help them, for they could not see the enemy firing from below.

Even as the three men watched, however, events took a dramatic turn. At a command which could clearly be heard on the summit, some sixty Boers, rifles at their shoulders, suddenly stepped out from concealment at a point just below the knoll and delivered a volley at point-blank range at the exposed Gordons on the promontory. Simon realised that they must have wormed their way up the mountainside while their compatriots below laid down covering fire. He could not help but admire the skill and soldierly prowess displayed by whoever was in command of the attack. The volley was devastating, and all but three of the little garrison on the knoll were killed. The survivors immediately fled back to the main perimeter along the narrow nek, bullets hissing around them.

Simon, Jenkins and Hardy flung themselves to the earth among the Highlanders who were manning the grassy crest which sloped down to the extended nek and who were attempting to return the Boer fire. But there was little cover and the superior firepower of the enemy below took immediate toll. Some of the Scots received five or six bullets in the head, and lying amongst them, Simon could hear the thump of the bullets striking home all around him, providing a grim accompaniment to the crack of the rifles and the shouts of the wounded. The Gordons were experienced soldiers, fresh from their successes in Afghanistan. Even so, the sudden apperance of a large number of enemy riflemen, followed by the accuracy of their firing at such short range, was too much for them. They scrambled to their feet and, kilts swinging, ran back in confusion towards the ridge behind them and the hollow beyond, almost stepping on the scouts in their hurry to find shelter.

'Stop!' shouted Simon, struggling to his feet. 'Open order. Face the enemy.'

'It's no good, bach sir,' said Jenkins. 'We'd better 'op it too, or we'll 'ave to fight the bleedin' lot on our own.'

The three turned and ran. 'Up to this kopje,' shouted Simon, and they turned to their right and scrambled to the top of Macdonald's Kopje, which commanded a view of much of the hilltop. They were greeted by Lieutenant Hector Macdonald, his revolver in hand, who commanded the Highland platoon manning the kopje.

'What the hell's happening to our men?' he demanded.

'They've just bloody run, bach,' panted Jenkins. 'Just bloody run they 'ave, see.'

'Rapid fire,' shouted Macdonald to his men. 'Tek the bastards as they come over the top.'

The three scouts added their fire to that of the Gordons on the kopje but it did little to affect the drama clearly unfolding below them. The flying Highlanders ran straight into the men of Colley's reserve who were now, at last – and reluctantly – moving towards the northern lip of the summit, urged on by their officers. The resulting chaotic swirl of figures now made easy targets for the Boers, who began pouring over the northern perimeter, shooting from the shoulder as they came, and the whole mass of defenders – retreating Highlanders, infantrymen of the 58th and sailors who a moment before had been sleeping or smoking in the hollow – now stumbled back towards the perceived safety of the ridge. As they did so, many of them dropped as they ran, caught in the back by the merciless bullets of the Boers.

'God, it's a massacre!' Simon shook his head in despair. 'Why doesn't Colley rally them?'

In fact, attempts to do so were now being made by the general and all of his officers. Cries of 'Rally on the right, rally on the right!' rose up to the kopje's defenders. These, however, merely added to the confusion, for Colley, Stewart and Fraser meant that the fleeing men should consolidate at the north-eastern side of the ridge, the officers' right, where a great clump of rocks offered cover. The men, however, swirled towards their own right, at the south-western end of the ridge, where the ground fell away and little cover could be gained. The Boers took advantage of this and poured in their fire.

Great swathes of slate-blue gun smoke now drifted across the depression at the mountaintop, bringing with it that distinctive acrid taste of battle that Simon knew so well. He licked his lips, desperate to remove the stinging dryness. The panic-stricken retreat from the northern face of Majuba's summit was like nothing he had ever seen before. Even at Isandlwana, where the redcoats were short of ammunition, overrun by the Zulus and outnumbered by forty to one, the soldiers had formed into resolute little bands and stuck together, presenting their bayonets to their assailants and, eventually, dying where they stood. He had never before seen British soldiers turn and run – but then he had never before seen the destructive effect of accurate modern rifle fire, delivered at such close quarters by expert marksmen.

And yet, glimmers of hope began to emerge. Through the gaps in the smoke he could see that many of the Gordons had rallied behind the low ridge and had been joined by men of the reserve. Simon could see officers stooping low and running up and down behind the line, trying to extend it on both flanks. There must have been at least two hundred troops now taking shelter behind the ridge. The Boers, however, now seemed have been reinforced and they covered the northern summit like a cloud of dun-coloured locusts, standing, kneeling, lying flat and firing, always firing, so that it became instant death for a defender to show his head above the ridge.

The ridge itself extended from Hay's Kopje, standing above it on the right, almost to the foot of Macdonald's Kopje on its left, where Simon, Jenkins, Hardy, Macdonald himself and the platoon of Gordons had a good field of fire across the Boers' position. Even

Simon, poor shot as he was, could see his rounds taking effect, and Jenkins, of course, was coolly picking off targets with precision. Yet Simon realised that the shooting of the young men lying around him seemed to be quite ineffectual. He turned to the Highlander at his side. 'What have you got your sights at?'

The Jock examined the ranging backsight standing up some eight inches from his squinting eye. 'It's four hundred yards, sorr,' he said.

'For God's sake, man. Who told you to set it at that? You're overshooting. Bring it right down.'

'Orders, sorr. We was all told at the start to fix at four hundred.'

Simon wondered anew at the rigidity of the army system. The British fighting man was trained to behave in battle as a brave automaton: to follow orders without question and to rely on the leadership of his officers. It was drummed into him throughout his training that he would obey orders *without a thought*. This produced courage and resolution, but it also removed most vestiges of initiative, and on that day on Majuba's summit, it meant that much of the British firing was completely wasted.

'Fire on open sights, you bloody fool,' snarled Simon, 'and pass the word on.'

Poor marksmanship, however, was not the only reason for the ineffectiveness of the shooting of the Gordons on Macdonald's Kopje. The position of the kopje should have given the platoon the opportunity to direct heavy enfilading fire at the advancing Boers. The spread-eagled Highlanders, however, were themselves now being subjected to intense and, inevitably, accurate sniping from the western base of Majuba. The top of the kopje was narrow and there was very little room for the men occupying it to take cover from the firing, coming now, it seemed, from all sides, for the burghers in the bowl below were also now shooting at the small group on its top.

The Boers' fire, in fact, was now ranging across all of what had seemed only minutes ago to be the safe positions of the British. The ground between the ridge and the northern lip undulated gently but the billows of stunted grass contained one distinct depression that was deep enough to conceal crouching men. This swept down roughly parallel to the ridge and it allowed the Boers to take position only forty yards from the British line. In addition, the enemy fire from higher up the slope behind was now overshooting the ridge and finding targets among the men of the 58th on the southern perimeter. As Simon watched, some of these men – already mauled at Laing's Nek and unnerved by the Highlanders from the northern edge who had swept by them in retreat – now themselves took to their heels, climbed over the edge and plunged down the mountain the way they had come only a few hours before.

'For God's sake,' hissed Jenkins, 'why don't the officers down there get bayonets fixed and order a charge?'

'Bit late for that,' said Simon. 'I think the men have all lost their nerve now. They're just keeping their heads down.'

As if to emphasise the point, it became clear that a separate party of burghers had climbed up the wooded eastern slopes of the mountain and were now subjecting the small garrison on Hay's Kopje to an intense fire. Simon watched, his perspiring cheek pressed hard against his rifle stock, as one by one the defenders on the kopje slipped away from their post and joined their comrades behind the ridge. He saw officers, swords in hand, berating them and attempting to rally others to retake the kopje, but it was useless. The will to fight seemed to have deserted all of the men now.

Suddenly, as if someone had given a signal, a great shout – more a spontaneous cry of despair than a rallying call – rose from the ridge and most of the troops there turned and ran back towards the southern perimeter and the path they had used to climb the mountain. Their officers, cursing, shouting, sometimes shooting their revolvers in the air, were left powerless to stop the rout, like islands in a fast-flowing stream as their men raced round them.

Whooping, the Boers rushed forward and emerged now, it seemed, from three sides of the summit. They stood, picking their targets and bringing down dozens of the running men as though they were shooting at pheasants in a field. The stricken troops, shot in the back, threw up their rifles and crashed to the ground, forcing their comrades in flight to jump over them as they tried to escape the incessant fire.

'Oh my God,' whispered Simon. It was little more than half an hour ago since that first withering volley had struck the Gordons on their kopje, so signalling the beginning of the battle proper. Within that time some of the most experienced troops in the British Empire had been reduced to a rabble. Through the swirling smoke, it could be seen that some knots of the British infantry were holding up their hands and surrendering. One or two desperately tried to direct fire from the top of the ridge but they were soon shot down. Some of the Boers had now reached the edge of the northern rim and were standing silhouetted there, calmly taking aim and firing down the mountainside at the running troops. It seemed that only the remnants of the little platoon on Macdonald's Kopje remained unbeaten.

'Where's the general?' asked Jenkins, wiping the back of a powder-stained hand across his moustache.

Simon peered through the smoke and caught a glimpse of that familiar straight-backed figure, revolver in hand, standing at his command post behind the ridge. As he watched, he saw him slowly turn and begin to walk back, following his fleeing troops. Then one shot rang out – symbolically individual among the general crackle of musketry – and Colley spun round and fell.

'Keep firing.' The call came from Lieutenant Macdonald. 'They will not take this kopje. We make a last stand here.'

' 'E's mad,' spat Jenkins. 'What are we goin' to do, bach sir?'

For a moment Simon laid his cheek on the turf, not daring even to look at the tumult below, for a large number of Boers had now turned their attentions to the little band on the kopje and bullets were once again cracking into the rocks at the edge of the little knoll. Then he looked up at Jenkins.

'There's nowhere to go, 352,' he said. 'We make a last stand here.' He risked a look over the edge. A ring of burghers were now beginning to climb up the little slope to the top of their position, while others were laying down fire to cover their ascent.

'Rapid fire at those bastards climbing,' shouted Macdonald. 'Those below won't fire for fear of hitting their own men. To the edge now . . .'

The three scouts joined the little ring of Highlanders who now moved to the edge of the kopje and levelled their rifles at the climbing Boers below. But Hardy, who had been coolly firing his Winchester repeater, lying, like the rest, on his stomach, suddenly rose and stood tall on the edge. With one swift and familiar movement he drew his Colt, and fanning the cocking mechanism with his left hand began blazing away at the enemy below. For a brief second, seeing him outlined against the blue sky, Simon marvelled at the heroic figure he cut – tall, slim-hipped, wide-shouldered, the perfect warrior – before he shouted, 'For God's sake, Al, get down.' But it was too late. The first bullet caught the Texan in his left thigh and the second in his chest. He doubled up and fell back into the comparative safety of the hollow at the top of the kopje.

Simon and Jenkins bent anxiously over the fallen man. He was perfectly conscious but his breathing was already laboured and blood was oozing from the wound in his chest. He smiled.

'Ooh, lads,' he said. 'That's me done an' all.'

Jenkins looked puzzled. 'What's 'e sayin'?' he asked of Simon.

Hardy turned his head. 'What's t' matter. Don't thee know a bit of reet Yorkshire when tha' 'ears it?' He was grinning, but the grin turned into a cough and a trickle of blood came from his mouth.

From somewhere near, Macdonald was shouting, 'Keep at it, lads, they're falling back.'

'Don't talk, Al.'

'Noo.' Hardy turned a wan face to Simon. 'Ah knows an' thee knows ah'm finished, lad. But got somethin' to ask of thee afore ah goes. Top pocket of me shirt. A letter. Tek it out.'

Simon did so and went to hand over a blue envelope. Hardy grimaced and shook his head. 'Noo. Keep it. It's from me muther. Picked it oop at Newcastle. Never 'ad time to reply. Promise me, lad, that tha'll write to 'er and tell 'er that ah died fightin' the Queen's enemies. She'll feel all t' better fer it.'

'Of course, Al.' Simon turned the envelope over. Written on the flap in an untutored hand was 'Mrs Edna Hardcastle, 17 Moorland Road, Batley, Yorkshire, England'. He looked up at the Texan. 'But Al – your mother is English?'

The drawn face lapsed into a grin again. 'Aye. Better 'n that. She's

Yorkshire. So am I. Never bin to America in me life. Name's not Al Hardy. It's Albert Hardcastle. Kept a tripe shop in Skipton.'

'A tripe shop!' Jenkins's voice reeked of indignation.

'Aye, tha knows. Cow's stomach an' all that. Lovely with onions. It were best tripe shop in Yorkshire. Sold it to become a scout with Custer. Got a fortune for t' place.'

The firing in the background seemed to have receded and Simon realised that Macdonald must have ordered a ceasefire to nurture ammunition until the next attack on the kopje. He turned back to Hardy. 'But you said you'd never been to America.'

'Sorry, Simon.' Hardy's voice was now fully reflecting his weariness, and blood was oozing down his chin. Jenkins wiped it away. 'In my imagination, that is. Yer see . . .' He tried to sit up, but Simon gently pushed him down again. 'Yer see, always loved the American West. A pal who emigrated from Batley sent me them dime magazines from New York. Yer know – Custer, Buffalo Bill, Wild Bill Hickok an' all that. Then in Bradford I met a Texan who spoke with this Southern twang. I loved it an' copied it – I was always good at amateur dramatics in Skipton. So when I sold the shop, I decided to *become* a Custer scout. 'Ad the buckskins specially made in Leeds, bought the pistols from a fancy shop in London and decided to tek a trip through Africa . . .'

His voice tailed away and Simon wiped another dribble of blood from the corner of his mouth. 'Don't say anything more, Al,' he said. 'To us you epitomise the American prairie, and always will.'

'But Al.' Jenkins had gripped Hardy's hand in earnest enquiry. 'I must just ask you . . .'

'No.' Simon shook his head. 'Let him be, 352. He doesn't need to say anything more to us.'

The wounded man managed another lopsided smile. 'Think I do, actually, Simon.' He turned to Jenkins. 'Why didn't I go to America?'

Jenkins nodded.

'Because I knew I'd be found out over there. Anyway, I knew all about it, in my head that is. Knew Bighorn off by heart, though you, Simon,' he turned his head, 'found me out a couple of times. North 'n South, moose an' all that.'

Simon summoned a smile.

'But the shootin', Al.' Jenkins was insistent. 'You're so bleedin' good at it. Springin' out from those rocks, drawin' from your 'olsters an' shootin' down those Boers. 'Ow did you learn all that?'

'Practice, lad. Night after night in t' summer, up on t' moors, firin' away. But those blokes I killed . . .' He swallowed hard and then coughed up more blood. ' 'T were first time I'd tried it for real. Nearly died, I was so frightened. That's why I was a bit slow a-drawin'.'

He nodded to Jenkins, but his voice was now no more than a whisper. 'You tek Custer an' look after 'im, and you, Simon, 'ave me Colts. I always meant to tell yer one day but never got around to it. You've given me the time of me life . . . loved every minute of ridin' with yer . . . Don't forget to write to me . . .'

The voice died away and gradually his eyes hardened and then set, looking unseeingly beyond them to the smoke drifting across the bright blue African sky.

Macdonald's voice rang out once more. 'Here they come again. Back to the rim.'

Swallowing hard, Simon closed the dead man's eyes, seized his rifle and scrambled back to the rim. As he did so, he realised that, of Macdonald's platoon, only a handful were left – insufficient to man it. The lieutenant himself had jettisoned his pistol and drawn his great basket-handled claymore. As he and Jenkins reached the edge, two carbine barrels were poked in their faces, and suddenly the rim was full of Boers scrambling it, their rifles levelled.

On his hands and knees, Simon saw Macdonald raise his sword, only to have it knocked from his hand by a carbine barrel. He glimpsed the fiery little Scot swing a fist and then be felled by a rifle butt. Simon dropped his head and said, 'Put down your rifle, 352. It's all over.' Wearily the two men regained their feet and raised their hands above their shoulders to face the row of rifles.

'Those two there. Shoot them now.' The voice came from behind Simon and he turned to face, once again, Baron von Bethman. The German's arm was no longer in a sling, and he was impeccably dressed in well-cut black jacket and riding breeches and boots, although his face was blackened by powder from his rifle, which he was now hurriedly attempting to reload. He had obviously taken a full part in the fighting. 'I order you to shoot them,' he shouted as he fumbled. 'You see they wear no uniform. I know them to be spies. Execute them now.'

A dozen rifle muzzles were raised – if a little uncertainly – and pointed at Simon and Jenkins. ' 'Ere,' shouted the Welshman, 'you can't shoot men in cold blood. We've just surrendered, look you. It's against the rules of . . . whatsit . . . civilised warfare, see.'

Jenkins's cry made the Boers pause for a second. Then von Bethman levelled his rifle. 'If you don't, then I will.' He slid the bolt to thrust the round into the breech, and Simon looked down the rifle barrel into the distorted face of the man who had shot Anna Scheel.

'Stop.' A voice rang out from the edge of the kopje top. Then followed a command in Afrikaans that made the Boers lower their rifles.

A large man, bearded of course, and with lank greasy hair hanging down from under his hat, climbed on to the summit and pushed down von Bethman's rifle. 'We Boers don't kill men who have surrendered,' he said.

'But I am accredited to the Boer command here,' said von Bethman. His voiced exuded authority as well as irritation. 'I know these men to be spies. They should be shot immediately. I order it.'

'You don't order my command to do anything. These men are my prisoners. I know them to be British scouts.' He turned to his men and spoke quickly in Afrikaans, so that they indicated to Simon, Jenkins, Macdonald and the remaining Gordons to precede them down the awkward slope of the kopje. Below them, the acrid smoke was clearing and the bowl at Majuba's top was littered with the bodies of the British dead.

Simon, his heart still pounding, looked hard at the Boer commander and then recognised the grim features of the man whose head he had cradled in his lap as he wiped away the blood from the wound caused by a horse's hoof in a gully in southern Transvaal.

'Hello, English,' said Gideon ter Haar. 'Now we are even. The next time we meet I have the right to kill you. But let's hope we are not fighting then. It would be a pity, *ja*?'

282

Chapter 15

On the main field of battle, the dejected group picked its way over and between the bodies towards the centre of the plateau, where the rest of the prisoners were being herded. The scene was heart-wringingly distressing to British eyes and ears, for rows of inert infantrymen lined the ridge, tracing its configuration in the tortured postures of the dead. Here, it was difficult to place a foot without treading on the remains of some poor creature, and Simon estimated that about sixty or seventy corpses lay in small groups where a stand had been attempted. Many more sprawled beyond, marking the path of the flight to the southern lip and testifying to the accuracy of the Boer shooting. Groans and cries for help from the wounded accompanied the little party's progress towards the centre. They passed the prostrate figure of General Colley, his head shattered by a bullet fired at close range.

Ter Haar nodded. 'Your general, eh?'

'Yes,' said Simon. He frowned in a conflict of emotions. 'Not a good general, I fear,' he said, 'but a good man.'

The Boer grunted. 'He was not a good man to start a battle on a Sunday and defile the Sabbath.'

'I don't think he wanted to fight today. He just wanted to take the hill.'

'Ja. But he was stupid if he thought we would let him sit up here. So he started the battle. Stupid and wrong, and the Lord has punished him.'

'Excuse me, sir.' Simon was surprised at Jenkins's unusually deferential tone. 'Those are our things there. Would you mind if we picked up our bedrolls?'

Ter Haar shrugged. 'All right. You will probably be sleeping in the open tonight. But take nothing else.'

Jenkins broke away and picked up his and Simon's rolls, slung them under his arm and then rejoined the group.

'Why did you—' began Simon.

'Oh, we're goin' to need these, bach.'

Simon looked around for von Bethman and caught a glimpse of the German in the middle distance talking to the tall figure of General Nicholas Smit, who was wearing his distinctive white jacket. As he watched, they were joined by a man incongruously riding a white pony, which presumably must have climbed the face of the mountain carrying its rider. Simon recognised the man he had seen on his first reconnaissance of Laing's Nek, the Boer commander-in-chief, General Piet Joubert, and he wondered anew at the relationship the baron had forged with the Boer high command. He was obviously close to the leaders and had been allowed to take part in the assault with the rest of the burghers. Was he some sort of official delegate from the German government, or merely what he claimed to be: an arms dealer? If he was the former, then his views must carry weight with the Boer leadership. If, however, he really was merely an armaments salesman, then perhaps it would be just his word against Simon's.

Now von Bethman turned and gestured towards the little group of Highlanders. Was he again demanding that the scouts be shot out of hand as spies? Simon realised that he was trembling. To be shot in cold blood would be a pathetic end to this miserable adventure.

There was no further intervention, however, and the group joined the main party of prisoners, who were told to squat on the ground in the centre of the basin. The baron and his companions had now disappeared, but a line of Boers was now strung along the southern perimeter, taking leisurely shots at targets down below – presumably British troops who had been flushed out of hiding places among the bushes and crags. The cheers that went up reminded Simon of the shouts of joy when a well-aimed ball toppled a coconut at the local fair he visited in Wiltshire as a boy. He felt sickened as he watched. Then he remembered that Colley had left two separate contingents of

284

troops on the long climb up Majuba. They had been instructed to dig in. Would they be able to offer succour to the fleeing survivors, and would they be strong enough to fight off the Boers who would surely now be organised to offer pursuit?

Jenkins sniffed. 'What do you think they'll do with us, bach sir?' he asked gloomily.

'Well, I can't see Smit or Joubert allowing von Bethman to have us shot.' Simon spoke reassuringly but he was far from confident. The German certainly seemed to possess some kind of standing with the Boer command, and the spy story carried a grain of truth in that they *had* operated behind the enemy lines in the Transvaal, so to speak. But he noted that Colonel Stewart was among the captives. If the worst came to the worst, he would surely confirm their status as scouts and therefore combatants, even if they did not wear uniforms.

'Why did you make such a fuss about our bedrolls?'

Jenkins gave a half-smile. 'I stuffed poor old Ally's pistols in me trousers under me jacket, see. Bloody things were stickin' out all over the place, so I've tucked 'em between the blankets.'

Simon groaned. 'Oh lord. Let's hope they don't search us.' Yet he felt a spasm of hope. If they were sentenced to be put up against a rock face and shot, at least they might be able to go down fighting.

Eventually the captives were made to stand and the march down the mountain to the Boer lines at Laing's Nek began. Simon realised that it was, indeed, a much easier route than that taken by the British, although, of course, the close proximity to the enemy's encampment would have made it impossible to make the ascent that way. It now began to rain, and as they stumbled down the steep hillside, Simon felt his heart wrench at the plight of the wounded – they had all looked to be British – left on the mountaintop. The Boers had seemed to have no medics among their numbers and Simon had noticed only one English doctor attempting to tend those of the fallen still alive. The other doctor had presumably been killed.

The Boer lines were reached and the prisoners were herded together in what appeared to be a horse compound at the rear of the trenches. This time, Simon was able to look around him at leisure and was surprised to see the rubbish that littered the Boer positions – another painful reminder that this British column had been beaten not by trained, disciplined soldiers but by civilians, men who almost seemed to be out on a camping holiday. He sighed.

'Mr Fonthill? Mr Jenkins?'

The enquirer was a boy, surely no more than fourteen years of age, although he was dressed as a Boer guerrilla in miniature: baggy jacket, dirty flannel trousers, large boots, slouch hat, bandolier slung across his breast, and carrying what was very much a full-sized Westley Richards rifle.

Simon stood. 'No,' he said carefully. '*Captain* Fonthill and *Sergeant* Jenkins.' It could be important to stress that they retained the right to be addressed so – although, strictly speaking, Jenkins did not.

The boy was not impressed. 'The general wants to see you. Come now.'

'Which general?'

'General Smit, of course.'

Simon felt a small surge of relief. At least he was known to Smit, who would remember him as Colley's messenger. And he recalled that Colley had maintained a high regard for his Boer opponent. An 'honourable and fine man' would surely not have them shot out of hand.

'Very well,' he said. 'Lead on.'

The two followed their diminutive guide through the lines until they reached Smit's tent. Simon noted that Jenkins still carried their bedrolls under his arm and was not sure whether to be glad or sorry. If they had to fight for it, then Al's pistols would be their only hope – perhaps they could grab a pair of horses and flee. On the other hand, a quick search could make them appear to be assassins.

He turned his head and whispered to Jenkins. 'Once we are inside, just place the blanket roll on the ground. We don't want to provoke a search.'

'Very good, bach sir.'

They were led to the same tent where Simon had delivered Colley's

286

letter to General Smit. Inside were a group of some eight or nine Boers, all standing, most of them middle-aged or elderly, with long beards and broad-brimmed hats. On the right of the group stood a bare-headed Gideon ter Haar, appearing much younger without his hat, and in the centre, General Smit with Baron Wilhelm von Bethman at his side. Simon caught his breath. But for the absence of chairs and tables, it could have been the setting for a court martial. Nevertheless, he forced a wry smile.

'Congratulations on your victory, General,' he said. 'I have to admit it was overwhelming.'

Smit nodded. He looked a most incongruous general, with his beard ragged and falling on to the rumpled waistcoat worn under his white jacket. 'Your people cannot shoot,' he said, his face expressionless. 'I am told that we have captured or killed two hundred and eighty of your soldiers for the loss of only two of our men killed and a handful wounded.'

The figures made Simon wince. How could such an expenditure of ammunition by trained soldiers produce such poor results? He remembered the rifle sights, set at four hundred yards. Von Bethman was staring, his pale grey eyes seeming almost transparent.

Simon inclined his head. 'With respect, General,' he said, 'I must remind you that you have won a battle, but not the war. General Sir Evelyn Wood will shortly be arriving at Mount Prospect with reinforcements. The forces of the empire will be arraigned against you.'

'Yes, Captain, but we have the Lord of Hosts with us. It was He who provided this victory for us on His day, the Sabbath, and He will not desert us. But,' his countenance became even grimmer, 'I have not called you here to gloat. The baron here has laid charges against you and your companion and has demanded your execution. I wish to hear what you have to say in your defence.'

'Then I must first hear the charges.'

'Of course. Baron?'

Von Bethman took a pace forward and half turned to face the silent group behind him. 'This man,' he said, gesturing towards Simon, 'is a spy who organises the gathering of intelligence for the

British. He calls himself a captain but he wears no uniform and operates behind your lines. This other . . .' he groped for words to describe Jenkins, 'this *peasant*, masquerades as his servant but is really his bodyguard. I discovered their true identity at Bloemfontein, where Fonthill seduced my sister-in-law and persuaded her to pass information to him about Boer movements.

'You will remember, Herr General,' he continued, 'that when you took a force to cut the British lines of communication at Ingogo, a British armed column met you there, instead of the usual mail picket. I am ashamed to say that they had been warned of your intentions by the Countess Scheel, my countrywoman, under the influence of this man. I followed her and saw her leave the British camp and conduct a meeting with her . . . her . . . spymaster here.'

Von Bethman was now standing with legs far apart, like a bantam, his face flushed. 'I realised that she presented a continual source of danger to your cause. They were about to ride to the British camp, no doubt conveying further information about the siting of your positions on Laing's Nek, and I fired at the Englishman. Unfortunately, the countess stepped in front of her lover and was killed. The bullet was intended for him.' Dramatically, the German now pointed a finger at Simon. 'This man was to blame and he should now pay the penalty.'

A silence fell on the gathering, and somewhere in the distance the sound of hymn-singing could be heard. The Boers were paying thanks for their victory. Simon felt a gentle nudge at his elbow and realised that Jenkins had not put down the bedrolls.

'Well, Cap . . . Mr Fonthill?' Simon realised that the craggy visage of General Smit could have been the model for a hundred Victorian paintings of Jehovah.

He cleared his throat. 'It is *Captain* Fonthill, sir,' he said evenly. 'It is true that I am no longer a serving officer, having resigned my commission. My companion is not *a peasant*,' he spat out the word, 'but a very brave soldier who has fought by my side at Islandlwana and throughout the recent campaign in Afghanistan, and earned the rank of sergeant. We are not spies but bona fide scouts for the late General Colley, having been commended to him by General Sir

Garnet Wolseley, who I believe is known to you. Our role can be confirmed by Colonel Stewart, General Colley's chief of staff, who has unfortunately also been captured.'

Simon felt his voice begin to rise but made an effort to remain rational. He was arguing for his life and that of Jenkins. He regarded the faces opposite. Von Bethman's, of course, was flushed and exuded hate, but those of the Boers, behind their long beards, seemed dispassionate, almost disinterested. They had reason to bear malice towards the British, but they were fervent Christians too, professing a high moral code – although Christians who took delight in potting soldiers as though they were running bucks. Which way would they vote this morning: like cruel Old Testament priests, or modern benevolent victors? He must appeal to their brains. He *must* stay rational. He gulped and continued.

'It is customary for British officers to continue to be addressed by their rank once they have left the army. So there is no deceit there. We did not operate behind enemy lines because there are no lines. After war was declared by the attack of your countrymen, General, on British troops at Bronkhurstspruit, General Colley ordered my sergeant and me to ride into the Transvaal to scout routes for him to advance and relieve the British garrisons there. But we were *not* operating behind your lines because – and this is important – Her Majesty the Queen maintains sovereignty over the Transvaal, despite your declaration of independence. So we do not consider that the border between the Transvaal and Natal constitutes an enemy line. That is what this war is all about, of course.'

He paused, but the stern faces opposite gave no indication that these debating points were striking home. He went on. 'We were captured by a Boer patrol but escaped. Later, we were overtaken and had to fight for our lives to cross the Natal border. In that skirmish I had the opportunity of taking the life of that gentleman there,' he indicated ter Haar, 'but did not take it.'

General Smit raised an eyebrow. 'Kornet ter Haar?'

Ter Haar nodded. '*Ja*. That is true, General. I was injured and he bound my wounds.'

Simon shot a quick glance at von Bethman. The German's former expression of arrogant superiority, of certainty that his closeness to his allies and the force of his charges would prevail, had now been replaced by a suppressed fury. His elegant thin moustache had been sucked beneath his lower lip and his face wore a look of angry frustration. Simon felt a brief moment of exhilaration. He sensed that this cool, logical answering of the German's points was winning the argument. How now to confront his relationship with Anna and the charge that they were lovers? Anna . . . He saw again the waxen image of her dead face as she lay in his arms. Immediately his caution vanished and he pointed a trembling finger at the German.

'I am no spy,' he shouted.

'Steady, bach,' whispered Jenkins. 'Don't lose it.'

But it was too late. The tiredness resulting from their night march and the strain of fighting for their lives on the kopje now descended on him and removed all restraint.

'I am no spy,' he repeated, his voice high and unregulated, 'but this man is a murderer. A coward who shoots women. It is he who should be executed. He is nothing more than an assassin.'

The silence that followed the accusation was broken by von Bethman. A slow smile had spread across his face, as though he had won a battle, and he turned to General Smit. 'Herr General,' he said softly, 'I think I can solve this problem for you. I am a gentleman, and no doubt this man here,' he nodded towards Simon, 'considers himself of the same class. He accuses me of the worst kind of crime in civilisation. As a gentleman, I have the right to demand satisfaction, and I therefore challenge him to a duel – but in this case, given the grave nature of that accusation, it must be a duel to the death . . . and I assure *Mr* Fonthill that my sword arm has fully recovered. I will therefore carry out myself this justified execution.'

'Oh no,' breathed Jenkins. 'Now you've done it.'

Simon felt the blood drain from his face, but he set his jaw. 'I am at your service, Baron,' he said.

Slowly Nicholas Smit nodded his head. 'I do not know about this duelling,' he said. 'I fear it is not the way of the Lord. But we are not lawyers and I do not know how we could have resolved the truth of these charges. If you both wish to fight to the death on this matter, then so be it. In the end, the good Lord will decide. Now, how do you wish to conduct this matter? I want no part of it, although I suppose I must delegate someone to see fair play.'

'Excuse me, my lord and General bach.' Jenkins had stepped forward, incongruously still holding their bedrolls.

'For God's sake shut up and stay out of this,' hissed Simon. 'What do you think you're doing?'

But Jenkins was already addressing the puzzled assembly. 'I 'ad the honour,' he explained, 'of bein' second to Colonel George Winterbottom when he fought the Earl of . . . er . . . Glamorgan on the beach at Rhyl, and I acted in the same capacity in Hyde Park when the colonel duelled with the Honourable Freddie Chumley. I therefore, gentlemen, 'ave 'ad some experience of these matters. Now,' he turned to a frowning von Bethman, 'you, my lord, 'ave delivered the challenge to the captain 'ere and therefore you will agree, I am sure, that the captain 'as choice of weapons? Yes?'

The baron clearly disliked the way in which Jenkins had assumed an air of command, but had no alternative but to assent. '*Ja*,' he scowled.

'Very good, my lord. Then, as it will be difficult to find a pair of, whatchacallem, duellin' sabres on this field of battle, like, the captain will choose pistols, won't you, sir?'

Simon nodded his head in glum despair.

Jenkins gave the assembly one of his most magnificent face-splitting smiles. 'Very well then, gentlemen, as the . . . er . . . offended party, we 'ave the right to fight under our national rules, which 'appen to be those of the London Duellin' Society, which says the following.' He drew in a breath. 'Only one shot in each revolver, each cartridge to be inspected by both seconds before the shootin', see. Back-to-back start, twelve paces away, called out by both seconds – in English, see, 'cos we're the challenged party – then turn in own time and fire. All agreed? Good.'

The baron was still scowling. 'Wait a minute, man. Wait a minute. We don't have duelling pistols out here. We can't duel without them.'

Jenkins gave a half-bow. 'Good point, my lord. But I think I may 'ave the answer.' He turned to Smit. 'With the general's permission?'

Smit shrugged his shoulders and held out his hands in a bewildered fashion.

Jenkins slowly unwrapped his bedroll. 'I just 'appen to 'ave 'ere,' he said, 'a pair of antique American duellin' Colts, the property of our late colleague, which we was takin' 'ome to give to 'is grievin' mother, see.'

He unfolded the bedrolls and slowly produced the long pearl-handled revolvers, like an auctioneer exhibiting a prize lot.

'Now don't worry, gentlemen, because these are not loaded, but I think you will agree that they are fine pieces of work and will do as good a job as duellin' pistols as anythin' out of the . . . er . . . Royal Mint.'

With great decorum he handed a revolver each to von Bethman and to Simon. Simon took his by the barrel, looked in amazement at Jenkins and shrugged his shoulders. Von Bethman, however, received his revolver with growing interest. He laid it in his hand, smoothed his fingers along the seven-and-a-half-inch barrel, inserted a finger in the trigger guard and swung the gun around by it before settling the butt in his hand. He studied the blue-grey metal and then looked up at Smit.

'These are forty-five calibre and will easily kill a man at twenty-four paces,' he said. 'They will do the work and I am therefore happy to duel with them, if you, Herr General, will keep both of them overnight to make sure,' he glared at Jenkins, 'that there is no cheating with them.'

'Oh perish the thought, my lord,' assured Jenkins. 'Perhaps the general will select just two cartridges from the belt to be used by the gentlemen tomorrow and keep them safe as well, like.'

Smit received the revolvers, took two rounds from the belt and handed the lot to one of his staff. 'Do this fighting away from the camp,' he said. 'I do not want it to be an exhibition for our men. And tomorrow. You must not duel on the Sabbath. Otherwise, make your own arrangements.'

Von Bethman inclined his head. 'I have no German aides with me, Herr General. May I have one of your staff to act as my second?' He paused for a moment and then nodded towards ter Haar. 'Although not that man. He may be prejudiced.'

Smit turned and addressed his companions in Afrikaans. He was obviously asking for a volunteer rather than issuing an order. No one, however, came forward. It was clear that this group of middle-aged burghers found the whole idea distasteful. Eventually one of them sighed and inclined his head. 'Jan van der Wath will help you,' said the general. 'Let him discuss the arrangements with . . .' he paused, and a half-smile came on to his face, 'the sergeant here. Now, please excuse me, for I have much to do.'

The gathering broke up and von Bethman strode away without a glance at Simon and Jenkins, who immediately joined van der Wath and engaged him in animated conversation – with most of the animation being displayed by Jenkins. As he was escorted back to the compound by the fourteen-year-old, Simon took with him an image of the frowning Boer, his mouth half open, attempting to follow whatever it was that Jenkins was saying to him.

Back with the other prisoners, Simon slumped to the ground and thumped one fist into the other in frustration. Why oh why had he lost his temper? He realised that he had played into the German's hands. With little hope of extracting a sentence of death from the prudent Boers, whom he now realised would never have risked provoking world opinion by executing prisoners of war, the baron must have planned it all, provoking Simon to insult him before witnesses and so ensuring he had grounds to issue the challenge. He had known that Simon would accept – and so sign his own death warrant. For that was what it would be. His win in Bloemfontein had been a fluke, he knew that. There was no way that he could out-fence the master swordsman a second time, or out-shoot the seasoned duellist. And why oh why had Jenkins insisted on pistols? His untutored strength might, just might, have given him the advantage again with swords – and they surely could have used the Highlanders' claymores. But he knew that the baron would be a far better marksman and it would take only one bullet to do the business.

His head was in his hands when Jenkins joined him in the compound some twenty minutes later. The Welshman thumped to the ground next to him. Simon looked at him with bloodshot eyes, half expecting to find the jaunty chatterer of General Smit's tent. But Jenkins's face was set and his black eyes were steely in their intent.

'Now, bach sir, we've got some preparin' to do,' he said.

'What the hell do you mean, 352? And what was all that blathering about Colonel Whatshisname and the Earl of Something or Other? I've never heard of them.'

'Neither have I, bach sir. You landed yourself in it right an' proper, if you don't mind me sayin' so. You was doin' so well, arguin' like a lawyer, till you lost your temper. You gave 'im just what he wanted. So I felt I 'ad to do a bit of takin' charge, see. Just to make sure that we shortened the odds a bit, like.'

'How on earth have you shortened the odds by opting for pistols? For God's sake, man, you know I can't hit a barn door with one of those Colts. I shall have a bullet through my head before I've lifted my arm.'

Jenkins looked chastened for a brief moment, then his face cleared. 'Now that's not the way to look at it, not at all it isn't.' He leaned forward confidentially. 'The truth is, see, that the little German bastard is much better with the sword than you, I could see that back in Blowfountain. The few moves you've got – mainly charging straight at 'im and throwing the kitchen wringer at 'im, as far as I could see – well, 'e knows them now and they wouldn't work at all this time. An' 'e would 'ave taken great pleasure in cuttin' you to pieces slowly, like. An' I wouldn't want to stand by an' let that 'appen.'

Simon sighed. 'Oh, I see. You favour a quick death over a slow one. Is that it?'

'Now, now, sir. Don't be pestimist . . . passimiss . . .'

'Pessimistic.'

'That's just what I was goin' to say. Now, we need to put a bit of work in before tomorrer. Oh, by the way, we are 'avin' this battle just after dawn, up at the top there at that place where we first climbed up and found 'em all waiting for us. You remember that 'ill?'

'Yes, near the Nek. The British call it Deane's Hill now, I think.'

'Yes, well, up there. Over the top away from the trenches, I think.' His voice fell slightly. 'That Boer chap wants us out of the way a bit, so we're goin' to 'ave the duel by the little cemetery they've put up there, where the British chaps are buried.' Jenkins's face took on a wry grin. 'I think 'e thinks it will save a bit of time after, see.'

Simon smiled, despite his depression. 'How very pragmatic. Now what's this preparation talk? I have no pistol to practise with and I don't see that it would help if I did. I'm just no good at it.'

Jenkins got to his feet. 'Come on. I'll show you. Let's go the other side of that rock, away from the crowd. Preparation is the thing. 'E'll be too cocky to do any. But we'll show 'im.'

Together they went to where a large rock shouldered out from the hillside, revealing a small but level stretch of ground behind it containing only a few Boer ponies. Here the two men began playing a ghostly game unobserved by all but the ponies and two black eagles, wheeling high overhead. They stood back to back and then, at Jenkins's command, strode twelve paces away from each other, with the Welshman calling out the numbers. There, they stopped.

'Now,' cried Jenkins, 'I want you to turn round to your right, not your left, so's you present a smaller target as you turn if 'e's quicker 'n you, which I expect 'e will be. You've got to turn as quick as you can. Go on, do it. Yes, that's good. Do it again and raise your pistol 'and as though you've got the Colt in it. Hmm . . .'

He strode towards Simon. 'The thing to remember is this: on 'earin' "twelve", turn to the right and stop when you're side on. Don't fire chest on. That'll give 'im too big a target. But turn quick and raise your Colt quick. That's all you do that's quick. The rest is slow, see. Real slow. You take aim *slowly*. Don't worry about 'im shootin' at you. You've got to make sure that you 'it him, so take your time with your aim. Now,' he sniffed, 'I don't mean that you've got to 'ang about all day, because your arm will sag if you hold it up too long, so: turn quick, arm up quick, make sure of your aim and then squeeze the trigger and don't snatch at it – just like with a rifle, see. Now, let's

295

do all that again, imaginin' you've got one of old Ally's big shooters in your 'and.

'Yes, that's good. Now, one more important thing. We don't know how the Colts will shoot, but I think I remember old Ally tellin' me that they shoot a bit 'igh. So don't aim at 'is head. If you do, you'll probably kill a bird. Aim just below the arm that's pointin' at you. It's a short distance so there shouldn't be too much of a . . . what d'you call it? Yes, deviation, that's it. So if it kicks 'igh, you'll get 'is 'ead. If it shoots low, you'll ruin 'is prospects of marriage. If it's straight, you've got 'im through the 'eart. And we want 'im dead, don't we? Now, let's try again – aimin' this time.'

For well over an hour the two men practised the routine, like small boys pretending to be duellists; Jenkins calling out the steps, and then both men turning, right arms extended and thumbs and forefingers making imaginary pistols. At the end, with darkness beginning to descend and rain falling again, Jenkins declared himself satisfied. 'Now,' he said, 'with a good night's sleep and old Ally watchin' over 'is pistols, like, I reckon you can take this little bugger to the graveyard in every way, bach sir. I am very confident.'

Simon regarded him closely. Was dear old 352 just talking to keep up his pupil's courage? Yet the great grin that curved up his servant's now bedraggled moustache seemed sincere enough, and the black eyes that sparkled at him carried no trace of dissembling. Something of the Welshman's confidence began to transmit itself to Simon. After all, those great Colts of Albert Hardcastle's never seemed to miss – ah yes, but there were two of them, and von Bethman had the other! What the hell. Simon crawled into his bedroll, his head spinning, and tried to sleep as the thin rain began its task of completely soaking him and his bedding.

It was a relief to get up before dawn. Van der Wath and the young boy came to escort them up to the top of Deane's Hill in the half-light. The rain had lifted and the first rays of a watery sun were probing the dark clouds to the east, but the prospect on the top of that plateau was sombre, to say the least. They walked past the line of trenches from which those rifle barrels had protruded so devastatingly a few weeks before and trudged on down a declivity towards where rows of rough wooden crosses could be seen. Simon felt his legs trembling. The right sort of morning and the right sort of setting in which to die, he thought. Yet Jenkins strode on, head high, a half-smile crinkling his face.

Von Bethman was waiting for them near the cemetery. He had dressed with care: polished riding boots, riding breeches and white shirt opened to the waist, revealing a tanned, well-muscled but surprisingly hairless chest. Simon wished he had been able to wear something a little more respectable than his sodden flannel shirt and worn corduroy trousers tucked into mud-stained boots. He felt at a disadvantage, as though his dishevelled appearance was letting his country down. He became aware that a third man was present at the scene, carrying a leather bag. At least the Boers had found a doctor!

The fourteen-year-old trotting at his side looked up and said: 'Good luck, English.'

The Boer second divested Simon of his jacket and opened his shirt to the waist to ensure that no padding or shield had been inserted to divert a bullet. The sudden cold made Simon suck air in through his teeth, and Jenkins looked at him quickly, but Simon nodded reassuringly. Then the two opponents were called together.

In rough, heavily accented English, van der Wath explained 'the rules of this game'. It was clear that he immediately regretted using the phrase, but ploughed on nevertheless. 'The two seconds will examine the guns and the cartridges and then you will take your guns and stand back to back. At the command "Walk" you will walk away from each other in a straight line for twelve paces. The seconds will count the paces. At "twelve" you will turn, remaining upright, and fire. You have one shot only. Is this understood?'

Simon nodded. Obviously the Boer had been briefed by Jenkins on 'the rules of the game', although God knows where the Welshman had got them from. In fact, the little man's enthusiasm – there was no other word for it – for the pistol duel still puzzled him. Still, it was no use conjecturing about that, not when he was about to fight for his life. A series of images flashed through his mind: his mother, in tight brocade, looking at him in disapproval; his father, sad and puzzled, sitting at his bedside in the regimental hospital at Brecon after he had missed the battalion's sailing for Zululand; Alice, gently kissing him in a mud-walled room in Kabul; Anna, Anna . . .

'The seconds will inspect the revolvers.' The pedantic tones of the Boer interrupted his reverie. With care, both guns were examined by van der Wath and Jenkins, the chambers rotated to ensure that no other rounds had been inserted and the barrels held to the sky to test their cleanliness. 'The cartridges.' These were taken from the Boer's pockets and the first given a cursory examination by him before it was handed to Jenkins. 'This is for your man.' The Welshman looked at it carefully before inserting it into Simon's Colt, rotating the chambers so that the round was level with the barrel, and retaining the revolver. 'Now for my man,' and he handed a second round to Jenkins.

Here, for the first time, Jenkins betrayed a sign of nervousness. He dropped the cartridge, quickly retrieving it and brushing away a strand of grass, before inspecting it solemnly and then handing it back to van der Wath with an apology. The Boer wiped it carefully before inserting it into the baron's revolver, rotating the chamber to ensure that the gun was ready to fire.

'Now, take your guns and cock them, stand back to back and walk when the order is given.' For the first time, the tone of the Boer's voiced softened a little. 'I would remind you, gentlemen, that you do not have to fire to kill. I think that the Lord may have seen enough killing at this place.'

'No.' Von Bethman's voice was clear. 'I shall kill him.'

'Very well. Walk! One, two, three . . .'

Simon's legs were now quite steady and he concentrated hard as he paced. *Turn to the right quickly. Raise your arm quickly. Then aim slowly, slowly. And kill the bastard.*

'Twelve!'

Simon whirled in a flash, raising his arm and pistol hand as he did so. But he was aware that von Bethman had turned even more quickly, and as he levelled his revolver at the German, aiming just below his gun arm, he sensed rather than saw the other's revolver spit flame and heard the bark. A micro-second later, he pulled his own trigger and closed his eyes waiting for the bullet to crash into him.

He was not sure how long he stood, but his eyes were still closed when he heard the cry of 'Doctor!' Slowly he opened them and saw the figure of von Bethman sprawled on the ground, a neat black hole in the centre of his forehead, just above his eyes.

'I knew the bloody thing would fire high.' It was Jenkins, of course, by his side, but a white-faced Jenkins, with perspiration standing out on his brow. The Welshman reached out and took the revolver from Simon's hand and then grasped his palm. Simon became aware that Jenkins's hand was trembling as he took it. 'Bloody well done, bach sir. Bloody well done.' The Welshman's lower lip was quivering under his huge moustache.

'Oh God,' breathed Simon. 'Oh God.'

'Give me the revolver.' Van der Wath had bustled over. Behind him, the doctor was bending over von Bethman, but his bag was unopened.

'Is he dead?' asked Simon.

'People who take a forty-five-calibre bullet in their brain usually die. Now, Joseph here,' he indicated the fourteen-year-old, who was looking up at Simon with wide eyes, 'will escort you back to the compound. No more shooting today, I think, Mr Fonthill. We will clear up here.'

The three walked back in silence and were met by Colonel Stewart at the compound gate. 'Where have you two been, eh? Bad news here, I can tell you.'

'What's that, sir?' Simon was glad that the bad news prevented him from answering the question. He did not want to talk about the duel. To Stewart, or anyone. Ever.

'It looks as though young Robertson, the chap we left in charge on the spur lower down to look after the horses, dug in well and gave a good account of himself when the Boers attacked him. But he was not supported by the first redoubt the general set up on the advance.' He snorted. 'The feller in charge there packed up and went back to Prospect, leaving Robertson and the survivors to fight their way back under heavy Boer attack. At least, that's what the Boers tell me.' He looked quizzically at Simon. 'I must say, you fellows did well up on

Macdonald's Kopje. You were the last to surrender, as far as I could see, and if I ever get a chance I will give you credit – and for getting us to the top of bloody Majuba. Funny thing's just happened, by the way. Joubert, the Boers' commandant-general, has just called in and given Macdonald's sword back to him. He said that "a brave man and his sword should not be parted". Nice touch that, eh? Boers are not bad chaps really.'

Simon nodded. He thought of them shooting down on the unarmed refugees fleeing from the battle, of their ready acceptance of von Bethman's story, and of their smug faith that the Almighty was *their* God and only theirs. Then he remembered ter Haar keeping his pledge and Colley's tribute to Smit. 'Yes, Colonel,' he said. 'Perhaps not bad chaps really, but very strange people for all that.'

'What's goin to 'appen to us prisoners, then, Colonel?' asked Jenkins.

'No idea. It depends upon whether Sir Evelyn decides to attack once he gets to Prospect with reinforcements. If he does, I suppose we stay in the bag.' Stewart frowned. 'But I can't see Gladstone letting the war continue after this mess. So maybe we'll be let out soon. God knows.' And he strode away.

The two friends sat together in companionable silence. 'Do you know,' said Simon after a while. 'I don't much care, really. But one thing's for certain – I don't want to see or experience any more killing for a long time. I think I have just about had enough.'

Jenkins nodded sympathetically. 'Amen to that.'

In fact, the prisoners were kept in genial captivity – the Boers could not refrain from joshing them about their poor shooting – for another two weeks, while rumours spread that a truce had been agreed and peace talks were being held. Jenkins soon regained his customary joviality and resumed his role as officer's servant, as well as exhibiting his old lag's efficiency in scrounging and stealing food and other creature comforts. Among his prizes was a sheet of tarpaulin that he rigged against a rock to provide shelter from the rain that now punctuated their days. Simon, however, became withdrawn and introspective. He declined to join an informal officers' mess that Stewart had created and spent his days making a crude wooden cross, upon which he carved 'Albert Hardy Hardcastle. Texan soldier. Fell in action 27/2/81.'

Then, on an appropriately sunny day, they were told that an armistice had been signed and that they would be allowed to take whatever belongings they still possessed and march back to Mount Prospect. Before leaving, Simon received permission to climb Majuba and plant his cross. In fact, Al had been buried in a communal grave in the centre of the plateau at the top, but Simon and Jenkins hammered in the cross there anyway. The flat top looked barren and empty, only spent cartridge cases showing that a bloody battle had taken place there only days before. If there were ghosts there, they were too new to make their presence felt.

Waiting for them at the gates of the compound as the last of the prisoners filed out were Gideon ter Haar and Jan van der Wath. The latter carried Hardy's great Colt revolvers.

'You were taking these to your dead comrade's parents,' he said in his grave voice, 'and you must complete your mission.'

Jenkins had the grace to look ashamed. The Boer turned to Simon. 'That man was not representing the German government, you know,' he said. 'He was just selling us guns. We needed him. But we didn't like him.'

There was no question about to whom he was referring. Simon summoned up a grateful smile and nodded. 'Thank you.' He thought for a moment and then added quietly, 'The countess had a son, you know, living in Essen. Perhaps your people could inform Krupps, so that the family could be told. You will, of course, say what you please, but perhaps the details of her death could be . . .' he faltered for a moment, 'well, obscured, for the sake of the child. An accident, or something like that . . .?'

Van der Wath nodded gravely. 'I think the matter has been overlooked but it should be done. I will talk to the commandant-general. As to the baron . . .?' He left the question hanging.

'Again, that is for you to decide. But he lived by the bullet, of course, in more ways than one, so perhaps the truth should be told here. He was a famous duellist, you know.'

'Very well.'

The four shook hands. 'No more killing now, English,' grinned ter Haar.

'No more killing, my friend. Goodbye.'

Three days later, Simon and Jenkins were sitting in the lee of their tent at Mount Prospect, sipping coffee and watching the evening sun bring out the details of the rock faces and terracing at the top of Mount Majuba. The soft light made it look quite unintimidating, even beautiful now – the 'Hill of the Doves' indeed. The mood of introspection that had settled on Simon since the duel had remained with him, and Jenkins, seeing the signs, had spent most of the afternoon tending to General Custer, his much-appreciated legacy, in the horse lines. Now he had returned, and the two sat together in silence, clutching their mugs and looking across at Majuba, the scene of so much slaughter so few days ago.

'There is one thing I can't understand,' said Simon at last.

'What's that then?'

'How did von Bethman miss me? He fired first – I saw him – and he was reputed to be a crack shot. I was only twenty yards or so away from him and even I didn't miss. He certainly didn't fire to one side deliberately. He swore that he would kill me. He *wanted* to kill me. How on earth did he miss?'

'Well . . .' Jenkins looked away. 'Perhaps 'e was too 'urried, see. Even the best shooters miss sometimes, look you.'

Simon shook his head. 'I've been thinking about it and I can't understand it.' He looked at Jenkins sharply. 'You didn't distract him in some way, did you?'

Jenkins looked shocked. 'Who, me, bach sir? Certainly not.' He held up his hand. 'On my mother's deathbed, I didn't distract 'im.'

There was something about his friend's denial, however, that made Simon frown. It was too specific. All right – he hadn't distracted the German. But had he done something else?

Simon put down his coffee and shifted to move closer to Jenkins. 'I think it's time, 352,' he said slowly, 'that I had the whole truth about this damned duel. Why did you jump in with all this bloody nonsense about the London Duelling Society – I know there's no such thing – and insist on using pistols? Come on, now. I want the truth.'

302

A look of righteous indignation settled on Jenkins's face but left it as soon as he saw the gleam in Simon's eyes. 'Oh all right, bach sir,' he muttered. 'But you've got to promise not to be annoyed.'

'I'll promise no such thing. What did you do? Come on.'

'Well.' Jenkins looked at the ground. 'The little bugger was goin' to kill you right enough, I could see that. I could also see that them Boers thought that this duel would be a nice let-out for them, see. As I told you, swords wouldn't be any good for you this time, but . . .' his voiced tailed away and he looked up with a great grin, 'I 'ad an idea about pistols, see.'

'Go on.'

'While you was all talking, I slipped me 'and under the blanket and took out a cartridge that were left in old Ally's guns an' put it in me pocket. Then I showed 'em the guns an' gambled that the baron bloke would fall in love with 'em and agree to use 'em.'

'Yes, well, I don't see where that gets us.'

'That night, I got the cartridge out of me pocket, took off the lead bullet and shook out about two thirds of the powder inside the case, leaving the primer and enough powder to cause a bang and a flash, like, but not enough to send the bloody bullet on its way into your belly, see. Then I put the bullet back.'

'So you switched the cartridge in von Bethman's Colt? But how on earth did you do that? I saw van der Wath put the thing in the revolver with my own eyes.'

Despite himself, Simon was now thoroughly intrigued and Jenkins sensed this and warmed to his narrative. 'Ah, well now, bach sir, that's not what you saw at all, see. To explain, we 'ave to go back a bit. You remember 'ow old Ally was always so good at cards?'

Simon nodded.

'Well, 'e was good because he cheated, bless 'im. Now, I knew this and I didn't care too much because 'e never asked me for the money 'e won. But I reckon 'e made a fair bob or two from the blokes from the 58th and other regiments 'e played with – and I bet 'e made more money from cheatin' at cards back 'ome than 'e ever did from that bloody shop. Trouble is, see, I couldn't see 'ow he was doin' it. So in the end I gave up and asked 'im. 'E didn't mind and 'e did 'is best to show me, though I could never do it properly. An' I'll never try it in a proper card game. If I was found out, them Jocks would kill me, see.'

'Well, how did he do it?'

' 'E was just quick with the cards, and most of the time 'e palmed 'em. You'll remember 'e'd got big 'ands. The trick was in distractin' attention so that whoever you wanted to fool was lookin' the other way while you did it. Simple, really – but you've got to practise, look you.'

Simon spoke slowly. 'You mean you palmed the good cartridge and replaced it with the one with little powder in it, so that it never left the barrel?'

A beaming Jenkins nodded. 'That's right. Now, do you remember that I dropped the good cartridge when it was 'anded to me?'

Simon nodded.

'That's when it was done. I picked up the good cartridge with me left 'and and, if you remember, put it into me right 'and to give it to that Boer chap who was the German's second. Except that I didn't. I just pretended to. I kept it back in me left 'and, because I already 'ad the 'alf-empty round in me right, so I just passed that one over, pretendin' to brush the grass off it an' all. I 'ad 'alf turned me back so that it looked natural that I should pass the thing with the 'and which was nearest, you see.'

'Show me.'

Jenkins scratched his head, then reached into his pocket and took out two well-worn pennies, seemingly identical. 'Now,' he said, 'they've both got the Queen's 'ead on 'em, but one's dated 1871 and the other 1873. So they're different but look the same. Right?'

'Right. Do get on with it.'

'Well, I'm doin' me best, but magic don't come easy, look you. Now, watch. You give me the '71 penny into my left 'and, see, and I've got the '73 one concealed in me right. I drop the '71 coin accidentally – or so it seems – and pick it up, covering it with the ends of me fingers, then pass it over into me right 'and. Except I don't. I keep it behind me fingers and then present the '73 coin in me right 'and to you. Look. I'll do it again.'

He did so and Simon shook his head. 'Damned clever. But what a bloody risk you took, 352. What if it had gone wrong – if you'd done it clumsily so that they saw, or something like that?'

Jenkins blew out his cheeks. 'That was the thing. I knew I was taking an 'ell of a risk, but I couldn't think of any other way. So while you was sleepin' the night before, like, I was up all night practising. I was a bit buggered in the mornin', but I 'ad to put a bright face on it. You see, the other 'alf of the whole bloody thing was that you would be good enough to shoot 'im, so I 'ad to encourage you. And you were, God bless yer, after a bit of trainin' that is. But I was right relieved when it was over, I can tell you.'

Simon remembered the pallor of Jenkins's face and the perspiration on his forehead. 'So,' he said slowly, 'I didn't kill von Bethman. You did.'

Jenkins's eyebrows lifted and his face assumed an expression of great consternation. 'No, bach sir. No. No. Now don't you go thinkin' that. I didn't kill the bugger. You did. I just stopped 'im killin' you, see.'

The two held each other's gaze for a moment and then, slowly, Simon reached out his hand to Jenkins. 'Three five two, this is the umpteenth time you have saved my life – and this time was by far the most ingenious method. Thank you. Thank you very much. Without you, that bastard would have shot me dead. There's no doubt about it.'

Jenkins's round countenance broke into a relieved smile. 'Well that's all right then. I thought you was annoyed for a minute, see. Anyway, you've done the same for me a few times, so we'd better stop countin', 'adn't we? What's next for us, then?'

Simon mused for a moment. 'I think I'd like to go home. We have to go to Yorkshire anyway, don't forget – although I think I'll keep the Colts, for I am sure that Mrs Hardy – sorry, Mrs Hardcastle – won't have need of them. You will come with me, of course. Then we can think about what to do next.'

Jenkins pulled a glum face. 'Domesticity then, is it?'

'Not for long. Just long enough to sort ourselves out, so to speak.'

'What about . . . um . . . you know.'

'Alice?'

'Yes.'

A slow, sad smile broke on to Simon's face. 'I hope she's happy. I think I'll write her a letter at last. Get me a bit of writing paper and then you'd better start packing.'

Jenkins's own face mirrored the smile. 'Very good, bach sir,' he said.

Author's Note

What was fact and what fiction? Most of Fonthill's adventures are woven around factual events, and so the descriptions of the build-up to the war and of the three battles in it are as accurate as a plundering of respected sources can make them.

Simon, Jenkins, Hardy, von Bethman, Anna, ter Haar and van der Wath are all fictional characters, of course. But Sir George Pomeroy-Colley, although a forgotten figure now, was a high-profile military leader in Victoria's Britain, and until he met his tragic end was indeed regarded as the coming man of his time. I based much of his conversation in the novel with Simon and others on his letters. President Brand, Commandant-General Joubert and General Smit were real figures, as were Colonel Stewart, Major Fraser, Lieutenants MacGregor and Macdonald and young Elwes. The latter really did cry 'Floreat Etona!' a few seconds before a bullet took his life on Deane's Hill, and somehow Joubert did ride his pony to the top of Majuba.

Colonel Stewart went on to garner fame four years later by winning a victory at Abu Klea in the abortive march to relieve Gordon at Khartoum, only to be mortally wounded the next day. The heroic defender of Macdonald's Kopje, Lieutenant Hector Macdonald, did, of course, receive his sword from Joubert and went on to be lauded as 'Fighting Mac' and become a major general, only to take his own life in a Paris hotel room with a charge of homosexuality hanging over him. He did so, it was rumoured, on the advice of the Prince of Wales, that perfect example of fine Victorian morality.

I confess to cheating somewhat with the other Mac, Captain

MacGregor, who charged with Simon across that bullet-swept plateau above the Ingogo. I have him die by a sniper's bullet behind the rock bastion, the defence of which did save the British from encirclement that day. In fact, quite predictably, he was killed on horseback as he led the charge to the rocks. I gave the gallant man life for a few hours after that because I wanted him to have the opportunity of explaining why any professional soldier leading foot soldiers across a plain against a well-entrenched enemy consisting of the best marksmen in the world, who were urged to kill officers first, would be so idiotic as to ride a horse. I felt the reader deserved *some* sort of explanation. There is no evidence to suggest that the explanation I give is what MacGregor would have said, but I feel in my bones that it is.

Majuba, of course, although a bloodbath, was really no more than a skirmish by modern standards in terms of forces deployed and casualties sustained. But it was very significant in its way. An armistice – mainly engineered by the indefatigable President Brand – led to a negotiated truce, which satisfied no one. The Boers of the Transvaal, under the emergent President Kruger, were later to break the terms of the agreement and to grow ever more anti-British, while Imperial Britain itched to avenge Majuba. It had its chance eighteen years later when the Second Boer War broke out (the British called the affair of 1880–81 the First Boer War, while to the Afrikaners it has always been revered as the Transvaal War of Independence). In that conflict, the leaders of the British Army were to show that they had learned virtually nothing about the military effectiveness of rifle fire directed by skilled marksmen. It was as though the battle of Majuba Hill had never taken place.

J.W.